THE WORLD GASH, A VAST VOLCANIC FIELD, IS SPREADING ACROSS KRYNN'S SEABED . . .

and it moves with a mysterious purpose. If something isn't done to stop it, it will poison the oceans and annihilate thousands of species. And once the oceans die, so too will the continents.

Apoletta of the Dargonesti and Utharne of the Dimernesti, representing the two principal aquatic races of sea elves, convene a Conclave to address the crisis. When undead attack the Conclave, Apoletta and Utharne decide to lead a joint expedition of their estranged species on a journey to the World Gash to confront the peril.

Apoletta and Utharne's mission to save the oceans will introduce them to new species and dire threats—and will bring them into the World Gash's dark heart . . . face to face with its most terrible secrets, including the ghosts of their own pasts.

Saving Solace
Douglas W. Clark

The Alien Sea
Lucien Soulban

The Great White Wyrm
Peter Archer
(March 2007)

THE
ALIEN
SEA

LUCIEN
SOULBAN

Champions
THE ALIEN SEA

©2006 Wizards of the Coast, Inc.

Published by Wizards of the Coast, Inc. DRAGONLANCE, WIZARDS OF THE COAST, and their respective logos are trademarks of Wizards of the Coast, Inc., in the U.S.A. and other countries.

Printed in the U.S.A.

Cover art by David Hudnut
First Printing: August 2006
Library of Congress Catalog Card Number: 2005935529

9 8 7 6 5 4 3 2 1

ISBN-10: 0-7869-4082-4
ISBN-13: 978-0-7869-4082-0
620-95618740-001-EN

U.S., CANADA,
ASIA, PACIFIC, & LATIN AMERICA
Wizards of the Coast, Inc.
P.O. Box 707
Renton, WA 98057-0707
+1-800-324-6496

EUROPEAN HEADQUARTERS
Hasbro UK Ltd
Caswell Way
Newport, Gwent NP9 0YH
GREAT BRITAIN
Save this address for your records.

Visit our web site at www.wizards.com

*To my mother who helped forge the
nature of my convictions,
and to my father who helped forge
the strength of those convictions.*

*Thank you Marcelo Figueroa for
introducing me to Margaret Weis.
And thank you Margaret Weis
and Pat McGilligan for your
patience, for your direction, and for
believing in me enough to give me so
tremendous an opportunity.*

PROLOGUE
A Sum of Things

She'd been watching him for over an hour: the way he moved beneath the water, how he touched the ruins of the broken city. He was comfortable in the ocean, but not born to it; that much she knew. He floated upright when there was no need for it.

As her father had said, humans who dared the deep oceans always felt a need to point their heads to the surface. It was a reminder of where they came from.

"We should kill him," Dionasis said. His eyes glittered like fierce sapphires as he gripped his trident of polished black coral harder. The cushion of water suspended his long green hair.

"Is that council talking," she asked, "or fear?" She studied the faces of the four male elves with her. Dionasis's gaze remained unwavering, but two others looked away.

"Slyphanous?" she asked the second man of seaweed-green skin. His old eyes met hers. "What is your word in this?"

The older sea elf stroked his flowing white beard. "I worry," he said, careful in word and thought, "that this KreeaQUEKH heralds an invasion force."

"KreeaQUEKH," Dionasis repeated with a sneer. "Kill him, I say. These surface locusts hunt our whale brethren from their wooden pods!"

1

"Yes," Slyphanous said, "but I also hear they are enemies of the minotaurs."

"Neither makes them our allies," she replied. "Hatred is easy, but I'm unwilling to seal his fate over our assumptions. Who among us has dealt with humans?" she asked then quickly stopped Dionasis. "And I don't mean slipping aboard their vessels and assassinating their sailors."

Dionasis frowned at the comment but said nothing. Nobody else spoke. She returned to studying the human in his red robes stitched with a luminous thread that attracted curious coral fish. The human tried to touch the fish, but they scattered.

"He knows spellcraft; that much is obvious," she said.

"How else would he survive without it?" Slyphanous said, his speech filled with the customary pauses that lent him a thoughtful mien.

"Indeed. Since neither his species nor his profession as spellcaster is of mystery to me, I will speak with him alone."

For the first time, Dionasis's features softened. "No," he said, touching her forearm. "What if he attacks?"

She smiled. "I've faced down blood sharks that could devour whales in one bite. I can manage here. Besides," she said, smiling, "if we all face him, he might feel threatened. Perhaps lie to protect himself. Alone I have a better chance of determining the truth."

Dionasis let go, albeit reluctantly.

Again she pondered the human's presence. That he had found his way this far down piqued her curiosity; here, the oceans crushed the hulls of ships with the fists of gods, and the great vortex in the sea above claimed an endless march of lives. This one, however, had arrived of his own volition; he might be the first to reach the bottom alive.

She followed the red-robed human, aware that her companions trailed close behind. She watched the way he touched the ruins of the great underwater cavern. His caress was intimate and reverent, his gaze filled with constant awe. He drifted through the cobblestone streets, a ghost of the ocean. The buildings curled up around him, their windows and doors open in silent hymn, their skin covered by barbed growths of coral.

He could not hide his smile . . . as though he were home. She appreciated the sentiment. The sea was her home as well.

Slowly, the city rose along a cliff wall toward the cratered roof of the cavern; the human followed its rise with a slow pirouette. He emerged into an air pocket. It was a large crater in the ceiling that canopied the structures resting on the great ledge. The cliff wall pushed the ruined buildings into the dry air; their mighty spires stretched upward to scrape against the cratered ceiling. Water turned the streets into shallow rivers and polished smooth the cobblestones with the gentle ripples of waves. Garlands of moss hung from the arms and necks of the human-looking statues, their stone eyes staring at rock sky.

The human reached the gray marble steps of a tall building with giant columns lining the front, and he walked out of the water. At first he wobbled, and she caught herself from rushing forward to help him.

What am I doing? she wondered.

The red-robed human had obviously been under water for some time. He continued to sway, his body still affected by waves he could not feel.

She understood. For all her little experience walking upon dry land, that her feet remained drawn to the ground was disconcerting—dizzying even. No such force existed in her oceans. She motioned to her companions to remain back, far from her.

The human finally succumbed to the land-sickness and sat heavily upon the stairs, water lapping at his feet. She remained hidden, however, behind a building corner and beneath the waves.

The red-robed human glanced around the cavern, apparently appreciating the odd growth of creeper vines that thrived in the moist air and clawed up the smooth-walled buildings. He marveled at the luminescent moss that grew everywhere and flourished in vibrant yellows, reds, and blues.

As he studied the ruins, he wrung the water from his long brown hair. His young features seemed frozen in awe.

"Daganant sariosos ot man phobo," the human said aloud. For the first time, he stared at her hiding spot in the shadows. Not directly at her, perhaps, but in her direction. He knew she was there.

"I'ya dososha et makili redorbore."

She hesitated, on the verge of diving back down.

Do not mingle with the air-breathers, her thoughts screamed. The voice, however, was more her father's than hers; she was always of too curious a mind to heed caution.

She avoided glancing back at the others. Instead, she reached into her pouch and pulled out a small ball of salted sea wax mixed with soot. She muttered a small phrase; the wax dissolved between her fingers and tickled her throat.

Prepared for the task, she floated to the surface and drifted closer. Her long locks of silver spread out upon the water's dark surface, only her head visible. Her pearl white skin and emerald green, almond-shaped eyes must have had a suitable effect upon him. He inhaled deeply and smiled.

"Don't worry," he said. "I won't harm you."

She looked at him and cocked her head. "I doubt you could," she said and reveled at his shocked expression. Her voice still tickled from the magic.

"You speak in the common tongue?" he said, eyebrows raised.

"Obviously," she replied.

He laughed easily.

"I do," she said, drifting closer to the human. She stood upon the steps. Her hair fell to the side as she emerged from the water.

His face reddened, and he looked away. "Oh! I . . . ah . . . I'm sorry," he said.

She hesitated, confused at his reaction.

"You're . . . ah . . . unclothed," he said.

She had to look down before she understood his meaning. She was bare chested, and even her long hair did not conceal her nudity. A gentle, genuine laugh escaped her lips. She'd forgotten about the human sense of propriety.

"I am not embarrassed," she said. "Why should you be?"

"It's just that . . . you're naked!" he said.

"Oh," she replied. "Am I your first?"

"Excuse me?" he asked, his eyebrows raised. He still looked away.

"Am I the first woman you've seen unclothed?"

"No, no," he said. "I've seen plenty of women naked—well . . . no, I didn't mean plenty . . . it's not as though I make a career of it." He laughed nervously.

She smiled. Most humans she'd met stared at her body and not her eyes. She'd had to teach a few of them lessons when they'd acted improperly. This red-robed human, however, was respectful. She didn't expect that from a would-be invader.

"Am I . . . is this . . . the City of the Kingpriests . . . Istar?" the human asked, desperate to change the conversation.

"Why do you ask?"

"I'm an explorer," he said. "Why, have you seen others like me?"

"No," she admitted. "But you're the first to arrive here . . . alive."

He must have heard something in her voice, recognized the change in her demeanor.

"Oh," he said. He glanced at her, appraising her with renewed appreciation and perhaps some fear. "Will I be the first to leave here alive?"

Guilt welled up in her breast. He seemed innocent in things—wonderstruck, really. The thought of death robbed him of that quality. She wanted to assuage his fears, but she couldn't, for her people's sake.

5

"That depends," she said. "Why have you come here? And please, say it to my face."

The human finally looked at her, into her eyes. "I came seeking treasure and knowledge," he replied. "I'm looking for the Tower of High Sorcery that fell with the Istar during the Great Cataclysm. I was hoping to recover artifacts from it. Are you one of the survivors of Istar?"

"No," she said. "But it is home to us now. Who do you represent?" she asked.

"Nobody," he replied. "I'm here merely to explore. My curiosity is my only master. I wish to learn more about this place."

"How much is that knowledge worth to you?"

"My life, I believe," he replied. "This place may well be my tomb. I found my way down here, but the vortex of the Blood Sea blocks my return."

She nodded. The mysterious whirlpool above the sunken city protected it from interlopers.

"And if you returned, who would you tell of this place?"

"Nobody," he said, his reaction seemingly genuine. "What's the use of adventure if everyone else can do it as easily? This was to be my tale of bravery. Nobody else's. Besides, who would believe me? People prefer to remember this place in song and parable. Moment by moment, the surface world forgets this place was ever real."

"Why?" she asked. "Why would they forget such great treasures?"

"Because," he replied, "we humans remember only that which touches our lifetime. And we are ignorant to all else."

"Does that apply to you?" she asked.

"No," he said, laughing. "I plan to live for a very long time. At least I hope to. . . ."

"Be careful what you wish for," she responded before hesitating. "Explore the ruins," she said, finally, "but be warned that I am watching you."

With that, she dived into the water; her four companions had drawn closer to ensure her safety. The human called after her, however, and she resurfaced.

"Wait, wait," he said. "Who are you?"

"I am Steward of Istar" she responded with authority—and loud enough for her compatriots to hear. She then whispered, "My name is Apoletta."

He smiled. "Zebulah," he whispered back. "Mine's Zebulah."

ACT

Dimernost and Hygant

I

CHAPTER
A Conclave of Unequals
1

Discourse was too polite a word for the arguments. The delegates spoke over one another, launching into tirades and interrupting each other by shouting even louder.

"Where were you when—"

"—safe on the surface, never having to endure the deep—"

"—Brynseldimer, may he never breathe water again, razed our—"

"This again! We will not take blame for what—"

"—we helped as best we could, but we had our own issues—"

"—the undead finding refuge beneath, they are—"

Apoletta inhaled warm salt water through her gills and exhaled in exasperation, a stream of bubbles frothing through her mouth. If anyone noticed or took umbrage at her apparent frustration, they said nothing. Instead, they continued arguing.

The delegates floated around a large, circular slab of coral that hung suspended in the water; braided ropes of seaweed tethered it to the high ceiling above. Dozens of docile green and white lantern fish, oblivious to the disputes, continued to swim about, illuminating the dome's interior with the radiant light of their innards.

Apoletta studied the Conclave's delegates, marveling at the antagonism that spilled forth. The humanlike children of the sea, while numbering a handful, stood in solidarity with the powder blue shoal elves of the Tide-Dancer clan. It wasn't surprising for the Dimernesti elves and children of the sea to have formed such tight bonds. Only the shoreline's border of sand separated the land-dwelling sea children and the shallow-water elves.

Meanwhile, the normally calm merfolk quarreled with two ocean striders. It took either a foolish mind or strong heart to quarrel with the striders; Apoletta couldn't decide which, with whale skin for flesh, black-and-white patches like a killer whale, sharklike eyes, and a mouth full of serrated teeth, the twenty-foot-tall striders could have devoured the fish-tailed merfolk whole. And yet they argued, floating almost nose to nose.

To the side of the argument rested one sea giant who appeared thoroughly amused at the delegates' antics, and the monastic brathnoc who stood outside the debates. Apoletta wasn't sure what to make of the brathnoc. With gray skin, wide faces, almond-shaped eyes of yellow that blinked like a fish's, and mantalike patagia connecting their arms to their legs, they kept their own council. All of them wore belts of kelp, from which they occasionally removed a leaf and chewed on it.

"What troubles you?" Slyphanous asked in his typically slow, thoughtful manner. He floated behind Apoletta but leaned forward enough to whisper in her ear.

"I now understand why the gods made the oceans so vast," Apoletta said, motioning to the arguing delegates.

Slyphanous smiled but shook his head. "I know you," he said. "What bothers you, hmm?"

"The Dimernesti were to help us in this Conclave," Apoletta said. "Instead, they have yet to pick a delegate to speak on their behalf. I'm here alone trying to—"

"Still avoiding the question," Slyphanous interrupted. "We discussed this matter yesterday."

Apoletta sighed. "You are right." She nodded to the balcony overlooking the circular courtyard where they waited. "Look at that child of the sea," she said, meaning one particular woman with long black hair who drifted in the water. "She sits as a trusted advisor to the Dimernesti. 'Mirror cousins' is what their two people call one another because they share the shore and the ocean's glassy surface."

"You're jealous," Slyphanous said.

"I am," Apoletta admitted. "We Dargonesti once shared the Dimernesti's trust, the one the children of the sea now seem to enjoy. Our rift has grown titanic in proportion."

"Well," Slyphanous said, shrugging, "isn't that why you helped organize this Conclave? To rebuild that trust? As leader of Istar, it is up to you to lead the way."

"I know," Apoletta said with a sigh. "I just wish I had more help."

Slyphanous nudged his head toward the delegates.

"Very well," Apoletta replied with a wry smile. After straightening the folds of her yellow oyster-silk robes, she inhaled more air than she needed from the water and rose up, above the table. Apoletta waited for everyone's attention.

That failed.

She continued to wait to be acknowledged.

That, too, failed.

The arguments had taken precedence over all civility and decorum.

Apoletta looked back at Slyphanous. He shrugged. She reached into her reagents pouch and focused on the waters of the domed ceiling of latticed coral, well above everyone's heads. Apoletta motioned, her hands sweeping through the water; electricity raised goose pimples on her skin while the small roll of seaweed disintegrated in her hands.

Apoletta inhaled, tasting the salt water rushing through her mouth and past her gills. A large sphere of water vanished from where Apoletta indicated. The heavy ocean rushed in to fill the sudden void with a loud crack, displacing enough water to nudge delegates and scatter lantern fish. Even the table slab of coral swayed.

A general, momentary silence followed.

"Now that I have your attention," Apoletta announced, "I wish to continue."

"We haven't finished!" the merwoman Athiana exclaimed, her body covered in linked seashells, her scales glistening with rainbow hue. "We refuse to continue this Conclave until the ocean striders grant the Spearfish Tribe access to the fishing grounds along the Salt-Bite Ridge."

"But few are the fish," the ocean strider Shakhall replied. "We barely eat. Hungry are our children."

"Because you've thinned the fish with your great appetites!" Athiana said.

"And the ocean is scarce of bounty, say I. The dead-who-live pollute the waters. Afraid are the fish."

"Please, please!" Apoletta pleaded. "I understand your grievances, I truly do. But there are greater issues at stake, issues that demand our attention."

"Your so-called World Gash, is it again?" a male Dimernesti said, his blue aquiline features marred by a vicious sneer and the scars of a harsh life.

"It is not *my* anything," Apoletta said, her temper rising. "It is our problem. I wish you to listen to someone knowledgeable. Someone with experience in this—"

"You're wasting my time," the Dimernesti said, his manner and tongue coarse.

Others murmured in agreement.

Apoletta's stomach turned into a balled fist; she wanted to slap each and every one of them. Never before had she seen such obstinacy. Then again, the gathering before her was the first time the various species of the seas had come together in such a fashion. Perhaps she should have expected it, though she'd assumed they'd willingly address what she believed was a common problem.

THE ALIEN SEA

Instead, they ignored the Conclave's purpose and aired their many grievances.

The merfolk argued over hunting domains. The influx of undead seeking easy sanctuary beneath the waves concerned the ocean striders. The shallow-water elves, the Dimernesti, harbored grievances against Apoletta's people, the deep-water elves of the Dargonesti. The amphibious children of the sea sided with the shoal elves on principle. And those were just the races that chose to voice their concerns. Along the edges of the high dome stood a smattering of representatives and curious third parties who had yet to join in.

If Apoletta were to unite these disparate delegates, she couldn't back down, nor could she show any weakness. She certainly couldn't be silenced by one Dimernesti with an inflated view of his own opinion.

Apoletta faced the shoal elf and fixed him with her emerald gaze. "A waste of time?" she asked. "Live in ignorance if you so wish, but who are you, may I inquire, to commit your people to your own short-sighted folly?"

"Me?" the Dimernesti said proudly. "I'm Guild Master for the Dimernost Traders. Most powerful guild there is in these waters."

"Then you may speak for the Traders, but you do not speak for the Dimernesti. Who does? Let me hear his voice in this . . . not the words of some self-appointed lackey."

The angry shoal elf kicked forward, his skin flushing a deeper blue; he reached for a serrated iron-shell knife.

"Hold!" a voice roared from the balcony. It was a male Dimernesti, close to Apoletta in age, his hair white and tied in a ponytail. He was larger than the shoal elves, with a wide chest and broad shoulders, but he still bore the customary almond eyes, thin ears, and light blue skin.

"Utharne," the first Dimernesti hissed, his hand dropping away from his knife. "This ain't no temple matter, here."

"Yes, but, I'm not here on temple matters," the white-haired Utharne replied quickly. He spoke in a deliberate manner as though hiding nervousness.

Not nervous, Apoletta thought. Intense.

"The Speaker of the Sea asked me to speak on her behalf, no, no, not you," he said, wagging his fingers.

The other Dimernesti hesitated; his hand dropped to his side.

Utharne flutter-kicked to Apoletta. "My apologies," Utharne said, whispering. "I'm Utharne of the Fallen Shores. It's a pleasure."

"Apoletta of Istar," she responded. She noticed the chain of painted shells dangling from Utharne's neck. "Our two peoples were to host the Conclave in tandem," Apoletta murmured, hoping she had at last found an ally among the rival clan.

"Our people don't care for this Conclave," Utharne replied. "Don't believe it absolutely necessary. But . . . I think our two people have drifted far enough apart, don't you? This is too important an event to destroy through mistrust."

Apoletta surrendered a generous smile, one that carried her unspoken relief.

"Wonderful," Utharne said, his eyes alight, then he turned toward the assembled delegates. Apoletta returned to Slyphanous.

"Did that rude Dimernesti say something about temple matters?" Slyphanous whispered.

"Did you see the necklace around Utharne's neck?" Apoletta asked quietly.

Slyphanous shook his head.

"The shells were painted. Blue flames."

"Abbuku?" Slyphanous asked. "This Utharne's a follower of the Fisher King?"

"A priest or a druid of Abbuku, more likely," Apoletta said, curiosity stitching her eyebrows high. "But he serves the Fisher King, regardless."

"I thought the shoal elves turned their backs on the gods,

hmm? Blamed them for their imprisonment under the Dragon Overlord."

"Brine, you mean," Apoletta said. "So did I. A mystery for later, perhaps."

The domed chamber was large enough to serve as a womb for a pod of fully grown whales, and still there would have been room to move. Lantern fish, their chests pulsing with a bright mustard glow, swam idly among the delegates. They provided light in tandem with the amber growths of crawlerweed that covered the dome's lower walls in deep thickets.

The dome's ceiling measured over sixty feet high, with four thick beams of coral converging on an open geode with purple crystalline walls two feet in diameter. The dome's surface, however, was lace-like, with wild patterns etched through the thin coral.

The delegates floated outside the circular table slab with its pockmarked surface; Utharne and Apoletta hovered above it. Onlookers, mostly curious Dimernesti, watched from the balconies overlooking the floor.

"On behalf of the Speaker of the Sea," Utharne proclaimed, "greetings! And yes, welcome to Dimernost, the only surviving Dimernesti city . . . but not the last, we hope."

"And as Steward of Istar, on behalf of the Speaker of the Moon and the Dargonesti cities of Watermere and Istar," Apoletta added, "I also welcome you to this Conclave and thank you for making this important journey."

"And why are we here?" a member of the brathnoc delegation asked, his words a hiss across the waters.

Utharne smiled broadly and bowed to Apoletta before swimming to the side of the table where two empty chairs waited. Slyphanous stood behind the second one.

Apoletta studied the assembled delegates before diving into the meat of the matter. "I have informed you of the threat we all face. While the troubles that brought you here are grave, I believe they are symptoms of a greater crisis."

"This World Gash, you speak of?" the female ocean strider asked.

"The World Gash is aptly named," Apoletta said. "It is indeed a wound, and if we do not act, perhaps a fatal one at that."

"You're being overly dramatic," a merman said, slamming the butt of his green trident into the table.

"Sadly, no," Apoletta replied, ignoring his crude gesture. "But if my words as diplomat will not move you, then perhaps another approach will. Hear the words, not of an ambassador, but of an explorer. Brysis." She motioned to a large archway measuring fifteen feet in height. For the sea giant and ocean striders who'd used it, it was a tight fit, but it dwarfed the woman and star-nose dolphin who emerged from its shadows.

The woman was Dargonesti, her hair gold and cut uncharacteristically short, and her skin the deep blue of the inky voids. Barklike bracers sheathed her arms and shins; she wore a seaweed and chain poncho that tattered into long strands, along with a matching loincloth. A rapier rested on her hip.

If the young woman looked tough, with her hardened physique and a wicked scar stretching across her left cheek and jaw, she seemed tougher for her companion, the star-nose dolphin. Its purple-gray body was thick, its beak ivory white. While the normally exuberant star-noses were known to swim alongside ships and perform spectacular aerobatics, this particular dolphin seemed anything but friendly. A collar and vest of toughened seal leather and turtle scale covered his upper body; sea urchin spines erupted from his vest, while orange plates of treated spinefish scales sheathed his fins and tail.

In short, the dolphin looked menacing, deadly.

Apoletta nodded to Brysis before joining Utharne. All the delegates appeared suitably impressed, as Brysis took her time swimming to the table.

"Is that a—yes it is! A war dolphin!" Utharne said to Apoletta.

"Indeed," Apoletta said.

"I have heard about them," Utharne said. "Dargonesti who don't like living as elves and instead tie themselves to dolphin forms. . . . Is that right?"

"The Land Shorn," Apoletta said, explaining the nature of these once-elves. They believed their humanoid bodies were ancestral vestiges of their lives on land, something completely unnecessary to life in the oceans. The Dargonesti and Dimernesti both hailed from dry-land elves, and though they bore some resemblance to their surface kin, the Land Shorn wanted to widen that gap by becoming a different species entirely. "He is second-generation war dolphin."

"Wonderful!" Utharne exclaimed. "But what does that mean exactly?"

"One parent Land Shorn, one dolphin. He was born as a dolphin with no ability to return to elf form. Otherwise, he is as intelligent as you or I."

Apoletta wasn't sure she approved of the ritual steps the Land Shorn pursued to change forms, but who was she to question the gods? Land Shorn priests managed to attain the god Abbuku's blessing to shapeshift into dolphins when all other Dargonesti could turn into much smaller porpoises. Those who succeeded in the Cavern Trials of the god were permitted to live as dolphins.

"Wonderful," Utharne whispered. "Are there many like him?" Utharne asked, a delighted twinkle in his eye. Brysis and her companion took their place above the table.

"More and more," Apoletta said then grew quiet as Brysis spoke.

Brysis floated above the table, studying the delegates. She'd faced down many horrors these past few years, but this moment somehow unnerved her. Still, the ocean had all but winnowed the fear from her heart, and she was poised for the responsibility.

"I am Brysis," she said, batting away a curious yellow-maid fish. She matched each stare with her own imperious gaze. "This is my guardian, Echo Fury."

A few of the delegates nodded back respectfully. The female ocean strider smiled at her, happy to see her friend. Brysis was likewise grateful for Ashkoom's presence.

"I was a handler for Istar's Royal Stable of Dolphins," Brysis explained. "But a few years ago, I was assigned to chart the new currents."

The delegates nodded. They understood the necessity of that action. When the three moons disappeared from Krynn's ceiling, the world lost its magic; spell-casting seemingly ceased. To those living beneath the waves, however, the disaster was far greater in consequence. The moons controlled the flow of tides, the various arteries of the body ocean. Without the moons' regulating touch, currents changed direction and migration patterns shifted alongside the known spawning grounds. The sea races had to relearn everything they knew, infants in an ocean they once ruled as masters.

Then disaster struck again and confounded all with the arrival of the dragon overlords, wyrms the likes of which Ansalon had never seen. The defilers remade the continents and ruined millions of lives before heroes brought them low.

"We know the evil of the new currents," Brysis continued. "We have lived them."

"Some of us did," the Dimernesti with aquiline features muttered.

Brysis spun to face the voice, but she caught Apoletta's glance. Apoletta shook her head slowly, and Brysis, despite the thorn nestled in her chest, swallowed away her rage.

Brysis continued speaking, relating her experiences, reliving them with each word. The three moons had returned several decades after vanishing. It signified the return of magic, the return of the gods who'd been mysteriously absent. Istar sent several groups to explore the oceans again after the dragon overlords had been usurped. Brysis had been among those mapping the arteries that ". . . stretched from the Blood Sea. Down south past Habakkuk's Necklace. Into the Bay of Balifor."

The aquiline Dimernesti snorted derisively. Brysis was not amused.

"Arrowawk!" Utharne said, calling the Dimernesti by name.

"What?" Brysis demanded of Arrowawk.

Arrowawk, ignoring Utharne, looked around the table to ensure his audience was listening. "I hear you Dargonesti consort with humans," he said.

"We have saved human sailors from drowning," Apoletta interjected, trying to hedge Brysis from confronting the obnoxious shoal elf. "What of it?"

"Didn't know you were so cozy as to be using their words," Arrowawk said. " 'Habakkuk's Necklace?' 'Bay of Balifor?' Names don't mean nothing to us true children of the oceans."

"Unlike us," Brysis said, her voice a knife's edge, "the humans learn from one another. They benefit from each other's knowledge . . . and daring. They don't cling to their shores like frightened children scared of the deep."

Angry protests erupted from the balconies and from the Dimernesti who swam around the table. Arrowawk's eyes widened in anger; his hand slipped to the pommel of his blade. That was all Echo Fury needed. The war dolphin thrust himself between Brysis and Arrowawk and bayed in an ear-splitting shriek that caused everyone to wince.

Both Apoletta and Utharne bolted from their seats and interposed themselves between Arrowawk and Brysis. Utharne hissed to

Arrovawk in whispers too low for Brysis to hear, while Apoletta chastised Brysis and Echo Fury with her glare.

"I told you! This was a poor idea," Brysis muttered.

"It's not your place to decide!" Apoletta said, matching Brysis's angry gaze. "If you will not help, then do me the service of keeping your mouth shut! There is more at stake here than your ego!"

The words stung Brysis, but she wasn't one easily cowed. The wrong words rose to her lips, and she didn't care. She raised her voice. "Ego has nothing to do with this! Your so-called delegates are acting like children."

Again the delegates cried out in anger. Even the normally jovial sea giant lost his customary grin.

"But you know what I say?" Brysis said, rising higher above the others. "Let the World Gash swallow them. What do they care if its volcanic fields are spreading? Or that the crater expands. Do they care to know why fish are harder to find?" Brysis said, fully aware of the hush that had settled over the chamber. "Because they're dying—from the foul vapors rising from the World Gash. Storm clouds of ash blanket the region! And there's nowhere the fish can flee. The poisons follow them on the currents!"

Brysis paused a moment, inhaling water to catch her breath. Nobody spoke; the eyes staring at her were a mix of fright, pity, and scorn. She didn't care.

"Go on," Brysis said. "Complain about the fish. Ignore the answers lying at your feet. Forget the scores of undead that migrate here because. . . ." A tired laugh escaped her lips. "Because they've come to feast. I have seen thousands of fish crystallized instantly in the yellow, sulfurous waters above the World Gash. I've seen the blubber boil on whales caught in columns of steam. I have seen precious friends die. . . ." She couldn't continue any longer. Her strength flickered; she felt horribly tired and two centuries older than her features suggested. Brysis turned her back on the delegates and swam for the welcome darkness of the tunnel. Echo Fury fell in at her side. Soon they were gone.

"Well," Utharne said quietly. "That didn't help, I should say."

"No, I'm sorry, it didn't," Apoletta replied, watching Brysis and Echo Fury vanish into the tunnel. "August delegates," Apoletta appealed to the assembled, "I suggest we rest for an hour and regain our focus. We have much to discuss."

"Please. Dimernost welcomes you as a second home," Utharne added then continued under his breath, "family squabbles included."

The delegates swam away from the table, their foul moods evident.

"Dinner?" Utharne asked. "I mean, would you join me? For dinner?"

"I—" Apoletta began before glancing back at the tunnel through which Brysis had disappeared. "I'm sorry," Apoletta said.

"You want to go after her?"

"She's angry," Apoletta said. "That doesn't excuse her behavior, but her expertise is invaluable. Since her first foray into the World Gash, she's returned time and time again to explore its periphery . . . and lost a little something each time, I think. We need her."

Utharne looked dubious, but he shrugged. "My friend and I will have dinner alone, then. Your choice," he said. "But I'll admit. Part of me is curious what she'll say next. It's all very . . . exciting, yes?"

"I'll speak with her," Apoletta said. "She can be reasonable."

Utharne nodded and smiled. "See you in an hour," he said.

The ocean felt wonderfully cool, the blankets of night sky slowly bleeding away their day-borne heat. Dimernost sat several hundred feet beneath the waves, where red, yellow, and blue fell away, and everything turned gray for human eyes. Apoletta knew this through the humans she'd met in her long lifetime. To the sea elves, however, the ocean retained its rich tapestry of colors, even in places as far as the deep abyss. The aural fish still glowed with a golden sheen, the avonage darters were still a creamy, sublime blue.

Apoletta rose toward the surface, hovering momentarily to study the city below her. Unlike Istar, which humans had built before the gods sent it tumbling beneath the waves, Dimernost was a true city of the seas; it possessed almost no roads, few streets. The Dimernesti had no more need for them. Instead, the buildings lay shoulder to shoulder, with hooded doors and windows mounted on the ceilings, staring up to the heavens. Only a few alleyways and forgotten avenues remained, zigzagging wildly through the cluster of structures.

Of all the squat buildings, only a handful rose higher than two stories, save the occasional tower or the pregnant belly of some air dome. The domes contained the homes of surface dwellers, forges, and several ale houses. Thick swatches of coral comprised the rooftops, though in places it grew as thin as lace. Lights from crawlerweed bladders, lantern fish, and even underwater fire called Urione's Flames sparkled through the small gaps—a starry sky mapped on the seafloor. Even with all the illumination, it was difficult to discern the city's true size. It rose and dipped below an expansive coral field that spread out for dozens of miles. Mounds of wild coral growths hid several buildings and covered many domes—a city built through its hills rather than upon them.

The shoal elves were busy rebuilding Dimernost, restoring its former grandeur. Apoletta could still see the damage inflicted by the dragon overlord, the damage that the Dimernesti tried masking, tried forgetting. They grew coral over every structure and tore down those scarred places that would appear too distinctive even with the coral sheath. In a few years' time, Dimernost would become a hidden capital, sheltered from prying eyes and no more distinguishable from any other coral field in the area.

THE ALIEN SEA

While Dimernost seemed bucolic compared to the more ornate structures of Watermere and Istar, Apoletta found it peaceful, serene. She kicked herself skyward, the two lantern fish keeping her idle company with their soft glow. They served as welcome escorts, even if Apoletta had to encourage their presence by baiting the water with tiny morsels of sea-moss. But the sun had set, and the three moons hid behind thick clouds, sharing whatever secrets moons shared with one another. Without the lantern fish, Apoletta would have been able to glean little in the darkness.

Voices emerged from the darkness and guided Apoletta to her mark: Brysis, with her low, angry tones; Ashkoom, the ocean strider, with her surprisingly soft voice; and the occasional burst of squeals from Echo Fury.

Echo Fury is aptly named, Apoletta thought.

A moment later, Apoletta found Brysis hovering a hundred feet below the ocean's calm surface. What little light shone from the three moons—black, red, and silver—died in the first dozen feet of water. Brysis appeared to be brooding. Even Echo Fury seemed unhappy, if that look were possible for a dolphin. Ashkoom smiled and bowed to Apoletta.

Apoletta returned the courtesy.

"I will return," Ashkoom said. "But remember my words. They will do well by you, they will."

Brysis offered a half smile, more conciliatory than genuine. "Thank you, Ashkoom," Brysis said. "Your words helped, if you can believe it."

Ashkoom smiled and kicked herself back down toward Dimernost. The Steward of Istar turned her attention to Brysis, who studied the ocean below her. Apoletta recognized the look. Brysis knew she'd done wrong, and for that she bore the appearance of a child awaiting her reprimand; an impatient edge also flickered in her face, one that betrayed the caged, pensive animal anticipating release. Echo Fury, however, simply swam around Apoletta and Brysis, choosing to remain neutral.

25

LUCIEN SOULBAN

"If you're here to chastise me—" Brysis began.

Apoletta raised her hands, stopping the younger female. "You are reasonable," Apoletta said, "so I will speak with you reasonably. We need the Dimernesti's help—"

"Yes," Brysis said, immediately defensive, "but they refuse to see—"

"We need their help," Apoletta repeated softly. She explained that whatever misgivings existed between their two peoples, they must be mended there, that night.

Brysis, however, said that the Dimernesti didn't welcome allies. They sought retribution for what Brine did, and they blamed the Dargonesti for not sharing their fate.

"Like all things, evil has two parents—action and inaction," Apoletta responded. The dragon had enslaved and slaughtered the Dimernesti, and nobody dared help them openly, neither the Dargonesti nor the gods. Apoletta knew they should have helped more than the pittance they did, but the oceans changed and turned the Dargonesti into frightened children. She believed the Dimernesti had every right to be resentful.

Brysis disagreed. Yes, they had a right to be angry; she understood better than most the strength anger offered. What she didn't like was their insistence on remaining victims.

"Ah," Apoletta said. "Victims to their own fears?"

Brysis nodded. "If you ask me, the shadow of Brine lingers over them. They're still afraid. They're waiting for the next horror to appear. Apoletta, these people are resigned to another terrible fate."

"Then shouldn't we help them?" Apoletta countered.

"No," Brysis said. "I say we go our separate ways . . . before they drag us down too."

"Then we'd compound folly with folly, following one bad example with another. I'm staying to help them. Our two people can only be strong together. And I think we can reach them through the assistance of Utharne, but I need your help too."

Brysis was quiet a moment. She frowned and bit her lower lip. "Fine," she said finally. "But only because I don't want you facing them alone."

Apoletta laughed despite herself. "The shoal elves are not the enemy."

"We'll see," Brysis said before diving back down toward Dimernost. Echo Fury cast Apoletta a sorrowful look before racing after his friend.

Apoletta sighed. She felt tired; the arguments seemed older than her. She'd spent years trying to convince the other Dargonesti they needed these alliances for their mutual survival.

Istar, her beloved city, once lay beneath the aegis of a great vortex called the Blood Sea. The Dargonesti of the sunken city had felt secure in their rule until the vortex calmed and formed a placid sea following a terrible season called the Summer of Chaos.

With the vanishing of the whirlpool, Istar no longer remained sheltered from the events that shattered the world. And in truth, Apoletta found relief in that. The Dargonesti of Istar had to grow and evolve as the other races had done. They had to mend old ties. The Conclave could dictate shoal- and deep-elf relations for decades to come.

Apoletta exhaled the air in her lungs that kept her buoyant and dropped back into the darkness of the ocean below. She didn't swim; she spiraled down slowly with the lantern fish for company. A moment later water surged against her back. She'd settled into a warm current.

As good a place as any, Apoletta thought. She turned toward the two lantern fish and darted her head forward, blowing bubbles in their face. The startled lantern fish dashed away, their glow dying immediately. They returned home, to the reefs below. Darkness encompassed Apoletta, and with it the strange hum of the vast ocean.

The warm current was weak, but Apoletta let it wash over her back; she closed her eyes, her thoughts drifting.

Zebulah. Mine's Zebulah.

Apoletta's eyes drifted open. "Zebulah," she whispered. Had it really been that long? She still remembered that first night when they had met. It was yesterday; it was an eternity.

Yes, she realized, forever is truly that long.

Sadness overcame Apoletta, its rough pinch familiar against the back of her throat, but it did not weaken her. It haunted her with a flurry of images that settled in her thoughts, a flutter of memories caught in glances. She closed her eyes to better see them. Zebulah stood on the water's edge, smiling at her; she and Zebulah spoke, their quiet voices echoing off forgotten walls; she held Zebulah in her arms. Zebulah. . . .

Apoletta smiled at the memories, however fleeting they seemed. His voice still rang true, to her delight, his laughter echoing in the chambers of her heart. She carried that in her prayers, in her dreams, and into the current. . . .

"Father Abbuku, Mother Kisla, carry my words on this current so that they may one day find Zebulah. Bring his whispers back to me though the decades divide us—"

"Apoletta."

The voice startled Apoletta, her prayer dying on her lips. It felt as though it had come from inside her own ears. Her eyes flew open, and she spun in the current, trying to locate the speaker. There was no one.

"Apoletta," the male voice said again.

Apoletta tried sensing direction, but the voice scattered, drifting first one way, then another. She advanced forward before turning back again. The voice lingered. It toyed with her.

There was a noise.

She barely had time to react to the flurry of movement behind her. As she spun, panic welling in her throat, hundreds of fish burst forth from the darkness, disgorged from a shadow's throat. They rushed past her, entire schools that were nothing more than blurs of yellows, reds, and blues darting around her body. They filled her

28

vision and obscured sound with the fluttering of fins. Something had driven them to panic. Apoletta caught the scent, a sickly rich putrescence, an acrid smell of decay. It filled her gills with each breath, and it chased the fish with reeking tendrils.

Death had arrived.

Apoletta could hear it, whatever it was. It swam through the water with slow, ponderous beats. The cloud of fish left her, vanishing back into the mouth of darkness. All of a sudden she was alone in the inky waters, the safety of the city far below her, its faint lights a cruel reminder of the distance between them. Apoletta lay absolutely still, floating and making as little noise as possible. Every sound projected through the ocean with ease, and even the drum of her heart felt as though it sent forth ripples through the water. She drew her breath in measured weight and willed her heart to slow. She tried seeing farther, but the ocean was full of veils.

The plodding beat approached, and the smell of death thickened. The waters tasted foul, but Apoletta endured their acrid tang. She listened carefully, moving her head from side to side like an axe-head shark, trying to better place the sound. The beats grew louder. Her vision, like all Dargonesti, was superior to that of most fish, but at that moment, it failed her.

The beating was nearly on top of her. It sounded large, and while she'd faced great adversaries before, she was ill equipped for an open fight then and there. Only her spellcraft was at her disposal, but that would have to do.

Apoletta mouthed a quick prayer to the Fisher King and concentrated a moment. Her outline blurred and her body distorted, her silhouette bleeding into the surrounding waters. All Dargonesti shared this ability for camouflage, and often made a game of it as children when hiding from one another. Apoletta would be harder to see in the dark waters.

No sooner had the effect taken hold than something emerged from the gloom. A large jester-whale drifted into view, its great tail beating in a slow tempo that drove it deeper. Lips naturally curved into a wedged smile on its bulbous head revealed long whalebone teeth that could trap shoals of krill. Its course would take it under Apoletta by some fifty feet.

Apoletta was about to laugh in relief when she noticed something strange. Her voice caught in her throat.

Wounds cut into the jester-whale's blubber peeled its skin open in loose flaps. Pale and mottled gray flesh covered the beast, while it smiled with black and broken teeth. Apoletta held her tongue as the beast swam beneath her, seemingly unaware of her. A white film covered its eyes, and the smell of decay threatened to gag her.

The whale was dead, Apoletta realized, and it was swimming straight for Dimernost.

It was undead, that much Apoletta understood, not that she professed herself an expert in the matter.

Apoletta swam behind the whale, trying to overcome the heavy fetid stench and turbulent waters. It had not noticed her and instead remained intent on its course. The lights of Dimernost brightened, and Apoletta's chest tightened in panic.

Alone out there, Apoletta knew that warning the others would attract the whale's attention. It would turn on her. If she didn't act, however, the whale might attack an unprepared Dimernost.

Apoletta slowed a moment, drawing upon another ability of her species, also used in Dargonesti childhood games. She focused long enough to draw forth four spheres of yellow light. They filled her with the warmth of good memories. As a frightened child, she had called the lights "friends" and had made them dance to her pleasure. She launched the spheres from her outstretched fingertips and sent them chasing after the whale.

The whale ignored the four lights dancing about its head. It continued on its way. Apoletta prayed the guards in the city below had noticed the faint glows surrounding the whale. In case they hadn't, however, Apoletta imagined a porpoise, head blunted without the beak of a dolphin and its size smaller. The sensation of melting lasted a brief moment, then Apoletta's body, clothing, and possessions shifted into the shape of a small, albinolike porpoise. She felt stronger, faster.

Apoletta shot through the water, chasing after the whale with its dancing lights. She opened her mouth and uttered a series of high-pitched squeals, knowing her porpoise voice traveled far ahead in the water, enough perhaps to alert the guards below. Surprisingly, the undead whale ignored her and continued stolidly on its course.

Brysis skimmed slowly over rooftops, lost in reflection. She had reacted badly, she knew, and felt annoyed at her own actions. Apoletta did not deserve her rancor, but Brysis could not help herself; her mercurial temper slipped out at inopportune moments, her tongue a poor cork for her volatile thoughts. Brysis sighed. Knowing what she knew of the World Gash, she'd grown especially impatient the past few short years.

The distant squeals barely pushed through Brysis's thoughts until Echo Fury nudged her gently. She looked at him, but he stared up, above the city. Brysis followed his gaze and saw the four yellow spheres in the distance. Their wan light seemed to touch upon the body of something exceptionally large, but Brysis could not discern its shape or nature. She could, however, hear the panicked squeals.

"Porpoise?" Brysis asked Echo Fury. Her eyes widened in horrified recognition. "No! Damn it! That's Apoletta!" Brysis turned to the growing crowd of Dimernesti sea elves who had swum up from their homes to investigate the disturbance. "Guards!" Brysis shouted. "The Dargonesti ambassador is in trouble. Guards!"

Without waiting for a response, Brysis and Echo Fury launched themselves skyward, hurtling upward toward the yellow lights. In mid-kick, Brysis changed into a porpoise; her body warmed, her muscles tightening into steel cords. Echo Fury squealed in appreciation and accelerated even faster because Brysis no longer slowed the two of them down.

They came within two hundred feet before seeing the whale. Another fifty feet and they understood its nature. The two swimmers arced away from the beast, uncertain of its intentions. They honed in on Apoletta's cries from somewhere behind the whale.

The cries suddenly died; Apoletta's voice had been silenced. Brysis and Echo Fury propelled themselves forward, spurned on by the worst of fears, but before they could move past the whale, a bright light flared before the beast's face. The whale jerked in reaction, and a disquieting moan tore past its mouth.

Apoletta had grown desperate, uncertain whether her actions had merited any attention. The undead whale had reached within two hundred feet of Dimernost without diverging from its course.

Whatever is necessary, Apoletta thought, and she accelerated up to the fluke of the whale before shapeshifting again back into her elf form; she would need her hands and voice for the task she planned.

Apoletta drew upon ancient arcane lore, and the ball of heat she envisioned filling her belly. She borrowed from the reservoir of both and wove a quick spell with the threads of her whispers.

"And by dawn, the coming of the light had saved them all," she whispered, recounting the closing sentence of one of her spell-fables—spells woven into the lines of Dargonesti parables. The dancing yellow spheres vanished; a brilliant white light erupted before the whale's face. Apoletta intended her last-ditch effort to alert those in Dimernost; the cataracts covering the jester-whale's eyes suggested the creature would be immune to the effects of the mystical flare. The whale, however, reared and bucked, not so much blinded as startled. That surprised Apoletta.

How did I affect it? she wondered. The creature is blind!

As the light died, Apoletta spotted more shapes in the water. To her left appeared a porpoise and the sure shape of a large war dolphin.

Brysis and Echo Fury!

Fur-lined sea otters—seven in total—also approached the whale. Apoletta recognized the Dimernesti even before the city guards shifted from sea otters back to their elf bodies. Their thick brush retreated into their skin, and in their hands appeared polished coral tridents; they kept themselves between the whale and Dimernost, now a little more than one hundred feet below.

The whale hesitated, uncertain. Then it shuddered violently in spasms that contorted its face and arced its back to such extremes that it seemed to threaten to snap its spine.

"No!" a pair of voices cried from below. Apoletta looked down in time to see the ocean striders, Ashkoom and Shakhall, clawing at the waters in their mad dash to reach the whale. "Get away from it! Flee! Flee!" they shrieked.

Too late.

A tearing sound issued from the whale, and the wounds and open flaps of blubber ripped open from within.

Dozens of hands appeared inside the whale's wounds and pushed at its sides, tearing further open the flaps of blubber. The whale uttered a horrific howl of pain before something choked off its voice. Skeletons and water-bloated zombies, by the score, filled the whale's mouth and clawed their way over its tongue and out past its teeth. Desiccated and pale creatures, their eyes glowing with malevolent hatred, pulled themselves up through the bulging blowhole.

Everyone froze in horror at the incomprehensible sight before them: dozens of fell undead tearing their way out of their foul vessel, the jester-whale. Before anyone could react, the undead swarmed over the Dimernesti guards, overwhelming them.

Screams and the blood of the living filled the water.

Undead rained down upon Dimernost.

The two ocean striders were the first to react; Shakhall muttered an expletive and pointed to the undead pack tearing the guards apart. Water rushed past Apoletta and a vortex of bubbles appeared below the mob, pulling several of the zombies and skeletons off their victims. Ashkoom, fury in her war cry, tore into the undead. They swarmed over her quickly, but she returned the favor, equally relentless in her assault. She snapped skeletons in half and swung her enormous falchion with frightening grace.

Apoletta tried spotting Brysis and Echo Fury, but the undead had filled the water. Two of the creatures that had emerged from the blowhole swam toward her, or rather clawed their way through the water. Apoletta's only salvation in the matter was that those particular undead were not water born. They could not swim as well as she. Forcing herself to calm a moment, Apoletta brought her hands before her and gestured in the water. The flame in her belly spread its warmth through her arms.

"The dolphins, leaping through the sun, brought fire back from the heavens," she said, whispering another spell-fable. Instantly, four darts of light swirled between her outstretched hands before coursing outward. All four missiles homed in on the lead undead charging forward. The foul creature dropped back, the darts striking like fast punches. The one behind it, however, redoubled its efforts to reach Apoletta. It shrieked in the water, its voice a wail of unholy rage.

Apoletta prepared another spell, calling to mind an appropriate fable. The fell creature was almost upon her, snapping its needlelike teeth in anticipation of its victim.

Out of nowhere, a blur of movement shot past the undead creature, which froze in shock at the sudden wound, like a second mouth, that stretched across its belly. It turned to find its attacker, Echo Fury with his bladed fins, and when it was distracted, Brysis appeared behind the creature and ran it through with her rapier.

Brysis smiled at the creature's death struggle, even as its companion recovered from Apoletta's missile barrage and kicked toward her.

Mistake, Apoletta thought. She drew strength from the warmth in her belly. Her fingertips tingled. She brought to mind again the fable of the dolphins leaping into the sky to bring the sun's flames back to the ocean; in doing so, the dolphins reputedly carried warmth and light to the first travelers who ever ventured beneath the waves.

Four more glowing darts appeared in Apoletta's hands; four lights streaked forth, over and past Brysis. They struck the creature swimming up behind her, slaying it with precise lethality. Brysis stabbed her target one final time; it slumped forward and sank slowly.

"Thank you," Brysis said.

Apoletta nodded and surveyed the battle scene. The whale was sinking, its large mass dragging it down below. All the guards were dead or had fled to Dimernost to help with the defense; the undead were in Dimernost now, terrorizing and murdering.

Apoletta headed for the two ocean striders engaged in the fight of their lives, but as Apoletta and Brysis approached, Shakhall cried out.

"Attend to those below, you must. We shall handle these ones!"

Apoletta nodded, but Brysis hesitated at the sight of Ashkoom's wounds. Apoletta grabbed Brysis by the arm.

"Down," Apoletta ordered.

Brysis didn't resist. They dived down with Echo Fury joining quickly.

Screams emerged from Dimernost as they approached, and to Apoletta's horror, the fighting appeared to be centered on the Conclave's dome.

Utharne swam through the waters of the empty temple, his eyes probing the darkness.

"Where, where, where are you, my friend?" he asked, half aloud, half to himself. He searched the ceiling with his eyes; the temple arched up, three stories held aloft by rows of stalagmite growths of coral. He almost missed the black figure darting between columns.

"I have you now," Utharne cried; thick fur covered his skin, and his features melted into the face of a sea otter. He chased after the black figure; it barked in apparent amusement and skittered away, allowing Utharne to give chase.

The seal Utharne chased was black, beautiful, and wonderfully sleek. Its skin caught light like a mirror and glistened. Only an unusual birthmark marred its ebony hue, a blue flame upon its brow much like the flame on Utharne's shell necklace.

Sea otter chased seal through the temple with a childlike exuberance to their game. They rounded columns and swam around marble statues, their play almost improper in the house of worship.

"Oh, I'm sure Abbuku wouldn't mind," Utharne told the rare visitor before winking at the seal. The seal barked its approval.

The pair raced past the seaweed tethers of a hanging brazier made from surface-forged iron when the seal stopped suddenly. Utharne almost collided with him. Instead he turned back into his elf form and panted.

"Enough of the game, eh, Brine-Whisker?" he asked.

Brine-Whisker said nothing; he sniffed the waters instead. Utharne understood and waited quietly. He, too, sampled the seawater rushing through his gills.

"I see," Utharne said. Without another word, the two left the sanctuary of the temple just as the guards trumpeted their warnings through conch-shell horns.

Screams erupted from the building as Apoletta, Brysis, and Echo Fury approached Dimernost from above. While the undead focused their attacks on the dome, several ventured into adjoining buildings on lethal explorations.

Apoletta hesitated; the scene was one of pandemonium. Several Dimernesti guards were already dead, their bodies desiccated, skeletal, and impossibly ancient before their time. Brysis immediately took to beheading them. Apoletta raced forward and grabbed her arm.

"In the name of Krijol!" Apoletta said, swearing on the warrior-goddess's name.

"Those killed by the undead could return as undead," Brysis said. "Please. Unless you wish to face an unending army!"

Apoletta's resolve weakened at the thought. She nodded and released Brysis. The younger sea elf continued decapitating the dead, while Apoletta pushed down toward the dome.

Part of the dome's ceiling had collapsed, revealing the interior. The undead that entered seemed of many types, ranging from the hate-eyed creatures that had attacked Apoletta earlier, to a handful made of tattered robes with glowing eyes. Apoletta recognized others as lacedons, foul flesh-eaters of the sea, their mottled green skin and bony limbs wreathed in seaweed.

The sea giant was lashing out with his jagged lance, impaling the advancing undead. To Apoletta's dismay, however, several delegates already lay dead; two of the merfolk appeared ravaged, their coral and shell crossbows near their floating bodies. Several brathnoc, too, had fallen, though the survivors rallied to blind their opponents with sticky jets of ink that they fired from their hands. Two brathnoc had succumbed to their species' battle frenzy and were attacking the undead with unequaled fury. They fought using their barbed red tails that the brathnoc delegates normally kept hidden.

Apoletta entered the dome proper through the cracked ceiling.

LUCIEN SOULBAN

The warmth in her belly flared into a raging ball of fire in her chest. There was blood in the water. These abominations reveled in the carnage, basked in the misery they spread. To the undead, it was a pitiless game, and Apoletta could neither fathom it nor allow it to continue.

Apoletta reached into her pouch to produce a swatch of seal fur tied with a bit of twine around an amber rod. Her lessons in magic, returned and the sensation of power sang its chorus.

"And though dim the sky," Apoletta uttered, her voice a growl, "so much the better to witness her fury!"

Upon the stroke of her last word, Apoletta unleashed a bolt of crackling lightning and directed it against a trio of the tattered-robed undead that were advancing on the brathnoc. Two vanished in the lightning strike, their shrieks echoing through the dome. The third barely survived.

Several of the undead, their inhuman faces contorted by confusion and fear, turned toward Apoletta.

"Come to me!" Apoletta shouted, her words angry but foolish. The creatures outclassed her, but then she intended her voice serve another purpose; it rallied the surviving delegates to strike back. When several of the undead, the hatred in their eye sockets smoldering, turned to attack Apoletta, the sea giant swung the lance above his head. He brought it down, impaling another creature and shattering the floor with the weapon.

The remaining undead decided the sea giant was the greater foe and charged him; they crawled over his large frame, and Apoletta cursed their cunning. Any spell she sent against them would hurt him as well.

The sea giant was strong, but the dozen fell creatures attacking overwhelmed him one cut at a time. Apoletta grabbed a trident from a dead guard and charged, joining two merfolk and the black-haired child of the sea already in the fray. Nobody approached the two brathnoc who fought with wild abandon, their screams sending chills down Apoletta's spine.

THE ALIEN SEA

Apoletta barely avoided the wild swing of the sea giant, swimming under the lance as it struck a nearby wall. The clamor echoed through the water, the din piercing her ears. She came on the lacedon with a bloody maw, and sank her trident into its back. It fell away, shrieking, but before she could strike at it again, something raked its claws across her back. Apoletta spun around with the trident, catching a second lacedon in the face.

It snarled and hissed at her, but she kept it at bay with her weapon. Her wound bled, and while her back burned from the toxins delivered by the lacedon's claws, Apoletta knew it wasn't a bad enough wound to cause the usual accompanying paralysis.

Apoletta jabbed and parried the creature, her skill with the weapon far greater than its skills with a snapping mouth and sharp claws. It swam around her, cautiously looking for an opportunity. Apoletta turned to follow its movements. Suddenly it stopped and grinned nastily. Apoletta realized her mistake: the lacedon had maneuvered her around; the lacedon she had injured a moment earlier was behind her.

The push of water was unmistakable; the creature at Apoletta's back snarled and snapped, its razor fingers inches from cutting into her jugular. Apoletta raised her trident in both hands at the same moment she kicked upward. She lifted the trident over her head, and arched her back. The trident's prongs caught the charging lacedon in its neck while she completed a backward flip. The lacedon sailed beneath her. Apoletta sank her weight into the trident, driving the creature into the floor, the prongs impaling its neck.

Unfortunately, the trident wedged into the undead's spine, leaving her unarmed to face her other opponent. It charged forward. Apoletta drew an obsidian dagger from the leg sheath hidden beneath her gown. She struck out, catching her opponent across its forehead. The lacedon's assault did not abate, however, and it barreled into her.

The lacedon sank its fetid teeth into Apoletta's shoulder; she cried out and immediately paid the creature several blade thrusts to its belly. It grunted in pain and bit harder; finally, it stopped chewing her shoulder and simply fell away, its eyes vacant and its stomach torn open.

Apoletta pressed her palm into her shoulder to staunch the blood flow, but the situation around her remained dire. Badly injured with cuts across his face, the sea giant was still enduring the tattered-robed foes that threw themselves at him with savage intent. The generally pacifist brathnoc had tried to blind their opponents but to little avail, while a handful of Dimernesti guards and the black-haired child of the sea were fighting the stragglers.

Apoletta wrenched the trident from her adversary and leaped back into the fray, first helping the beleaguered brathnoc. A few well-placed jabs with her weapon and another undead fell. Another took its place and another after that. She dispatched them, her movements growing heavy and slow, her wounds aching. In between quick glances, she noticed that the sea giant had fallen and appeared close to death, though thankfully he had eliminated several of the undead. A few guards and one battle-enraged brathnoc were still fighting.

Suddenly, one of the dead guards floating near the floor twitched . . . then another. Two dead guards moved, their eyes drained of reason or compassion, their limbs already stiff. Dread, much like cold water, filled Apoletta's belly, turning her heart to ice.

Apoletta pushed herself between the brathnoc and the remaining undead. She turned to the delegates and hissed, "Escape while you can. I'll draw their attention."

One of the brathnoc, however, pointed with webbed fingers. Apoletta followed his gaze to the ceiling, where a serene-looking Utharne and a seal floated down through the hole and deep inside the chamber. Apoletta marveled at the black seal, for upon its forehead, like a flame straddling a candle, was a lick of flickering blue flame.

THE ALIEN SEA

As Utharne stretched out his arms, the undead took notice immediately. Some hissed, but every single one of them retreated a step. The priest of Abbuku pointed at the dozen or so undead before him and shouted with the voice of a struck bell.

"Heed me, unhallowed! The Fisher King demands you submit or *flee!*"

The flame on the seal's forehead grew in intensity as Utharne swept his arm forward. The undead wailed in terror before five of their tongues turned to ash. Three lacedons as well as one of the pale creatures with the gaze of feral hate and a tattered-robed undead, froze in place. Their skin cracked and flaked. Almost instantly, the three disintegrated into muddied clouds of ash.

The seal swam into the dome's chamber and headed straight for the injured sea giant. As it swam by the remaining undead, they scattered, forcibly pushed away. The seal swam up to the sea giant and waited there, protecting him.

The surviving undead scurried away. They poured out the hole into the dark ocean, but Apoletta did not feel vindicated yet. She swam after them, her fury pushing her forward. She wanted the beasts to pay for their actions, for the deaths they had inflicted.

Outside more guards waited, having dispensed with the undead elsewhere. They attacked the slower-moving creatures, but the agile lacedons easily avoided the scattered guards and escaped. Apoletta's heart raced, and her limbs weighed on her heavily with numb exhaustion, but still she pursued them.

Apoletta pushed herself until she was within striking distance of an injured lacedon. She hurled her trident, an expert throw that struck the lacedon in the back. It dropped away into the dark water.

Only then did Apoletta realize her error. Two hundred feet above the wan lights of Dimernost, she'd just thrown away her last, best weapon. Too exhausted for spellcraft, she was alone again in the inky darkness. The other lacedons scattered into the murk.

Carefully, Apoletta tried listening, despite her beating heart.

Something out there moved. It displaced water with a caressing hiss.

She was not alone.

Apoletta remained still, trying to locate the sound. She turned to face the presence, but whatever it was remained just outside her field of vision. She caught glimpses of it, a large snow-crest shark, possibly. But its skin seemed odd.

It's armored? she thought but almost instantly realized that it was swathes of thick, blood-hued coral that covered its flanks and the flat of its head and nose. Then she caught a glimpse of something else, something farther out that exuded a soft glow.

It took Apoletta a moment to recognize the luminous thread stitched in arcane patterns. Shocked, she darted forward and caught a glimpse of a red-robed figure floating in the distance, on the curtain's edge of shadows.

"Zebulah," Apoletta whispered, her voice robbed of its breath.

"Apoletta!" a voice cried out.

Apoletta's heart stopped, but the voice was that of a woman. It had come from below.

Apoletta looked down to see a concerned Brysis, Echo Fury, and four guards swimming up to meet her.

Apoletta looked back to the robed figure, but he was gone. Apoletta darted forward, but Echo Fury swam in front of her and stopped.

"We have to go!" Brysis said, growing more concerned. "Several undead escaped. Utharne wants everyone inside Dimernost. Now."

Apoletta listened to the water, but she couldn't hear anything over Brysis and the others. "Shh," Apoletta instructed.

Everyone fell dead silent; Apoletta searched the surrounding ocean with her eyes and ears, but there was nothing.

"Apoletta," Brysis whispered. "Please."

Apoletta looked at the group and recognized their wide-eyed, almost pleading expressions. Apoletta nodded. "You're right," she said. "We should return."

THE ALIEN SEA

Apoletta gave the dark waters a final glance before heading back down to Dimernost; Brysis and the others followed.

Zebulah? Apoletta thought. What's happening?

CHAPTER
Aftermath
2

Utharne scurried among the injured in the dome, trying to bring them comfort. He'd spent his time praying to the Fisher King and using his healing crafts to stabilize the badly injured. Utharne was spent and could heal no more; instead, he and Brysis applied salves and unguents to help the remaining wounded.

Apoletta did what she could with quiet whispers and words of encouragement. Finally, when a moment presented itself, Utharne swam over to Apoletta. The marvelous seal was with him, though without the flame atop its forehead. It still bore a blue-flamed birthmark.

"How are you?" he asked gently. "I mean your injuries. Can I see to them?"

Apoletta shook her head. "Thank you," she replied. "Save your crafts for those who need them most."

He nodded, a tired but appreciative smile on his lips.

Apoletta motioned toward the sea giant who lay against the dome's curved wall and asked about his condition. Utharne informed her Boddenson would require rest but that he would recover.

"Good," Apoletta replied. "And who, might I ask, is this?" she asked, reaching out to pet the seal.

The seal squinted with pleasure; Apoletta stroked the fine fur on its head.

"This," Utharne said, "is my friend, Brine-Whisker."

"He's beautiful," Apoletta replied, studying him. "But what was that blue flame I saw on his head?"

"Briney is. . . ." Utharne hesitated. "I must remember not to call him Brine. He's my holy symbol, my touchstone with the Fisher King. It's how I perform miracles."

"Ah," Apoletta said, smiling. She'd heard that Dimernesti priests once possessed living symbols of their faith. "But I thought those were in the old times."

"Before my people shunned the gods," Utharne said. "There's no shame in telling the truth. Hard, yes; shameful, no."

"I'd like to know more when we have time," Apoletta said, smiling.

"Wonderful," Utharne said.

Shouts intruded on them both, and Apoletta turned to find Brysis arguing with Arrovawk and several shoal elves.

"What now?" Apoletta said, all raw nerves. She and Utharne swam quickly before the two parties could come to blows.

"What's going on, Arrovawk?" Utharne asked.

"Explain yourself," Apoletta told Brysis.

Both parties launched into their tirade before either Apoletta or Utharne could stop them.

". . . sea wench was cutting the heads off our guards . . ."

". . . fools don't realize that the dead return to life . . ."

". . . think they can walk all over us Dimernesti . . ."

". . . too frightened to pull their heads from out their—"

"Enough!" Apoletta shouted, her voice echoing across the dome's interior. Everyone went silent, shocked by Apoletta's outburst. But the childish display of her subordinates and her shallow-water cousins angered her as much as the loss of so many lives burdened her thoughts. Even then, her thoughts also lingered on the figure in the red robes. All the commotion and uncertainty frightened her.

"We lost many tonight," Apoletta said, her words measured carefully to ensure everyone heeded her every last word. "They did not die for you to bicker like children! See to the wounded and prepare the dead. They deserve dignity this night . . . from both of you!"

"I'll prepare the dead and make sure that they're actually, you know, dead." Utharne said.

Brysis and the Dimernesti guards appeared humbled by Utharne's statement; they bowed their heads and nodded before swimming off to help the injured. Only Arrovawk challenged Apoletta's stare, but before she could react, a soft purr came from Utharne.

"Arrovawk," Utharne said, "I'll drop you where you stand. And it'll be kind business compared to what the good woman here would do to you."

Arrovawk hesitated then dropped his eyes. He left them alone.

"Sorry," Utharne said.

"We both have reason to be sorry," Apoletta said, staring at the injured and their tenders. "But we also have larger concerns, far larger than we realized."

"Yes, we do," Utharne said. "The other delegates are heading home as soon as possible, starting tomorrow at dawn."

"We can track them all down later," Apoletta said with a deep sigh. "For the moment I'm more concerned with your people. Are you still with us?"

Utharne sighed. "I . . . I don't know. I mean, you know that many Dimernesti opposed the Conclave. Now, well, this attack has renewed their doubt and opposition. In a strange way, it has given them new reasons why we should shun outsiders."

"I will not see this Conclave die."

Utharne grinned. "Good. Then we will work together tomorrow."

"Sleep," Slyphanous said.

Apoletta turned her head and stared across the stately room at Slyphanous. He stood at the room's balcony, the only entrance into her chamber. Two Dargonesti in armors of polished crab shell and leather stood behind him, looking out across the city. She lay in a bed of green fan-leafs with a covering of furs.

"I wish I could," Apoletta said.

"May I come in?" he asked.

Apoletta nodded.

Slyphanous entered the room and paused, studying Apoletta carefully. "What happened out there?" he asked finally. "And don't tell me it was the attack. When Brysis returned with you, you were strangely discomposed. Shaken."

Apoletta smiled. She had a right to be shaken, given the circumstances. But then again, perhaps she did not. She'd faced truly horrific adversaries in her centuries as Istar's warrior queen and stalwart defender. In the decades following the Dargonesti expedition to explore Istar, she had found and faced many terrible creatures that had taken roost in the sunken city. The centuries after were not much better either.

"You acted as though you saw a. . . ."

"Ghost?" Apoletta responded. "I did see a ghost tonight."

"More undead?" Slyphanous asked.

Apoletta sighed. "No. I saw someone dressed in red robes. I . . . I heard a voice too. I think it was . . . Zebulah."

Brysis watched the ocean strider Ashkoom for a while before she turned to Echo Fury.

"I need to do this alone," she said.

Echo Fury gave an upturned flick of his head before darting away.

Brysis breathed in deeply, trying to ignore the blood spores lingering in the water; the currents were rich with the smell of death.

She swam up to the ocean strider who floated fifty yards above the dome, staring out across the dark water.

Brysis floated near Ashkoom for several long moments before speaking. "I'm sorry for your loss," she said. "Shakhall was—"

Ashkoom offered a torn smile, but it faded when her thin lips quivered.

"I'm so sorry," Brysis repeated, a lump swelling in her throat. She wanted to embrace the ocean strider, but the giantess's size prohibited it. Instead, she lay one hand on Ashkoom's arm and blubberlike skin.

The ocean strider shook her head. "Nothing to be done," Ashkoom said, staring out. "Beheaded him myself, I did," she whispered. "Better for all."

"Are you staying?" Brysis asked.

Ashkoom shook her head again. "At first light, I travel home. Shakhall's children must be told."

"This is my fault," Brysis said. "And don't say it wasn't. I invited you and Shakhall here. Persuaded you the Conclave was *necessary*." Brysis's laugh was derisive.

"Bring us here, you did," Ashkoom said. "And perhaps fault does lie with you. But we are glad we came, we are."

"Glad?"

"I will miss Shakhall, I will," Ashkoom said, interrupting the much smaller sea elf. "But the cause was worthy, it was."

"Was?"

"I told the delegates the undead are greater threat, I did. This proves me right."

"But," Brysis said, hesitating, "this proves what we've been saying. It's the World Gash at play here."

"How?" Ashkoom said. "You see with your own eyes the dead-who-live, you did."

"Yes," Brysis said, "but the undead come from the World Gash, where they have safe harbor. I know it. I can't prove it yet, but I know it as well as I know my own name. That area is blighted and poisoned with sulfur. Nobody threatens them there."

"What would you ask?" Ashkoom said. "That I stay? I cannot. Shakhall's children must be told. To purify his spirit and prepare his bones for the Spawning Deeps."

Brysis understood. Those ocean striders on the cusp of a natural death sensed their time approaching and went to a secret place called the Spawning Deeps. It was a mass graveyard filled with their bones and possessions. Although solitary creatures in life, the ocean striders believed they shared their aquatic hereafter in the company of others; their heaven was abundant with fish, and it was the only place they could finally become a community without hunting everything around them to extinction.

"After you are done," Brysis said. "The Conclave needs you."

"The same Conclave you mock?"

Brysis grew silent, the comment a well-deserved slap. She hadn't always been so short tempered; once, her patience and compassion matched Apoletta's and Utharne's.

"Not any longer do I mock," Brysis said quietly.

"I'm sorry," Ashkoom said, obviously embarrassed. "The comment is undeserved, it is."

"No," Brysis said in quiet tone. "It—look, you can't judge the Conclave by my foolish actions."

"You are passionate, not foolish," Ashkoom said, correcting her with motherly concern. "It is why I like you."

"Passionate," Brysis said, laughing. "I like that. But it doesn't change anything. The Conclave needs allies; I understand now. And the more people band together, the more others have the courage to join. Please, give this a chance."

Ashkoom was quiet a moment. "Very well," she said finally. "But if you're to sway the others, you will need proof of your words."

"Yes," she agreed. "I need proof."

"That the World Gash is the danger you say. Only then will others like the brathnoc or tritons join."

Tritons, Brysis thought. Those would be worthy allies. The triton war with the reptilian sahuagin occupied their attention and resources, however.

"Could you speak with the tritons? On our behalf?"

"I will, after Shakhall. And if your Conclave survives this night."

Brysis nodded. "I know," she said. "I pray it does."

Slyphanous sat at the edge of Apoletta's bed. She sat with her back against the wall, the covers to her hips and her long, beautiful silver hair undulating gently. And they argued.

Slyphanous said that the red robes could have belonged to any of the neutral Wizards of High Sorcery. It was their mark. Apoletta countered with the fact that runes adorned the stranger's robes, runes stitched with luminous thread, the same as Zebulah used to have. Slyphanous asked if Apoletta had ever met any other red-robed wizards from the surface to know if such runes were unique. Apoletta admitted she had not.

Slyphanous sighed. "Apoletta, my dear. I know you miss Zebulah, but he left us decades ago. He must not have survived. Not all these years."

"Why not?" Apoletta asked. "His magic kept him young for nearly a century when we were together. Why not?"

"Because," Slyphanous said gently. "Magic fled our world, for what? Over three decades? Zebulah had nothing to preserve his youth during that time. . . ." Slyphanous trailed off.

"What are you saying?" Apoletta said.

"You must face the possibility," Slyphanous said. "Likely he long ago drowned."

"No," Apoletta said, instantly rejecting the notion. It stung her to think that, even though it wasn't the first time someone had mentioned that possibility.

"He couldn't survive the deep. Not without his spells," Slyphanous insisted. "When he fled, it was likely to his doom."

"No," Apoletta said. "I don't believe that. He was resourceful and. . . ."

Slyphanous waited a moment before asking. "And?"

"And," Apoletta said, "I saw him tonight. Heard him. I know I did."

Slyphanous sat there, thinking. He finally nodded. "Very well," he said. "Then if you truly saw him tonight, then you must ask yourself this: What was he doing out there?"

Apoletta shook her head. "I . . . I don't know. But I will tell you this," Apoletta said, "I intend to find my husband."

The undead attack rattled everyone. Many more delegates believed that isolation was the key to weathering catastrophic events. The brathnoc left first, their words devoid of pretense or animosity. They spoke curtly; that was how they communicated.

"Thank you. We're not interested in the Conclave. Good-bye." And with that, the mantalike brathnoc left as first light scattered across the ocean's surface.

The blue-haired merfolk were even less cordial.

"The attack was inexcusable," the merfolk delegate, Athiana, said. "That an enemy force managed to approach your city so easily is a frightening and damning testament. No wonder the dragon Brynseldimer scattered your people so effortlessly."

Apoletta marveled at the change in the once mirthful and friendly merfolk; they'd become so brutal and callous, she wondered if seawater wasn't the only thing the dragon overlords had poisoned when they altered the lands.

Utharne, however, responded calmly. "Brine . . . Brynseldimer," he corrected, "hurt your people as much as he did ours. So I have to wonder. Are you angry with the Dimernesti? Or with yourselves?

For being victimized a second time last night?"

Athiana's eyes flared with violet intensity, and she looked ready to strike down Utharne. Utharne seemed more curious of her reaction than worried. Athiana spun away and left with a flutter kick that almost displaced Utharne.

"That was, um . . . not very pleasant," Utharne said with a grim smile.

Ashkoom left next with the decapitated body of her mate. Brysis said her farewell to the ocean strider, as did Apoletta. Before Ashkoom could leave, however, Apoletta asked her for her opinion of the whale that had carried the undead.

The ocean strider stared at the corpse of the whale, which was still lodged in the collapsed building where it fell. Shoal elves were hacking it into smaller pieces and spreading the remains among the coral groves north of Dimernost.

"One of the dead-that-live," she responded grimly. "It is all but mindless. The dead-that-live hide inside it. It swims; they steer it by pulling its muscles."

That made sense to Apoletta. Her flare spell that caused the whale to jerk did not affect it directly, but it startled the undead hiding inside who peered outside to steer.

After Ashkoom left, Apoletta turned to Utharne and nodded. It was time.

CHAPTER
The Speaker of the Sea
3

The days passed with nothing to span the hours except for the string of arguments and accusations. The Dimernesti disliked the presence of their Dargonesti guests, and they used the undead attack to strengthen their support and to push forth their isolationist policies.

"From the First Cataclysm," a sleek shoal elf said, his green hair braided and his age marked in the centuries, "when the great mountain of fire crashed into the sea and destroyed Istar, we have been at odds with our so-called cousins."

The Dimernesti were united once, Apoletta knew, but when the Cataclysm that sunk the proud city of Istar altered the terrain, the disaster nearly obliterated the Dimernesti cities that lay in shallow waters. Tidal waves raced across every continental shore, barreling over shoal elf communities, a million hammer strokes of the gods striking the anvil of Krynn. The Dimernesti, devastated by the instant loss of home and culture, became nomads.

"Where were they when the disaster struck?" the shoal elf demanded.

"Unfair and untrue!" Apoletta responded. She turned to bow to the Speaker of the Sea, Nuqala.

The leader of all Dimernesti, Nuqala wore her age like a beautiful crown. A veil-like robe covered her body, while beneath, oyster-silk strips coiled around her limbs. Despite her white hair and weathered features that bespoke centuries of hardship, her eyes glistened sharply.

"Forgive me," Apoletta said, "but I must protest."

The Speaker of the Sea, sitting on her balcony throne high above in the interior of the hollow tower, nodded.

"My people flocked to your aid," Apoletta said, turning to the various clan representatives, "but the Dimernesti turned us away."

"Clearly your guilt has authored its own version of history," the shoal elf replied with a harsh laugh. "We of the Blooded Shore Clan know the truth! Did the gods not forsake you for twelve years for your selfishness? Because you refused to help others? You retreated into your own cities and forgot we ever existed."

"Retreated!" Apoletta said, returning his incredulous laugh. "Yes, the gods forsook us and then forgave us! But before then, in the first year after the Cataclysm, to you alone we offered help! Your people slapped our hand away as often as we offered it."

"It was jealousy," Nuqala said, her voice soft but resonating within the hollow tower.

Utharne, who stood at her side, offered Apoletta a lopsided smile, but it vanished quickly.

"Jealousy?" a female representative with powder blue skin demanded.

"Yes," the Speaker of the Sea said. "We were jealous that the Dargonesti had not suffered as we had. So we refused their help."

"Well!" the Blooded Shore representative said. "I, for one, am glad we refused their help." He looked around for support, pleased with himself.

"The Clan of the Emerald Shell agrees," said the Dimernesti female with powder blue skin. "Or we would have suffered the Dargonesti's betrayal when they refused to help us following the Second Cataclysm—when Brynseldimer plagued us."

"The Sunstrider Clan disagrees," said a male Dimernesti named Gavalothus, whose skin was striated in two shades of blue.

Apoletta knew him well and was glad for his support.

Gavalothus continued. "Dargonesti envoys from Istar, from Apoletta herself, gave us two dragonlances."

An audible gasp echoed through the room.

"You had dragonlances?" the Emerald Shell elf asked, her brows furrowed.

"Had, yes." Gavalothus looked uncomfortable. "With the Dargonesti's help, we launched an attack against Brynseldimer."

"And *failed*," the Blooded Shore representative said with a laugh. "Never send a Sunstrider to do a Blooded Shore's job."

"Job, Inserrifa?" Gavalothus said, addressing the Blooded Shore elf. "You mean sell the dragonlances to the highest bidder? Isn't that what you do best?"

Inserrifa kicked forward with a roar, his outstretched hands ready to strangle Gavalothus. Before anyone could react, the water between the two representatives became translucent with ripples. The iris-shaped column of water swelled outward, pushing both elves backward.

"There will be no fighting in this house . . . my house!" Nuqala said, her angry voice echoing through the hollow. The remnant flicker of spellcraft danced around her outstretched hand. She stepped off from the ledge of her throne and floated down, her long white hair a regal cloak that fluttered above her. When she landed, each representative fell to one knee and bowed his head. Even Utharne and the Speaker's guards dropped from their perch and bowed. Apoletta motioned for Slyphanous to do the same as she followed suit.

"Rise, Apoletta of Istar," the Speaker said. "You are mouthpiece for the Speaker of the Moon and thus stand equal to me."

Apoletta gratefully did as instructed. Although she'd ruled over Istar as its steward, she felt humbled and small in the Speaker's presence. Nuqala was the oldest Dimernesti; a survivor of the First

Cataclysm and the Second, she embodied their history, and she deserved everyone's respect.

"We are a proud people," Nuqala said to Apoletta; she placed her finger under Apoletta's jaw and brought her head up. The Speaker's eyes were of such light green that they seemed gold. "And in equal strokes, our pride has both cost us and allowed us to survive."

The Speaker turned to the others.

"And you! Children of Dimernest and Brandis Soleyya, I will not abide division and bloodshed between us anymore. Are you so petty as to believe this Conclave is solely to the Dargonesti's benefit? Whether you agree with their actions or not, Dargonesti have never turned on Dargonesti since the days of Urione. Can you claim the same? Blood feuds? Hunting domains? Raiding parties? Go! Retire for the night and return tomorrow. You face longer days than the ones that preceded you, that much I promise. We will repair this rift! Go!"

Shaken, the representatives rose to their feet and swam out the tower's archway, mumbling their apologies. Apoletta was about to follow when the Speaker of the Sea stopped her with a gentle hand.

"Not you, Apoletta of Istar. Nor you, Utharne of the Fallen Shores. I have a grave task for you both."

"I will not lie," the Speaker said, sitting upon her great chair in her balcony perch high above the tower floor. Her guards, their armor made from the thorny red carapace of large crabs, took their positions on either side of her throne. "Our position is perilous."

Apoletta and Utharne said nothing as they floated before her. They simply listened to the female elf whose voice carried the wisdom of her long years.

"My people are scattered, thanks to Brynseldimer. He kept us hostage. We fractured." Nuqala sighed and remained quiet a long moment.

Finally, Apoletta asked how they could help, trying to stir the Speaker from her thoughts.

"I'm afraid you can't," the Speaker said. "In fact, I fear we agreed to the Conclave when we ourselves weren't ready."

Both Apoletta and Utharne drifted forward, concerned.

"Surely we can't give up? Not now," Utharne said.

"Please, Speaker of the Sea, we cannot turn back from this course," Apoletta added desperately.

The Speaker nodded. "I understand; I truly do. Though I will admit to my own reservations about the Conclave."

"How so?" Apoletta asked.

"My people were jealous of you, our deep-water cousins, for not suffering as we had. We could have used your help, but we went our own way and suffered for it. That said, there is some blame that remains at your feet."

Apoletta bit her tongue. She wanted to respond, this argument was age old between the Dimernesti and Dargonesti. Both sides blamed one another for events. Apoletta had to admit she herself wasn't sure how the Dargonesti initially failed the Dimernesti. When the Cataclysm had befallen the world, the Dargonesti refused to help the surface world. For that, the gods robbed their priests of miracles and their wizards of spells. Not until Nakaro Silverwake quested for his people and recovered the artifact sword Tideripper did the gods forgive the Dargonesti and restore their magics, after a twelve-year drought. Even then, Dargonesti had made the first effort to help the Dimernesti following the Cataclysm. Above all other species, they tried to help their cousins.

Unfortunately, neither could Apoletta ignore the fact that animosity existed between the cousins.

"My people," the Speaker began, "may have rejected your help, but your people gave up on us too easily. We were hurt . . . devastated.

The tidal waves swept in, leaving ruins behind, and then they swept back out, flattening the ruins. Every family lost three members or more. I had five brothers and three sisters I will never know. And when we became jealous at what you managed to preserve, when we refused your help, your people acted like small children and sulked. You stopped helping us or anyone because we hurt your pride. The surface world suffered for it, and eventually, you did as well."

Apoletta wanted to respond, but the words lodged in her throat. She couldn't argue; Nuqala's statement smacked of the truth.

"I . . ." Apoletta began. "I'm sorry. On behalf of Istar, if that is what we did, then I am truly sorry."

The Speaker smiled softly. "We are a stubborn people— shallow and deep water alike. We are proud and therein lies our gravest fault."

"But is it so great, and forgive me for saying so, that we can't work together now? Get past the past, I mean?" Utharne asked.

"No," the Speaker said. "I am not giving up on the Conclave."

Apoletta felt relief, a sigh escaping her lips.

"But," the Speaker added with a tired smile, "we still have work to do before any Conclave can be successful."

"What, ah, what are you saying?" Utharne said.

"I have a task for you both. You say the World Gash is a dire threat for all our people. Then you must bring us irrefutable proof. Thus far, only the Dargonesti have laid eyes upon this place. Utharne, I wish you to go with the Dargonesti and bear witness to this World Gash. And take others with you . . . dissenters, even. Give our people reason to believe you through your eyewitness observation."

Utharne hesitated then bowed his head.

"How may I help?" Apoletta asked.

"I need your people to serve as guides. Show the doubtful the worst of what you fear. Give them a reason to forget our past grievances and a reason to unite."

"But what of the, you know, other representatives?"

"While you mount your expedition into the World Gash, I will try to mend the rifts among our own people. Maybe, then, when you return, we can renew our efforts to unite the tribes of Dimernesti and Dargonesti."

Apoletta and Utharne nodded, though one small matter bothered Apoletta.

"What troubles you?" the Speaker asked.

"I am sorry," Apoletta said. "I would not be so bold as to question your judgment."

The Speaker shook her head. "I have little time left to be troubled on issues of formality."

"Thank you," Apoletta said. "I have no issue with leading the expedition to the World Gash, but we must travel to Istar and Watermere first . . . to Takaluras."

Both the Speaker and Utharne looked at Apoletta, curiosity on their faces.

"We are not prepared to travel to the World Gash," Apoletta said. "Takaluras has the maps, the pathfinders, and the equipment we'll need for the journey. And while Istar is closer, I must also stop there and speak with the Speaker of the Moon directly. I must seek his permission. Otherwise, he may see my actions as an affront to his authority."

"Then take Utharne and the others with you to both places," the Speaker of the Sea said, "to convince Treyen Silverwake of the expedition's importance."

"Your wisdom humbles me," Apoletta said.

"And your spirit humbles me," the Speaker said. "I can understand why your Speaker of the Moon entrusted you to protect Istar. He chose wisely."

◆ ◆ ◈ ◆ ◆

"I like her," Nuqala said, studying Utharne. Utharne admitted he did as well. The two sat in the quiet of the tower, the guards

LUCIEN SOULBAN

having been dismissed outside. They spoke at length about the perilous journey ahead, about the fact that no Dimernesti had set foot in Watermere in centuries; Utharne's replies came in short sentences, if at all.

"Something troubles you," Nuqala said.

"It does?" Utharne said with a laugh. "You're too good at reading me."

She shrugged. "The voice carries the sound of the words, but the face is what carries their meaning. Only some words," she said, patting Utharne's hand with matronly affection, "are easier for me to hear than others. Now, what troubles you?"

Utharne hesitated. "I'm afraid of leaving you alone in your state."

She laughed. "May I remind you that I practiced the healing arts before you were born?"

"Yes," Utharne admitted, "but you haven't done so in ages. Do you still believe in the miracles?"

At that, the Speaker grew silent for the moment. Utharne understood why, even as she explained that she'd not reconciled herself with the gods. She still hadn't forgiven them for leaving.

The argument that Utharne and Nuqala shared rode out its familiar course. She'd seen far too much horror to be so forgiving of the gods. She'd outlived three of her children and two grandchildren, all lost in recent years. How could she forgive the gods for inflicting those days upon her people? Upon herself?

Utharne defended the gods, saying the Dark Goddess Takhisis had betrayed them all. Takhisis, not the gods, stole the three moons that regulated magic. In fact, it was the gods, including the Fisher King, who returned the three moons.

Nuqala shook her head. "You were once a father," she said gently, about to make a point.

Utharne blinked back tears; his wife, his children; the wound was so easily wrenched open. The pain was worse when it came unexpected, when the memories rushed back in before he could prepare. He looked away.

"Oh, Utharne," Nuqala said. "I'm sorry, my dear. I'm sorry."

"No, I'm fine. Yes . . . fine. Um, continue. Please," he said, though he could not face her.

"Tomorrow, perhaps," the Speaker said, her own voice dusked by sorrow, her own ghosts rediscovered.

"No," Utharne insisted. "I'm sorry. I don't mean. . . ." He hesitated. "I want to know."

The Speaker nodded. "I'm sorry for using your pain to make my own arguments," she said. "But as father and husband, you would have done anything to protect those you loved. And you did everything you could to save them."

"Yes," Utharne whispered.

"And are we not the children of the gods? Should we not have expected their protection? Against the mountain that crashed into the ocean? Against the tidal waves that devastated us? Against the depredations of Brynseldimer? Against Takhisis? How can I forgive them for what I have seen in less than four centuries?"

Utharne inhaled, but the explanations and speeches he might have offered others felt hollow here. He understood her pain, and that frightened him. "I don't know," he admitted, turning to face her. "I want to know; I want to learn why they took my family. But when all's said and done, I . . . I can't expect to know!"

"Are you afraid of the answer?"

"No!" Utharne said then calmed himself. "No. I don't ask because it seems. . . ." He sighed. "Because it seems selfish. I see others with greater burdens. Burdens? Is that the right word? Yes, yes, burdens. And then I feel selfish for my self-pity. That's why I don't ask."

The Speaker smiled gently. "Yet now you understand my position, my dear boy."

Utharne said nothing but nodded.

The Speaker laughed softly. "Whatever I feel about the Conclave and about the gods, I must do what is right for my people, first and foremost. The Dimernesti do need this alliance. And they need their gods to give them strength."

"But the people, they follow you. You set an example by leading us."

"Yes, but I measure my life in months now, not years. And I fear I won't be around long enough to enter this new day with them. I can only usher them through the threshold and, if I'm wise enough, close the door behind them."

"Speaker?" His voice choked.

"Hush. Let me finish," Nuqala said. "We are a changed people, and yet we still insist on holding on to the past. We are not our mothers and grandmothers, who survived the First Cataclysm. They died years ago but bequeathed a birthright of hatred and anger to their children. This must change. Who we once were is no longer important. Before I die, I would very much like to see a glimpse of who we might become."

"I don't know what to say," Utharne said, awed by the Speaker's wisdom.

"Say nothing. Help our people grow. Reconcile them with the gods. Go, see the World Gash, and bring back detailed accounts of its malice. Visit Watermere and impress upon the Dargonesti the need for unity."

"But how will this help us grow? I mean, what will that quest achieve?"

"It'll help our people see beyond their own troubles. I know this in my heart. You and I, we understand this sacrifice. Our people must as well. It'll stop their selfishness, their belief that their misery is the only one that deserves a voice. Now go, dear boy. Go before you tire this old woman too much." With that, the Speaker beckoned Utharne to lean in, and she kissed his forehead.

Ash floated in the water, a black snowfall caught in absolute suspension. And if it did fall at all, only the darkness below welcomed its descent; turbidity shielded the seafloor below and eclipsed the sky above, leaving naught but the gray limbo.

Wartide floated in that nothingness, lost to the true scale of his surroundings. The ocean felt colder than he remembered, the warmth lapped up by the thirsty waters.

A figure in billowing red robes that were stitched with glowing runes floated alongside Wartide. Where the red robes masked all hint of gender and shape, Wartide lay naked save for his loincloth. Where the red robes revealed the hint of ashen skin on the figure's hands, Wartide's flesh contrasted a rich blue. Where the red robe bore sharp, bright runes, Wartide's bone-dust tattoos seemed to bleed into his skin, the patterns no longer as crisp.

"You don't feel cold, do you?" Wartide said, studying his ashen-colored companion. Wartide could not easily discern his features; his companion's head was buried deep inside the cowl of his red robes. Were it not for the faint arcane rune work that spilled from the robes onto his skin, Wartide wouldn't see him at all. "Or maybe the cold is all you feel?"

His companion did not reply.

"You're thinking about that sea elf again." Wartide said. "You want to know who she is?"

The companion did not reply.

Wartide shrugged. "One of the delegates. She's Dargonesti, like I was before they cast me out. But I'm Blood Shoal now . . . Mahkwahb!" He flicked his ponytail over his shoulder, his hair caked and dyed with red clay.

The companion turned to Wartide and glanced over the sea elf's body with cold detachment, as though studying his hue.

"Ah," Wartide said. "You're wondering why her skin differs from mine? It's white, like pearls, her hair spun silver, yes? It's more and more common for sea elves to be of different hues. Are you infatuated with her?"

His companion turned away.

"You're full of questions tonight!" Wartide said with a laugh. "Is that why you didn't attack her? Back at Dimernost?"

His companion said nothing.

"Are you disappointed that I forced you to withdraw?"

Still nothing. They floated in the darkness, staring into the storm of ash.

"Would you like to know her name?" Wartide whispered. "I know her name, which is more than I can say for you."

The comment drew blood. The companion whipped around to face Wartide, the runes on his face and billowing robes glowing fiercely.

A smile flashed across Wartide's face, but it quickly turned into a discomforted grimace. Patches of crimson coral erupted from beneath his skin. No blood appeared, but the pain threaded his every nerve nonetheless. Within moments, a coral carapace—an articulated and form-fitted suit of armor—covered Wartide's body. From his hands grew a coral trident. Sharp coral spurs lined both weapon and shell.

"You wish to try me?" Wartide said calmly, smiling. "Later, perhaps. Master comes." His sharklike helm was free around the mouth. He turned to face the darkness.

The temperature of the water increased. The ocean below glowed, as though a fast-rising sun rose to greet them. Wartide turned toward the master and readied himself.

A column of steam bubbled up from below; at its core was a reddish hellfire that cracked and sizzled.

"All is ready, Master," Wartide said, bowing his head. "The attack drove a wedge into the Conclave. The sea elves won't soon recover."

"Good, I am pleased" said the Master. His voice shuddered the waters, making it difficult to see him. "Proceed with the next step. You know what must be done to earn my continued favor. Do not fail me, and I will reward the Blood Shoal beyond imagination's paltry reckoning."

"We shall do as you ask," Wartide said, bowing his head.

"Use this. It is of my creation," the Master said.

From the darkness, a large coral sphere floated into view. It spanned the length of a dolphin, and it appeared to be made of a delicate latticework of overlapping coral. It also shifted, its gossamer branches breaking and reforming into new patterns.

"The Legion Coral will serve you as it has served me," the Master said. "Now go. Prove your worth. Bring me victory."

With that, the column of steam and its lit heart returned to the shadows below, plunging Wartide, the red-robed figure, and the Legion Coral back into ashen darkness.

Wartide faced his companion. "Attend to the Legion Coral. I have other matters to address."

The red-robed figure hesitated before finally swimming away with some grace; the Legion Coral trailed in his wake, following like an obedient pet.

Wartide watched them leave with a grin before closing his eyes. He imagined sharkskin covering his body, his feet fused together into a mighty tail, his mouth and throat filled with teeth in sharp rows. His body melted, and he became that which he imagined.

Wartide, as a shark, tore through the school of fish. He ripped into them with dagger teeth, the coral carapace covering his flanks cutting them as he thrashed about. Within moments, carrion debris filled the waters around Wartide. Instead of feasting on the dead fish, however, he shifted out of his shark form. The scales and coral covering his body retracted in a brief surge of pain. It passed, leaving Wartide in his loincloth.

From a hidden pouch in his loincloth, Wartide removed a small fetish of a turtle attached to seal-leather string. He waved the fetish through the innards and dead debris of the slaughtered school before taking a small morsel for himself. A small mumble escaped his lips.

"It is motion," Wartide said. He waited for a response.

Within moments, a swarm of snap-bill sea turtles filled the water. Each as large as Wartide's head, the turtles swam all around him, gobbling up the feast he'd left for them. A few even took nips at him, drawing green blood into the water. Wartide was glad for their approval and let them continue; he spoke despite the discomfort.

"It worked as planned. He saw his beloved Apoletta and reacted as you said he would."

A voice swelled inside Wartide's head, shifting and changing with protean speed, like the surf crashing into the beach, like walking face-first into webs. *And in turn, Apoletta has heard his voice and will continue to do so. Now leave him to his curiosity,* the Voice said. *I will look after Zebulah.*

CHAPTER
The Journey
4

The three shark-blade whales raced through the water, faster than any current could carry them, for longer than any shark could sustain its bursts of speed. Despite their size at more than seventy feet in length, the shark-blade whales were agile and fastest among the krill-eaters. They had streamlined heads, like those of a moray, and equally sleek bodies.

Strapped to each whale was a seal-leather harness that spanned its girth. On the middle whale, the harness held a dozen supply sacks woven from ironweed and protected beneath large tortoise and clamshells. On the first and last whale, the harnesses latched together to form several rolls of lamprey saddles for passengers. A true saddle sat atop each whale for the rider.

The lamprey saddles were comfortable pouches that allowed the passengers to lie inside them, hugging the whale the way lampreys latched onto sharks as they fed.

Apoletta lay comfortably inside her fur-lined lamprey saddle and enjoyed the rush of water as it raced by. Her long silver hair danced behind her, and she gripped the hand stirrups tighter. She turned her head to look up, to the saddle above hers, from which perch Utharne was studying her.

"You're smiling," he said.

She nodded and faced the rush of water. "So I am."

Utharne smiled. "You wanted to ask me something? Earlier, wasn't it? When we left Dimernost?"

"It can wait," Apoletta said, closing her eyes and enjoying herself.

"Milady," Utharne said. "We're barely, what? A half day out of Dimernost? I am already bored."

Apoletta laughed. "The journey is still a few days in the making, thanks to these magnificent creatures," Apoletta said, patting the whale, "and you're already bored? The trip promises to be a long one for you."

"Well, I'll think of other things to talk about. Until then, what is it you wanted to know? Ask away."

"Very well," Apoletta said. She looked down to Slyphanous, but her advisor was asleep, his head tucked into his pouch. She turned to face Utharne and, with some embarrassment, admitted her terrible secret.

Names . . . she was horrible with names. She couldn't remember them to save her life. Utharne smiled broadly and said, "Of course. My name is Utharne——"

Apoletta laughed.

"Wonderful!" Utharne said. "Another smile. I think I could grow to like this new face."

"You mock me," Apoletta said, returning his grin. "I meant the others on this journey."

"Ah," Utharne said with a mischievous grin. Without further prompting, he pointed out the various members of the expedition. Apoletta already knew the pilot of the supply-laden whale. It was none other than the obnoxious Arrovawk, who protested——fought hard, actually——coming. But the Speaker insisted that he join the expedition, and Arrovawk ultimately obliged, albeit grudgingly.

Next came the rotund fellow with three different bands of green to his skin and a bald head. That was Briegan of the Fallen Shores, who piloted the last whale.

"Fallen Shores?" Apoletta said. "Like yourself? Is he your countryman?"

"No," Utharne replied, sadness in his eyes. "Can't be a countryman when you have no country. No, just Fallen Shores."

"I'm sorry," Apoletta said, apologizing, though uncertain of his meaning or her transgression.

"Never you mind," Utharne said lightly, continuing with the tour. He pointed to the crown of their whale, where a young Dimernesti sat, his skin a light blue and his jade-green hair adorned with hanging feathers of surface birds. That was Maleanki, a congenial lad who liked to finish other people's sentences.

Utharne rolled his eyes. "Try leading him in prayer. It doesn't work. Constantly trying to finish your blessings for you."

"He seems nice enough. And the soldiers?" Apoletta said, glancing back at the last whale; it carried ten Dimernesti men and four of the eight Dargonesti bodyguards assigned to protect her.

Utharne admitted he didn't recollect all their names, but the dour female Dimernesti in spine crab armor who was holding the turtle-plated shield was Vanastra. Apoletta blushed. She'd dismissed the captain as male on account of her shorn head, square shoulders, and broad chin.

Utharne continued laughing. "I won't tell anyone. I promise. She does get that misperception often, you know."

"Thank you," Apoletta said, grateful for not having made that error in the woman's presence.

Before the pair could continue speaking, however, the whales slowed. Maleanki pointed down with his sea-reed stick. Apoletta and Utharne both slipped out of their saddles. Brysis in her gray porpoise form, along with Echo Fury and Brine-Whisker, raced up to meet them, each bleating or barking loudly to gain the caravan's attention.

The whales halted completely; the Dimernesti and Dargonesti soldiers took to the water, their weapons ready. Four more of Apoletta's bodyguards swam over from the first whale.

"Your Highness, what's wrong?" a Dargonesti soldier asked. He wore black and yellow sharkskin armor and carried a wicked-looking serrated trident. Numerous scars marked his once handsome, angular face.

"We'll know the matter in a moment, Captain Ornathius," Apoletta said.

Brysis arrived with her two companions and immediately shifted free of her porpoise form. The water flushed with the warmth of her change.

"Below," Brysis said, gasping for air. "You must hear this. Bring the whales."

Arrowawk, bringing the second whale alongside the first, shot them all a suspicious look. "Why have we stopped?" he demanded.

"Trust me, sire," Brysis said, ignoring Arrowawk. "It's below the third cold layer."

"You're out of your mind!" Arrowawk said. "Ain't no way we're going that deep."

"Shut your mouth," Vanastra said, her voice rough for a female. She came up behind the assembly. "We go where Utharne goes."

Captain Ornathius of the Dargonesti straightened. "We go where Her Highness goes. We do not follow your priest."

Apoletta and Utharne exchanged exasperated glances.

"Yes you do, Captain," Apoletta said. "Utharne is my equal here. You follow his orders as though it were my voice that uttered them."

Captain Ornathius's skin darkened, but he bowed his head. "I did not mean to speak out of turn."

"And you, Vanastra," Utharne said. "You're to protect Apoletta and listen to her as you would listen to me."

Vanastra said nothing. She matched Utharne's gaze and offered a slight nod.

"Down?" Apoletta asked Utharne, who nodded.

"Down it is," Apoletta said with a shrug. "We'll break surface so the whales can catch—"

"Their breath?" Maleanki asked, interrupting.

"And so you might dress warmly," Apoletta said, taking the interruption as though it were her own words. "It will get very cold."

They scuttled across the ocean floor, seemingly chaotic in movement but somehow always advancing. Occasionally, they used their legs to leap through the water, sailing gracefully before landing and stirring the muck into torpid clouds. Red-orange carapace, bipedal, a long snout lined with a wicked array of teeth, and five red eyes mounted on eyestalks, the magori appeared frighteningly strange, alien creatures. At ten feet tall and chittering madly among themselves, they intimidated the most hardened veteran.

In their wake staggered various undead in myriad states of decomposition. With their bodies robbed of gases, they remained ground locked, though some of the incorporeal wraiths flitted erratically through the water like strange fish. On occasion a shadow moved over the rocks and ground with no body to cast its reflection.

The sea life knew well enough to stay clear of the unruly band, though schools of fish did trail safely behind, eating the floating carrion particulates left by the decaying undead.

Above the rabble swam several sharks, many of whom bore tribal tattoos drawn in squid ink on their flanks. With them swam the dark sea elf Wartide; his red-robed ally, Zebulah; and the Legion Coral sphere.

Wartide kept a constant eye on Zebulah, who simply continued staring out across the ocean floor, as though searching. Wartide knew what was coming.

Zebulah looked at Wartide, his face lost inside the folds of his red cowl, then out into the distance. With that, he swam away from the group, heading in another direction.

"You're heading the wrong way," Wartide said.

Zebulah hesitated but didn't turn.

"My spies report she left Dimernost. She swims in that direction," Wartide said, pointing east. "She's heading for the God's Throat to Watermere. We'll handle Silver Horn and the others alone if we must. But we need you for the fight with Anhalstrax."

Wartide watched Zebulah vanish into the turbid waters before nodding to a strange undead who'd been watching them both.

The undead creature who approached rode upon a desiccated antlered sea horse; the sea horse's once bright yellow skin had turned brown, its round eyes hollow sockets of flesh. Even its once proud antlers, which stretched out from the sides of its coronet like a cradle of horns, had broken and fractured. As for the rider, all that remained was naught but a pair of glowing eyes and skeletal hands that controlled the reins of its mount. The bare trace of its blackened, skeletal body flickered in and out of sight.

"Follow Zebulah," Wartide said.

The creature hesitated. Its barely visible black teeth clacked together in thought.

"Do not refuse me this, wichtlin," Wartide said. "You know whose favor I hold."

The wichtlin clacked its teeth together again, wheeled the sea horse around, and rode it into the opaque waters.

Wartide watched the wichtlin leave. "Soon," he said. "Soon."

The ocean existed in layers. Sailors knew the world beneath their keel was unlike the world of sky and air. In the oceans colors died in the upper layers, and the monsters that breached the surface had no fear of man or minotaur. Strange sea life and alien water confounded both sense and sensibility. Even the pearl divers of Saifum's Sea Reach feared their seas. To them, fear meant respect, and respect meant survival. To them, the gods never intended man, elf, and dwarf to know the secrets hidden just beyond the abyssal darkness stretching far beneath their feet.

The sea elves, however, acted less fearful but no less respectful. The ocean acted and reacted as a living, breathing thing. The unseen breath of the gods carried the tides; the currents served as their gods' veins, and the sea elves felt blessed to swim in its holy arteries.

The Dargonesti believed the ocean marvelous for all its subtleties. And the first subtlety they learned—understood—was colder water was heavier, more sluggish, than warm water. Therefore, the deeper one ventured, the colder it became. The Dimernesti, who did not swim in the depths, did not understand this subtlety. But the Dargonesti could distinguish the different layers: from the first cold layer, where the sun no longer warmed the deep evenly, to the third, where temperatures were easily half those of the surface.

Apoletta watched her Dimernesti companions, half in worry, half in admiration; she'd never seen shoal elves venture so deep. To their credit, not a one complained. They didn't wish to appear frightened. Instead, they gripped their seaweed and whale-skin cloaks tighter around their bodies and appeared in awe of the terribly dark world.

Vanastra remarked how it felt as though the ocean tried to push her up, to which Apoletta mentioned it was the nature of cold water to do that. Brysis bade them to listen carefully, impatience in her voice.

Everyone stopped speaking, stopped aspiring air through their mouths and out their gills. Then Apoletta heard what worried Brysis, the creaking groans that filtered through the ocean . . . indistinct and distant . . . and everywhere.

"Whale song," Apoletta said. She closed her eyes.

The Dimernesti appeared startled. Even Arrowawk admitted he hadn't heard the likes of it before. Apoletta explained how sounds acted differently down there. The cold layers of the water acted like a thin floor to the layers above; it muted sounds, returning only the murmur of echoes. Down there, the surface was silent, but down there, because the water was colder and heavier, sound moved differently.

"It sounds like many whales," Vanastra said.

"It is," Brysis said, outstretching her arms as though bathing in song. "The whales of this region drop down here to sing. Their voices carry for leagues."

"Do you understand them? The whales, I mean?" Utharne asked, stroking Brine-Whisker's skin.

"No, but they're troubled," Brysis said. "I've heard the warning songs before."

"Warning?" Apoletta asked. "Warning of what?"

Brysis shook her head. "I wish I could say. But they warn of danger." With that, Brysis turned to face the whales. It was only when she did that Apoletta realized the three pack whales were facing in the same direction. They appeared to be listening intently.

"No," Apoletta whispered, realizing the direction they faced.

"What's out there? I got turned around. Anyone else turned around?" Utharne asked.

"Out there lies the enclave of Hygant," Briegan said.

"The brathnoc capital," Apoletta said. She looked to Brysis. "Are the brathnoc in trouble?"

Brysis shrugged.

Everyone was silent for a moment, the whale song echoing gently.

"No, no," Arrovawk said. "Bad enough you dragged me on this fool's errand. I ain't making a detour!"

Utharne looked to Apoletta, throwing her a questioning look.

"They've embraced a peaceful life," Apoletta said. "They may be in trouble."

"Peaceful?" Vanastra said, chuckling mirthlessly. "My father can never swim properly, thanks to a brathnoc's lashtail."

Captain Ornathius nodded. "I must agree with Vanastra. The brathnoc have only recently embraced peace . . . it hasn't been totally accepted."

"I saw them fighting the undead," Arrovawk said. "Demons, they were. Best we leave them. If they're in trouble, it ain't an undeserved fate."

Apoletta stared out across the cold expanse. Her eyes searched the turbid waters, as though seeking answers in the gloom. There was something amiss with the brathnoc, Apoletta feared. They had seemed unsettled and unusually silent at the Conclave. And the whale song was another sign.

Utharne drifted closer to Apoletta. She sighed, offering him a tired smile.

"If the brathnoc need help, then maybe we can use this to our advantage," Utharne said.

Apoletta smiled. "So there is a politician under those priest's vestments. What are you proposing?"

"Help the brathnoc now and earn their trust later?"

"Devious," Apoletta said. "I approve."

"Change of plans," Utharne said, turning to face the expedition's members. "We're going to——"

"Hygant?" the young Maleanki said.

Utharne smiled politely while Arrovawk groaned loud enough to attract his whale's attention.

"Send a messenger," Apoletta instructed Captain Ornathius. "Advise Watermere we'll be arriving later than anticipated."

CHAPTER
Hygant
5

The journey did not lack for arguments, but the Dimernesti appeared glad to be closer to the surface. The world sounded clearer to them, and their bodies were better tuned to the buoyancy and warmth. Apoletta had to admit that while she missed the cooling touch of her deep-water home, the surface felt more alive, more vibrant. Sounds sometimes rang with abnormal—almost painful—clarity, but she grew inured to the effect.

Finally, on the third day of their journey, Brine-Whisker, Brysis, and Echo Fury returned from scouting ahead. Apoletta knew they approached Hygant. She and the others swam alongside the tired whales, their weapons at the ready.

They swam in brathnoc waters now, Brysis said. Captain Ornathius offered to announce Apoletta's presence to Hygant, which earned Vanastra's challenge to perform the same for Utharne.

Utharne sighed and bade they both go. Apoletta and he waited for the others to leave.

"So like children," Apoletta said, shaking her head. "My father's curse is upon me."

Utharne laughed. "Too true. They do act like jealous siblings. Perhaps that's a good sign for our two people."

"One would hope," Apoletta replied.

The delegation waited outside the Hygant Forest, a sprawling green mass of warm-water kelp. The smaller stalks rose to the height of an elf's torso, while the thickest measured the girth of whales. They all formed a tangled thicket of algae weeds on the ocean floor that rose hundreds of feet to tickle the underbelly of the sea.

The forest's breathtaking green contrasted sharply with the blues of the water. Spiny urchins littered the floor; bouquets of thick fronds flowered along the stalks, while schools of fish darted in and out of the gently swaying forest. Apoletta surveyed the massive forest, spanning dozens of miles in either direction.

Arrovawk, Briegan, and Maleanki were herding the whales through the rich clouds of krill and shrimp when Captain Ornathius and Vanastra returned. Everyone crowded around the pair as they related their story to Apoletta and Utharne. The brathnoc's Synod had agreed to meet with the delegation, though Vanastra added they didn't appear happy with the unexpected visit.

"I'm not sure this is wise," Vanastra said.

"This isn't about wisdom," Utharne replied. "It's about necessity."

Apoletta stared into the dark undergrowth of the forest, beneath the canopy of fronds. Several brathnoc guides floated there, waiting to escort them into the city.

The delegation entered the Hygant Forest and immediately fell silent, in awe of their surroundings. The kelp stalks rose above them, corkscrewing and winding their way upward. Their thick stalks lay covered in sheaves of leaves that undulated on the mild current like ghostly fingers; all waving in unison first in one direction, then another. Kelp floated upon the ocean's surface, forming a canopy that allowed little light through and rendered the underside dark. Fortunately, large yellow bladders growing from the stalks glowed softly and lit the kelp forest. The spherical nodes measured several feet across and kept the stalks buoyant with the gases trapped within.

Apoletta marveled at the strange world. It was by far the largest kelp forest she'd seen, and its breadth of creatures stole her breath. Black sea snails and slugs slowly marched up and down the stalks; bloat fish and slime mackerels darted in and out of the forest; dog dolphins chased one another in frantic games; sea serpents shot through the waters on crooked arrow paths.

The five brathnoc escorts remained typically silent as they fluttered and kicked and guided themselves on their outstretched patagia. Two had unfurled their elegant but thorny lashtails, certain warning that while the brathnoc had eschewed violence in their culture, it remained within their capacity.

Not that the Dargonesti and Dimernesti guards had forgotten. With their grips steady on the pommels of their own weapons, they watched the surrounding forest and listened with keen ears.

Thankfully, the journey ended uneventfully. The delegation found itself venturing over the woven canvas of Hygant itself, the city of the brathnoc. If the brathnoc made little distinction between the name of their forest and that of their settlement, it was for good reason. They'd woven Hygant the city from Hygant the forest.

No building in the city had walls. Instead, long strands of kelp that remained connected to the stalks had been woven together to form the floors and ceilings of structures. It was a city of gigantic hammocks, of giant webbed pavilions. Anywhere from four to twenty stalks formed the pillars of any particular home or business; the brathnoc had bent more stalks at near right angles to create floor and ceiling beams. They had then braided smaller strands of kelp over and under one another before fastening each end to the nearest stalk. The brathnoc also wove floors and ceilings in that fashion.

The guides led the delegation above the city, which itself rested a hundred feet above the seafloor. Curious brathnoc peered from below, but none ventured upward. Apoletta noticed other delegation members marveling at the truly exotic domain. Only Brysis seemed unimpressed, indifferent almost. It took Apoletta a moment to realize she was studying something. Apoletta followed Brysis's gaze downward, eventually spotting a fish seller, his treated wares gutted and hanging from thorns. Apoletta had heard that the brathnoc eschewed raw meat to control their ancestral war lust. She felt at a loss to explain Brysis's curiosity.

A question for later, she thought.

Finally the guides escorted the delegation into what appeared to be a clearing. Although the stalks grew thicker than ever in circumference, Apoletta wondered if they'd somehow reached the end of the Hygant Forest expanse; she quickly realized the reason for the clearing.

"My word," Utharne said, cradling one arm around Brine-Whisker. Everyone stopped, awed by the spectacle below them.

The forest hadn't thinned. In fact, they'd entered the very heart of Hygant Forest. The canopied pavilion before them was huge in proportions. Its pillars numbered more than one hundred stalks, with another two or three hundred bent and woven to form the solid cradle for the floor and ceiling. No stalks ascended above the pavilion with its tent-poled ceiling. They were in the eye of the green hurricane . . . in the empty heart of the forest.

A guide swam up to Apoletta, but Captain Ornathius quickly interposed himself between them. The guide seemed surprised.

"Captain," Apoletta said, "I'll be fine."

The good captain never removed his gaze from the brathnoc, but he did slip to the side.

"Only two," the guide said.

Both Vanastra and Ornathius objected, but Utharne and Apoletta stopped them.

"I will go," Apoletta said.

"And, yes, certainly . . . you won't be without my company," Utharne said.

"Wouldn't it be wiser for me to accompany Apoletta?" Ornathius asked sharply.

"If you're so worried about her," Vanastra replied, "then perhaps you and your soldiers should remain here to guard her. Cleric Utharne and I can meet with the brathnoc."

Apoletta shot them both a withering look. The two soldiers realized the brathnoc had been studying them with wary gazes. They nodded and apologized in low voices.

"You have your two," Brysis said, turning to the brathnoc guide. "Don't give us reason to come after them."

Apoletta stifled a groan. "We'll be fine," she said. "Wait here."

Utharne kissed Brine-Whisker on his forehead. "You too, troublemaker," Utharne told his companion, who barked in reply.

With that, Apoletta and Utharne accompanied the brathnoc guide down to the giant pavilion.

Heavy fronds fell from the ceiling all the way down to the woven floor. Two brathnoc footmen pulled aside the leaflike curtains and allowed their visitors inside.

The pavilion inspired greater awe inside than out, if that was possible. The entire ceiling sloped upward and lay covered in a bloom of yellow bladders that kept the ceiling aloft. While the light they produced individually was of a soft cast, together they conspired to rival the sun's luster.

From the ceiling, curtains of leafy fronds drooped to the floor. The brathnoc had pulled them to the side, revealing thick stalk pillars covered in more glowing bladders. Despite that, the curtains filled the pavilion's interior like a house of veils and limited sightlines to mere yards.

THE ALIEN SEA

The brathnoc guides waited outside and motioned for Apoletta and Utharne to continue ahead without them. While uneasy, Apoletta did her best to appear calm. Utharne, however, simply gawked at their surroundings and seemed more than happy to examine the pavilion's interior. The pair swam forward, carefully moving past curtains and around pillars, seeking their hosts. The water tasted spicy; their gills tingled at the scent of the kelp. Slowly, Apoletta realized her anxieties had diminished. She grew less worried about facing whatever lay inside the pavilion and, in fact, felt more buoyant, less tied down by the weight of her body. She felt almost as though she might float away.

At the center of the pavilion, Apoletta and Utharne stumbled across their host. A brathnoc elder with a long lashtail, likely a member of the Synod, floated before the black wood mast from some giant ship that extended ceiling to floor. The brathnoc was busy carving the wood into intricate, fluid patterns, some tale related in flowing pictograms. Apoletta wished she understood how to read the brathnoc language. From ceiling to floor, long kelp vines wound their way down the mast.

The elder's black skin glistened in the light. His patagia were large, larger than any Apoletta had seen. Had he extended his hands fully over his head, they wouldn't snap taut; instead, they undulated at the frill's edge like that of a skirt-snake. And on the matter of snakes, his legs melted into a single rapier tail that ended in a hardened thorn.

The elder carved another symbol into the wood before pushing back and examining his handiwork. Satisfied, he shot a jet of ink from his hand, staining the wood and his latest entry. Only then did he turn around, almost contorting himself to face them.

"Do you like it?" he asked, his voice like a snake's.

"It's lovely," Apoletta said. "What's it for?"

"An accounting," he said. "My people have much to atone for."

"Ah," Utharne said, obviously uncomfortable.

81

"I'm surprised you came to our humble city," the elder said. "But we still aren't interested in your alliance."

"Forgive me," Apoletta said, "but I do not know your name."

"Of course you do," the elder said, turning in upon himself. "I am Brathnoc."

"Well, yes. Of course you are," Utharne replied. "We meant your—"

"I know," the elder said. "I speak for my people. Therefore, my name is my people's."

"Of course," Apoletta said, interjecting herself into the exchange smoothly. "Brathnoc, do you also speak for the Synod? I've seen none other here."

"And you shan't," Brathnoc replied. "I speak for the others, yes. They hear through my ears and speak through my mouth with their floral voices."

Apoletta and Utharne exchanged glances, uncertain what to make of Brathnoc's strange words and his snakelike tone.

"The Brathnoc to whom you spoke upon arriving, and the one to whom you speak with now, are not the same."

"Apologies," Apoletta said. "We are woefully ignorant of your culture. But my people and Utharne's would like to rectify that."

"Quite impossible," Brathnoc said, his face shifting through myriad expressions. "I fear that is not going to happen, sweet lady. The answer is no. Perhaps some day but not today. Perhaps we should listen to your pleas. But now is neither the time nor the place. You might say, the foolish mind closes his ears with his hands. But the more foolish, if you'll recall, listens to all that is said. Perhaps another time. A discourse for anon."

"Well," Utharne said, offering an accommodating smile. "That's certainly disconcerting, if you'll forgive me. For saying so, I mean."

Brathnoc shook his head. "Forgive me, but I suppose I do speak to myself when channeling their voices. But I'm afraid the majority has spoken."

Although Apoletta hated to do so, given the display of voices and facial gymnastics Brathnoc manifested while speaking for the Synod, she felt compelled to ask.

"May I ask why this decision?"

"Allow me," Brathnoc said, the voice intended for all the others and not merely Apoletta. "Our people, though valiant for what they've eschewed, must first discover who they are and who they're to become before we can consider joining others as equals. Our society, our kinship to one another, is newfound. The change alone is difficult to embrace."

"But our people share your unease," Utharne said. "Believe me, I understand exactly how you feel. It's frightening, terrifying actually, to extend your hand in friendship. Especially after everything that's happened. But my people are willing to give this, this, um, alliance a try despite our fears . . . trepidations, yes! Another good word."

"That is your decision. I must make a different one for my people."

"But—" Utharne said.

"Thank you, but I'm afraid you came for nothing," Brathnoc said. He curled away, almost knotting himself.

Utharne appeared crestfallen, but Apoletta wasn't so easily rebuffed.

"Are you in some kind of peril?" she asked pointedly.

Brathnoc turned around. "Pardon," he said.

"Are you in peril?" Apoletta repeated. "Do you need our help?"

Brathnoc shook his head slowly, obviously confused by the question. A litany of hissing "Noes" spilled from his lips. "Why?"

"The whales sing songs of danger," Apoletta said. "They sing from these very seas."

"Yes! We heard it," Utharne said diplomatically. "Impressive, really."

Brathnoc said nothing for a moment; then another voice sang from his lips. "Danger, yes! Of course. Perhaps I can explain. West of the Hygant Forest, an ancient shark hunts. It is a large beast. Quite large. Attacks and eats whales and other sharks regularly. Too large to enter the Hygant, thankfully. We're quite safe, therefore. Though I'd avoid the western seas. I'm sure that's what the whales were singing about."

"Yes," Apoletta said slowly. "That must be it. Thank you for your time."

Utharne cast a worried glance at Apoletta, but she shook her head. It was not the time to argue.

"Thank you," Brathnoc replied. He was about to turn away again when he was struck by an afterthought. "Speak with the quartermaster for whatever provisions you need. I suggest you leave as soon as you can. Forgive me, but strangers make my people uncomfortable."

"Might we spend the night in the Hygant?" Apoletta asked. "Our whales are tired."

Brathnoc offered a slight nod. "Away from the city," he said.

Apoletta and Utharne offered their thanks and left.

Apoletta and Utharne swam back, glancing on occasion at their escorts. The four brathnoc kept a respectable distance, well out of earshot. The two sea elves discussed their meeting with the Synod, about how eagerly the elder seemed to dismiss them, wondering whether he was just imagining those voices in his head.

The caravan of whales and passengers rested at the edge of the forest's clearing. None of the brathnoc ventured close to the sea elves, despite their curiosity, and kept their distance respectable. None lingered to watch.

Vanastra and Captain Ornathius appeared relieved for Apoletta's and Utharne's safe return. Brine-Whisker barked happily and danced around Utharne. Utharne stroked the crown of his head, leaving Brine-Whisker squinting in utter satisfaction.

Most everyone crowded around the pair for news.

Naturally, Arrowawk asked if they could leave immediately, Vanastra asked if they were prisoners, and Briegan asked if they could rest the night, for the whales were—

"Exhausted!" Maleanki said, interrupting.

Only Slyphanous and Brysis remained quiet, preferring to listen. Apoletta and Utharne held up their hands to stop the barrage of questions and informed their compatriots that far from being prisoners, the brathnoc *wanted* them to leave . . . only, they weren't going to leave.

Apoletta turned to Briegan. "Do the whales still hear the warnings?"

Briegan nodded toward the whales. Apoletta realized they faced the same direction, listening quietly.

"Utharne, a moment please," Apoletta said.

Utharne nodded and whispered something in Brine-Whisker's ear. The seal darted away, through the waters. Apoletta motioned to Brysis, who floated a short distance away, her arm draped around Echo Fury's fin. Brysis swam over while Echo Fury burst away to chase the agile Brine-Whisker. The others watched them warily.

The trio clustered together, talking in low whispers.

"I do not believe the brathnoc," Apoletta said in a low voice.

"Are we in danger?" Brysis asked.

"Um, no?" Utharne said, looking uncertainly at Apoletta.

"I do not believe so," Apoletta said. "But I'm sure they're lying about the seas west of their forest. I do not think a giant shark plagues them."

"Brysis. Did you notice anything? Out of the ordinary, I mean," Utharne asked.

Brysis nodded. "Earlier. While swimming over their city. Did you see their fish?"

"What? The ones gutted and prepared?" Utharne asked.

"No," Brysis said. "Their array of fish. Not their preparation."

"What of it?" Apoletta asked, watching her carefully.

"Too many species," Brysis said. "Fish from colder waters, fish from warmer waters. Even some I couldn't identify. Many weren't indigenous to this area."

"Prepared fish last longer, correct?" Apoletta said. "Couldn't they have been caught by other brathnoc communities and brought here?"

Utharne smiled. "No, no," he said. "But I think I understand what she is saying. There aren't any other peaceful brathnoc."

Brysis nodded.

"These brathnoc," Utharne said, "are the first and only peaceful ones. Hygant is their first settlement. All other brathnoc outside the Hygant are still, um . . . wild. Is that a good word? Wild?"

"More like *savage*," Brysis said. "There are no other brathnoc communities like this one. The others move as bands. They raid and kill. Then they leave when no fish remain. The good ones, the changed ones, live here. They feel safer together."

"When the brathnoc of the Hygant first appeared at Dimernost's borders," said Utharne, "we almost attacked them. What a dark day that would have been! They told us about their city, which is impressive, given its age."

"How old is it?" Apoletta asked.

"Ten winters old," Utharne replied, "I think. A little older maybe. And it keeps growing. Now . . . why did these brathnoc become peaceful? I don't know. I mean, they certainly didn't say why. We asked, trust me, but they're reserved . . . or secretive."

"No matter," Apoletta said. "I wish to explore the western seas beyond Hygant tomorrow. Find out why the whales are so troubled and why the brathnoc see fit to lie to us. We risk offending them, but I feel it is necessary." She looked to her companions.

"A mystery," Utharne said. "Wonderful!"

"New species of fish," Brysis said. "I'm sure that'll delight Echo Fury's palate."

"And Brine-Whisker's as well," Utharne said.

THE ALIEN SEA

"Unlikely friends," Apoletta said with a smile.

Utharne nodded. "Come. Let us give the others the bad news."

"I want to see Arrovawk's face when you tell them," Brysis said, chuckling to herself.

The night was pleasant despite the surroundings. The sea elves rested between the giant stalks of kelp on the bountiful seafloor, with its abundance of sea urchins and snails. Supper consisted of a pleasant bounty of howler crab and glass-skin lobster, sea urchin and kelp fruit. Brysis groomed Echo Fury with a fish-comb and sang him soft lullabies; Utharne prayed while a normally playful Brine-Whisker kept a sedate vigil nearby; Vanastra and Captain Ornathius ran their soldiers through drills, well within competitive sight of one another; Briegan and Maleanki attended to the whales.

That left Arrovawk, Slyphanous, and Apoletta seated on rocks around a bloom of yellow kelp bladders. An uncomfortable silence lingered until Slyphanous pulled out a conch shell marked with small holes. He nodded to Apoletta.

"May I honor you with a song?" he asked.

Apoletta smiled her gratitude and kept her grimace hidden. Slyphanous was loyal and astute but certainly not musically adept.

Slyphanous blew gently into the conch, drawing forth three half-strangled notes, before singing:

In time there was, a daughter there was

In time there were, three moons there were

In time—

"No, no, no! Stop your caterwauling, you banshee of the seas!" Arrovawk cried rudely. "You're hurting the poor whales! Ain't they suffered enough?"

Slyphanous's eyes widened, and his mouth opened and closed while searching for something to say. Finally the words came. "My songs are elegant melodies—"

"Like the Abyss they are! Threatening to swallow my soul!"

While the pair carried on their argument, Apoletta seized the opportunity to leave her seat, a bare whisper of a "Pardon me," on her lips as she slipped away.

She swam, her long strands of silver hair flowing freely in her wake. Behind her the heated words continued.

"Well, I shall continue singing," Slyphanous said in protest, now racing over the lyrics as though to catch up with them. "In time there was, a daughter there was—"

"Well, I know a few chanteys myself!" Arrovawk said, singing even more loudly. "One-tail Jewl was an ugly lass, with two great shells and a scaly—"

And that was all Apoletta cared to hear. She swam up to Briegan, who was stripping blood leeches from the whale's belly. He cooed softly in its ear, keeping it calm.

"She's beautiful," Apoletta said.

"Salystra. My whale," he replied with a happy nod. "Her ancestors have been serving alongside mine for centuries."

"You're a Dimernesti Trade Rider?" she asked.

"That I was. My entire family, in fact. We'd like to think we're what kept the Dimernesti from drifting too far apart. We brought goods and news to the outlying communities, your ladyship."

"It's Apoletta, please," she said. "I have never stood on formality among my own people. I will not ask it of you."

He nodded. "Kind of you," he replied, uncomfortable. "Er, what can I do for you?"

"Utharne," she said cautiously. "You and he are both of the Fallen Shores, yet he says it is nowhere anymore. Were the Fallen Shores a place? Or is it a mark of sorts?"

Briegan inhaled softly, his eyes searching hers. It took him a quick moment to compose himself. "The Fallen Shores," he said carefully, "are a bit of both. And they weren't one place, but many. They . . . no longer exist. The dragon overlords saw to that. My shoal village was one of those overrun when the dragon Malys devastated Balifor. Never knew we were there, but he poisoned the waters good, he did. We were . . . lucky," he said cautiously, as though uncertain he could use such a word, given the circumstances.

"Lucky?"

Briegan went back to tending the whale. "My entire village survived. We escaped Malys's notice. We escaped. But others . . . others weren't so lucky. Malys and Brine claimed far more lives than they had a right to—lives of far greater worth than they possessed. Many Dimernesti lost their villages, or their homes, or their friends. Or their families." Briegan looked over to Utharne. "Some lost all four."

"I didn't know," Apoletta said softly. "I'm sorry."

Briegan shrugged. "We have a new home now. Dimernost welcomes all who hail from the Fallen Shores . . . the lost places. And Dimernost has grown strong again. We have a city. I think our nomadic days are behind us. We can weather the storms together."

"I hope so," Apoletta said. "Our people have much to learn from one another."

Briegan nodded his appreciation. In the background, Arrowawk and Slyphanous continued bickering. Apoletta realized the Dimernesti and Dargonesti soldiers had both halted their training regimen and were laughing among themselves at the exchange.

"Ah, you're daft!" Arrowawk said. "Everyone knows mermaids are the strumpets of the seas!"

"Merfolk are a beautiful, elegant people!" Slyphanous cried in protest.

"Beautiful? Hah! Not the ones I seen. Ugly lot. Kept sunning themselves on the rocks and the gulls kept throwing them back in the water!"

"You, sir, wouldn't know a mermaid from a . . . a walrus!"

"Sure I would," Arrovawk said with a grin. "Walruses kiss better!"

The soldiers burst out laughing.

Apoletta thanked Briegan for his time and complimented Salystra for her beauty. Briegan nodded and went back about his business.

With the journey tomorrow, Apoletta suspected she might need the aid of her spells. It was time to study more spell-fables, perhaps the one where the sun refused to enter the waters or the song of the loyal steed that followed Daydra Stonecipher when she forsook the land to become a sea elf, to fight her sister, the Sea Witch Sagarassi.

"And tritons," Arrovawk was saying, "I hear they carry them big tridents to compensate for their—"

"Sir!" Slyphanous cried, utterly scandalized. "Is there a sea creature you won't slander?"

"Not any that don't deserve it," Arrovawk said triumphantly.

Dimernesti and Dargonesti soldiers laughed loudly, and even Utharne, eyes closed on his meditations, cracked a smile.

Apoletta smiled, not for Arrovawk's humor or Slyphanous's predicament, but because the fractious sides were laughing together. She enjoyed the moment before turning to her studies.

The caravan of whales departed early in the morning, before the sun warmed the upper blanket of ocean and the kelp flowers opened. The caravan traveled beyond the edge of the Hygant Forest, far enough that their brathnoc escorts no longer followed them. Apoletta and company then skirted around the Hygant Forest to reach the westernmost seas.

Another evening interrupted their journey. Apoletta spent the night studying spell-fables etched on whale-bone cylinders and enduring Slyphanous's songs. Arrovawk spent his time, and his ribald lyrics, with a more appreciative audience: the soldiers. Apoletta wasn't sure which was worse, but Vanastra's and Captain Ornathius's elves seemed to enjoy Arrovawk's company.

Early dawn of the second day, the delegation continued its trek. The morning had not yet waned when Brysis returned in porpoise form, Echo Fury racing alongside her. She bleated out several energetic chirps to Apoletta before turning and swimming back the way she had come. Apoletta told the others to follow.

The three whale riders kicked their mounts into long sprints, and the sea elves clung on for dear life. They sailed over giant coral beds with wide latticelike flowers and scattered clouds of dartlike bluefish. Finally, the seafloor dropped away at the edge of a large, jagged crevice. It stretched away in either direction, infinite like the shoreline.

Whale song filled the water, as did a myriad of other noises—clicks, whirrs, thumps, and others that defied description. The three shark-blade whales soared over the crevice, their passengers peering down into what they expected was darkness. What they saw instead was a river of color, of blues and grays, reds and greens, a river of sea life.

Brysis and Echo Fury dived down, darting among the migrating animals. Apoletta and Utharne both slipped free of their lamprey saddles and swam down. Brine-Whisker followed, and the soldiers scrambled to catch up and protect their charges.

The river seemed endless and as unusual a collection of sea life as Apoletta had ever seen. There were whales—krill feeders and fish eaters alike—dolphins and shy porpoises, schools with hundreds of brightly colored fish, different-sized rays, slow jellyfish and belligerent men-of-war, sharks by the dozens—though few of the real killers—and squid and octopuses. There were many new species, fluid creatures that oscillated from one geometric form to another, swarms of crablike insects that moved like ink-colored currents, and flattened lampreylike creatures with sword-blade bodies. They numbered in the thousands, and they filled the trench, taking advantage of the fast-moving current that allowed many to simply glide when they tired.

Apoletta and Utharne slowly swam through the caravan of migrating animals, careful not to frighten them. Almost immediately, the migration separated the elves from one another. Animals of all colors and species swam past them, calm to the new arrivals in a parade of strangers. Apoletta reached out and stroked the faded blue flanks of a cloud-sailor shark. A giant dew-head whale passed above her, casting her in shadows.

Then a school of darters flitted past her. Following them was a scarred bell-ghost, with its long tendrils that threatened to sting anything that approached it too closely. Apoletta moved out of its way and watched the ephemeral creature float past her.

Utharne swam around a black-eyed squid to reach Apoletta. Together, they marveled at the migration, which was unlike anything either of them had ever witnessed. Even Apoletta, who had seen animals flee the onslaught of Chaos and the poison of the dragon overlords, could not remember anything as spectacular. Then the pair remarked on the taste in the water as it passed through their gills.

It was sulfur. With a sick lurch in her stomach, Apoletta suddenly realized what was happening.

Before Apoletta or Utharne could move, however, many voices cried out in a terrifying shriek. The noise came from above. A dozen half-naked brathnoc, wearing naught but kelp belts, their lashtails flowing freely behind them, swam over the crevice's lip and dived into the river of animals.

Apoletta and Utharne both blanched, blood draining from their faces. These were not the peaceful, monastic brathnoc they'd just left, but the ancient berserkers of the seas.

The brathnoc dived past the migrating animals, lashing out with their sharp tails and inflicting horrible wounds. Frightened creatures scattered in every direction, taking flight. All manner of creatures raced past Apoletta in their panicked flight. A large dolphin pushed her, and she lost her balance. Schools of fish, confused by the flurry of movement, dashed past. Small fish entangled themselves in Apoletta's long, free-flowing silver hair, and pulled at her in their panic to escape.

Utharne raced toward Apoletta and earned the lash of a tentacle across his back. His blood filled the water, but the smell of it mixed and vanished in the blood of so many injured creatures.

More creatures spun and battered Apoletta. As Utharne reached her, so too did Brine-Whisker. The clever little seal darted around the fleeing animals, the blue candlelight flame on his forehead glowing fiercely. Brine-Whisker swam around Apoletta, also trying to shield her from the onslaught. The flame grew brighter. Utharne touched Apoletta's shoulder, and a warmth flowed through her body; she felt assured, safe. Those animals that came close enough to strike the trio veered abruptly away.

Apoletta, Utharne, and Brine-Whisker hovered at the center of the storm, watching the animals scatter in panic. That's when one of the marauding brathnoc noticed them. He screamed with indescribable rage and charged straight for them. Utharne only just saw the brathnoc when Apoletta reached into a pouch and threw out a pinch of red, blue, and yellow silt.

Moving her arms, Apoletta shouted, "And Daydra found a world without color, save for that which she brought with her."

Each mote of the floating dust exploded with light and became a rainbow of bright colors whose bands clashed and collided. Several fish in the violent rainbow's path fell unconscious, but the brathnoc clutched his eyes, screaming in pain and fury. He flailed about, striking at the surrounding waters.

In response to their companion's anguish, the other brathnoc converged on the screams. Enough animals had scattered, thinning the river of creatures well enough to see. Apoletta noticed the clusters of sea elves who'd banded together for protection and now more than two dozen brathnoc who swam about looking equally confused. Everyone eyed each other, fear and uncertainty in their faces.

"Wait," Apoletta shouted, hoping to avert a fight.

"Peace, peace," another brathnoc with black spots across his back shouted.

Three brathnoc converged on their blind companion and, with practiced skill, held him steady. One of the three brathnoc, a female, removed kelp leaves from her companion's belt and stuffed them into his mouth, earning herself bite marks in the process. She did not seem to notice.

To Apoletta's surprise, the berserk brathnoc calmed down, his anger somehow quenched. His sight returned as well, and a mollified gaze replaced the feral stare that had fixed Apoletta moments before.

The other brathnoc did not move, but many were removing kelp leaves from their belts and eating them as well. The brathnoc with the black spots on his back swam up to Apoletta.

"You must come with us," he said.

"Is that a threat?" Captain Ornathius demanded, swimming over to them.

"Come with us or the sea elves will never be welcome in our waters again."

Apoletta sighed. She looked to Utharne, but they understood one another well enough. They did not come here to make enemies of the brathnoc. They possessed enough adversaries.

The sea elves once again found themselves in the clearing between the Hygant Forest and pavilion. They awaited word from the Synod for an audience. Until then, they tried to appear calm but could not help but notice the gathering crowds of brathnoc who hid between the stalks of kelp, watching them. Their whispers filled the water, and many chewed on the kelp leaves.

Apoletta and Utharne quietly swam among their companions, trying to assuage their fears. Brysis and Echo Fury ignored the growing crowd, while Arrovawk made a show of staring right back at them.

Finally, tired of waiting themselves, Utharne and Apoletta simply sat down on a kelp-covered stalk. Brysis and Slyphanous joined them, as did Brine-Whisker. The soldiers and whale tenders kept watch, however, ready to move at a moment's notice.

"If I can ask?" Utharne said, stroking Brine-Whisker's head. "Your spell—it was a spell, wasn't it? The one with the colors?"

"Yes," Apoletta said. "It is a spell."

"Yes, yes, I thought so!" Utharne said, excited. "I've seen spells, obviously, many times in fact. The Speaker of the Sea has many accomplished spellcasters with her. It's just the way you cast that spell . . . it was unusual. No magical words I didn't understand. More like a story!"

Apoletta smiled and nodded. "Our spell-fables. When the three moons in the sky vanished, magic vanished alongside them."

"Yes, yes, I remember. Horrible times for us all. Horrible. Many miracles silenced. Even the gods became lost to us," Utharne said, scowling at the memory.

Apoletta continued, explaining how her people had searched for reasons magic had failed them. At first they thought the gods were punishing them again, but even in places such as Urione, where the priests made no secret of their adoration for the Maelstrom Goddess Zura, magic had fled. Everyone shared their fate.

"I remember Dargonesti messengers visiting my home. Searching for answers, obviously. But I had none to give."

Apoletta nodded. "Afterwards, we believed, perhaps, that magic itself remained . . . that only our connection to it had failed. My people searched for new means to cast our spells."

"The spell-fables?"

"Not exactly. In searching for answers, we delved into our past and rediscovered our legacy." Their history recounted how Daydra

Stonecipher made her journey from land to the ocean, how the
Dimernesti Purifiers became the first Dargonesti and fought wars
against a breed of creatures called koalinths in order to survive,
and how Nakaro Silverwake pleased the gods and returned magic.
Apoletta smiled at the last thought. She had known and cherished
Nakaro, once. To the elves Nakaro's name carried the weight of his
legend, but to Apoletta, how like a father he was to her, and she like
a daughter. She continued. "In essence, each served as a reminder
of how we struggled, persevered, and eventually thrived. We drew
comfort from our fables, from our past trials. So without magic,
we set about turning our existing spellcraft into something that
honored our history, to remind ourselves that struggle has always
been part of our heritage."

"You did this? I mean, not to diminish your accomplishment!"
Apoletta laughed.

"We hear that often," Slyphanous said. "But Apoletta is a gifted
wizard and she has seen much of Krynn's history unfold, so she
carries that wisdom."

"You are too kind," Apoletta said. "But we must thank the gods
for their hand as well. When the three moons returned, Solinari,
the silver moon, rewarded our faith, our ingenuity. It was difficult
at first, but we quickly discovered which stories empowered us
enough to draw forth the magic."

"Wonderful," Utharne said. "And all Dargonesti are capable
of this?"

"Not all, hmm," Slyphanous said with a sigh. "Purists espouse
their own method; it's caused a small schism."

"Purists!" Brysis said, snorting. "You mean the esteemed wizards of Watermere."

Apoletta explained, seeing Utharne's confusion. "Our principle
cities are as different as the three moons and the lands whose skies
they grace. Urione is a dark place where Zura holds my people's
hearts."

Utharne shook his head and expelled water from his lungs in

disgust. Zura, also known as Zeboim, was a foul dark goddess who made undead of her followers.

"I feel the same way," Apoletta whispered. "In Urione, Zura's magic holds sway. In Watermere, the purists rule and whisper in Treyen Silverwake's ears how our magic is to be distrusted. Then there is my city, that of Istar, where we created the spell-fables."

"Um, sorry for interrupting, but what of Darthalla and Dargonest?"

With some reluctance, Apoletta tried to explain. "Ever since Darthalla nominated their own Speaker of the Moon—"

"You have two Speakers of the Moons?"

"Depends who you ask," Brysis interjected. "Darthalla nominated Aquironian as their Speaker. And Dargonest swore allegiance to him. Watermere shunned both cities. But Darthalla and Dargonest believed they had little choice. The journey to Watermere was dangerous and long without magic."

"Yes, well . . ." Apoletta said, trying not to become embroiled in the political quagmire that had been raging for some years. That Darthalla and Dargonest chose a new Speaker of the Moon was understandable in her eyes. Perhaps it wasn't what she'd have done, but she understood. That they refused to follow Treyen Silverwake of Watermere since magic had returned and easy communication had been reestablished was something she could not support, however. "Regardless, the Dargonesti may not be as united as we once were, but we are trying to rebuild our ties."

Utharne smiled. "Not so unlike us, eh?"

Apoletta offered an embarrassed smile in return. The matter bothered her, especially since she'd been trying to convince the Dimernesti to join forces with her people.

Thankfully, the arrival of five brathnoc saved Apoletta from further discomfiture.

"The Synod will see you now," the lead brathnoc said, his skin as gray as his tone. He pointed to Apoletta and Utharne. "Only you two may come."

"No," Brysis responded. "I'm coming as well."

The brathnoc shook his head. "No, only them."

"Not this time," Brysis said. "If the Synod will not hear me, fine. They'll never know the danger that faces your paradise."

"Brysis," Apoletta hissed but stopped. She could think of no way to stop the hotheaded sea elf.

"The danger that you face," Brysis continued, undeterred, "will curdle your precious kelp leaves. It will wither your stalks. You'll have nothing to quiet your anger. Your rage. And all this," she said, motioning at the forest, "all this will turn to dust by your own hands. Now tell me, messenger, is that worth the Synod's ears?"

The messenger hesitated, but the water tasted of salt and oil. Apoletta recognized the smell of fear. The messenger chewed on some kelp leaves thoughtfully before finally relenting.

"Come," he said, including Brysis in his gaze. "But you will all wait outside until the Synod says otherwise."

Brysis smiled in response, despite Apoletta's angry gaze. Utharne, uncomfortable, swam to the others to tell them to behave themselves in his and Apoletta's absence.

"We'll speak of this later," Apoletta whispered to Brysis.

"Later, you'll thank me. You need my voice," Brysis said, typically curt. "Trust me. The brathnoc know little of diplomacy. They know much about the seas, however. In that, I speak their tongue far better than you do."

Apoletta went quiet at the comment. She knew Brysis was right, and that thought stung her. Her attempts at diplomacy had failed; perhaps they needed a heavier hand here. Brysis understood the primordial demands of the ocean. Perhaps the brathnoc answered to the same instincts.

Utharne returned, saving Apoletta from further comment; the three sea elves swam toward the pavilion, the brathnoc in their wake.

◆◆◆◆◆

THE ALIEN SEA

It did not take long for the Synod to meet with all three elves. Still, the request seemed like a heavy burden to the brathnoc, who always appeared on edge. They spoke with an impatient sigh, their manners growing increasingly brusque.

Nonetheless, Apoletta, Utharne, and Brysis entered the pavilion under the escort of six guards and found themselves gathered around the same black mast and Brathnoc himself. The guards waited at the edge of the veil-walled chamber while the mouthpiece for the Synod swam about, agitated and obviously upset with recent events.

"You betrayed our trust," Brathnoc said, moving about as he spoke.

Apoletta looked at her companions. Brysis seemed ready to fight his words with equally volatile ones of her own, while Utharne obviously preferred to placate Brathnoc.

"You lied to us," Apoletta said.

"We owe you nothing," Brathnoc said, his voice growing shrill under the influence of a Synod member.

"True," Apoletta said, "but the fact is you need our help."

"Really, and how is that, I wonder, hmm?" Brathnoc asked in an entirely different tone.

"The migration we saw," Brysis countered. "That's why you refused to join the Conclave. What do you care of the World Gash? Especially when the World Gash is pushing all these animals through your waters. Its currents are working to your favor. You have all the food you'll ever need without ever venturing far."

"If others were to learn of the bounty that flows through here," Brathnoc said with a feminine lilt, "we would have to face more enemies, take to war again to save ourselves. We cannot abide losing either our hunting grounds or our peace."

"The kelp," Apoletta said. "It soothes your thirst for blood?"

Brathnoc remained quiet a moment before sighing and speaking in a masculine tone. "Yes, and more. We came here, a small pack of nomads, looking for food. When we ate the plant, it dimmed the red haze of our thoughts. We could think clearly . . . as though for the first time. We remained and lured more of our brethren here, to give them clarity."

"You said 'and more'?" Utharne asked.

Brathnoc nodded slowly and held up one hand, as though to silence some unheard voice. "The Synod exists through the kelp. It has touched our thoughts. Given us something we never possessed. Even amongst each other."

"What?" Utharne asked.

"Empathy," Brathnoc said, his voice filled with awe at the concept. He went on to explain how once, the brathnoc were nothing more than savages; how the Hygant Forest had saved them and given them such fruitful hunting grounds.

It was Brysis who shook her head sadly. "Surely you know this won't last."

"Why not?" Brathnoc asked in one voice, before shifting to multiple voices in tone and pitch. "Who's to say it shan't? It sounds like a threat? Was it a threat? You have no proof of your claims. Perhaps she's right! Send them out! Let them speak!"

Apoletta, Brysis, and Utharne watched, fascinated by the display of Brathnoc struggling with himself. His features contorted; his body went rigid one moment and relaxed the next. He shut his eyes, focusing on the voices in his head. Finally, his original hiss of a voice emerged.

"Explain yourself," Brathnoc said, his gills flaring in rapid breath. The effort taxed him.

"We're not threatening you," Brysis said. "Yes, the World Gash is driving fish away, and to you. But that's because it's expanding."

"So you've said."

"So I've seen. The volcanic fields are active; tremors collapse the surrounding cliffs."

"Even if that is true," Brathnoc said, "it shan't threaten us for several generations."

"The World Gash itself won't, it's true," Brysis said. "But its poisons are spreading on the currents. You can't tell me you don't smell it in the trench."

"The animals carry it on their skin," Brathnoc said dismissively. "Nothing more."

"No," Brysis said. "It's the water that carries the taste. But"—Brysis raised her hand to stop the Brathnoc from arguing further—"let's say the World Gash or its poisons won't touch you for years. Generations, maybe. What about the migrations?"

Brathnoc smiled. "If the World Gash expands as you say, then it will only herd more animals through our lands. And we are not greedy." Another voice emerged from Brathnoc's wide lips. "We only kill those we need. We allow the others to continue forth."

"Yes," Brysis said with a smile, "but soon . . . soon the World Gash will drive others from their homes. Aquanox, the Dragon of the Deep, dwells between the World Gash and you. As do tribes of sahuagin and koalinth. Once forced to migrate, they will go where the food is plentiful. They will follow the migration. Straight to here."

Brathnoc's eyes widened in horror as the implication struck him. The shark-people, known as the sahuagin, and the brathnoc despised one another. Their battles were bloody and ruthless, both species driven to mutual ferocity by the taste of blood.

"And that's only the beginning of your woes," Brysis said, pushing her advantage. "The water in the trench acts like a river. It will grow more poisoned. Already the coral there dies. Once that happens, hungry animals will search beyond the trench banks for food. And they'll find the kelp forest waiting. Once they realize it is there, more animals will come. They will strip it clean."

Brathnoc appeared panicked by the thought. Without realizing it, he reached over to the kelp growing around the black mast and plucked a leaf from it. He ate it, calming himself and squinting in pain. Turmoil obviously gripped the Synod, and Brathnoc shut his lips to stop the words, stop the anger from escaping. After chewing on several more leaves, he spoke at last, his voice unlike any of the others. It was deep and resonated with such calm authority that even Brathnoc himself seemed affected.

"You speak your words with the conviction of truth, young elf. But is that the truth you believe for yourself or the one you have seen for us?"

Brysis hesitated. Apoletta could see her considering the answer carefully, for which Apoletta was grateful.

"It's the truth of experience," Brysis said carefully. "What I've seen is true. The World Gash expands unchecked. It'll certainly displace the sahuagin and koalinth of the region. What escape route they'll follow, I don't know. But they'll follow the food, and much of that food swims through here. As for the animals, they'll go hungry. The sulfur and the starving animals will strip the coral in the trench. They will begin hunting beyond the current. Hygant is a garden they cannot—they will not—ignore."

"But with an alliance," Utharne said, sensing opportunity, "the Dimernesti can help you, oh most certainly, yes. Your people can plant kelp fields in Dimernost in case, you understand, something happens here."

By the look on the mouthpiece's face, Apoletta realized that the brathnoc were not well versed in agriculture. They were still hunters learning to live in one place and take advantage of the already abundant kelp crop of the forest.

"The Dargonesti can teach you farming," Apoletta said. "Growing plants, keeping provisions for emergencies."

"Yes, yes," Utharne said excitedly, "all that. And, well certainly, everything else you'd expect in an alliance. Trade and, perhaps, our help in defending yourselves."

Brathnoc considered all that for a moment. "And what would you demand in the exchange, I wonder?"

"That you join the Conclave as full participants," Apoletta said. "We need help to fight the spread of the World Gash."

"Yes, and some hunting rights to help feed our people," Utharne said. "Many Dimernesti are returning to the fold. I'm afraid we'll strip the local waters of their bounty."

"Perhaps we can also study the animals," Brysis added. "There are many species I've never seen before. We don't know what remedies or qualities they can offer both our people."

Brathnoc quietly mulled it over. "My people must consider this carefully," he finally said. "Your words have merit, but we've known nothing but turmoil thus far. We need time to adjust."

"Forgive me for saying so," Apoletta said, "but our age is one of turmoil. The world will not wait for you, as it does for none of us."

"I understand," Brathnoc said. "Give us time to debate the matter, but do not expect us to arrive at our decision soon. Perhaps by the time you convene another Conclave, we'll send emissaries to listen . . . participate perhaps."

"Wonderful!" Utharne said. "That's all we can ask."

With that the three sea elves left the lit pavilion, glad to have gained some small victory in their mission. They swam back to the delegation and prepared for their departure to the far north, where Watermere lay.

ACT

Watermere

II

CHAPTER
Unexpected Company
6

A poletta."

A dark figure leaned over her prostrate body, whispering her name in her ear.

"Apoletta."

She awoke with a start and looked about. She was still in camp, in a private tent. And she was alone. They were three days removed from Hygant, having taken several rapid currents on their journey to Watermere.

After removing the heavy leather-quilt blanket that kept her weighted down, Apoletta swam out through the tent's flap.

Everything in the camp was as it should be. The three whales, still asleep, floated above them. Their faces were contorted, reflecting their strange, troubled dreams. The caravan's passengers slept in the silted clearing of the coral field, surrounded by hedges of coral lances.

Still half asleep, Apoletta tried to rouse herself. She tugged at her oyster-silk cloak, drawing it closer about her shoulders. The cold numbed her; it was not the kind of cold one normally found in deep waters, but another kind of chill. It started inside of her, in the marrow of her bones, and radiated outward. She shivered.

"Apoletta."

She turned again, trying to locate the unknown speaker. She could see nothing, and everyone slept still, including the guards on night watch. They slumped on the seafloor, their pockets filled with stones to weigh them down.

Everyone appeared caught in the pitch of some fitful dream. Apoletta watched Utharne and Brysis, Slyphanous and Echo Fury, all unconscious as though overtaken by exhaustion. Only Brine-Whisker remained awake; he lay next to Utharne, watching him carefully and standing guard. He looked to Apoletta, a tiny coil of blue flame curling from his forehead. She looked to the others again. It took Apoletta a moment before she realized their lips were moving. All who slept were murmuring in their sleep.

"Apoletta." All whispered her name.

Apoletta shivered.

Am I still dreaming? she wondered. The water felt ephemeral, as though she might fall through it as easily as her hand passed through rain. Brine-Whisker, however, did something she'd never seen him do before. He narrowed his large, thoughtful eyes and growled at the whisper issuing forth from Utharne's blue lips.

"Apoletta," a distant voice said.

Apoletta turned and pursued the voice; an odd compulsion that pulled at her drew her away from the camp. The reckless action frightened her, but she felt too lethargic to panic or to resist. Instead, despite herself, she filled her lungs with air and floated upward, into the sky of indigo waters.

"Apoletta," the voice insisted. It sounded like Zebulah.

She struggled against the gauze filling her thoughts but to no avail. She was going somewhere against her will but to see someone she desperately wanted to see. After a moment of swimming with half-hearted kicks, she felt something move alongside her. It was Brine-Whisker. Apoletta almost cried from relief for his company.

Together, the pair swam into the deeper dark of the water, where the seafloor dropped away and turbid darkness awaited them in every direction.

Brine-Whisker sensed the intruder before she did. He snarled again, the blue flame on his forehead glowing bright. A cowled figure on the edge of darkness skittered away, as though pushed by the light.

"Zebulah?" Apoletta asked.

The figure wore red robes stitched with runes of glowing thread. Apoletta, feeling stronger, touched Brine-Whisker's back. He understood; the blue light faded, drawing some of the darkness back toward them.

"My love," Apoletta whispered. "I know you. Please. Let me see you." She tried to advance forward, but Brine-Whisker approached with her; his wan blue flame pushing Zebulah back.

"Please," Apoletta told Brine-Whisker, but the seal refused to budge. He shouted an angry bark and would not move.

"Zebulah," Apoletta said, turning back to the robed figure. "Let me see your face."

The figure chuckled, a cold, empty laugh that said good humor was the last of his qualities. Yet he pulled back his cowl.

Zebulah floated there, but he was not the Zebulah she remembered. Apoletta gasped, her eyes dancing over his features. The glowing runes that adorned his robes carried over onto his face. They stood out against his sallow, gray skin; but the sigils could not compare with the unholy emotion blazing in his eyes. The Zebulah Apoletta remembered had counted himself as human. That creature, however, was no longer mortal.

It was undead.

"Who are you?" Apoletta demanded, now certain in her horror that the foul thing was not her husband, not the human she had met and loved decades ago.

The creature said nothing; it studied her, its gaze cold, analytical.

"No," Apoletta said, mentally preparing one of her spell-fables. "You are not Zebulah. What are you? A replicate? An illusion?" She produced a copper piece from her pouch—a coin she'd found in

Istar centuries ago, which had remained in her possession since. She turned it over in her hands and drew upon the heat in her belly.

"When Stonecipher first dipped her head beneath the waves," Apoletta incanted, "she heard the ocean's thoughts and murmurs."

The thrum of the surrounding deep vanished, replaced by whispers. The red-robed undead did not move, but neither did it appear frightened by the spell. Apoletta focused on its unflinching gaze, her mind a sword that cleaved through its skull to reveal its most immediate thoughts. They filtered in far quicker than Apoletta anticipated. She knew it—knew him—already. His thoughts fell open at her feet as though carelessly thrown.

"Zebulah," Apoletta whispered. Apoletta wanted to refute the undead thing, but the more she fought the truth, the more it grew self-evident. The way he moved, the way he spoke, he was Zebulah but stripped of his humility and the kindness she remembered. She tried to read his surface thoughts, to glean more information, but encountered only empty holes and patchwork memories.

"What happened to you?" she asked.

More faded memories appeared, snippets of Zebulah's life as human . . . of Apoletta turning her back on Zebulah while sea elves clutched him—betrayal.

Apoletta's eyes widened. "I never betrayed you," she said. Her strength returned with the surging tide of her anger. It did nothing to stem the scratching inside her ribs, however, the horrible awareness that recognized her former husband in the shell of a creature before her.

More memories flitted into view, contradictory ones that Zebulah remembered and seemingly could not reconcile: fleeing Istar in fear of Apoletta, yet touching her lips while she lay in his arms, their most intimate moments revealed in the mind of something undead. The undead Zebulah was not a loving participant in those affairs, but an unwelcome voyeur, someone tainting Apoletta's memories with his presence.

"You," Apoletta said carefully, "you are Zebulah. My husband."

Her voice shook, trembling with her love for him.

Zebulah focused on his name. He still saw himself as human. In his thoughts, he kissed Apoletta a thousand times in a thousand different places on her body.

"No!" Apoletta said, her stomach clenching at the notion that the creature knew her so intimately. "Maybe once, but not anymore! Zebulah is dead."

Memories of Apoletta turning her back on him. Memories of him fleeing Istar.

"I didn't betray you," she said, nearly shouting. "I . . ." and the words died in her mouth.

Memories of Apoletta leaving Zebulah. Memories of Zebulah seeing himself for the first time as undead, examining the dead fingers attached to his dead hands, attached to his dead arms. Apoletta leaving Zebulah. Zebulah becoming undead.

"No," Apoletta said, her voice soft. "I didn't do this to you! I wouldn't have. I loved you."

Zebulah's eyes froze. He touched his lips, perhaps remembering the brush of a lost kiss. He looked at Apoletta, the anger and rage in his eyes gone; only a curious sadness remained. Confusion. He looked away, suddenly shy.

And in that action, Apoletta saw everything she remembered of her husband. "Please," she begged, "don't go. Tell me: What has happened to you?"

Zebulah paused. Shattered memories appeared and vanished like fingers leafing through the pages of a torn book. He searched for the right memory, but none came to mind.

Apoletta tried moving forward, but again Brine-Whisker followed her and drove Zebulah farther back into the darkness.

In that moment voices called through the waters. Apoletta heard her name again, this time shouted by her friends. Brine-Whisker barked loudly, and the blue light on his forehead brightened. Zebulah drifted away, pushed by the candlelight's horizon.

"Wait!" Apoletta said. "Where are you going?"

In Zebulah's thoughts darkness appeared, waters of the deepest black, where ash fell slowly in perpetual winter. That was home now.

More shouts carried Apoletta's name, closer than before. Swimmers approached quickly; Apoletta's friends swam to her rescue.

"I can't lose you again!" Apoletta said.

Thoughts of her and Zebulah, still somehow human, together in the inky blackness and ash fall, embracing one another in a grip that not even the centuries would shake loose.

"I cannot come with you," Apoletta said. Then she sensed something moving in the shadows of Zebulah's memories. Something else lived there. She saw Zebulah bowing to the darkness.

"Who is that?" Apoletta said.

Apoletta's friends called out to her. She could see them now, swimming for her. Brine-Whisker's flame was a beacon that drew them.

A fleeting image caught Apoletta's attention. In the darkness of Zebulah's memories, something long and serpentine flowed, its beating wings propelling it forward.

"Dragon," Apoletta said.

Then another image appeared, one of a sea elf, his skin a dark blue and his hair colored with red clay.

Mahkwahb, Apoletta realized.

"You will serve Blazewight," the dark blue sea elf in Zebulah's memories told Zebulah. "This is not a dragon in the way you suppose. This beast is more cursed than you. And he despoils the sea with his taint. Come. You'll see."

"Get away from her," someone below them shouted. It sounded like Utharne, but Apoletta could not tear her eyes away from her husband's.

"Where are you?" Apoletta demanded.

More images raced through Zebulah's thoughts. She saw underwater vistas where threads of lava threw up curtains of steam. Ash sailed downward in lazy drifts.

"The World Gash?" Apoletta said, uncertain.

"In the shadow of the impaling throne," Zebulah said, his voice sounding cracked and broken, like a dust-caked organ neglected for years. It hurt him to speak. He started to swim away.

Before Apoletta could rush forward to stop him, Utharne swam between them, Brine-Whisker at his side.

"Heed me, unhallowed! The Fisher King demands you submit or *flee!*" Utharne shouted.

"No," Apoletta called out, trying to stop Utharne, but Brysis was upon her, holding her back.

Zebulah dismissed the priest's effort with a flick of his wrist and let the darkness swallow him. Apoletta broke free of Brysis and swam forward, tearing at the water as though tearing at the curtains between Zebulah and herself.

Alas . . . Zebulah was gone.

At the camp, Utharne listened to the tangled mess of conversations and confusion. Slyphanous waved at people to quiet them, but that only fueled the arguments.

"Her husband?" Arrovawk asked loudly.

"Lower your voice!" Slyphanous said, looking back at the tent where Apoletta slept. She'd been through a terrible ordeal.

"An air-breather?" Arrovawk said, still as loud.

"Yes, a KreeaQUEKH," Captain Ornathius replied, grimacing at the thought.

"What of it, Ornathius?" Brysis said.

"It isn't proper!" Captain Ornathius responded.

"Here, here," Arrovawk said.

"Apoletta's concerns are her own," Slyphanous said, still keeping his voice low. "And I care not what Watermere thinks of the matter. She is the First Mother of Istar! We found a city in ruins. It was she who rebuilt portions of it so that we might have a home. She saved the Heroes of the Lance from drowning, she fought in the war against Chaos, she helped us discover the spell-fables, and she brought us together. She deserves your respect!"

"She answers to the Speaker of the Moon. And he certainly didn't approve of Zebulah," Captain Ornathius responded.

"What's a Zebulah?" Arrowawk asked.

"Her husband," Maleanki said with a wide smile.

At that moment, Utharne chuckled, the absurdity apparently lost on everyone else. The others stopped chattering and stared at him.

"All of you," Utharne said. "Have you thought about it? Zebulah, I mean? Thought about it really? You're arguing about her marriage when the problem, the real problem I think, is that Zebulah is undead. As in dead but not quite. As in the attack on Dimernost is likely connected to him. Connected? Is that a good word? Yes! Connected to Zebulah's appearance here."

Nobody spoke for that moment.

"How long were they married?" Utharne asked.

"A century. Thereabouts," Slyphanous said.

"Can KreeaQUEKH live that long?" Vanastra asked, her brows furrowed.

"Apparently," Brysis said.

"Zebulah was an accomplished magician," Slyphanous said. "He extended his own life, and he could breathe water."

"But what happened to Zebulah?" asked Utharne. "When magic vanished, I mean?"

"I am not comfortable discussing Apoletta's affairs!" Slyphanous said.

"Please," Utharne said. "It's important."

Slyphanous thought on the matter before answering. "Very well," he said. "Zebulah survived in one of Istar's many air pockets. But that did not last long."

"What happened?" Utharne asked.

"Apoletta cast him from the city."

Everyone's eyes widened.

"I did not hear that!" Captain Ornathius said.

"Why?" Utharne asked.

Slyphanous shook his head. "No, I've betrayed my lady's confidence enough tonight. If you wish to know, ask her yourself. Enough people already have treated her affairs as their own," he said, looking directly at Captain Ornathius.

Ornathius actually blinked; Slyphanous stared at the rest of them with a gaze that challenged any of them to dare speak. Finally, he left the circle and went to sit outside Apoletta's tent. The others drifted away to catch what remaining sleep the night had left for them. Utharne considered the matter quietly and petted Brine-Whisker.

"You were brave," Utharne told his companion. "I'm proud of you."

Apoletta kept her voice soft, just strong enough to catch Slyphanous's attentions. Peering into the tent, he was shocked to see her awake and kneeling just above the silt-covered floor.

"What's the matter?" Slyphanous whispered. "Can't sleep?"

Apoletta stared at her advisor. "I heard you speaking," she said, "with the others."

Slyphanous stammered, suddenly embarrassed. "I . . . I'm sorry, my lady. Sorry indeed. I meant nothing by——"

"No, no, old friend," she whispered. She motioned for him to approach.

Slyphanous sat upon the water, inches above the floor.

"Do you miss him?" Apoletta asked.

"Zebulah?" Slyphanous said. "I admit I do. He was an agreeable fellow, even for a human."

"I miss him," Apoletta responded.

"I know," he said. "But you and I both know that thing tonight was not your husband."

"No, he is still my husband, but," Apoletta said, stopping

Slyphanous from arguing, "but I recognize that he's changed. I would be a fool not to."

"Changed? He has died and become something foul," Slyphanous said, his brow furrowed.

"Zebulah is trapped," Apoletta said. "He serves a master, and I suspect his master is to blame for his condition."

"You cannot save undead. Only their destruction frees them. And even then. . . ." Slyphanous trailed off.

"I know. But neither can I allow Zebulah to . . ." she continued, searching for the right word, "persist like this. He's in pain. Trapped. I must save him."

"Saving him might mean killing him," Slyphanous said with some care.

"I know," Apoletta whispered. "But I cannot let him endure this way. I intend to liberate him, though first I must deal with his so-called master. For that, I need your help."

"Mine?" Slyphanous asked, surprised.

"You're the only one I can trust in this matter."

Slyphanous sighed and shook his head. "You know I serve you without hesitation," he said. "What is your wish?"

"At dawn break, take two of Captain Ornathius's soldiers and travel to Istar as fast as your porpoise forms will carry you. I need you to retrieve something for me. Meet us in Watermere when you have it."

"Have what?" Slyphanous asked.

Apoletta smiled and explained her plan, much to Slyphanous's dismay.

The wichtlin hovered high in the water. Its antlered sea horse looked about impatiently, but the wichtlin held the reins tight. It looked down at the distant camp then up again, in the direction Zebulah had fled.

THE ALIEN SEA

With a smile, the wichtlin clacked its teeth and laughed, its voice a thin, whispered hiss. It pushed its sea horse forward. They dived through the water, racing back to Wartide.

CHAPTER
The Storm of Silt

7

"Zebulah's back," said the dark sea elf.

"Where?" Wartide asked, peering about. All he could see were the combined forces of undead, magori, and Mahkwahb.

"He's trailing us and in a foul mood. He obliterated one skeleton with a fiery spell after it ventured too close to him. Everyone is swimming outside his reach."

Wartide said nothing. In their journey Wartide's band had accomplished one of their master's tasks, destroying Silver Horn, an oceanic forestmaster who protected a large expanse of verdant red and yellow coral fields. The oceanic forestmaster, a creature whose hindquarters were a dolphin's fluke and whose body and head looked like a horned white horse with flippers, had fought well, but Wartide soundly defeated the creature. That was one less impediment to his master's success; for others, they would need Zebulah's help.

The wichtlin approached.

"What happened?" Wartide asked.

The wichtlin hissed and whispered, words spilling backward from its lips. The words sounded unintelligible and maddening to anyone listening. Wartide, however, simply nodded at the information.

"You're certain he found them?" Wartide asked.

The wichtlin clacked its teeth in response.

Wartide dismissed the wichtlin and the three tattooed sharks swimming next to him. The sharks and wichtlin bolted from their places and raced on ahead, vanishing into the turbid haze.

A rush of pain swept through Wartide as his mouth stretched wide and his coral-armor broke through his skin to cover his shark form. He raced after a school of fish and tore into them. Turning back into elf form, he waved the turtle medallion through the chum.

"What is your wish," he asked with a soft mumble.

A family of sea turtles appeared and nibbled at the carrion cloud. Again, Wartide endured their bites.

"Warn Blazewight," a woman's voice said. "Impress upon him the threat Apoletta and her band poses. I will see that some survive the ordeal to come."

Although that surprised Wartide, he never hesitated in his service to her. "As you wish," Wartide said, never voicing the one question he wanted desperately to ask.

Why?

Ashen clouds caught in perfect suspension surrounded Wartide. He squinted harder, squeezing his eyes shut; the ash, the waters black as ink, and the deep cold were all illusions. Wartide realized he was far from his master's home, but whenever he envisioned that dark place, he felt almost as though he'd conjured a bit of himself there.

Something of gigantic proportions moved through the darkness; the violent *hiss-pop* of water turning to steam rose in pitch. Despite the heat emanating from Blazewight, Wartide felt colder than ever.

"You have my attention," Blazewight said from the darkness.

"We've slain Silver Horn," Wartide said. "We are proceeding to the savage-claw crabs. We'll use a few undead as a carrion meal to lure the crabs into a trap before striking. Afterwards, we move to attack Anhalstrax."

"I approve," Blazewight said, his voice shuddering the waters. "Is that what you wished to hear? My approval?"

"No, my lord," Wartide said. "I wouldn't bother you with such trivial matters."

"What, then, requires my attentions?"

"My spies learned that the Dimernesti and Dargonesti have sent a delegation to Watermere. I think they've uncovered your plans and will use that to forge their alliance. They will come here, next, in force. They may even reach Anhalstrax before we do."

"What!" Blazewight demanded, his voice like thunder.

The waters stilled except for the odd *hiss* and *pop*. Finally Blazewight spoke again, his voice sending the water into turmoil. "I shall use the power of the Impaling Throne. I will deal with them."

"You are powerful and mighty," Wartide said, bowing.

"They will not survive the night," Blazewight responded. "Where are they now?"

"Northeast of the Blood Sea and the minotaur isles. They approach the mouth of one of the God's Throat, but which one and how far they are, I know not."

"I will lash the Northern and Eastern Courrain Oceans with the greatest storm seen by mortal eyes."

Wartide floated in place, bowing deeply. "They cannot survive your wrath."

"I know they cannot," Blazewight responded.

For a long time Wartide was unable to speak or move. Finally, he opened his eyes and found himself floating in warmer waters of deep greens and sparkling blues. He became a shark and immediately tore after his small army. He had to warn them all. . . .

They were in the Eastern Courrain as well.

THE ALIEN SEA

Storm-crafting something of a hurricane's magnitude is an art, and as with any art, it must begin slowly, with a gathering of ingredients. No tempest springs forth from nothingness. The magic to summon and drive a storm must follow its own devices, or the result will be a short-lived gale.

The storm began with winds, and as all birds know, the most powerful of the winds live high above the lands, above most clouds. The storm summoned by Blazewight began there, in the loftiest of winds called the high stream.

The spell agitated the upper stream, forcing it to move faster than normal; the birds below quickly sensed something amiss and flew for safety. The agitation of the upper stream affected the lower depths, warm air mingled with cold air, and the clouds filled with heavy moisture. The waters of the sea grew choppy and the swells rose.

The winds accelerated, and the waves became moving walls of water. A hurricane formed soon after—purple clouds, ragged lightning, lashing rain, and fierce winds.

The tumult emerged from seemingly nowhere. Apoletta's caravan had neared the surface for the shark-blade whales to swallow another few hours of breath when Brysis remarked on the brooding gray clouds that were racing across the quickly eclipsed sky.

Utharne examined the sky above with faint interest.

Brysis pointed to the east, where a wall swept the horizon. The storm appeared ugly with purple cauliflower thunderheads and a skirt of utter shadow. Only random licks of lightning illuminated the undergrowth between the sky and sea. It was moving quickly.

"A typhoon?" stout Briegan said. "In these—"

"Waters?" Maleanki said, finishing his sentence. "Yes, it is odd."

"Too odd," Apoletta said, watching the storm. "It moves too quickly."

"Really?" Utharne said, squinting. "How can you tell? I can barely see above water, you know. Poor dry sight. Hate the surface, really."

"No, no," Brysis said, growing horrified. "It's moving fast, yes, too fast!"

The wall of clouds had advanced rapidly, lowering the gap between the horizon and the caravan.

Everyone cried out to see the high waves. The darkness beneath the clouds seemed to undulate. The storm had quickly crossed closer. And that's when they first felt it—the slow, heavy drag of water being sucked toward the storm.

"Tidal wave!" Vanastra screamed. "Dive!"

Most of the others needed little encouragement. They dived beneath the surface, though some, half in a shocked daze, lingered too long.

The steady rumble grew in pitch. Apoletta struggled downward and away from the tidal wave, but she felt sluggish. She fought harder, changing into a porpoise to swim faster. Around her, others already had shapeshifted. Brown-furred sea otters and gray porpoises were kicking harder to escape the growing pull.

The ocean floor appeared in the murky indigo. Apoletta kicked harder, but the heavy silt was agitated, obscuring her sight as powerful waves streamed the sand over dunes. The sea grew murkier by the moment, though in some places she could see the stony bottom.

Apoletta struggled to reach the seafloor, her torso and fluke aching from her frantic, exhausted crawl. In the dim recesses of her thoughts, Apoletta wondered why the ocean floor seemed closer to the surface. A panicked scream answered her question; she looked up in time to see the tidal wave had peeled away the top layers of the sea, leaving less than a hundred feet of depth. The roar of the massive waves advancing toward her was deafening.

It might be me who is screaming, she thought.

Apoletta's felt like driftwood; she was numb with exertion. The ocean floor retreated. She saw her companions ducking into a large undergrowth of coral. Briegan and Arrovawk released the whales, letting them try to escape. She called out for help from somebody, but her breath came in ragged strokes and nobody could hear her anyway.

Within moments, the ground vanished as upturned silt filled the water.

She twisted around. It was then that Apoletta spotted the dark cut of a narrow trench to her left. It appeared and vanished amidst the turbulence. The trench was no more than a couple of dozen feet deep and a handful of yards across, but it might protect her. With renewed hope, she angled for one last attempt to reach the trench.

The approaching thunder shook her bones. The trench lay only a few feet away, the lip near enough to grab on to. To Apoletta's dismay, however, the silt curled up and swept skyward.

With a last push, Apoletta dived over the edge of the narrow trench, nearly skinning herself on its jagged lips. It was too tight for her porpoise body, so she changed back into her slim elf form. Her fingers scrambled for purchase on the cliff's brown rocks, and she squeezed inside. The tidal wave rolled over her, hammering her down with a fist of water that slammed through the narrow gap. She grunted at the pain and careened against the walls, pushed hard inside. She fell and continued plummeting. Rock outcroppings rose to meet her, and she deftly avoided one before slamming into another.

She felt a sharp pain in her shoulder, followed by a knife-stab of agony in her upper chest. She tumbled head over heels, again and again, until finally Apoletta stopped long enough to peer up and see the rolling sea rush past her deep trough. Then, to her horror, thick waves of silt flooded into the trench, muddying the waters and covering her.

Apoletta choked, the silt turning to paste in her mouth and gills. She kicked up, swimming through the slush that rapidly filled her trench. The silt smothered and blinded her, the walls pressed in on her. Apoletta's hair grew heavy with filth; she fell back into the trench under the steadily growing weight, coughing and gasping for clean water.

The tidal wave continued on its way, sweeping across the ocean. The crests of the following waves were nearly as high, their troughs almost as deep. The waves gouged the ocean like giant hands that dug at the seafloor, unearthing mountains of silt and muck.

The violent ocean turned a brownish color; the sky above was bruised black. Birds, caught in the wild downpour that followed the tidal wave, drowned or were whipped apart in mid-flight. Furious lightning pelted the sea, destroying those fish not already crushed between the killing waves. In short, the great storm killed with ease and pleasure, and death was an arbitrary broker.

Silt continued to fill the trench, trapping Apoletta in muck. The weight was tremendous, and Apoletta felt herself being sucked down into the quicksand.

Is this how drowning sailors feel? Apoletta wondered. She gasped for air but drew little from the muddy waters. Desperate, she plunged her only free hand into the muck and reached into a pouch. She prayed she'd found the right one.

Apoletta's fingers wrapped around something familiar just as the silt reached up to wrap around her neck and smother her mouth. With a last gasp, Apoletta croaked out, "And though robbed of land, Daydra could swim alongside the swiftest dolphins!"

THE ALIEN SEA

A strange warmth flooded through Apoletta's legs as the spell took hold. Her muscles tightened; strength returned to her limbs. With a powerful kick, Apoletta pushed her upper body free of the silt and grabbed for nearby rocks. With all her strength, she pulled and pushed herself out of the trench. She emerged back into a din, her breath gone.

The thunder and waves pounded Apoletta, sweeping her up toward the tumultuous skies. The magic she'd cast to escape remained with her, though. She kicked toward the surface.

Apoletta could see the lightning flashes in the sky above. She kicked harder, desperate to break the surface, which seemed to retreat from her outstretched hand. Suddenly, her stomach lurched, her leaden lungs felt as though they'd dropped into her feet, and the wave was pushing her up at an alarming speed.

She broke the surface, gasping for air and riding the crest of a giant wave more than a hundred feet above the ocean below. She choked on thick sea foam, her lungs and gills hiccupping on bubbles. For a moment, vertigo overtook her; she slipped through the sea foam and fell through the air, skidding down the wave's cliff. Apoletta breathed as quickly as she could before sliding off the last slope and plummeting into the ocean again.

Suddenly, in the murky waters, some unseen net entangled her. It gripped her wrist and knotted about her legs. Only when she pulled at the net did pain sear her scalp. She realized that she was entangled in her own hair.

There was little choice or deliberation; Apoletta pulled her seashell knife from its sheath, cutting frantically at her hair. The ocean carried away her silver locks, and slowly Apoletta liberated herself.

She broke the surface again in time to be carried skyward on the back of another giant wave. She breathed as quickly as she could, diving over the crest of the wall of water before it could collapse atop her. She choked on the waters thick with silt and the thick froth of sea foam, and angled herself for another leap off the wave's cliff.

It promised to be a long night.

The tidal wave and the storm that drove it continued along their path, eventually striking and breaking their backs on the western mountainous shores of the Blood Sea Isles. Only then did they dissipate, the dark clouds eventually shredding in the high winds.

At last the shrill cry of gulls prodded Apoletta awake. She raised her head; her scalp and neck burned under the light of the bright sun. Apoletta floated on the ocean's surface, clutching a—

Whatever it was suddenly dived underwater, startling her. Despite her blurry vision, she stared at the creature that swam away—a giant sea turtle with a green shell.

Apoletta was both stunned and exhausted. Her head felt strange; only when she touched her unevenly shorn hair did she vaguely remember cutting it off in the midst of the storm.

No clouds graced the sky, which appeared as blue as the waters. Nothing disturbed the mirrorlike surface—the winds gone, the waves silenced, and yesterday's violence a dim memory. Apoletta sank beneath the surface, immediately grateful for the cooling touch of seawater on her dried skin. When she sank no more, she kicked her way to the bottom, her movements slow and gentle but her body complaining all the way.

Sharks filled the water, drawn to the dying and wounded sea life. They mostly ignored her, though Apoletta kept her dagger ready. The ocean was deep again, but with a different seafloor than the one she remembered. The waves had churned the silt and deposited it again into a smooth blanket. Except for outcroppings of rock, surviving coral fans, and briars of thorny lashers, the ground appeared pristine and flat. It would not last; already a mild current fashioned rows of ribbed dunes, while translucent mantis crabs, with their clear carapaces, left footprints behind in their search for the plentiful carrion.

Apoletta glided over the strange new landscape, searching for her friends. Despite the solemn beauty of her surroundings,

Apoletta grimly wondered how Slyphanous and his two escorts had fared. The Blood Sea rested nearby, so she hoped Slyphanous had escaped to safety within the bowl of islands and land. Meanwhile, she would focus on the others. Only Apoletta did not recognize her surroundings, did not know where to start looking.

Fortunately, they found her first. Echo Fury and Brine-Whisker rushed toward her, barking and squealing with pure joy. She swept an arm around each of them, grateful to see them alive. Brine-Whisker appeared unhurt, while Echo Fury bore a bruised flank. One of his armored fins had cracked.

Echo Fury dismissed her concern with a chirp and instead gently pushed his beak against her short hair.

"Ah, yes," Apoletta said, feeling self-conscious. "A story for later."

Echo Fury swam around Apoletta and angled his dorsal fin to her. She smiled and stroked his crown. "No, I'm well enough to swim," she replied.

Both Echo Fury and Brine-Whisker darted away, forcing an aching Apoletta to keep pace. Thankfully, they did not have far to go.

Silt covered the coral growth where the others had sought shelter. It was a coral cave, Apoletta realized. Only the entrance lay exposed, and even then it bore the distinct impression of having been dug out in urgent fashion. Briegan floated there, tending to the bruises on one of their whales; the other two were missing.

"Briegan!" Apoletta said.

"Your Ladyship!" Briegan cried. "Thank the Speaker!"

"What happened to you all?" she asked, noting he appeared none the worse for wear. "How did you survive?"

"Utharne," he said simply. "His miracles kept us alive, kept the water clean enough to breathe."

"Where is everyone, then?"

"Some went looking for you. Arrowawk is looking for the other two whales."

"Was anyone hurt?"

At that, half of Briegan's face curled into a sad smile while the other half curled down as though he needed comforting. He nodded toward the cave, unable to speak.

Apoletta raced for the cave with its silt ramp descending down into the darkness. A low moan tore through the waters behind her; it was Briegan blowing into a conch horn, signaling the search parties to return.

The cave was surprisingly shallow, its walls sharp with broken coral lances. In the back of the cave, Utharne sat. He tended to Maleanki, who sat propped up against the wall, groaning softly. When Utharne saw her, his face changed from miserable to a grateful smile. Then he seemed to remember where he was, and the grin vanished. He returned his attentions to Maleanki.

Apoletta swam up beside them both and expelled enough air from her lungs to sit. Maleanki appeared badly hurt. The taste of his coppery blood filled the water, and he was bleeding profusely from his back. Apoletta was about to question why Maleanki sat with his wounded back to the wall when she gasped. Something had impaled Maleanki against the coral lances of the back wall.

"What happened?" Apoletta asked.

"We, ah, we rushed into the cave, but the waves pushed us even deeper inside," Utharne said, choosing his words carefully through clenched teeth. "The water shoved us! Maleanki was inside already. We, uh, we all fell upon him. He struck the wall. We did this. We ourselves did this!" Utharne stared at her, his face torn by grief. "I can't heal him. I have nothing left. My miracles were spent keeping the rest of us alive. Even if I wanted to, I couldn't cure him. Not without removing him. But he's impaled on the coral. And even if I . . . if I remove him, he'll bleed to death instantly. I might as well . . . I might as well just kill him and end his suffering, but I can't bring myself. . . ."

Apoletta pulled Utharne into her embrace, his body wracked with heaving sobs.

"I'm sorry," he muttered against her shoulder. "I'm sorry. Everyone, they . . . they look to me for answers. I tried. I tried. But I can't do anything."

"It's not your fault," Apoletta said, her voice soft. "Perhaps you are right. Perhaps it is time to end his suffering."

Utharne pulled away from her, his eyes wide. "I can't. I can't. Not again . . . not again!"

Uncertain what he meant, Apoletta placed her hand gently against his cheek. She could see only that some distant wound had reopened inside him, forcing him to relive a past torture. "Shh," Apoletta said, stroking his cheek, trying to calm him. "Then say a prayer to guide him to the Fisher King. I'll stop his pain."

"I don't know if I can," Utharne said, his eyes bloodshot green. "How, uh, how do I ask? I mean, how do I pray to the gods when I. . . ." He paused, trying to find the words. "When I can't forgive the gods for this."

"I understand," Apoletta said. "But despite how you feel, Abbuku still provided you strength to cast your miracles, did he not? To save the others?"

Utharne nodded.

"Then perhaps Abbuku understands your anger. Besides, you do not pray for yourself. You pray for him," Apoletta said, looking at Maleanki.

"Yes, I pray for him," Utharne repeated in a whisper. He looked back to Apoletta. "Forgive me."

"You owe me no apologies," she said. "We'll pray together. I'll release him."

Utharne seemed to regain his sense of purpose. He searched deep into Apoletta's eyes. "You've done this before," he said.

Apoletta smiled ruefully. "I regret that I have. When magic fled, I discovered the best medicine was often mercy."

Utharne nodded. "I remember that lesson well," he whispered. "We'll pray together."

Other than young Maleanki, a soldier named Anariannial also died that night, his body wedged with crushing force between two rocks; three others under Vanastra's and Captain Ornathius's commands were missing. They never reached the cave. The survivors left the bodies of both Maleanki and Anariannial inside the cave, covered in silt.

Most everyone seemed grateful to have found Apoletta, perhaps even Arrovawk, though his gaze was as venomous as always. No doubt he blamed Apoletta for their predicament, and he made a point of demanding that the Dargonesti compensate him for his lost whales. Apoletta was too exhausted to argue. Brysis trimmed her hair as Arrovawk ranted, evening out the rough jags of the once proud tresses to shoulder length.

After a day of rest and recuperation, the ragged caravan ruefully resumed its journey to the northeast, away from the Blood Sea Isles, to a place called the God's Throat.

CHAPTER
The Defiler's Breath
8

The sea elves called the seafloor framing the continents The Ledge. Beyond The Ledge, the seafloor dropped into the Median Ocean, the name of the layer below the sunlit belt, where the waters measured thousands of feet deep and sunlight failed to penetrate. Beyond the Median rested the Yawning Deep, a frightening, mysterious layer that began miles down and was supposedly devoid of any life.

Nothing could have been farther from the truth, though convincing the Dimernesti companions of that proved an epic struggle in itself. The shoal elves, with Apoletta's promises and Utharne's prodding, left The Ledge. They dropped into the frigid Median Ocean, their complaints as bitter as the cold they felt.

Strangely, the deeper the reluctant Dimernesti ventured, the more their complaints faded. Utharne cast spells upon Salystra, the surviving whale, to give her breathing assistance, and even Arrovawk had to admit, albeit grudgingly, that he grew more comfortable with the waters. Apoletta smiled and told them to wait.

Finally, after what felt like an hour of descent, the water warmed and a silvery light emanated from below. The fish returned in breeds that turned the heads of the Dimernesti. They had never seen the like of those species that the Dargonesti had long beheld in their explorations of the Yawning Deep: long serpentine fish with clawed appendages, blue scuttle crabs as large as horses, and yellow bladder fish that swelled to more than eight feet in diameter before contracting and propelling themselves forward. The coral, sponges, and algae grew in great profusion and variety, their colors sharp reds, sunflower yellows, creamy greens, and royal blues.

The silver light came from everywhere and nowhere, like tricks of shadows in the corners of one's eyes. Utharne had been silent company the past two days, and he simply marveled.

"I've heard of these places—pockets, correct? Wonderful," he muttered.

"In some places in the Yawning Deep, light and life return to us," Apoletta said, smiling in the soft glow that lit everything evenly. No shadows were cast there. "It is a reminder from the gods that there is no place on this world that Solinari's light will not find."

Utharne nodded. "Yes, yes, I understand. It's rather like we're beneath the stars and the silver moon's glow. It's much like a clear night on the surface. Wonderful," he repeated.

"When the moons vanished," Briegan asked, "what happened to these places?"

"Vanished with Solinari," Brysis said. "Like they never existed. Like a phase of the silver moon itself. A window that could close at any moment."

"But when the moons returned," Apoletta said, "these places reappeared as well."

After a few more long moments, they came upon the edge of a deep chasm. It stretched wide at several hundred feet, tapering to a point at one end and extending into the diffused light at the other. The chasm stretched down far below them, the silver light unable to illuminate its seemingly fathomless darkness. The glow ended less than two hundred feet down, but it illuminated the spiral columns half protruding from the cliff walls and the giant face of horrific features carved into the corner of the chasm's lips.

THE ALIEN SEA

The face measured longer than the span of a minotaur's galleon from its brow to its chin; swatches of incandescent mother-of-pearl covered its surface. Where the mother-of-pearl had fallen off rested a strange green rock whose striations looked like muscle fibers.

More unusual than the bright material covering the face were its features and the strange, trembling howl that issued from inside of it. Of the first oddity, its features, they bore nothing similar to elf, human, dwarf, or kender. Instead, its features were squidlike, with tentacles for a jaw and two angry, narrow slits for eyes. The face appeared to be moving, thanks to the shimmering mother-of-pearl and the strange silvery light playing across its surface; the tentacles shifted and swayed while the eyes danced in their narrow sockets.

Of the second oddity, a strange, continuous howl issued from the tentacle-lined mouth. Needlelike teeth rimmed the puckered maw, which measured more than thirty feet in diameter. The mouth extended into a throat-tunnel that vanished into the darkness of the cliff wall. From the tunnel issued forth an unusually strong current that spat out from the trench. It was the unusual current that produced the howl.

"A Defiler's Breath!" Arrowawk said. "You're mad if you think we're riding a Defiler's Breath."

"I've been using them for centuries," Apoletta responded mildly. "They are our fastest currents."

"Currents of the Abyss usually are the fastest, yes!" Arrowawk replied. "But there's no way I'm taking that route."

"It doesn't lead to the Abyss," Brysis said. "It's perfectly safe!"

"Really? And where does it go?" Vanastra asked, furrowing her brows.

"To Watermere!" Captain Ornathius replied, annoyed.

"No, that is not what I mean," Vanastra said. "The current may travel to Watermere, but where does it start?"

"Nobody knows," Brysis countered.

"But the Dargonesti have traveled many of the God's Throat currents," Apoletta said. "They have never caused us issue."

"When the three moons vanished," Utharne asked, appearing uncomfortable, "did the currents suddenly cease?"

"Your point?" Brysis asked.

Apoletta caught Brysis's eye and motioned for her to remain quiet. Brysis appeared impatient, however.

Utharne sighed. "Forgive me, Brysis, but your people did the same thing we did, didn't they? Sent explorers inside? The mouth tunnels, I mean?"

"Yes," Apoletta admitted. "We examined three of them, and no"—she interrupted Utharne and Vanastra quickly—"of those who ventured the deepest, not one returned."

"We examined two," Utharne said. "The same fate befell our explorers."

"But have you used these currents on occasion?" Apoletta asked.

Utharne nodded, albeit reluctantly. "Yes," he admitted. "When absolutely necessary."

"Please believe me when I say this is one of those absolutely necessary times," Apoletta said.

Utharne thought about it, everyone's eyes on him. "Well, yes, I can see that," he finally said. "We'll use this route."

Arrowawk threw his arms up in exasperation but said nothing further.

"Prepare yourselves," Apoletta told everyone.

Preparations consisted of tightening their packs on the whale and ensuring nothing would fly off during the violent journey.

"Thank you," Apoletta whispered to Utharne.

"I admit I have my reservations. About using a Defiler's Breath to travel. But I trust your judgment. Just tell me this, why the sudden urgency to reach Watermere?"

Apoletta thought a moment before answering. "Something is happening in the World Gash," she said. "I don't know what or why. I have a deep feeling that time is urgent. Only a feeling, an instinct, but my instincts have always served me well. We must be swift."

"And you feel this because of your husband?" Utharne said. "Pardon me for saying this, but because he is undead, I must be skeptical. You can't trust the undead. Did he say something to you?"

"Well, he didn't exactly speak, but yes—"

"Then it may be a trick," Utharne said.

"Yes, there's that possibility—"

"He could be misleading you, Apoletta."

"Perhaps, but—"

"Undead cannot be trusted."

"Let me finish!" Apoletta said, snapping loud enough that everyone stopped and looked at them. They returned to their work with an obvious ear on the conversation. Only Brysis decided against decorum and swam over to the pair.

"What's the matter now?" she asked.

"It's nothing," Apoletta replied.

"It's private," Utharne said at the same moment.

Brysis grunted, disapproving. She crossed her arms. "I'm not leaving. Involve me or continue pretending. Please," she insisted.

Utharne sighed. "Zebulah told her he was at the World Gash."

"And you believed him?" Brysis said to Apoletta with raised eyebrows.

"This has nothing to do with Zebulah!" Apoletta said fiercely. "We must explore the World Gash and bring back proof of its evil. You all know that. This is the fastest possible means. I am going, regardless of Zebulah and whether or not you all choose to follow."

Both Brysis and Utharne looked startled at her sudden vehemence.

"Your reasons for going this way," Utharne stammered, "that's what I was questioning. I'm sorry."

Apoletta stared at Brysis, inhaling deeply to cool her temper.

"I, too, am sorry," said Brysis at last.

Apoletta whirled and swam away.

Apoletta and the others stared down into the deep chasm, ready to descend into the stream of the God's Throat—what the Dimernesti called the Defiler's Breath. Utharne swam up next to her, with Brysis following close behind.

"I'm going to the World Gash with you," Utharne said.

"I'm going too," Brysis said. "To keep you both from getting lost. And don't get any ideas. I'm doing it for Quayseen." With that, she dropped into the trench and motioned for the others to follow. Echo Fury swam on her heels.

"Who's Quayseen?" Utharne asked.

"Her mentor," Apoletta said. "He died in the World Gash. A story for later, and one better shared by her." Apoletta swam after Brysis, the Dargonesti close behind. She looked back to see Utharne shrugging toward the others before diving after them.

The God's Throat traveled swiftly over hundreds of miles. It moved faster than the full sprint of shark-blade whales and would cut the journey to Watermere by two days. The water carried a natural luminosity from living motes that cast light whenever disturbed.

The ancient current also smoothed the walls of the trench to a glassy slickness, polishing the cliffs into featureless, rolling hills. It wore down any outcroppings.

Occasionally, one of the Dargonesti soldiers or Brysis would unfurl a strong leather cloak, grab two edges in each hand, and create a makeshift sail. The sail pushed them well ahead of the expedition and allowed them to scout ahead. They'd then return by drifting at the current's edge, which slowed them, and dive back in when the others appeared.

Speaking during the journey proved nearly impossible. To breathe, they tilted their heads to the side and gulped at the sea so the rush of water didn't tear their gill membranes.

Occasionally, when they needed to rest or recast water-breathing spells, they emerged from the trench and camped. At those points, however, they lay well beyond the pockets of Solinari's light, inside the bitter chill of the Yawning Deep. The darkness hedged their vision to mere feet, and their only illumination came from hag-fire fish with their firefly eyes and the filament of light from the trench. In those cold and seemingly barren places, the expedition rested and ate. Then they dived back into the fast stream.

Despite their reservations at using the Breath, Briegan and Arrowvawk proved quite adept at managing the current. And the whale, without complaint, followed them to the stream's diminishing point. There the trench opened out into a wide plateau that basked in Solinari's glow and the current seemingly evaporated like a sigh exhausting itself.

The coral submerged itself beneath Wartide's shifting skin, causing a moment's discomfort. He studied the scene of carnage below. They'd halted the migration of two thousand savage-claw crabs, each some two yards across, before the crabs could reach the World Gash. The intelligent crabs acted with one impulse: to feast on the carrion left in the wake of the spread of the World Gash. Once Wartide and the other sharks caught the queen crab and tortured her, however, her followers collapsed from sharing her pain. The magori and undead treated themselves to their victory meal, tearing their opponents apart and peeling back their carapaces to sup on the tender white meat.

"We leave tomorrow, back home," Wartide said to another Mahkwahb floating next to him. "We'll deal with Anhalstrax along the way."

"Do we have enough magori and undead for the fight ahead?" the elf asked. "The last two battles depleted us."

"Reinforcements are already there, harrying Anhalstrax. Once we arrive, we can finish the job."

"Master will be pleased."

"Not for long, he won't be," Wartide said, grinning. "When we attack Anhalstrax, be sure to keep the magori between you and it."

"What of the undead?"

"They serve Her. Therefore they serve us," Wartide said.

"Even Zebulah?"

Wartide's smile deepened. "Especially Zebulah."

CHAPTER
Watermere and Respite
9

The expedition arrived at the borders of Watermere with Apoletta and Utharne in the lead, followed by Vanastra and Captain Ornathius swimming shoulder to shoulder. Behind each commander swam their soldiers in single file, again abreast with each other. Brysis, Briegan, and Arrovawk took up the rear with their small train of animals.

At Apoletta's insistence, Dargonesti and Dimernesti approached in equal stride to indicate the importance of their shoal elf guests. No Dimernesti had visited the domains of Watermere in centuries, at least not in any official capacity.

Watermere's vistas seemed better suited to the kingdoms of air-breathers than to the deep. Solinari's light glowed there, blessing the waters with warmth. On the stretches of coral ridges and kelp fields rose high-towered castles sculpted from the very bedrock and polished to glassy smoothness. The fortifications had no castle walls strung between them. What was the use of walls when everyone could swim over them?

In the kelp and seaweed fields, farmers guided large sea turtles harnessed to plows, while fishermen used nets strung between two fast-moving porpoises to snare schools of fish.

Most everyone stopped to stare at the guests as they swam

by, and a few Dargonesti soldiers in polished crab-shell armor swam ahead of the expedition once they discovered Apoletta was with them. Up above, a Dargonesti patrol rode astride two killer whales and kept in sight of the expedition.

At each village or community along the way, people gathered to quietly watch the expedition's passage. Utharne stopped once to offer a quick prayer at a village shrine dedicated to Abbuku, the Fisher King. Apoletta watched him pray for a moment, knowing he did so to show the others they shared a faith in common. The Dargonesti villagers, although wide eyed when Utharne arrived, appeared mollified when he offered his prayers.

The expedition continued forward until they met with an honor guard of the Speaker's finest warriors. They rode well-muscled, lime-colored hippocampi, steeds with a horse's head and upper body, two front legs that ended in fins, and a lower body that tapered into that of a long-tailed fish. The soldiers and their steeds wore plating of gleaming brass and iron. Metalwork was near impossible under water, except in thermal forges where smiths hammered gold into jewelry. Most metal armor worn by the sea elves came from wrecks or was pilfered during surface raids; thus, armor was always piecemeal and transitory at best. She explained to Utharne that their armor came from the dwarves of the continent of Taladas.

The lead Dargonesti wore a helmet with red and orange butterfly fish fins as plumage. He jutted out his ample jaw and introduced himself as Captain Stormbrave. Apoletta introduced herself as Steward of Istar with Utharne as her honored guest and counterpart.

At first Captain Stormbrave barely nodded in Utharne's direction, a discourtesy that bothered Apoletta.

"He is mouthpiece for the Speaker of the Sea," Apoletta explained, "and is thus kin and kith to the Speaker of the Moon by the codes of conduct."

Stormbrave almost sneered, but he caught himself. Apoletta

stared straight at him, her gaze burrowing into him. He blinked, realizing his mistake. "An honor," he muttered to Utharne.

"And this is Major Vanastra," Apoletta continued firmly. "She commands the Dimernesti forces."

Stormbrave, uncertain, offered a quick head bow toward Vanastra and Captain Ornathius.

Apoletta continued, asking if Slyphanous had arrived yet, to which Stormbrave responded he had not.

"Wasn't he traveling with you?" Stormbrave asked.

"I sent him ahead to Istar to attend to a matter. The moment he arrives, bring him directly to me."

The captain nodded. Apoletta could see from the corner of her eye that Utharne was studying her. She hadn't explained in detail why she had sent Slyphanous off to Istar, and Utharne hadn't pried, despite his curiosity. Captain Stormbrave turned his hippocampus around and ordered two men from their steeds. He then offered them for Utharne and Apoletta to ride, with the two Dargonesti soldiers leading by the reins.

Apoletta complied, knowing full well the need to maintain the appearance of protocol and decorum in Watermere. If the Dargonesti considered the Dimernesti their barbarian cousins, then the Dargonesti of Watermere frowned upon Istar's citizens as their provincial brethren.

Utharne followed suit. Apoletta could see he disliked riding the fierce hippocampus, but he endured the experience with some dignity nonetheless.

Satisfied, Stormbrave led the honor guard. The expedition continued on its way to Watermere's capital with the guard heralding their arrival.

"Vanastra isn't really a major," Utharne whispered to Apoletta. "We don't have such ranks. She's simply their leader."

"Captain Stormbrave needs a dose of humility," Apoletta said. "Let's not give him reason to snub your people."

"Of course," Utharne whispered back.

As they continued, the fields and castles grew denser in number and more elaborate in construction. Soon, little natural seafloor remained; instead, a patchwork of harvesting farms and towns sculpted from the bedrock spread from horizon to horizon. They approached Watermere's capital, the city of Takaluras, which outsiders often called Watermere as well. The castles grew more ornate in structure, with high, winding towers that corkscrewed like coral spirals, colonnaded roofs, and long arcades. They appeared constructed of a variety of rich materials, from white alabaster to pale green jade coral to different shades of marble. This undersea city contrasted sharply with Dimernost, which the shoal elves had built low and beneath the coral fields. Instead, the Dargonesti built their structures for show and with little fear of predators. They had mastered their domain.

Utharne remarked on the streets and cobblestone paths between the buildings.

Apoletta said it was for sea turtles pulling heavy materials, but she also admitted it was a remnant of their land-dwelling days. At the time of its construction, the sea elves knew no other architecture and could not envision a city without streets. And unlike the original Dimernost, which fell during the First Cataclysm, Watermere never suffered such a calamity. Thus, they had had little reason to change their original designs.

They continued into Takaluras itself, the city of castles. The outside walls were actually giant forts yoked together shoulder to shoulder. Despite the small touches that differentiated each, they all appeared roughly uniform. They served as the city's main battlements, their clifflike walls rising above the surrounding seafloor. Beyond the castle battlements, the rest of the city rose even higher, as though elevated on a gigantic pedestal that began at the roofs of the forts and stretched for miles along their diameter.

The companions swam up along the outside wall and past windows before they cleared the forts and gazed upon the cluttered metropolis itself. Even Apoletta found it hard to distinguish where one castle began and another ended. They blurred together. Bridges and skywalks extended over one castle to connect with others, buildings wove in and around one another without even touching, and three or more citadels shared the same courtyard. Thanks to the chaotic jumble, streets stretched out like the patterns on brain coral. At the center of the hub sat a great tower whose crown faded into the glow of Solinari's diffused light.

The royal families of Watermere, known as the Speakers of Blood, consisted of its preeminent landowners. The families arranged and brokered marriages according to property values, and when two families joined through matrimony, they often linked their castles together through annexes, bridges, courtyards, and towers. Some landowners in the already crowded city built castles and extensions atop older structures. Thus, some fortifications rose to astounding heights, with old towers spearing the roofs of the new.

The landowners also decorated their castles in a myriad of ways. Seaweed vines overgrew the walls of some citadels, while seashell designs adorned the exteriors of others. They turned giant clamshells into doors, made scallop shells into windows, used spiral cone shells for columns, and employed turban cones as tower domes. Carvings in marble, jade, coral, and obsidian and murals of sea life completed the ornate facades.

Outside of castle walls and under the spider's web of bridges and floating annexes, the Dargonesti had built smaller buildings from stone, some of which sat flush with the castle walls, while small streets bordered others. The commoners lived here.

Apoletta informed Utharne of all this and more as they penetrated the city; he asked as many questions as Apoletta could tolerate.

Along the way they spied a variety of races, again to the obvious surprise of Utharne, who believed few outsiders came to Takaluras. They stared at merfolk traders bartering with Dargonesti fish vendors.

"No," Apoletta told Utharne. "You're right to wonder. Watermere has been isolationist in its past."

"But not Istar?"

Apoletta shrugged. "We also were, until I met Tanis Half-Elven."

"You met one of the Heroes of the Lance?" Utharne asked, his mouth open.

"I met several of them actually," Apoletta said. "We rescued them from drowning one time, but that was when they were mortals, before they became legends. As for Watermere," she continued with a smile, "Watermere changed with the vanishing of the moons and their return. After losing their connection to the gods after the First Cataclysm, Watermere treated the Second Cataclysm with utmost gravity. They sent out ambassadors to the other friendly races of the sea. This is the result. Tritons and merfolk are no longer strangers to Takaluras. And I hope the same will hold true for the Dimernesti one day."

Utharne nodded and marveled at the sights.

Finally, the expedition wound its way down the main thoroughfare, under bridges and past towers with curious onlookers lining their route all the way. They approached the imposing tower, which up close appeared even more impressive than at a distance. According to legend, the Watermere tower stood as sister to the Tower of the Stars in the elf forests of Silvenost, but it was not its twin in form or appearance. Watermere's Tower of the Moon spiraled upward, like a worm-shell with its curled whorls and tapering coil. It reputedly rose more than six hundred feet, but with Solinari's moonlit glow, the tower seemed to rise and diffuse infinitely into the light, its head shrouded at its height.

The royal masons built the tower from striated bands of silvery mother-of-pearl, deep green jade shell, jagged fragments of black obsidian glass, and red crystals from ruby oyster. Smaller spiral towers emerged from the Tower of the Moon's trunk.

THE ALIEN SEA

The base of the tower rose from a dome of delicate lattice coral sculpted in long ivy patterns. The dome itself topped a large citadel made from a variety of eggshell, jade, and smoky marble. It included stables and barracks with an adjoining field for the military exercises, as well as the royal residences for the family currently in power—Treyen Silverwake's family.

With the honor guard in the lead, the expedition approached the two-story gate with its jagged, thorny portcullis. A messenger wearing a loose tabard of green swam up to Stormbrave, and the captain stopped everyone with a raised arm. After conferring with the messenger, Stormbrave guided his hippocampus back to Apoletta and Utharne.

He informed them that the whale could rest in the giant stables. Major Vanastra's men would be shown to the barracks, but Major Vanastra would have a room in the officers' quarters. Utharne and Apoletta were invited to be guests of the royal quarters while Captain Ornathius and his men were to report to the quartermaster.

Apoletta asked for a moment alone. Captain Stormbrave offered a curt nod and pulled on the reins of his hippocampus. It snorted as he returned to the head of the honor guard.

"Brysis?" Apoletta asked, calling her up from the rear.

"I'm fine," Brysis said, approaching with Echo Fury. "I'll have chambers adjacent to the royal stables. I'll find Briegan and Arrovawk comfortable rooms for the night."

"Thank you," Apoletta said.

"Not a chance!" Arrovawk squawked. "Bad enough sharing a week in your company. There any dry quarters here?"

"Yes," Brysis said. She motioned in the general direction of a high pyramid. Air filled its interior, specifically to cater to those elves with a taste for smoking or drinking alcohol. "Perhaps you'll like the Rusted Bone Tavern. Strong drinks and women of loose morals."

Arrovawk smiled. "Dargonesti women? Could be worse."

145

"I'd prefer to stay with my men," Vanastra said.

"Yes," Utharne said. "I completely understand, of course. But we're guests. Might be prudent to play the part of the—"

"No," Apoletta said with a sigh. "Forgive me, Utharne, but she's right. Let her stay where she's most comfortable. The Dargonesti are going to have to learn how to relate to you on your own terms."

Vanastra offered a grateful nod.

The expedition dismounted from the hippocampi and parted company, with Apoletta and Utharne following Stormbrave.

A courtyard surrounding the citadel lay beyond the portcullis. It contained coral trees and shrubs of braided seaweed. Beyond the courtyard, the walls of the citadel rose eight stories high; Apoletta and Utharne swam through a giant double door shaped like a clamshell. They entered a large chamber with a domed ceiling and rows of columns. One wide-mouthed passageway led straight to the base of the Tower of the Moon. Along its length floated Dargonesti soldiers armed with long tridents.

Captain Stormbrave took Apoletta and Utharne to the royal quarters in the adjacent chamber. "The Speaker of the Moon requests your company for dinner this evening. Both of you," Stormbrave added as an afterthought. With that, he left the two in the hands of the servants.

Apoletta groaned in relief as her attendant took the coarse sponge and scrubbed the encrusted filth from her back. The attendant, a young elf maiden with light blue hair, had been working her way through different types of sponges of differing textures, breaking routine to occasionally rub Apoletta's back and legs with scented seaweed or smoothed seashells heated on thermal vents. Those same vents heated the room.

Apoletta gurgled something as she lay facedown on a bed of luxuriant seal leather and soft kelp bedding.

"Pardon?" the attendant asked.

Apoletta cleared her throat with an apology and said, "You have wonderful hands. I could use such treatment in Istar."

"Milady is too kind," the attendant replied. "But I could not depart Watermere. I serve the Speaker of the Moon."

"Mmm," Apoletta said in utter bliss. A moment later, another elf maiden entered the chamber and waited patiently. "Yes?" Apoletta asked.

"Pardon the intrusion, milady. Master Utharne has asked me say that he's gone to visit the Temple of Abbuku to pay his respects."

"Alone?" Apoletta asked, raising her head slightly.

"No, milady," the maiden replied. "He is with two soldiers from the honor guard. He said he will return in time for supper."

"Thank you," Apoletta said, dismissing the young maiden. She collapsed again, lost in delight with her treatment.

The two guards remained quiet, not that Utharne minded. He marveled at the city around him and swam slowly to enjoy the sights better. But if Takaluras were a spectacle to Utharne, so too was he a spectacle to it. Its citizens stared as he passed, immediately recognizing he was a stranger among them. Some gaped openly; others eyed him as he passed, but most just watched him out of the corners of their eyes, pretending they didn't care. He didn't mind the scrutiny, however. He felt privileged to be the first Dimernesti to be welcomed to Watermere in ages.

Brine-Whisker, however, was more curious and less shy. The excited seal darted over and under bridges, from vendor to vendor, through doors and out windows, often being chased away by some frightened shopkeeper, customer, or resident. He barked at every new thing he saw, as if announcing "this is mine" or asking "what are you?" Utharne grinned happily at his companion's mischief; the Dargonesti bore the treatment stoically as their Dimernesti visitor enjoyed the company of two honor guard soldiers.

Finally, they reached the Temple of Abbuku, which sat upon the roof of a great fort. Three colonnaded arcades stacked atop one another served as the temple walls. Utharne could see through the columns into the temple's interior, which lay open to the sky. An enormous tree of red and blue coral appeared to have broken through the fort's roof at the center of the temple, mushrooming open fifty feet above the seafloor. At its visible height, it was more than ninety feet tall, and the tips of its branches radiated with faint yellow, red, and green embers. Utharne recognized the fire-blossom coral but had never seen one that size. The tips glowed thanks to luminescent nematocysts—tiny venomous stingers that attracted small fish with their colors and killed them to feed the coral colony. The venom didn't affect anything larger than a seagull, but nematocyst wounds certainly stung fiercely.

While one of the honor guard went to seek out Abbuku's high rector, Utharne swam into the temple's main plaza. A briar patch of fire-coral covered the fort's roof, surrounding the tree's thick trunk. Utharne floated well above the seafloor and watched the colony of fish orbiting the coral monument.

A moment later the guard returned along with a bare-chested temple acolyte with bands of golden seaweed that snaked up his biceps. He bowed to Utharne.

"Welcome, Rector," he said. "The high rector is eager to meet you."

❖ ❖ ◆ ❖ ❖

"Remarkable," High Rector Falanthius said. He stroked Brine-Whisker's brow, gently touching the blue flame birthmark of the

Fisher King. Falanthius was portly and of long years judging by his white braided hair. He wore a simple gown of yellow silk and white stitching; upon his brow rested a crown of blue coral wrapped with strands of cobalt kelp. "I have not seen a living touchstone, oh, in many centuries now. Your kind is almost forgotten."

"My kind?"

The high rector smiled. "Forgive me, but our people, we've done much to appear sophisticated. Cast away our old customs. Turned our back on the wilds. Pity, really. We've forgotten the savage ways."

"Pardon?" Utharne asked, uncertain what the high rector meant by that.

"No, no. Not how to act savage," Falanthius replied. "We've tamed our borders. I mean, we've forgotten that the sea remains savage."

"I see."

"I envy the Dimernesti; your connection to Glorious Abbuku remains primal. As it should. It's a true faith."

Utharne squirmed, a little uncomfortable at the odd praise. "Our people long ago turned their back on Abbuku," Utharne admitted. "On all the gods, actually. The temple is barely a quarter full at prayer. And only on holidays."

"And why is that, might I ask?"

Utharne considered the matter carefully. "We're an angry people. The Dimernesti, I mean. The hammer strokes of both Cataclysms struck us as though our heads were the anvil. My people feel betrayed. It's not that they don't believe in the gods—no, no, certainly not. It's because they believe that the poison runs deeper in their veins."

"Hmm, the deep poison," mused Falanthius. "Well, then," he continued. "What of you and your story?"

"My story?"

"Yes," the high rector replied. "Was your faith not shaken like the others'?"

LUCIEN SOULBAN

Utharne nodded. "To the core, it seemed."

"Yet you did not abandon the gods?"

Utharne shook his head. "Actually, I did so, for a time. But it seems that the gods did not abandon me." With that, Utharne stroked the underside of Brine-Whisker's silken chin. The seal squinted. "You might say I did not choose him. He chose me."

"A miracle, to be sure."

"Yes," Utharne said. "But given the tragedies we have endured, it seems people expect a greater miracle in return. They expect a balance to things. I alone cannot stem the flood of Dimernesti who have abandoned their faith. My miracle is a personal one."

"Hmm," Falanthius said, his white brows furrowed. "It appears we have much in common, you and I."

"I thought the Dargonesti faith held true."

"In appearance only. But we are a fractured people. There are the Land-Shorn, who seek a new truth, and then there are the Purists."

"Purists? I have heard a little about them."

"Yes, well, they're a quarrelsome lot, expounding the purity of our lineage and the sanctity of our heritage. Ancestor worshipers. That's what they are, really."

"I'm not sure I understand."

Falanthius smiled and floated gently over to the only piece of furniture in the room—a marble throne trimmed with gold foil, an ornate jade headpiece, and a globe-shaped handgrip on the armrest. The room was certainly ostentatious; the walls of the high rector's reception chambers were decorated with sculpted coral murals. The detailed scenes depicted the lives of heroes and saints, all sea elves and all toiling and fighting in service to Abbuku. Falanthius sat in his chair, slipped his foot through a leather loop, and gripped the armrests' globes. That anchored him to his stately throne.

Falanthius explained how, when the three moons vanished, the Dargonesti sought answers and remedies from a variety of sources. In their search some fell away from the gods completely, one such faction being the Purists. They believed the Dargonesti were, in fact, two different people: those born of the Dimernesti Purifiers—the Dimernesti who reputedly left their brethren to become Dargonesti—and those born of Daydra Stonecipher. They considered those of Dimernesti blood inferior, while those of Daydra's line were deemed true Dargonesti.

"Daydra Stonecipher was never Dargonesti. Was she?" Utharne asked. "She was merely an elf who ventured into the oceans, right?"

Falanthius shrugged. No one knew for certain, he said. Legends did suggest she became a sea elf at one point, but otherwise the legends remained vague. The Purists existed in the confusion of the ancient tales, in their muddying. One legend indicated the godly artifact called the Greygem created the Dargonesti, another that they came from the Dimernesti, who themselves sprang forth from a gem called the Grathanich, which was likely the Greygem just the same.

"The Purists use their legends as proof that there are, in fact, two species of Dargonesti," Falanthius concluded.

"Are they strong? Here in Watermere?"

"In a manner. They believe that only someone of Daydra Stonecipher's lineage can be a true spellcaster. Naturally, they have a strong following among the wizards."

Utharne groaned. "Oh course. I understand now. Apoletta mentioned that Istar's use of spells—sorry, spell-fables—was not well received here."

"Of course not," Falanthius said. "The Purists claim magic comes from strict tradition, and what Istar does is a travesty of the Purist core tenet, of Daydra's gift."

"Um, I beg your indulgence for so many questions, but just how dangerous are these Purists?"

"Dangerous enough for the honor guard to provide for your escort."

"Me?"

"Yes, my boy," Falanthius said. "You are Dimernesti. You are considered responsible for creating the Purifiers, the weaker Dargonesti."

"Are we in any danger, then?"

Falanthius leaned forward and whispered, "My lad, you couldn't be in more danger if you and Lady Apoletta had entered a sea of sharks covered in blood."

Brysis entered the dark, cavernous chamber alone. She breathed a long, grateful sigh and felt herself emptying the sorrows of the world from her chest. She quietly removed the seaweed and chain poncho from her shoulders, unfastened the bark bracers from her wrists, and slipped out of her loincloth. Everything settled to the silt-covered floor with a muted crinkle of metal. She finally unfastened her belt and gently laid her rapier to the ground as well. She floated, naked, in the darkness, the water her only cloak.

Shadows filled the domed chamber, but she knew its dimensions. The darkness did not bother her. It brought her comfort.

Brysis swam slowly into the large hall that lay hidden below the Tower of the Moon, which extended for hundreds of feet in all directions. Any smaller, and it would have been cramped and cruel lodgings for its occupants. Brysis swam past the twisted stalactites of yellow coral that grew from the high ceiling all the way down to the floor. She finally reached the chamber's center, so marked by the marble medallion of a mariner's star embedded in the floor.

"I'm home," Brysis whispered.

The hall erupted into a gibbering cacophony of clicks; squeals; and high-pitched, staccatolike laughter. Dozens of shapes exploded from the surrounding darkness, the shadows unable to contain them any longer. Of course, they'd already sensed her presence, but they always played that game. A vortex of dolphins, smaller porpoises, and dog-sized star-chasers streaked around her, a squealing, joyous whirlwind of life that nearly spun her around. Brysis returned their joy, with a true and deep laughter she rarely allowed herself to express anymore. Moon-kissed and blunt-nosed dolphins, sky-racers and laughing-dart porpoises, all her friends were here. And they numbered in the hundreds.

In their voices, dozens of simple questions emerged; not in words, but in impulses and gestures. *Where were you? Why did you leave? Could you play with us? We missed you. We love you. The pod welcomes your return. . . .* And many more voices were drowned out by the most enthusiastic of cries and yelps. Brysis took to her porpoise form and joined the happy crush of mammals that clambered around her.

After an exhaustive hour of playing with her friends and answering their questions in ways they'd understand, she finally reverted back into her elf form and collapsed on the floor. She sat with her back against the wall, petting the half dozen companions who lingered.

A familiar face appeared and rested its head, blunt snout and all, on her lap.

"Hello Minnow-Tyrant," she said, stroking the dolphin's head. Her hand traveled down to touch his scars. They looked worse than they felt. The snub-nosed dolphins of the Royal Stables of Istar and Takaluras scarred easily, their gray skin welting into white scars permanently. The mapmakers of both cities used these special dolphins as living maps. They accompanied expeditions, where the cartographers carefully transcribed their discoveries on the dolphins. It was also why Brysis had removed her clothing. She could not afford to scratch the dolphins, scarring them accidentally.

"Did they treat you well?" Brysis asked.

Minnow-Tyrant bleated weakly.

"I know," she said. "You miss home. When they're done copying your map, I'll take you back to Istar. I promise."

Minnow-Tyrant said little else. He simply closed his eyes and enjoyed Brysis's company.

Brysis studied her old companion carefully. He looked tired, dispirited, perhaps. His once lustrous gray had turned ashen; his skin felt hot. Absently, Brysis traced the line of her expedition with Minnow-Tyrant, her finger following the map scar that traveled from Istar, down past the islands of Habbakuk's Necklace, all the way into the Bay of Balifor and the first recorded site of the World Gash. Brysis had accompanied the first expedition to find it, and Minnow-Tyrant had served as the first map of the region—a dubious distinction.

Without realizing it, Brysis touched the scar of the World Gash. Minnow-Tyrant started awake, as though stung. The scar was swollen and red. It looked fresh, the lines thicker. In fact, she realized, the lines were thicker than before. The scar had grown.

Brysis swam up to the stable master, a short sea elf who wore a perpetual frown. He watched her warily, obviously sensing her hostility.

Good, Brysis thought.

"Minnow-Tyrant!" Brysis said, "What's happening to him?"

"Happening?" the stable master said, one eyebrow raised.

"Did anyone touch him? Scar him?" she demanded.

"No," he said, his frown deepening. "He's grown ill, that's all."

"Then why are there fresh scars on his body?"

The frown faded, and the stable master sneered. "Impossible," he said. "Minnow-Tyrant is a Royal Dolphin. And he's feted. Nobody would dare touch him. That's against the law."

"And yet the outline of the World Gash is growing."

The stable master blanched. "Impossible," he said.

"No," Brysis yelled. "I treated his scars when Veloxua first mapped him. I was there! The lines were never that thick!"

The stable master open and closed his mouth, until finally he said grudgingly, "The royal cartographers sent to copy the map said the same thing."

"How would they know about the scar?" Brysis said, almost yelling.

"Not about the scar," the stable master said. "About their maps. They returned several times to copy the maps. But they said whenever they tried drawing the World Gash, their ink-jelly bled into the parchment. They've been unable to map the World Gash."

Brysis felt the blood drain from her face and limbs. Were the lines indeed shifting and growing? Was that a reflection that the World Gash itself was expanding?

Apoletta looked resplendent in her long, almost gauzelike white gown. The seamstress had cut long slits under the arms and along the legs to provide for ample movement while swimming. The gown, made of oyster silk, glistened with pearls and gold-plated shells. About her wrists and ankles hung gold bands linked with chains to two rings on each foot and each hand.

In a word, she looked beautiful. She even drew the gaze of the honor guard who waited at attention.

As she floated down the corridor, Utharne swam up to meet her. He looked harried and appeared ready to say something when he suddenly stopped and took stock of her. His eyebrows rose.

"You look wonderful."

"Thank you." Apoletta blushed. "But you're running late," she said, eyeing his tattered seaweed woven cloak and the leather apron worn over his loincloth.

"Oh, yes. Of course. I was—" His eyes widened suddenly. "Your hair," he said, eyeing the long, luxurious ropes of braided silver hair that spilled past her bare feet.

"My one conceit," Apoletta said.

"Regrown?" Utharne asked.

"Yes," admitted Apoletta, laughing. "With a little help."

Yet Utharne did not look at all happy or pleased.

"Why the suspicious glances?" Apoletta asked.

"We must speak. Privately, that is."

Apoletta nodded. They quickly searched the hallway until they found a small room with a fountain spewing a trickle of bubbles.

"We must hurry," Apoletta said. "It is discourteous to be late."

"You didn't tell me the situation was so grave. With the Purists, I mean."

"Yes," she answered, nodding. "There are some Purist zealots out there, but they bark loudly. That is all. Do not be concerned."

"They aren't dangerous? I mean, to you? I'm not worried about me."

"Dargonesti would never attack another Dargonesti."

"What about Uriona?"

"She never attacked other Dargonesti. She left Watermere to build Urione, but it was never a violent rupture. Yes, it is true, she consorted with the Goddess Zura and enslaved others, but she never turned against us, her brethren."

"Maybe she never got the chance. What about the Mahkwahb?"

"The dark sea elves!" Apoletta said, surprised. "You know much about our history."

"Well?" Utharne asked. "Am I right? Were they not Dargonesti who turned on you? Aren't they still . . . exiled? Yes, that's the word," he said to himself, "exiled, those Dargonesti who don't follow your codes? The Mahkwahb were many. What if they are in league with the Purists?"

Apoletta bit her tongue. She, like many of her people, disliked discussing the Mahkwahb and that dark period in Dargonesti history. Speaker of the Moon Imbrias Takalurion had exiled forty Dargonesti from Watermere. And in exile, they changed, their skin changing color and their hair growing coal black. They had turned cruel and evil. The current Mahkwahb bore little resemblance to their predecessors, but the stain remained.

"That was two millennia ago," Apoletta said flatly. "Yes, one poor specimen of our people occasionally emerges as an exception, but what you're suggesting implies the concerted actions of a whole group of Dargonesti. A conspiracy! That's impossible."

"Listen," Utharne said, keeping his voice even. "All I'm saying is that we might be in danger."

"Utharne, I. . . ." Apoletta hesitated, trying to find the right words. "We're going to be late. We aren't in any danger here, especially from my own people—"

"I'm sorry," Utharne said, his voice quiet. "I can't accept your reassurances. You haven't told us everything. The Speaker of the Sea is trying to bring the Dimernesti Clans together. Yes? She's in poor health. The failure of this mission would weaken her irreparably. I must think of her and my escort, even if I were tempted to believe you."

Apoletta sighed. "I know all that," she said, her voice turning angry in spite of her best efforts. "I never said we were perfect. This danger you speak of, it's all in your imagination."

"No!" said Utharne, raising his voice. "I have been warned, and now I am warning you. Apoletta, you have asked my people to change. For the alliance. But you never told us that your own people were so divided, or that by coming here we might be putting ourselves in jeopardy."

"There you are!" a voice said, interrupting. A young, bare-chested sea elf swam into the chamber. He wore the red skirt of a house squire. "We've been looking for you. Dinner is about to begin, and you must be seated." He looked at Utharne with an upturned nose. "Surely you're not wearing that?"

"Offer my regrets to His Highness and Speaker of the Moon, Lord Silverwake," Utharne said brusquely, swimming away. "I'm feeling ill and won't be able to enjoy his hospitality."

Apoletta could not speak, much less breathe. Nobody refused a meal with the Speaker of the Moon. The air had left her lungs, and her throat stung. The squire recovered quickly, however.

"Well . . . yes," he said, stammering. "Supper, yes, supper. We must go. We're running late."

Apoletta could not stop staring at the door through which Utharne had left.

CHAPTER
The Speaker of the Moon
10

Marble statues and carpets woven from seaweed fibers decorated the large dining hall. At the center of the room sat a long rectangular table made from engraved brass and set for a sumptuous banquet. On plates made from large clamshells rested an array of raw food: strips of red tuna, blue-tiger screamers dusted with crushed sea-olive seeds and brine-root, crabmeat stuffed inside kelp leaves, raw clams and scallops waiting to be opened and devoured, conch shells filled with glistening black and green caviar, caged lobsters ready to be boiled and eaten, glazed shark ribs lightly grilled over Urione's Flames, kelp fruit baskets . . . the list continued.

Apoletta sat in her high-backed chair and picked at her food, occasionally glancing at Utharne's empty seat. The Speaker of the Moon sat at the distant end of the table.

"You've made a home for Qualinesti refugees?" the Speaker asked. Treyen Silverwake was much younger than Apoletta, though his responsibilities had aged him beyond Apoletta's years. His braided gold hair had faded to white, and his features were pronounced. His cheekbones rode high while his nose sloped down the center of his face. One eyebrow curled upward, seemingly in perpetual curiosity. He wore a second skin of gold and silver, a thin,

159

polished, and form-fitting metal shell that sheathed his torso, arms, and shoulders. It extended beneath his silver and black skirt woven from some glossy material.

Apoletta nodded politely, though her low spirits had dimmed her smile. She explained how fifty Qualinesti made Istar home at her invitation. After Apoletta had met Tanis Half-Elven, she had tried reestablishing contact with the surface-living Qualinesti. It took decades before either species could make diplomatic inroads, and even then only after the fall of Qualinost did their friendship solidify. But in truth, she could hardly call her guests refugees, at least not anymore. They took to their new home with as much enthusiasm as any Dargonesti.

Treyen appeared surprised, frozen in the act of eating a crab-stuffed kelp roll.

The Qualinesti in Istar had undergone the Ritual of Change, Apoletta continued. They remained pale skinned, but had become water-breathers, though, she added with a wry smile, they had yet to develop a palate for raw food or seaweed.

"Ahh . . ." Treyen said. "The Path of Princess Vixa. Seems fitting that, like her, they should abandon their Qualinost heritage to become Dargonesti."

"It was hardly Princess Vixa's choice," Apoletta said too quickly before realizing her place. "I'm sorry," she said. "I meant nothing—"

"Hmm," Treyen said, mildly reproachful. He sucked the clam meat out from a shell. "As I was saying, your Qualinesti guests would do well to learn from her example."

"Yes, Speaker," Apoletta said. "It's because of Vixa's ancient tale that they accepted the idea of the transformation in the first place, though. . . ."

"Yes?" he asked.

"Well. They hope someday to reclaim the city of Qualinost from beneath the lake. And they've said that if they cannot raise it from the lake, then they shall live within it as we have done in Istar."

"Raise the city from Nalis Aren? The Lake of Death? Foolish."

"Perhaps," Apoletta said, "but their devotion to their city is admirable."

"It's sentimental folly," he said dismissively. "And lake elves? I've never heard of anything so preposterous."

"Yes, Speaker," Apoletta said, her eyes downcast.

"Now, what of this other folly with the Dimernesti and World Gash?"

Apoletta inhaled softly, trying to approach the subject delicately. "The Speaker of the Sea asks that we undertake an exploration of the World Gash to show her kinsmen the threat they face."

"And why does this matter concern us?" he asked, sounding annoyed.

"In truth," Apoletta said, "it doesn't concern us at all, if such is your decision."

"But?"

"I will not question your pronouncement in the matter," Apoletta replied, "but Dimernost seeks to put the old differences behind them. They know they need allies and that we would benefit equally. The trackers and warriors of the city are fierce, indeed."

"Yes," Treyen said. "Your report on the undead attack was quite interesting and edifying. Continue." As he listened, he nibbled on a handful of live shrimp, sucking them from their shells and leaving their carapaces floating messily around him.

"I fear if the Dimernesti cannot count on Watermere or Istar for support or help, then they will come to rely on Aquironian and the cities of Darthalla and Dargonest."

The Speaker stopped eating. He frowned at Apoletta.

"I'm afraid the brathnoc, if coaxed into an alliance, will ally with Dimernost, not us."

"Bah!" Treyen said, waving his hands as though shooing away pauper fish. "We have survived all these centuries while faring better than the Dimernesti and brathnoc. Our cities are too deep to touch and disturb. What do we really have we to fear?"

"Uh, well," she replied, startled. "Our deep seas are no protection against whim and fate. And the truth is. . . ." Apoletta hesitated.

"Speak," Treyen said.

Apoletta inhaled softly, using the cool water to flush the heat from her face. She rarely spoke with someone of a greater station than she. As a ruler of Istar, her words were usually listened to respectfully. She hated feeling like a lesser in Treyen's eyes.

Yet it was Treyen's father, Nakaro Silverwake, who'd chosen her to explore then rule Istar. He'd valued her judgment and had decreed that following his death, Apoletta would continue ruling Istar until she stepped down willingly. And the Dargonesti so loved Nakaro, the elf who brought back magic and redeemed his people to the gods, that Apoletta was accorded power by virtue of Nakaro's endorsement.

Apoletta decided to be bold. "The Dargonesti are splintering," she admitted. "The Purists are driving a wedge between our people. And the Land-Shorn, while loyal, are further dividing us by their politics. We may never raise a hand against one another, but we will grow further divided, and our society will be torn apart if we don't make alliances."

"How would alliances with non-Dargonesti solve this problem?" Treyen asked, intrigued.

"By opening our eyes to greater issues that affect all who live in the ocean. And these greater dangers unite us all. Yes, we've been fortunate to have escaped the cataclysmic troubles of the Dimernesti, but perhaps it's also made us complacent. Arrogant."

"You presume too much!" the Speaker said, though his tone was even.

His eyes darted away. Apoletta turned in time to see a red-clothed squire swim toward him. Treyen, without waiting for the squire to speak, said, "I know. Show him to his seat."

The squire promptly swam away. A moment later the squire returned with Utharne in tow. Utharne wore a beautiful burgundy sleeveless jacket and a burgundy and deep green sarong wrap about his waist. Someone had braided his hair.

"I beg your forgiveness for my late arrival," Utharne said, quickly glancing at Apoletta. "I hope I am not . . . too late." He bowed deeply. "In the name of the Speaker of the Sea, I offer you the solidarity and blessings of the Dimernesti people."

"On behalf of the Dargonesti people, I accept your gracious well-wishing and offer my own in return. I trust you're feeling better?" Treyen asked, watching Utharne carefully.

"I am. It's the cold and depth of the ocean that has tired me, I fear."

"I was told you visited our great city today," Treyen said courteously. He motioned Utharne to sit in the empty chair. "What do you think of it?"

Utharne sat. "It is beautiful beyond words. Unlike any place I've ever seen. The inhabitants of Watermere seem quite . . . um, what's the word? Cordial! Yes, quite cordial."

"Well," Treyen said, vastly pleased, motioning for Utharne to eat. He turned his gaze to Apoletta. "To hear Apoletta speak of it, she seems to think our society is on the verge of collapse."

Apoletta's mouth dropped open, but she quickly caught herself. Utharne, for his part, appeared thunderstruck, but he covered his astonishment by starting to eat. Apoletta tired of the little game with Treyen. Whatever his motive, it grated on her nerves.

"I did not mean to say that," Apoletta began carefully.

"Then what did you mean to say?"

She glanced at Utharne. Treyen watched both of them carefully.

"Please," Treyen said. "Proceed. We're all cousins here, are we not?"

"Very well," Apoletta said. "What I said was that our good fortune has bred in us complacency and a certain arrogance."

Utharne's eyes shot wide open while Treyen chewed his food mildly.

"Well, I'm sure arrogance isn't the right word," an uncomfortable Utharne offered.

"Then tell me something," Treyen said, directing his attention to Utharne. "If, as Apoletta claims, our good fortune has bred arrogance in our people, then what has the Dimernesti's misfortune bred in them? Are they a united people? Are they harmonious?"

Apoletta felt sorry for Utharne, to be caught in the middle of a fight he couldn't possibly understand and had no hand in starting. To his credit, however, and before Apoletta could rescue him, he met the Speaker of the Moon's disquieting gaze.

"It's hard to be harmonious," Utharne said, "when the times have stolen your family. Your home. But we try. And we survive. Nobody knows how to survive better than the Dimernesti. Nobody. We are artists at surviving."

"Yes, well," Treyen said, "we've survived as well." He spread his arms to indicate the lavish room, the very building that housed them, as proof of their success.

"Perhaps we've been fortunate thus far," Apoletta said. "That is all I was saying. That may be the best reason why peace has been kept between the Purists and the Land-Shorn."

"But should any calamity befall Takaluras," Utharne, beginning to understand what had transpired before his arrival, followed on her words, "will that amity prevail?"

"And if it doesn't?" Treyen asked reflectively.

"Then Dargonesti could end up fighting Dargonesti," Apoletta said.

"You cannot claim you know the truth," Utharne said, "without making a liar of someone else."

"The Purists assert that everyone else is lying," Apoletta said. "That is their cunning. The truth about the World Gash is a truth that will be proved paramount to all, and an alliance to fight the World Gash strikes a blow against factions at home."

◆ ◆ ◆ ◆ ◆

The meal ended abruptly. Treyen Silverwake dismissed Apoletta and Utharne with little explanation. They thought they might have convinced him, but he gave no clue as to his inner thoughts.

As they left the chamber, Captain Stormbrave waited with a cartographer, a female sea elf in a long strip of red linen that wrapped around her light frame. She carried rolled map skins tucked under her arm. Stormbrave bowed to Apoletta and Utharne, but Apoletta could see other matters preoccupied him by his pensive expression.

Stormbrave and his companion quickly entered the dining hall.

Apoletta and Utharne departed, swimming slowly through the corridors of the palace. Neither spoke for the first few moments, but when the apologies came, they stumbled out past both their lips in a rush.

"You were right," Apoletta said. "I have demanded more of your people than I have asked of mine."

"These misunderstandings happen."

"But my behavior was unacceptable. I truly admire your people," Apoletta said, stopping Utharne with a light hand on his arm. "And I respect you even more. Despite our differences, I can only hope my people conduct themselves with as much strength as yours have in the face of adversity."

Utharne smiled. "And your people are equally admirable. You still reach out to others in need, even though you don't share their misfortune. Compassion despite one's good fortune is rare."

"Thank you," Apoletta said, sighing. "I will not speak ill of Speaker Silverwake, but I wish he'd been more congenial."

"Actually, I expected his attitude."

"How so?" Apoletta asked.

"He was testing us, I think. I've seen the Speaker of the Sea do much the same."

"I did sense an ulterior motive. I don't understand, though."

"I don't think we're meant to. Understand, I mean."

Apoletta pinched the bridge of her nose. "Perhaps, then, it is time to sleep. I am glad we settled this . . . uh, issue between us."

"As am I. I don't like arguing with friends." Utharne bade her good night and departed for his quarters.

Apoletta swam for her room, but on arriving, however, she found Brysis waiting for her outside.

"We must speak . . . privately," Brysis said. "Is that your hair?" she added as an afterthought.

Apoletta summoned a servant to bring them food because Brysis had yet to eat. While they waited for the meal to arrive, the two sat in Apoletta's small salon, Brysis lying across the divan and Apoletta on a baglike chair made of soft sponge.

Brysis told Apoletta about the problem with Minnow-Tyrant and the maps. Brysis had informed the cartographers of her hunch that the strange bleeding ink affected all their atlases that included the World Gash. After considerable cajoling, they checked. It was true: All their maps, even the ancient ones with the Bay of Balifor on them, marked the expanding borders of the World Gash. And in each, the ink or scar appeared fresh.

Servants entered with a clamshell filled with the evening's menu and promptly left. Grateful for a meal, Brysis tore into the crab rolls and sucked on the squid pudding. Apoletta was going to wait until she had finished eating, but Brysis insisted on talking.

"The cartographers summoned advisors. The advisors summoned wizards. The wizards summoned priests. Then the priests suggested summoning the cartographers again. Idiots!"

"What did they all say?" Apoletta asked, drawing close to the edge of her chair.

Brysis shrugged. "They theorized—or rather droned. I couldn't keep up with their rambling. They were fond of their own voices. Finally they cast magic. Divinations or something."

"What did they uncover?" Apoletta asked.

"Illusions."

"Illusions . . . including Minnow-Tyrant's wounds?"

"That's what I wanted to know," Brysis said. "The white-robed wizard and a priest agreed that I had a point. A first, if you ask me. They said it's actually a curse. But not a direct curse. Something called a . . . um. . . ." Brysis tried to think of the word.

"Stigmata Curse?"

Brysis snapped her fingers and pointed at Apoletta. "Yes, that's it! The name of the curse. What is it? What do you know about it? The blasted wizard couldn't explain it simply."

Apoletta nodded. She explained that it meant the maps themselves weren't cursed. The region of the World Gash itself must have been cursed, and the power of the curse was such that it was reflected in places that bore the image of the World Gash, such as the maps.

Brysis said nothing for the moment. She simply eyed Apoletta with an exasperated expression. "That's what the wizard said," she said, obviously frustrated. "Exactly what he said. I don't see how it tells us anything that isn't obvious."

"Well," Apoletta said, engrossed in thought. "It means the maps are not cursed, the World Gash is. The maps are like mirrors of that curse."

"Why, then, is Minnow-Tyrant suffering," Brysis asked.

Apoletta didn't know.

Brysis grew quiet, but her face was twisted with emotions. Finally she said that Minnow-Tyrant wasn't the only one affected.

"Another dolphin?"

"No," Brysis said. "Minnow-Tyrant was with me on the first expedition into the World Gash, when we lost Quayseen. . . ."

"I knew him, of course," Apoletta said. "Quayseen was your mentor."

"Yes. And he died because of me," Brysis said, but before Apoletta could comfort her or disagree, Brysis waved away her concern. "I've made my peace with that. That's not the point."

Apoletta nodded and waited for Brysis to continue.

"Minnow-Tyrant was also with me . . . during the third expedition. That is when we tried mapping the World Gash. It was my turn to guard the camp. The expedition left for the day. They vanished for nearly a week. I searched for them, but I couldn't find them."

"I remember," Apoletta said. "Twelve Dargonesti explorers, Istar's finest, lost."

"Minnow-Tyrant found his way back. But he'd changed. Been witness to some horror."

"Oh, yes. There was another survivor, was there not?"

"Veloxua," Brysis said, nodding. "She was also with me when Quayseen died."

Apoletta remembered the story then. Veloxua had returned mad. Something in the World Gash had driven her insane. Nobody in Istar knew what to make of her affliction, so they had brought her to Watermere. But the priests of the city could not help her. They could only comfort her and treat her with balms.

Brysis feared that Veloxua also must have been suffering from the Stigmata Curse. She would visit Veloxua the following morning and find out the truth.

Apoletta thought about it a moment. "May Utharne and I accompany you?"

Brysis nodded.

"Then the matter is settled. Before we leave tomorrow, let me speak with the Speaker of the Moon. I'm sure he can be helpful."

"You think he knows? About the maps and Minnow-Tyrant?"

Apoletta smiled. "After tonight. I'm certain he knows."

As she'd promised Brysis, Apoletta rose early in the day and spoke with Captain Stormbrave. She requested an audience with the Speaker of the Moon. It was a fortunate coincidence, then, that

Treyen had already sent Stormbrave to find Apoletta.

Very quickly Apoletta found herself in the Speaker's private chambers, a large, circular room situated inside one of the smaller towers connected to the Tower of the Moon. The chamber encompassed an entire floor of the structure and commanded a breathtaking view of the seafloor below and the ocean sky above. A sweeping balcony broken by columns framed the chamber, and all of Watermere, dappled in silver light, unfurled below it. Eight members of the honor guard stood at the compass points of the balcony in pairs. Another two stood by the circular opening in the floor.

Bookshelves and two long marble tables filled the chamber interior. Upon each shelf sat books treated to survive the long-term effects of seawater. On one table rested bronze and copper devices of the arcane sciences, open books, and a variety of spell reagents in an equal number of containers. Dozens of unfurled maps rested upon the second table, covering it under thick layers of animal skins.

Apoletta waited patiently while the Speaker of the Moon hunched over the second table, studying the maps. She continued waiting until, finally, Treyen cleared his throat and looked up at her.

"Apoletta, do you know the difference between fate and consequence to one who can see the future?"

Apoletta shook her head. His odd greeting mystified her. "I admit I do not."

The Speaker looked tired, his eyes dark and his face drawn. Apoletta realized he had on the same armorlike skin he had worn on the previous night.

"Consequence is the future born of the immediate . . . the moment," Treyen said wearily. His shoulders sagged. "I speak in anger, and you react in anger. Or I speak kindly, and your reaction differs. Consequence is born of the moment and is not long lasting."

LUCIEN SOULBAN

Apoletta's face showed her puzzlement, she feared. Treyen studied Apoletta carefully, his eyes like hooks that fished deep inside her, and he was fishing for something. Apoletta could only stare back; no malice was in her gaze, just deference. While some nobles questioned Treyen's position as Speaker of the Moon, Apoletta had no doubt that he deserved to wear the mantle of his station.

"Fate," Treyen continued, "fate is that which remains immutable. I speak in anger, and regardless of your reaction, the outcome will be the same. Love, madness, anger, hope—it doesn't matter what I say to alter consequence, the fate remains the same."

"What are you saying?" Apoletta finally asked.

"I am saying," Treyen began, "I am saying that my questions may seem to badger. They humble. They incite. But it is the only way I can discern consequence from fate. That is the curse and blessing of my ability to envision the future . . . of all Speakers to see the future."

"Then last night?" Apoletta said.

"I'm sorry to say that was necessary."

"You were gazing into my future? Into Utharne's? What did you see?" she asked.

"I saw fate," Treyen whispered.

A chill shot through Apoletta's spine as Treyen's face sagged, as though everything he had envisioned were dire. She saw, for the briefest instance, an emotion she could not quite place.

Forgive me, it said.

"Do you see my . . . death?" Apoletta asked, suddenly disquieted by the thought.

"I cannot say."

"Utharne's?"

Treyen shook his head. He would not answer.

"Then why are you telling me this?" Apoletta asked, frustration choking her voice.

"Because it doesn't matter what I say. The outcome remains the same; it is tied to your fate."

170

"Does my fate have to do with the World Gash?" Apoletta asked, nodding to the maps with the black stains upon them.

The Speaker of the Moon cast a sideways glance at the maps. "He waits for you there."

"Who?" Apoletta stammered, even though she already knew the answer.

"Your husband," he answered evenly. "He is eternally lost and believes he has found an anchor to his past through you. But that is all I see. Something blocks me from staring into that eye of darkness. There are powerful elements at work, and they conspire."

"My husband does not matter," Apoletta said, straightening. "If you had spoken with me—asked me—I would have told you about him. I don't need to know my fate lies there. It is not because of my husband. What you call fate is really my resolve in the matter."

The Speaker smiled. "I know that very well, Apoletta," he said. "But have you considered that you aren't being given a choice? When I said that something conspires, I meant something conspires to draw you there. Everything that's happened so far has been intended to bring you to the World Gash."

"But why?" Apoletta asked.

"I truly don't know. I cannot see beyond that moment."

"It's a trap?"

"Yes, most certainly."

"But if I know it is a trap, then I may elude it," Apoletta said.

Treyen Silverwake shrugged, inhaling deeply. Water filled his throat, air suffused his lungs, and he drew himself up. His eyes cleared. "Do you know," Treyen said, "I never approved of my father's choice of you as Steward of Istar? Nor of your choice of mate. Nor your use of spell-fables. Nor your involvement with the Heroes of the Lance. In fact, almost everything you've done has been contrary to my wishes . . . had you ever deigned to ask my permission, of course."

"I know," Apoletta said gently. "But I remain a loyal servant of the Silverwake family and of the rightful Speaker of the Moon.

You are my pilot star. I steer my path in your light."

"But you do not steer your heart to my wishes, correct? As it should be, I suppose. You will make a good Speaker one day."

"Excuse me? Surely you mean a Speaker of Blood?" Apoletta said, referring to Watermere's senate of landowners.

"No. And to tell you the truth," Treyen said, "I wouldn't have chosen you. But the choice is not mine. Not really."

"Whose then?" Apoletta asked, filled with wonder and curiosity.

"Again, it is fate. Fate has made that choice for me," Treyen said.

Apoletta nearly protested when Treyen caught her gaze. He knew her thoughts.

"And fate has made that choice for you as well," he said.

Brysis and Apoletta swam through the waters in porpoise form. Utharne swam as a sea otter with Brine-Whisker at his side. The silver sheen of Solinari brought a soft glow to the land and lit the way ahead. The echoes of the city faded, and the thrum of the ocean returned to fill their ears.

Five large war dolphins, including Echo Fury, provided an escort. All five dolphins appeared fierce with their engraved brass plates protecting their fins and flanks. And where the flesh lay exposed, the scars from old battles showed.

Echo Fury's pod was renowned for their fierce disposition and their remarkable loyalty. Apoletta found herself grateful for their company and protection. Given events of the past week, Apoletta did not feel safe anywhere.

The group swam past the last of the roads, to the edge where Solinari's glow waned, and the ocean slowly surrendered to the growing midnight. There, the borderland village of Triastemus waited.

Triastemus appeared bucolic. The villagers there used simple bricks to make their scattered homes, which were surrounded by sea-wheat, kelp stalk, and mustard pod fields. Farmers toiled, using sea turtles and sea horses to pull their plows. The largest cluster of simple buildings squatted around a vent-well, a deep hole surrounded by a ring wall. Beneath the village rested magma springs that heated the water of the well and provided the entire region with warmth.

Brysis swam straight for the largest building, a communal lodge with a peaked roof and ironwood walls that stretched for a hundred feet in either direction from the open door. Apoletta and Utharne followed Brysis into the building, leaving the war dolphins to patrol outside.

Inside, the lodge opened into passageways that split off in three directions; doors lined each corridor.

Brysis motioned for Apoletta and Utharne to wait; she went to speak to an approaching, matronly looking sea elf with white hair and a yellow and orange toga.

"What is this place?" Utharne whispered.

"A hospice," Apoletta whispered back. "Those Dargonesti affected by incurable madness are brought here. There is no hope left for them."

Brysis swam back while the matronly sea elf waited.

"Her affliction has grown worse," Brysis said. "Her condition was affecting the others, so they moved her. Come."

The matronly sea elf quietly escorted the trio outside to a smaller building.

Another sea elf tended to Veloxua as Apoletta, Utharne, and Brysis entered. The caretaker was dressed in thick swabs of cloth, and in her hands she held rocks warmed at the well. The room was of a frightful cold that pierced bone and lung. The caretaker nodded and told Brysis, "I'll be outside," before leaving.

A bed, trunk, and chair adorned the simple chamber. Veloxua lay asleep, buried under layers of blankets. She seemed tall for an elf, her face long and thin; her bed-tousled hair was deep green, and her blue skin was unusually dark, verging on indigo. When she opened her eyes, Apoletta and Utharne recoiled. Inky blackness swam in Veloxua's eyes; her pupils floated in and out of the murk. Black ink likewise stained her lips.

"Who is there?" she asked, squinting to see despite her murky vision. A trickle of ink dribbled past her lips and plumed as it stained the water.

The deterioration of her friend obviously stunned Brysis. Utharne quietly reached forward and touched the diffusing ink. He pulled his hand back in alarm and rubbed his fingers.

Before anyone could stop her, Apoletta did the same. Bitter cold stung her fingers. Apoletta pulled away her hand quickly, her fingertips frosted white.

"Please?" Veloxua whispered, suddenly trembling.

"It's me; it's me," Brysis said, shaking herself loose of the fear. "Brysis. I'm here."

"Brysis?" she asked. "Please, take me from here!"

"I can't," Brysis said. "They're caring for you."

"How can you say that?" Veloxua said, crying tears of ink. The swirls in her eyes did not diminish. The temperature in the room grew colder. "They torture me!"

Utharne and Apoletta exchanged questioning looks. Brysis carefully pulled the sheets off Veloxua to examine her friend. Veloxua recoiled at the touch, her body stiffening. Brysis quickly placed her hand on Veloxua's cheek, trying to soothe her anxieties.

"Shh," Brysis said. "Nobody is trying to hurt you."

Veloxua wore a tattered seaweed woven gown. Apoletta could see no signs of bruising or bodily harm. She appeared healthy despite her pathetic circumstances.

When Brysis tried to console her, however, Veloxua grew more inconsolable. She insisted Brysis had to help her escape the horrors of that place. And the more she cried, the more the ink filled her eyes and trickled from her mouth and nose. A light cloud of blackness crowned her head.

"Veloxua," Brysis said, trying to control her own feelings. "We need to know what happened to your expedition . . . in the World Gash."

"Didn't you see it? You must have!"

"No, I didn't. I wasn't with you."

"But you're here now," Veloxua said, confused.

"Yes," Brysis replied. "We're both here. We're both safe."

"No!" Veloxua cried. She looked around in sudden panic, as though afraid someone had heard her. She whispered after that outburst. "We're not safe. Never again so long as the coral hungers."

"The coral?" Brysis asked. She shot Apoletta a miserable look, as though to say she'd been through the conversation before, too often before.

"It feeds, like the racing lightning. Its mother is the darkness, the cold ink."

Brysis straightened and looked at Apoletta. "Cold ink, Veloxua? What do you mean, cold ink?" she asked.

Apoletta realized it was the first time Veloxua must have mentioned that particular detail.

"The ink, the shadow?" Veloxua said, shaking her head. "I don't know. But it's so terribly cold."

"Where did you see this?" Brysis asked.

"In the trench," Veloxua said, speaking as though it should be obvious to Brysis. "The trench was filled with black ink. Didn't you see it?"

"No," Brysis said. "I didn't accompany you."

Veloxua cried, turning the water dark with her tears; a deep chill overtook the room. "Why are you being so cruel?" she said, grabbing Brysis by the arm. "Why do you leave me here?"

Apoletta leaned forward, afraid to ask the question, but asking regardless.

"Veloxua," Apoletta said. "Where are you right now?"

Veloxua grabbed Brysis by the arm in blind panic. "Someone else is here," Veloxua said, her whispers cracking.

"Just Apoletta and a friend," Brysis said. "You remember Her Ladyship?"

"No, someone else is coming," Veloxua said, hissing. She appeared to be listening to something. "Leave . . . save yourself," she said. With that, Veloxua's head snapped to a corner of the room.

Apoletta, Utharne, and Brysis all followed Veloxua's gaze. They listened intently, but the soft drone of the sleeping ocean held no other voices.

"Go!" Veloxua said. "I'll distract them!"

"Veloxua," Brysis said, "there's nobody coming. You're safe with us."

"No," Veloxua moaned. "They're here! Flee!"

"Where are you right now?" Apoletta demanded.

"Hide!" Veloxua cried.

"Where!" Apoletta repeated, trying to break through Veloxua's fear.

"In the black ocean," Veloxua cried. "In the trench! Can't you see me?"

And with that, Veloxua fell unconscious.

Veloxua rested beneath the thick covers; Brysis sat on the corner of her bed.

"Has this ever happened before?" Utharne asked gently. He, too, appeared shaken.

"No," Brysis replied dully. "She hasn't been coherent since the third expedition. But the ink. The cold. I'd never seen that, heard about that, before. And what did she mean she's *still* in the trench? Could that really be possible in some way?"

"I . . . I don't know," Utharne said, muttering. "I'll need Brine-Whisker."

Utharne slipped through the door to find his companion. Apoletta waited quietly, retreating into her thoughts, trying to remember some spell, anything that could help them or Veloxua. But her grade of magic could not combat curses or afflictions.

Apoletta jumped when Brysis touched her wrist. Brysis nodded toward Veloxua, who was muttering in her unconscious state. Veloxua's eyes remained closed, but ink curled upward from the gap between her stained lips.

"Apoletta," a voice whispered.

Apoletta blinked.

"Apoletta," Veloxua said, but she was not speaking in her own voice. The voice that squirmed past her lips was deeper by an octave and rough for its whisper.

"Apoletta." Veloxua's lips did not even move.

"Zebulah?" Apoletta whispered back.

Veloxua, eyes still closed, smiled.

Apoletta, Utharne, and Brysis felt exhausted, their ministrations bringing them into the late afternoon. Utharne, with Brine-Whisker's help, prayed and augured for Veloxua's benefit, but nothing significant came of it. Prayers to dispel, prayers to protect, prayers to restore, prayers to consecrate . . . none of them had the least apparent effect.

Veloxua had said nothing since whispering Apoletta's name, and the three companions had arrived at a frustrated impasse.

"Nothing!" Utharne said, throwing his arms above his head. "It's as though my prayers slip off her . . . no . . . through her. Yes, through her," he said to himself.

Apoletta nodded and quietly said, "I have one last idea to try."

The others looked at her, brows furrowed and mouths frowning.

"It's a spell," Apoletta said, "that allows me to hear the thoughts of others."

"Hear?" Utharne asked worriedly. "Only hear?"

"Yes. Only hear. They cannot influence me. I am in no danger."

Brysis inhaled sharply. "Listen to mad thoughts!" she muttered. Utharne looked away.

"We have little choice," Apoletta said.

When the others did not argue, Apoletta prepared the spell. She took her favored copper piece from her pouch. "When Stonecipher first dipped her head beneath the waves," Apoletta said, "she heard the ocean's thoughts and murmurs." The spell took effect immediately. Apoletta focused on the coin, and through the coin, she focused on Veloxua. Her hearing narrowed, becoming the sword's edge that cleaved through the noise of hair, skin, and bone. At first the rush of thoughts from everyone nearby seemed to pour into her head. Soon enough, though, the other voices dropped away. Apoletta filtered through each, discarding them and moving on to the next. Finally, she found Veloxua's voice.

The world suddenly lurched beneath Apoletta's feet. She no longer heard Veloxua's thoughts. A snowfall of ash filled her sight; the ocean itself was the darkest gray she'd ever witnessed. The bitter bite of sulfur curled her tongue back inside her mouth. Everything was strangely quiet. Veloxua's screams were muted by the absolute stillness. The water smelled like rusted metal. And the cold . . . a cold beyond the reckoning of the living, it was, cold as worn by Death for its vestments, so cold that Apoletta expected to see glaciers float past her with bodies trapped inside the ice.

Apoletta spun around, trying to find Veloxua's vanished voice. But somehow, the immense surrounding darkness engulfed her and swept away her sense of proportions. Apoletta turned and continued turning without ever coming back to where she had started. Finally, Veloxua whirled into view, her face calm with death's grace. Yet Veloxua continued screaming in the distance somewhere, her voice apart from her throat.

"Veloxua?" Apoletta asked, almost choking on the foul waters.

THE ALIEN SEA

"Where are we? Where are you now?"

"We are where lava turns sea to steam and where ocean floor drops into the Abyss. I live in the ashen rains, in the shadow of the twisted throne, the impaling thorn."

Veloxua looked down. The curtains of ash parted beneath her feet, and Apoletta caught a glimpse of the glassy seafloor covered in the wavering glow of magma fissures. A long black fissure, like a vein, snaked its way across the ground. Within the fissure, darkness bubbled and conspired. Suddenly the edges of the fissure crumbled and collapsed away into the darkness. The ocean floor cracked into baked mud scales and fell into the widening maw of shadow. Within moments, the trench had consumed the seafloor as far as Apoletta could see.

Apoletta could not move; fear froze her limbs and turned them into stone. In her life she'd held court with dragons and watched as the maelstrom sky over Istar rained fleets of whole ships, their minotaur sailors twisting in midair as they screamed plumes of bubbles. No horror, however, compared to the magnitude of the shadowed place where she stood.

Something moved in the darkness, and a pair of ember-lit eyes opened; glowing red cracks spread out from the eyes. It roared at Apoletta. The darkness exploded from the trench and raced upward, toward Apoletta, swallowing the ocean with an unquenchable thirst. And the eyes raced up too, eager to devour her.

Apoletta started, bolting from her nightmare. Utharne and Brysis were holding her down, floating mere inches from the ceiling. She'd been thrashing about, and from her icy lips trickled dying threads of ink.

Brysis eyed Apoletta. "In no danger, you say?"

They swam, harder and faster than ever. Halfway to Takaluras, Apoletta used her spellcraft to alert the others, sending forward her commands and instructions to Stormbrave, Captain Ornathius, and Vanastra.

When they arrived, Captain Ornathius and Vanastra were busy preparing their men, while both Arrowawk, looking red eyed, and Briegan readied the shark-blade whale, Salystra. Slyphanous waited for them as well, much to Apoletta's relief. Utharne and Brysis went immediately to attending to their duties. Apoletta embraced her advisor and friend.

"I heard what happened," Slyphanous said. "I'm sorry about Maleanki, about everything. I should have been there."

"No," Apoletta said. "I needed you elsewhere. You did well. Did you bring what I asked?"

"Yes," Slyphanous whispered. "It's safe with Captain Ornathius."

"You could not have come at a better time. I was wrong," Apoletta said.

Before Slyphanous could probe her statement, Stormbrave arrived astride his hippocampus. "I have spoken with the Speaker of the Moon," he said.

"And?"

"He bids you a fair journey. You will have more men at your disposal and four more whales. The whales are a gift to the Dimernesti for the ones they lost."

"Thank you," Apoletta said. "And please, if you will, deliver a message to Speaker Silverwake for me?"

"I suppose," Stormbrave said.

"Tell him this, these exact words. What matters to me is not the fate I meet. That was never the intention of my journey, or the path the gods set for me. It is how I meet my fate that matters. And thanks to him, I shall meet it bravely and with my eyes open."

Stormbrave cocked an eyebrow, but nodded; he rode away.

"You said earlier you were wrong?" Slyphanous asked after a moment.

THE ALIEN SEA

"About the World Gash," Apoletta said. "So terribly wrong. We are in peril. Every one of us. We must leave Watermere right away, or all is lost."

"Why?"

"The World Gash is not expanding slowly," Apoletta said. "It is spreading fast and far. And it is spreading with calculated fury. If we do nothing to stop it, the ocean will soon be hostile to our presence. We will be alien to it."

"But . . ." Slyphanous stammered, "how do you stop the World Gash, hmm?"

"This I do not know," Apoletta admitted. "But Utharne wishes to speak with someone who might, and . . . we must find Zebulah."

Anhalstrax, the aquatic dragon, was a long, sinewy beast with tiger stripes of blue on her green scales. Along her length ran kelp-like frills, while her sleek head and elongated snout seemed almost birdlike.

Anhalstrax patrolled her waters with a watchful eye. The oceans had grown stranger by the years, and more surface creatures found a home in the oceans since magic had returned.

Undead and the magori numbered many among the new arrivals. Bands of one or the other targeted Anhalstrax regularly, but she always repulsed their pathetic attacks with ease. Anhalstrax thought they sought her vast treasures hidden inside her well-concealed lair.

But as Anhalstrax swam under the canopy and between the jagged blue trunks of coral trees, bands of magori and simple-minded undead hidden in the forest attacked in a coordinated effort for the first time.

They swarmed around the dragon, though their weapons and paltry spell effects did little to harrow her. Instead Anhalstrax dispensed with them gleefully, slowing a score of attackers in the stream of her freezing black breath and crushing others.

Slowly, however, the acidic blood and entrails of the magori stung her badly, eating at her. The water killed the burns quickly, but Anhalstrax felt pain.

As Anhalstrax dealt with the intruders, another wave of magori and spectral-like undead swarmed over her. The second wave included sharks encrusted by coral that led the charge.

Mahkwahb, Anhalstrax realized, though she still believed she had little to fear from the new attackers, the dark sea elves. Still, the blows struck deeper and stung worse than before.

Although battle engrossed, Anhalstrax noticed the undead human wearing sigil-lit red robes, and the coral-encrusted shark that accompanied him; both kept their distance. The undead motioned toward Anhalstrax, and a large sphere of coral charged through the waters.

Anhalstrax could not move aside in time. She intended to coil out of the way, but no sooner had the sphere reached her than it exploded outward with dozens of barbed lances. Several spears punctured Anhalstrax, though even more cut through the magori and the simple-minded undead. The magori screeched in their chattering, gibbering tongue. The spears injected them with coral, flooding their veins with shards, calcifying their blood; the coral grew wild inside them, piercing their organs and covering their skin. In moments they were nothing more than coral statues, their mass assimilated back into the sphere.

Anhalstrax knew the effects all too well because the coral afflicted her too. The coral grew inside her, invading her organs, muscle, and bone. It grew and overtook the dragon's scaly hide, constricting Anhalstrax's movements, encasing her. The surviving undead, magori, and Mahkwahb backed away and eagerly watched the aquatic dragon's demise.

At last it grew difficult to breathe, the coral coating the dragon's gills and filling her lungs. And she suffered the worst from the coral spurs digging slowly into her body. Anhalstrax struggled hard, however, and in one last burst of strength, broke through the coral sheath and tore free. In moments Anhalstrax fled faster than anyone could follow. In her wake, however, lingered the dissipating clouds of green blood.

Wartide and Zebulah watched Anhalstrax flee. The Legion Coral reformed itself into a latticelike sphere.

Zebulah began to move forward, about to give chase, but Wartide shifted form, his skin becoming flesh again. "No," he commanded. "The dragon's infected. Let it weaken some more. It should be feeble enough when Blazewight arrives."

Zebulah cocked an eyebrow at Wartide.

"I know," Wartide said. "You're thinking the Master isn't strong enough to conquer Anhalstrax . . . wouldn't that be the pity!"

Zebulah studied Wartide, curious as to his remarks; the Blood Shoal elf offered him a lopsided grin.

"In time you'll understand," Wartide said. "For now let us weaken Anhalstrax more so that Master can claim his safe victory."

ACT

The World Gash

III

CHAPTER
Council of the Matriarch
11

Again they rode the currents of the God's Throat—the Defiler's Breath. The journey took only three days, cutting a week from their travels. A risky venture, to be sure, with koalinths and other fell creatures lying in ambush, but the size of their expedition intimidated such creatures and discouraged predators from attacking them.

In addition to Brysis, Slyphanous, and Utharne—and their respective animal companions—Apoletta counted five whales, more than twenty armed sea elves under the command of Captain Ornathius, and another seven under Vanastra. The whales fell under the steady supervision of Briegan, Arrowawk, and three Dargonesti riders named. . . .

"Utharne," Apoletta whispered from her lamprey pouch, "I've forgotten the names of our new riders."

Utharne smiled and said, "Fendalius, Hopethorn, and I believe the woman is Blue-Diver. Yes, yes, Blue-Diver, that's it. Shall I write down their names?"

"You shall do no such thing," Apoletta said in mock indignation.

Utharne chuckled. "However do you remember your spells quite well?"

"I have troubles with names, not spells. Do you know that before the Chaos War, we were visited, in turn, by each Master of the Wizards of High Sorcery? They came to me, Red, White, and Black, each seeking my council on finding the Tower of Istar."

Utharne nodded. He knew of the Tower of Istar, a fabled repository of artifacts and magic from the days before the First Cataclysm, when Istar lay beneath the open sun. Legends claimed it had survived the catastrophe but that the gods had turned it invisible.

"Heady company," Utharne commented.

"So heady that I actually forgot their names," Apoletta said, laughing. "I continued referring to them as Chosen of Solinari, Chosen of Nuitari, and Chosen of Lunitari. They must have believed it a curious Dargonesti affectation. To this day I still forget their names."

Utharne joined in her laughter.

The expedition finally reached the Whistler's Chain, a deep-sea mountain range south of the Blood Sea of Istar that divided the Southern Courrain Ocean from the Eastern.

Utharne had taken over the lead, much to Arrovawk's chagrin. Whistler's Chain was thick with mountains and rife with mining shafts that bore deep into the rock. The ancient passageways whistled when swift currents blew through them. Their construction was ornate with the same disturbing motifs of squid-faced humanoids that could be seen throughout God's Throat.

At long last, Utharne led the force to an enormous shaft struck into the root of the mountain. With a mouth far wider than the base of Watermere's Tower of the Moon, the shaft dropped away, angling under the mountain. The light came from the horde of spherical, tentacle-covered, and translucent star-orbs; like floating lanterns, their filaments and threadlike appendages glowed an uncanny blue-white. They rested inside the length of the shaft by the hundreds, but even their light could not illuminate its depths. Among their numbers swam enormous pulse-blooms, flowerlike creatures with long, deadly tentacles floating behind them.

The five whales sang in unison, a sudden, groaning dirge that gave everyone a start.

Arrovawk cursed, looking as though his drunken revelry in Watermere still afflicted him. Apoletta and the others hesitated uncertainly, but Utharne appeared unconcerned. He swam among the star-orbs and said they were safe enough, and Apoletta and Brysis agreed to accompany him.

Captain Ornathius and Slyphanous were suspicious of the whale song and the star-orbs, but Utharne explained. "Please," he said. "I've been granted a rare privilege . . . an honor that extends only to Her Ladyship and Brysis. Vanastra, tell them."

"They are safe," Vanastra said. "This is a holy place."

"What about the pulse-blooms?" Captain Ornathius asked, motioning to the shaft.

"Guardians against intruders," Utharne said. "They will not attack. Well, the three of us, I mean. We're quite safe. I assure you."

"Wait here," Apoletta instructed.

Thus commanded, both Captain Ornathius and Slyphanous bit their tongues.

"What about Echo Fury?" Brysis asked.

"Him as well, I'm afraid."

Echo Fury spat out a series of angry clicks, but Brysis spoke quietly to him. After a moment Echo Fury jerked away from Brysis and bolted. Brysis shook her head.

"He's angry with me."

"I'm sorry," Utharne said. "But fair is fair, I suppose. Brine-Whisker will also stay." With that, he motioned for Brine-Whisker to pursue Echo Fury. The seal barked once and swam after his compatriot. "Swim where I swim," Utharne instructed Brysis and Apoletta.

"Utharne," Apoletta whispered. "I've been patient with you up till now. I really must know who we are going to meet."

"She is called the Matriarch. She is a divine oracle. For Abbuku."

Brysis gasped. "The Matriarch? I thought she was legend."

Utharne shook his head. "No. In fact she's Abbuku's touchstone. In these lands, I mean. And we're keeping her waiting."

"But who is she? Why is she important?" Apoletta asked.

"She is possibly the greatest ally we have," Utharne whispered. "You'll see."

Quietly, they entered the shaft, dust motes in the mouths of gods; they swam feet to head. The soft light added an eerie glow to their countenances, bringing out unexpected shadows. Utharne followed a lazy, winding path that only he spied through the shaft, drifting first one way, then another, passing through clouds of star-orbs without touching them and past the featureless pulse-blooms. A strange creaking groan filled the shaft. It was reminiscent of whale song, but it felt far more ancient to Apoletta. For a moment, she swore she heard someone recite the history of whales spoken in one, venerable voice.

A pulse-bloom tentacle dropped into Apoletta's path, startling her. Out of reflex, she pushed away from the poisonous appendage. Suddenly, the star-orbs dimmed in unison, almost plunging the shaft into darkness; then they all swam toward her with their pulsing bodies.

"The path!" Utharne said, almost yelling in panic. "Keep to the path!"

Apoletta scrambled back to her position behind Brysis. The star-orbs stopped their advance and glowed softly once more.

Thankfully, the trio entered an enormous cavern through a giant hole in the ceiling. Although the cavern appeared naturally formed, the occasional spiral column or building wall surfaced through the rock face, as though the cavern had yet to digest its previous occupants. The cavern itself dwarfed anything Apoletta had ever seen or envisioned. It could have held Istar in its belly and added, perhaps, even Takaluras with the Tower of the Moon at full height. The stalagmites and stalactites lent it the appearance of a maw whose teeth had grown wild.

Apoletta had difficulty gauging the dimensions of the cavern, though the luminescent moss and star-orbs did much to illuminate what could be seen. And what could be seen, ahead of them, was a whale of titanic proportions.

"The Matriarch," Utharne whispered and bowed his head.

Brysis dropped her jaw, and Apoletta impolitely did the same.

The Matriarch was an albino whale; her ivory tail stretched back so far that it vanished into the turbid mists. Her blunt head measured the size of a mountain's peak, and the three sea elves felt like sand motes before her saucer eyes. Whether the Matriarch could see them, however, Apoletta remained uncertain about. Her eyes were milky white.

All around the Matriarch swam schools of fish and clouds of star-orbs. They constantly cleaned her body with their teeth and tentacles, eating at the spurts of coral or hardened carapace of barnacles encrusting her.

The Matriarch moaned again in a loud, strange voice that sounded like all the timbers of the world creaking; the water shuddered.

"You may each ask one question," Utharne said softly.

Brysis's eyes widened, and she muttered to Apoletta, "What in the Abyss do you ask a mountain?"

"I do not know," Apoletta said. "But . . . she's a beautiful mountain, isn't she?"

The Matriarch sang, as though pleased by the remark, a happy burst of noise that seemed to sweep through them. Images flooded Apoletta's thoughts, every moment to ever bring her happiness was remembered, unveiled anew, repainted in fresh colors, and joyously relived. In certain of these moments, Apoletta and Zebulah swam together; she rediscovered the wonders of the ocean through his eyes, laughed at what made him laugh, and recalled what she'd forgotten . . . or taken for granted.

Apoletta blinked and the images vanished, but she saw the same blissful smile on Utharne's and Brysis's faces, each experiencing their treasured memories.

"Ask," Utharne said. "And she will answer. If you wish, I will go first."

Apoletta and Brysis exchanged glances.

"I need to think hard about my choice," Apoletta said. Brysis nodded.

"Very well," Utharne said.

With that, Utharne swam up to the whale. Apoletta watched him grow smaller in proportion to the Matriarch. It took a few long moments for him to reach the huge creature, at which point, Utharne measured the size of a speck of krill. Then, to Apoletta's horror, the Matriarch opened her mouth long enough for Utharne to enter before closing it again.

Apoletta and Brysis raced forward, trying to reach Utharne.

Utharne floated past the rounded, column-wide teeth of the Matriarch and into her mouth; the whale's giant tongue seemed like a spongy, rosy road that curved down into the darkness of her cavernous throat. No stench greeted him or assailed his nostrils. It smelled as fresh there as the ocean after a storm. The Matriarch closed her mouth, casting Utharne into total darkness. He closed his eyes and thought of his question.

"How do we stop the World Gash?" he asked.

That is not your question.

No voice spoke to him but the shuddering echo of whale song. It filled his senses and touched something at the very core of his being. Few things ever reached him there, in his private heart and thoughts; the most primal of emotions—anger, love, sorrow—reposed there, the ones that his mind could not, or would not, silence.

"What do you mean?" Utharne asked, taken aback.

Another question lies closer to your heart. I hear it above all others.

Utharne shook his head, confused. But he knew what she meant. More than speaking the truth, the Matriarch exposed the

THE ALIEN SEA

truth; there was no possibility of deception, no mistaking the words of the god. Utharne could feel the question forming in his mind, but he didn't want to ask it.

Ask it.

"But I'm only allowed one. Question, I mean. And this isn't about me."

Ask it. It is the thorn of your heart.

"Please," Utharne said. "I don't want to know. I don't have the right!" But the truth already remained exposed, open for him to revisit and remember. The truth for him was a wound that never seemed to heal. The truth and the death of his family were one and the same, and Utharne could not seek one without finding the other. He couldn't experience the truth without reliving his own impotence to help his loved ones. He couldn't know the truth without, again, watching his wife die in his arms, holding the limp body of his son, or fighting the carrion crabs in a vain attempt to keep them from tearing his daughter's body apart.

Utharne wanted to ask one simple question: Why?

Why?

That encompassed everything he wanted to know: Why did you let the Dark Goddess Takhisis steal the world? Are not your children worthy of your protection? Why could you not find the world when it vanished? Are you not all-knowing? Why did you not bring back those who had died? Did they have to suffer from your mistakes? Why did my family have to die?

Why?

Then again, that was the one question he could not bring himself to ask. He feared asking the question. He feared the answer. His faith in the gods already had suffered its share of cracks; whenever Utharne questioned, the cracks deepened. Yet he sorely wanted to believe, not only to assuage his own pain, but also so he could help others.

The thought of asking why shook him to the very foundations of his being.

So, instead, Utharne had focused on the other question, and buried the one closest to his heart deeper. The thorn twisted in his heart, but he pushed away the pain.

"How do we stop the World Gash?" he asked again, his voice barely a whisper.

The song stopped momentarily. Silence accompanied the darkness for a while before the groan returned.

Seek the dragoness Anhalstrax. She will set you on your way. She lives in a cave under the Valiance Coral Fields. You will know it by the ships. But you must hurry.

The mouth opened and Utharne swam out, his limbs weak and heavy. Apoletta and Brysis had just arrived, and relief was etched on their faces. He waved off their concern and motioned with a flick of his head for the next one to enter. Apoletta and Brysis exchanged wary glances.

Apoletta entered without further ado.

That is not your question.

Apoletta blinked. Trapped inside the mouth of a giant whale—which, coincidently, required a great deal of trust in Utharne—in the absolute dark, hearing a strange song she felt more than heard, proved great hurdles to thinking clearly. It seemed her question did not satisfy the Matriarch, or she'd somehow offended Abbuku's oracle.

"Pardon?" Apoletta asked, hoping she'd misheard the Matriarch.

That is not your question. There is another question closer to your heart.

In a flash Apoletta saw Zebulah in her mind, but she quickly ignored the impulse. "Perhaps," she replied, "but it is not the question that my people can afford."

And if Utharne already asked about the World Gash, what would be your next question?

THE ALIEN SEA

"Hmm, a myriad of others," Apoletta replied, scarcely believing she was conversing with a giant whale. "But I am going to the World Gash for my own reasons."

Yes, you must go for the reasons that matter to you. The ones you shall find hardest to achieve. Right now, however, a question lies closer to your heart than all others. You will fight for the answer to this question most fiercely. That does not diminish your other questions. You would be surprised to learn how intrinsic one question is to the other.

Apoletta hesitated. She closed her eyes to ponder what the whale had said. She saw how asking the question about Zebulah might benefit her. However, that was entirely contrary to her idea of what she was doing that was most important: struggling to solve the riddle of the World Gash, helping to rally the Dimernesti, Dargonesti, and other sea races, and helping the sea elves change from a fractious race to a united one.

She desperately wanted to ask about Zebulah but had come all the way to the Matriarch to find out about the World Gash, not her undead husband.

Apoletta suddenly opened her eyes and prayed that her question was the right one.

"Very well," Apoletta said. "I trust in Abbuku, so I pray you will answer that question which best will help us against the World Gash."

Silence greeted her words for long moments before the whale's song finally returned in her heart and in her mind.

Zebulah is dead and must continue his course into the afterlife. That is not to say the dead cannot be saved. That is not to say all victories are complete.

The Matriarch's mouth opened.

Brysis floated into the darkness, the Matriarch's song swimming through her. She was its ocean; a much-needed smile lit up her face. She had yet to ask her question.

Ask.

Brysis opened her eyes. "I will not ask if I can save Veloxua. I must find a way myself. But . . . Quayseen and Shakhall . . . I wonder about them. Are they safe now?"

They swim with Abbuku, in the clear blue oceans. They hunt, they laugh, and they share stories of you.

Brysis smiled and let her tears wash through the water. "Please," she said. "Can I stay a while longer? Hear your song?"

The Matriarch obliged and sang the lullaby that whale mothers sing to put their children to sleep, even when age and distance have separated them. It was the one song whales could hear across any expanse, the one song that oceans still carried in their veins, long after mother and child had left the world.

The trio returned together, much to the relief of the others. Although members of the expedition brimmed with questions, Apoletta, Utharne, and Brysis did not speak in detail about their time inside the Matriarch. In truth, they said little about the experience, save for Utharne.

"Valiance Coral Fields. That's where we must go now," he told everybody.

"That's at least a day's swim from the World Gash," Vanastra said.

"I know," Utharne said. "And we must hurry. Our time grows short."

With no further delay, the expedition continued on its way.

CHAPTER
The Shipyard
12

Another day spent in travel, and the expedition of sea elves arrived at the edge of the Valiance Coral Fields. Once, the coral fields contained a rainbow's array of hues and an abundance of species: the flat flowers of tabular coral, the round masses of brain coral, the spiral leaf and veiny fan coral . . . all that and more grew atop the canopy. Below, the canopy contained a rich offering of sea fungi and tube mushrooms clustered around coral trunks.

What the sea elves saw before them, however, was only a graying, dying mass. The dozens of miles comprising the fields shrank steadily, thanks to their proximity to the sulfur-soaked waters of the World Gash. Many of the fish fled, leaving nothing to feed, or feed upon, the coral.

The fields appeared level, but Apoletta and the others knew better. They found a large gap in the canopy for the whales and passed into the true forest beneath. Thick trunks of coral grew from the ground and flowered fifty feet above the seafloor. Rocks covered the ground, except where the thermal fissures lay. Sharks filled the forest, each fighting for dominance over a stretch of the feeding ground. Silver- and white-tipped sharks, amberhead sharks, and ruthless axe-bones fed on the floating bodies and dismembered limbs of humans, sea elves, and magori. The stench of decay filled the water, and the presence of death and the World Gash turned the region a murky green.

"The whales aren't fond of this place," Blue-Diver, the female whale rider, commented. Her whale bucked side to side.

"True enough for all of them!" Arrowawk said.

"Something's wrong," Brysis said. "On your guard!"

"Out, out!" Captain Ornathius shouted.

Apoletta and Utharne looked about, vigilant for whatever lay in wait. That's when she spied the shark with inked tattoos covering its body. It charged them.

"Mahkwahb!" Apoletta shouted before gesturing to draw forth her spell. "The dolphins, leaping through the sun, brought fire back from the heavens!" The warmth in her belly flared, and four darts leaped from her fingers, dancing around one another in flight. The darts struck the shark, forcing it to veer away.

By then it was too late. Mad chittering voiced through the water, and more than a dozen magori emerged from the murky shadows of the brine.

"Dart-lancers!" Captain Ornathius yelled. Six Dargonesti soldiers transformed into war dolphins with thorny crab armor that covered their fins, snouts, and flanks. The six dart-lancers burst into action, moving through and past the magori.

"Retreat!" Vanastra ordered the others. "We'll hold them back!"

The Dargonesti and Dimernesti formed quick skirmish lines around the whales and delegates. They used tridents, hooked nets, and thin water-blades to hack and slice at any advancing enemy. Apoletta and Utharne unleashed what spells they could to help. The green, turbid waters seemed to hide an unending flow of enemies, however, and a smattering of undead trundled into view on the seafloor, groping toward the expedition.

From the corner of her eye, Apoletta saw the trade riders try to bring about their whales to escape back through the gap. Panic overtook the poor creatures, however, and the five handlers had a devilish time trying to maneuver them. Two whales struck each other in the process.

The careening whales blocked the sea elves from their escape route, unless some poor soul willingly ran the gauntlet.

Blue flames licked Brine-Whisker's brow, and Utharne cast all manner of protective and healing spells to keep his friends alive.

It was growing difficult to see. Adding to the confusion of murky water and the darting war dolphins and sharks, the sea elf soldiers used their blurred forms to become ghosts in the turbid fog. The magori countered by spewing forth mists to mask their movements. In moments the water turned into a thick soup, though the magori navigated with expert skill. Apoletta cursed; during the Chaos War, she had fought the magori when they had descended upon Istar. She'd forgotten their aptitude in navigating their own mists.

"Escape!" Apoletta said to Utharne. "I will protect you!"

"Truer than you know!" Utharne said. He touched Apoletta's arms and murmured a prayer. An infusion of warmth shot up Apoletta's arm and coursed through her body. Her muscles pulsed as though radiated. A shark burst from the gloom but immediately veered away from her and Utharne.

"You're protected," Utharne said. "Now, where is out?"

"I can't tell anymore," Apoletta said. She spied a magori below her and unleashed four darts of light against it. The darts struck true, and the magori vanished into the murky waters with a screech.

"When I move, hold on to me!" Apoletta said before shifting into a porpoise, her body warmer now and streamlined. She called out, using her voice to paint her surroundings with sound. Her voice echoed back to her. Moving shapes filled the waters.

Apoletta sensed that escape lay above them, but five giant shapes blocked the way. Wailing, the whales were overcome by fear.

While Apoletta could see more clearly as a porpoise, she could not cast her spells. Instead, she called out to Brysis.

Within moments, both Echo Fury and Brysis—in porpoise form—arrived, slamming indistinct shapes out of the way.

Apoletta asked about the others, but Echo Fury was already moving away, barreling through the waters and battering at anything that blocked his way. Brysis followed. Apoletta waited for Utharne to grab on to her before she raced after Echo Fury.

Echo Fury swam erratically; Apoletta assumed he saw things that she could not and tried to follow him move for move. Finally, they emerged from the thick, soupy water in seas friendlier but no less green. There were fewer sharks and none with tattoos.

They traveled a short distance, eventually finding refuge under a coral ledge. Echo Fury remained outside on watch, while the others returned to their natural forms.

"What's happening here?" Utharne asked. "Mahkwahb, magori, undead . . . all working together?"

"We must find Anhalstrax," Apoletta said.

"What of the others?" Utharne asked.

"Send them a message," Brysis responded.

Apoletta nodded and cast her whispers to Vanastra, Captain Ornathius, and Slyphanous, telling them to hide and await instructions. She prayed they still lived to hear her.

The companions swam in the direction of the ship graveyard, with Brysis leading the way through the murky green waters. Echo Fury and Brine-Whisker were instructed to keep their voices quiet lest they attract enemy patrols.

Brysis practically vanished in the green waters as she darted from shelter to shelter. They hid in the hollows of coral trunks, under ledges, and behind sharp rocks. They suffered scratches and cuts but bore their hurts silently. Their enemies, no more than shadows in the dark, seemed everywhere. At last, Brysis reappeared, motioning.

THE ALIEN SEA

A great wall of wood loomed ahead in the murk. It was a ship, rent in half by some terrible force. Empty sockets for portholes stared back at the three sea elves. Brysis, without explanation, slipped through the large crack that halved the wreck. Echo Fury and the others followed without hesitation.

They swam through the eerie dark of the upturned ship, through the down-slanting deck, the gutted hold, and along its sheared edge before reaching another crack in her ribs. They could see beyond to the mast of a second ship that beckoned in the gloom. A third ship rested on its ribs to their right, topped by the remnants of a fourth. They'd entered a graveyard of ships: rusted iron, eaten cloth, and bloated wood.

Brysis swam forward under the shadows of masts, over splintered decks, and through gashed hulls. They weren't alone. The chitters and clicks of the magori sang out around them; the groans and hisses of undead surrounded them. Brysis ignored the larger vessels, the great ships and galleys, and instead flitted among the small dhows and fishing boats, staying hidden. Still, the undead and magori seemed to infest the place.

Finally, Brysis stopped. The graveyard ended at the edge of a broken seafloor separating the ships from a sizable mountain of rock with a prominent cave mouth. They'd run out of cover.

The magori with blood-splattered patterns on its carapace skittered across the seafloor. Every so often, it stopped at a hole and thrust its hands inside. It would often emerge empty handed, but finally it found something. A moray eel bit its hand and held on with a tight grip. Pulling the moray off would rip the magori's flesh on the eel's needlelike teeth. That would be too painful. Instead, the calm magori waited; sooner or later the eel would open its mouth to breathe again. Biting, for the moray, was suffocation.

The moray opened its mouth to inhale, and the magori grabbed it by the neck. In one swift motion, it bit the moray's head clean off and ate its prize. It didn't hear the movement behind it until it was too late. The armored dolphin slashed by, cutting the magori with a bladed fin. The magori shrieked, its wound opening deep, but the dolphin had already vanished. The magori shrieked again, alerting the others of danger.

Apoletta watched in revulsion as magori and undead crawled out from the holes and cracks in the broken ships and joined in pursuit of the intruder. Brysis appeared unfazed, however; Echo Fury was a fast swimmer and already safely away.

Brysis, Utharne, and Apoletta camouflaged themselves in water, turning into turbid hazes, and raced across the open field. Brine-Whisker kept pace alongside them, staying low to the seafloor. They arrived at the large cave mouth, seemingly undetected, and found the savaged remains of undead, magori, and a couple of Mahkwahb strewn about. Apoletta hoped Anhalstrax would recognize friend from foe.

The large cave mouth held a rotting galley. Beyond it lay a large tunnel, its walls crosshatched with claw marks. Inside the tunnel, the temperature grew warmer, and the water tasted rancid. Refuse from many broken ships littered the floor: snapped steering columns, broken masts, a myriad of sailors' possessions, and sometimes even their skeletal remains.

The three exchanged glances. Finally, the tunnel widened into a cavern, but barring their way was a large barricade of debris. Scavenged from the graveyard, the flotsam made a wide wall stretching across the cavern that rose to half the tunnel's height. It created a bottleneck that forced attackers through a narrow opening.

Suddenly, a giant dragon's head appeared from behind the battlement. The giant dragon opened her mouth to reveal a row of bloody teeth.

The companions cried out in unison.

"We're allies!" Apoletta cried.

"The Matriarch sent us!" Utharne said.

"Friends!" Brysis said.

Anhalstrax did not seem in a mood to listen. Her head lurched forward, spewing forth an inky black cloud that engulfed them and filled the tunnel. A bitter, barren cold overtook Apoletta, rattling her bones and infecting her with a heavy fatigue. She could not move; she could not think; she could barely see, her eyes blinking rapidly. She saw Utharne and Brysis grip themselves tightly, as though squeezing out the heat from their own bodies.

Only when Apoletta began to feel a little warmer did she realize that Anhalstrax was studying them with a fierce cobalt stare. The dragon had spared them, for the moment.

"P-p-please," Apoletta said, her teeth chattering. "M-M-Matriarch s-sent us-s."

Then, to Apoletta's surprise, Anhalstrax relaxed, and in doing so, looked suddenly spent, on the verge of collapse. Apoletta noted the damage wrought against her. Her yellow and green fringes were cut, torn, or missing entirely; burns scarred and twisted the edges of her mouth and the corners of her lips; strange patches of coral encrusted her wounds.

"Have you come to save me?" Anhalstrax asked, her voice surprisingly sweet and melodic.

Unfortunately, Apoletta, Utharne, and Brysis could only offer blank stares. Where could they start with their story? And how could they save a dragon from its foes?

"Ah, I see," Anhalstrax said. "You've come as my last witnesses, then."

Treasures ripped from the holds of the ships or dragged from other shipwrecks filled the magnificent, high-ceilinged cavern. The bounty included piles of coins in metal chests, a multitude of weapons scattered about, jewelry of elven and dwarven make, metal statues, silent figureheads of human maidens and minotaur chieftains, the gilded flanks of an elf swanship, perfect white-oak oars, engraved wheels, and even an iron boathouse of gnome crafts-manship. Artifacts from the surface crammed the cavern; some seemed ordinary and useless to a dragon, while others glittered with untold wealth.

Anhalstrax riveted their attention, above all. Her lilting voice, for all its beauty, weighed heavy with untold sadness. Whatever afflicted her was beyond Utharne's power to heal or help.

The companions related their purpose to the dragon, and in turn, Anhalstrax explained her plight. She told them of the attacks; while her frosty breath did little against the undead, she said, they fell easily to her claws and mouth. The magori, however, with their acidlike entrails and poisonous blood cost her dearly with every bite or talon swipe.

Apoletta could not help but notice the twisted burns on Anhalstrax's face.

When Utharne reached out to touch one of those crusting coral growths, Anhalstrax snaked away that segment of her body.

"Do not touch me there," she said. "I've seen the magori die horribly for that honor. It is a weapon the Mahkwahb and undead wizard employ, a sphere of coral that acts like a cancer."

"Undead wizard?" Apoletta asked, blanching.

"Yes. He wears the colors of the red moon, Lunitari, but his magics are blighted."

"What does this do? The coral, I mean," Utharne said.

"It eats at me," Anhalstrax said. "Devours me a little through my blood and wounds."

"Can you not stop it?" Brysis asked.

"No. I can only forestall the inevitable. It comes and goes. I wait for the sphere to attack, and I fight it off, but I grow weaker with each assault. At least my cold breath pains it. That pleases me."

Silence descended upon them a moment. Suddenly, Anhalstrax's head bolted up.

"I hear them moving outside. They will attack again, but . . . there's something else out there. You must leave!" she said, her tone suddenly urgent. "You don't have long. Behind that shield!" She indicated a giant iron ram plate that once adorned the prow of a minotaur ship. "You will find a passage leading far beyond here. Flee!"

"Could you not come with us?" Apoletta asked. "Surely you can shift form?"

"I cannot anymore, alas," Anhalstrax said. "Once infected by the coral, I lost that ability. I tried and almost died when the pain tore through me. The coral will not change with me. No. You go, flee, escape."

"We can't leave you," Brysis said.

By now, Apoletta could hear the magori and undead rustling outside the cavern. They did a poor job of sneaking about.

"You must!" Anhalstrax said.

"How do we stop the World Gash?" Utharne asked, stammering.

Anhalstrax appeared at a loss, as though the question were too great for so urgent a time. Finally, she pointed to the artifact of a great silver seal, partially hidden among the treasures. The artifact measured Apoletta's size and depicted the same tentacle-covered face found at the mouth of the God's Throat. Inscriptions wound their way around its edges.

"They are an ancient race," the dragon said quickly, "born before the elves, ogres, and humans learned how to master the oceans or remember their history in words. These squid-people, these eaters-of-minds, were not of this place, and for their cruelty to other living things, the gods vanquished them from here. You'll find your answers etched on that seal!"

Apoletta looked at the seal. "We cannot carry it."

"Then read it. Can you do that?"

"Yes!" Apoletta said, swimming over to the artifact.

"I will hold them off for as long as I can, but when I say 'escape,' I mean you should do so as swiftly as you can! Apoletta, listen to me!" Anhalstrax roared.

Apoletta, frightened, spun around to face the dragon.

"None of you will come to my aid," Anhalstrax said. "Do you understand?"

"Yes," Apoletta whispered, her heart pounding.

"Let my death be in sacrifice and service to Abbuku," Anhalstrax said.

The others nodded, not knowing how to respond.

"Very well," Anhalstrax said, with a nod to herself. "I will tell you this. If you wish to enter the World Gash, do not go through the sulfur clouds. There is an ancient well . . . the Dead Well. It is where I found this seal."

"I've heard of the Dead Well. But I was never able to find it," Brysis said.

"It is west of here. Find the whirlpool of sharks. They smell the death from the Well but cannot reach it." Anhalstrax looked to the cave mouth. "Hurry," she whispered. "The Dead Well is a maze, and accursed at that, but I have marked a safe passage through it with my claws. I hid the entrance beneath a thicket of thornweeds. Good luck to you all," Anhalstrax said. "And do not dare to stray from the path I marked!"

Apoletta swam to the silver seal and pushed engraved mahogany boards off it; they wafted slowly to the floor. The seal was old and battered, the silver depreciated of its original luster, but Apoletta could see and read the engravings easily enough.

Behind Apoletta, Brysis and Utharne cleared the way to the escape passage hidden behind the large ram plate. Brine-Whisker and Echo Fury swam around, preparing for a fight.

Her gaze riveted on the seal artifact, Apoletta ran her fingers across the engraving, marveling at the fine work. She recognized the language. "It is Sacayasse," she murmured. Sacayasse was one of the original languages of the elves when they were first learning to speak and communicate.

"They come in force!" Anhalstrax roared.

The companions turned in time to see Anhalstrax raise her foreclaws. The water at the barricade churned into a froth of thick bubbles. The underwater wave blocked the entrance; magori and undead threw themselves against the solid mass, but to no avail.

"Hurry!" Anhalstrax said.

Unfortunately, the wall did not impede all the undead. Several creatures with tattered cloaks for bodies slipped through it with ease. They crawled over Anhalstrax's body. Fearless Brine-Whisker charged forward, his blue light blazing on his brow. Even Anhalstrax seemed awestruck by Brine-Whisker's courage, for she did not protest.

Utharne, as well, swam forward, his arms raised. "Heed me, unhallowed! The Fisher King demands you submit or *flee!*" The gray dead scattered, swimming back through the wall.

"For this once," Anhalstrax said softly. "Thank you, Chosen of Abbuku."

Apoletta was focused on the ancient script. If the seal hailed from the age of the squid-people, then the writing did not. Elves wrote the words long after, she realized. Apoletta reached into her pouch and produced a pinch of salted sea wax mixed with soot.

"The words of the sea were strange to her, but in time she understood them as her own." The wax dissolved in Apoletta's fingers, and the words were hers to know. She ran her fingers over the script as she read, scarcely pausing to reflect on their significance. She slowly rotated, head over foot, following the script as it followed the curve of the seal. Utharne and Brysis gathered behind her, eager to understand the message.

"Enemies of our fathers, the primordial ones . . . squid-walkers of the deep . . . lords of ancient places," Apoletta muttered loud enough for her companions to hear. ". . . Be warned of their evil . . . feasters of flesh, brain, and thoughts . . . no evil is spared them. . . ."

"I cannot hold them!" Anhalstrax cried shrilly. With that, the churning waters fell away and a flood of magori, undead, and Mahkwahb descended upon the dragon. She spun and spiraled, smashing foes against walls, floor, and ceiling.

Despite their promises, the companions could not stand by. Abandoning the seal artifact, they swam forward to help Anhalstrax with their spells, their blades, and their lives even. The dragon, however, guessed their intentions; she motioned desperately, fashioning another wall of churning water between her and the companions, cutting them off from her plight.

"No!" Brysis screamed, but Utharne grabbed her by the shoulders.

"We promised," he said, his voice miserable.

Brysis and Utharne could only watch in horror as Anhalstrax fought the invaders. Apoletta forced herself to return to the reading. She stumbled across a familiar phrase.

"Utharne, Brysis, listen to this," she said. "To the unhallowed place they traveled, to their last bastion these peoples unnamed. Blessed by the shadow of the impaling throne, the twisted thorn, they turned sea to ash and opened doors that never ought to have been opened."

Turning toward the others, Apoletta caught a terrible glimpse of Anhalstrax. The dragon was fighting well, fighting to the last, her body covered in wounds.

Apoletta forced herself to look away. "The Impaling Throne . . . that is what we seek!"

"Flee!" Anhalstrax cried, at once louder and weaker than before. That's when the unmistakable roar of a second dragon tore through the waters and shook the walls. Apoletta knew that awful sound, as well as the primordial fear that accompanied it. Her mind screamed for her to run, yet she could not help but turn and watch the horror unfold.

A cloud of steam flooded through the cave mouth, shattering the battlement apart and engulfing Anhalstrax. The wall of water collapsed, and both Anhalstrax and her attackers screamed and screamed as something brought the water to boiling pitch.

The magori, the undead, and the Mahkwahb swarmed over Anhalstrax. Wartide and Zebulah, with the Legion Coral at their side, watched as their forces overwhelmed the dragon, uncertain as to why she'd cast a second battlement of water behind her. She'd effectively put her own back to the wall and cut off any room to maneuver.

Despite that, Wartide smiled grimly, readying his trident. "How often does one have the opportunity to fight a dragon?" he asked with a grin. "Tell the Legion Coral to stay. I don't want it killing my men again." He charged forward and yelled back at Zebulah. "To the victors go the dragon's horde!"

Wartide did not know whether Zebulah followed or not, nor did he care. He advanced on Anhalstrax, dancing around her, striking and moving away from her undulating, serpentine body. Only when a bolt of sizzling lightning struck the dragon did Wartide notice Zebulah floating off to the side, unleashing his spells. Anhalstrax was clearly dazed. Wartide used her confusion to his advantage, stabbing with his trident and weaving, stabbing and weaving.

Wartide fell into battle-lust. With Anhalstrax near death, Blazewight could finally take her. Only then would Blazewight emerge from his hiding place inside the ribs of a great ship.

With a realization that turned his blood to ice, Wartide turned around just in time to see the wall of steam emerge from the green murk of the tunnel mouth, scalding everything.

"Flee!" Anhalstrax roared, obviously trying to scare her attackers.

Wartide's master bellowed in return, his voice shaking the cave walls. Some of the Mahkwahb, magori, and undead turned to face their cruel, overeager master, too slowly it seemed. Others, Wartide among them, knew to try to escape the deadly cloud.

Only it was too late. Wartide felt the approaching heat burn into his back and draw blister bubbles to the surface of his skin. It wouldn't be long. The steam cloud would kill him.

Then, to Wartide's astonishment, Zebulah swam past him at amazing speed. Wartide recognized the spell that propelled the wizard. Zebulah grabbed Wartide's wrist and dragged them both to the extremities of the steam cloud. They screamed, as the searing pain peeled and instantly blistered their skin. But as the water wall dropped, Zebulah dragged Wartide to shelter amidst the dragon's vast horde of curios and valuables.

Apoletta, Brysis, and Utharne watched in horror as another dragon entered the cave. At least, Apoletta believed it to be another dragon. Ribbons of steam wreathed its body, and what glimpses they caught of its skin showed something strange and blackened and cracked. Even its claws seemed charcoaled. Wingtips, like the fins of a giant shark, rose in the steam before vanishing in the blur. Through the steam, filaments of red light shone through in jagged patterns. Its eyes likewise glowed red.

Apoletta felt a deep chill. She recognized the second dragon as the creature she had seen in Veloxua's thoughts.

The two dragons fought inside the steam cloud while undead, magori, and Mahkwahb fled or drifted, lifeless and ruined, their flesh scalded clean off.

Brysis grabbed Utharne's and Apoletta's arms. Numbed, Apoletta allowed Brysis to drag her to the passageway. Echo Fury and Brine-Whisker entered first, followed by Utharne. Only Brysis and Apoletta remained as a terrible snap filled their ears, followed by tearing noises. Brysis and Apoletta turned around to see a decapitated Anhalstrax tumble through the water like a limp ribbon. Her head followed a moment later.

Sickened, Apoletta was about to enter the tunnel when she spied a familiar red-robed figure. He had hidden in the treasure trove behind a fallen marble statue of a human warrior. Apoletta drifted a step forward before Brysis grabbed her arm.

"We need you," Brysis whispered urgently.

Apoletta nodded. "I know," she said. "He'll pay for this, I swear."

The two sea elves vanished into the darkness of the passageway before anyone spotted them.

Wartide watched Anhalstrax plummet, both her head and body striking the floor with muted thuds. For a moment, only Blazewight's beleaguered, raspy breaths filled the cave. Then the steam cloud seemed to shift and undulate and move.

"You have served me well," Blazewight said to no one in particular. "Withdraw from this place now. I will seal it until you return to retrieve its treasures for me."

"What of the wounded?" a Mahkwahb asked.

The question did not please the dragon. He turned on the dark sea elf, instantly engulfing him in the scalding cloud. The screams of pain were short lived.

"I will not be questioned!" Blazewight said, biting and snapping to punctuate his statement. The steam cloud moved back through the tunnel on its way outside.

Dutifully, the magori and undead withdrew, crawling and swimming as quickly as they could. Only the Mahkwahb lingered to attend to their wounded companions, dragging them along as best they could. Wartide watched Zebulah simply turn and leave; he swam after him, awkwardly keeping up.

Wartide smiled at Zebulah, who appeared confused by his own actions in saving Wartide earlier.

"You and I," Wartide said. "I guess we're friends."

Zebulah scowled.

"And I think you underestimate your importance in this situation," Wartide said.

Zebulah did not respond. Instead, they left the tunnel as one of Wartide's surviving lieutenants, Naranthil, swam up to join them. They had barely cleared the tunnel mouth when the cloud of steam surrounding Blazewight erupted in a red glow. A gout of flame surrounded by ribbons of steam gushed out from the cloud and struck the rocks over the cave's mouth. The action precipitated a cave-in; the tumbling rock crushed the survivors still trapped in the tunnel. A moment after the avalanche settled, a couple of the undead slipped through the boulders. They appeared none the worse for wear.

"I'll fetch a healer," the gaunt Naranthil said, leaving Wartide to rest on the ground.

The undead wizard watched impassively, his brow wrinkled.

Zebulah turned to Wartide and studied him,

"Patience, my friend," Wartide responded with a knowing smile, despite his injuries. "Patience." With that, Wartide fell unconscious.

Apoletta's energy was spent. Brysis sent Echo Fury to find the others. Within a few hours, Echo Fury had rounded up the survivors of the expedition.

The two groups embraced like long-lost friends, though sadly, one whale and its rider, Hopethorn, had not survived the attack. Neither had several Dargonesti and Dimernesti soldiers who valiantly stayed behind to protect the retreat. In all, seven sea elves and one whale died in the skirmish.

In a panic Apoletta went to search the remaining whales for her package. Captain Ornathius caught her gaze and touched a wrapped seaweed pack strapped to the flank of Salystra. Apoletta felt embarrassed for her selfishness, but relieved nonetheless.

"We must part ways," Apoletta told Captain Ornathius.

Apoletta met the cries of complaint, the questions, the refusals, and the stunned stares with motherly patience. She and Utharne explained how the size of the expedition had become a hindrance. Stealth was their greatest ally and wasn't possible with such a large force.

The only one who cheered was Arrowawk until Apoletta said, "Arrowawk, we need you most of all."

Arrowawk glowered at them. "What for?"

"Yes," Brysis asked. "What for?"

"My views," Utharne said, "are suspect? Yes, yes, suspect, that's the word. To the other Dimernesti, I mean. We need Arrowawk to be a second set of eyes, and to report what he sees."

"No, no! I lost three whales on this fool's errand. I ain't risking more."

"I can't force you," Utharne admitted.

"You're damn right about that!"

"But without you," Utharne said, "we fail our people. We fail the Speaker of the Sea."

Arrowawk opened his mouth then shut it. He opened it again, again saying nothing. "That's unfair," he replied finally.

"Yet it is the truth," Apoletta said. "If you accompany us and tell the others what you see, in earnest, then both the Dimernesti and Dargonesti will be in your debt."

Arrowawk's eyes narrowed. "This debt? It wouldn't include trading rights with your people?"

"Certainly," Apoletta said.

"And the brathnoc?"

Utharne sighed. "We'll discuss them later."

"Then I'm your elf, but I ain't lying for you."

"We're counting on it," Utharne responded. "We need your honesty."

"What about me? I refuse to leave your side," Captain Ornathius said brusquely.

"Captain, I need the expedition escorted safely to Dimernost," Apoletta explained.

"In truth, that isn't my concern," Ornathius said. "You are my concern, and I have already been remiss in my duties, letting you vanish from my sight. Forgive me, but I refuse. And do not order me to leave. I will not. Let Vanastra take the expedition to——"

"No!" Vanastra said, cutting off Ornathius. "Utharne is my responsibility. Where he goes, I follow."

Apoletta exchanged quick glances with Utharne and Brysis.

"Very well," Utharne said. "Briegan, you are now in charge of those we must leave behind."

"You may each bring two men," Apoletta told Ornathius and Vanastra.

"Bring the whales to safety," Utharne ordered Briegan. "The remaining soldiers will protect you. You and they are brothers now."

Briegan nodded. So did the soldiers. There was no longer suspicion between them. Even the attitude of the new soldiers from Watermere had softened. Everybody drank the same water, ate the same food, shared the same shelter, spilled blood in the same cause.

"Go to Dimernost," Utharne ordered. "Let nobody make you feel unwelcome there. You've earned your seats at our tables. Briegan will see to that."

Apoletta offered Slyphanous a sad look as she approached.

"I can guess. I'm not going with you, am I?" Slyphanous asked.

"I'm sorry, my friend," Apoletta said. "Where we go, we will need those skilled in spells or weaponry."

"Have you heard him sing? That might be his best weapon," Arrovawk said and added quickly, "No, I'm sorry, Slyphanous. I wish I could trade places with you." He offered Slyphanous a grin. "You bloody banshee of the seas."

Slyphanous nodded and bowed his head slightly. "I'll await your return," he said to Apoletta. "Please do return. Istar needs you, so settle this business with Zebulah."

With that, the others bade their quiet farewells and parted company without further thought. They quickly dispersed in the murky green. Nobody, save Apoletta, noticed the package that Ornathius carried on his back.

After Blazewight left, the waters cooled to tolerable levels. Wartide rested inside the bowl of a sunken caravel, upon a bed of silt and wood. His wounds had all but healed, but the exhaustion remained. He awoke when he sensed movement nearby. Naranthil waited, unwilling to disturb him.

"What is it?" Wartide asked.

"One of the undead that survived the cave-in, a wraith, saw three sea elves inside the dragon's cavern. Two were Dargonesti, one Dimernesti."

"Did one have long silver hair?"

"Yes."

"Did the avalanche bury them?"

"I sent him to check the cavern. A few magori were inside, dying, but nobody else. The wraith says there was a hidden passageway."

Wartide shifted position, smiling. "Do the magori know about the passage?"

"Not anymore," Naranthil said, returning his grin. "The wraith is one of ours. He fed upon the magori."

"Good," Wartide said. "You've done well. Tell the wraith to

keep his mouth shut. He'll be amply rewarded when we return to claim the dragon's horde for ourselves."

The lieutenant nodded. "What of the three sea elves?"

"Find out where the passage leads. Go west and take the Legion Coral with you. Thin their numbers, but leave the silver-haired one alive."

"The coral is too unpredictable. It may kill her as well."

Wartide closed his eyes, but his smile widened. "Have faith," he said. "Have faith that she'll die when we want her to."

CHAPTER
The Dead Well
13

Apoletta and her compatriots were only a few hours from the World Gash, with the ocean growing increasingly agitated. Sulfur tinged the water enough to irritate their eyes and gills. The temperature increased, and everything grew murkier, cutting visibility down from dozens of feet to mere inches. Their world was reduced to a thick soup. They could see no farther than the outstretched reach of their tridents. They heard sound as heavy and sluggish, thanks to the minerals in the water.

Were it not for Echo Fury and the two dart-lancers accompanying Ornathius, they would have been virtually blind. The dolphins swam in wedge formation ahead of the companions, listening for trouble. They also possessed an additional strategy since they'd rested long enough for Apoletta to study her spells and repeat the one she'd used on Veloxua to examine her thoughts. Rather than focus on one person, however, Apoletta used the spell in a novel way, communicating with Echo Fury and the dart-lancers.

Apoletta could not employ the spell for long and not if she was moving in the water, but as the dolphins sensed their surroundings, she was alerted to their perceptions.

After hours of traveling in such exhausting fashion, one of

the dart-lancers returned and assumed sea elf form. "Sharks," he whispered.

"Mahkwahb?" Brysis asked in a low tone.

"Not certain," the dart-lancer said. "They're all circling but moving strangely."

"Bring us within fifty feet," Apoletta said.

The dart-lancer shifted form again, metamorphosing into a war dolphin. He slowly swam ahead of the group, staying within sight. After a few long moments, he was rejoined by the second war dolphin and Echo Fury, who were circling back.

Apoletta reached for the familiar copper coin and cast her spell to perceive the dolphins' thoughts. She focused her listening until one shark, followed by another, swam through the sphere of her spell. She immediately understood why they seemed "strange."

"The sharks," Apoletta whispered. "They're half dead."

"What, you mean undead?" Brysis asked.

Apoletta shook her head. Not undead, she explained, but exhausted to the point of dying. They knew only to swim and swim until they died. That narrow circle of the ocean had become the sum territory of their existence. They'd forgotten the world beyond, as though they were cursed. And they weren't alone. Other fish were also swimming in the area, half dead.

Brysis asked if that meant they were in danger, but Apoletta did not know the answer. Perhaps the curse affected only simple-minded creatures since it hadn't affected Anhalstrax. Still, she warned the others to swim clear of the dying sharks.

The expedition floated down to the seafloor. The smell of death, the pungent aroma of exposed entrails, and the overpowering odor of decay sickened them. One of the Dimernesti spewed a cloud of vomit, and the others immediately swam away from the retching sea elf. The sharks would be attracted to anything they could stomach.

The refuse of death littered the ocean floor in the form of shark, fish, and other animal carcasses. Their bodies were desiccated and stringy; some showing bite marks where hungry sharks had ravaged them after death. The floating pieces of decaying creatures made the water too filthy to drink from, too filthy to breathe.

"Find the thornweeds," Apoletta said, nearly gagging.

"Keep watch for us," Brysis asked.

Apoletta, glad for the distraction, sent her thoughts out, searching. After a moment she sensed a strange, chaotic mind. Apoletta had never before imagined the mind of a magori, but the creature's violent, single-minded hunger for causing suffering and bedlam was unmistakable. Unfortunately, as she perceived the magori, it, too, perceived her. Apoletta saw herself through its senses, all vibration and electricity.

The magori screeched. Apoletta cried a warning in return. More screeches filled the waters.

Apoletta fumbled for a pouch and pulled forth a smaller bag and a candle too wet to light. It did not matter.

"And in that moment, Daydra discovered the ocean could be friend and foe alike!" Apoletta incanted, and the candle sparked to life with a small flame despite the wet wick. She spoke directly to the magori. "The sharks are a greater danger to you." A ball of light inside her stomach flared as she felt her fingers plucking at the spine of the magori.

The magori screeched again. Apoletta could no longer see it, but she felt the spell take affect. It went to attack the sharks, drawing some of its brethren away as well if Apoletta and her compatriots were lucky.

The companions raced across the seafloor, desperately searching for the thornweed patch, but carcasses carpeted the ground. Apoletta searched as well, listening in horror as the sounds of battle filled the water. She was at a disadvantage; the magori were blessed with sight unaffected by the filthy water. And it grew more difficult to see after the magori began filling the water with their mist.

Something above her moved, swimming hard and fast at her. The magori materialized out of nowhere, just inches away from slamming into her and crushing her skull under its weight. Ornathius tackled her, pushing her out of the creature's path. The magori struck the ground but immediately scrambled to its feet. Ornathius lunged with his trident. He severed several of the creature's eyestalks. The magori backpedaled into the mists, screaming.

"I told you I wouldn't leave you!" Ornathius declared, searching the gloom.

Apoletta nodded gratefully. She was busy concluding her spell, one begun right after the magori's attack. Four bolts of light leaped from her fingers and went flying into the gloom. The creature screeched again.

"Thank you!" Apoletta said at last.

A dolphin cried out. Apoletta recognized a summoning call.

"This way!" Ornathius said, moving toward the sound.

"No!" Apoletta said. "Utharne! Vanastra! They do not understand dolphin calls! We must find them."

Ornathius hesitated a moment. "First you!" he said.

"I will not leave them!"

"I have no intention of letting them die! Can you hear their thoughts?"

"Yes, I have one spell of that nature remaining."

"Then it'll be easier to cast it from a safe place, and escape afterwards!"

Apoletta fought her overwhelming concern for her friends, the panic and duty that confused her reasoning. Finally, she nodded.

Ornathius and Apoletta shifted into porpoise form, the warmth flooding their bodies and their enhanced senses pushing back the murk. They swam for the cries of the dart-lancer. Around them, magori struck at them with spears and sickles, but the two proved too quick to be caught easily. Of greater fortune, the sharks had stirred from their exhaustion and were attacking the magori, distracting them from the sea elves.

THE ALIEN SEA

The two sea elves skimmed the seafloor, past decaying and bloated corpses. The thornweed patch suddenly appeared; the dart-lancer cried out desperately. Apoletta saw the hole leading into darkness between the thick, thorn-covered vines.

Apoletta shifted out of her porpoise form and cast her last spell to hear nearby thoughts; she prayed her friends remained within its range. Ornathius, still as a porpoise, ordered the dart-lancer to go where she bade. The captain would stay behind to protect her.

". . . by the might of Abbuku. . . ." She heard Utharne as he cast his miracles.

She was nearly overwhelmed by the wild fight she was sensing. But she pointed toward where she sensed Utharne, and the dart-lancer burst away to his rescue.

More thoughts filtered into her consciousness: Brysis, searching for the voice to guide her to the thornweed patch; Echo Fury, delighting in the battle; Utharne, grateful for being rescued.

"Call them!" Apoletta said.

Ornathius cried out. Several magori also heard the chirps, but Apoletta saw that the growing swell of sharks had locked them in combat. The sea elves were a mere handful compared to the magori, but the sharks numbered dozens more than the magori. The thoughts of all the brutal creatures filled Apoletta's mind, swirling and clashing.

Brysis arrived a moment later, as did Echo Fury. Magori acid had half melted the dolphin's armor, but the toxin was diluted by the ocean water, and the dolphin would survive none the worse for wear. Apoletta focused on Arrovawk and located him next. She pointed to where she sensed his thoughts, and Brysis swam away with Echo Fury in tow.

Utharne, Brine-Whisker, and a Dimernesti soldier appeared next with the dart-lancer. Brysis and Echo Fury returned moments later with Arrovawk.

"Saved by a dolphin!" Arrovawk cried with indignant horror, but Apoletta could hear the gratitude in his thoughts.

Suddenly, before anyone could act, one magori screeched. Apoletta sensed thoughts filled with panic. The others joined in. Apoletta was nearly overwhelmed by their fear of something they called "slaughter coral." The magori were trying desperately to flee.

"Down, in the hole, now!" Apoletta shouted.

The second dart-lancer appeared, followed by Vanastra. They were swimming wildly, anxious to escape something. Apoletta cried out to tell them to follow the rest.

Something on the periphery of her spell caught Apoletta's attention; it was a new thought, one so alien that she nearly broke concentration. Whatever chased Vanastra and her companion was truly monstrous. Apoletta discerned hunger, avariciousness, and worse. Single-minded and determined, the thought represented a consuming, destructive force.

And where that thing passed, it absorbed and ruptured the other thoughts surrounding it. In moments, all Apoletta could hear were the agonized screams of the tortured dying. Apoletta dispelled her magic, flinging herself away from its fiery passage.

A sea otter and dolphin appeared out of the gloom, racing ahead of the sharks and magori that fled the approaching killing force. A sphere of latticework coral followed a moment later; it shot out lances that impaled shark and magori with hunger's indifference. The coral spread inside the wounds of its victims. Crusted growths raced over their bodies and exploded out of their mouths and eyes.

Horrified, the sea elves froze at the savage sight. The latticework sphere bore down on Vanastra and the dart-lancer. Both would die, so one acted. Vanastra shifted out of her form, and spun to face the coral, screaming for the others to turn and flee.

The coral barely slowed as it slammed into Vanastra. The lattice flowed over her body, hooking itself into her skin. Vanastra was smothered without even a scream. She struggled against it for bare moments before it swallowed her whole.

THE ALIEN SEA

Apoletta screamed in fury; Utharne grabbed her and pulled her into the hole behind them. "Shapeshift!" Utharne shouted, breaking into Apoletta's shock.

Almost immediately, everyone turned into porpoise, dolphin, or sea otter, and as one they vanished down the hole, into a carved cylindrical passageway. The coral sphere would not be denied, however. It, too, crashed into the hole and immediately began to spread across the curved wall, covering every surface with its poisonous touch.

The cylindrical passage was rough at its mouth, but on the inside it smoothed out to polished stone. Its surface appeared glasslike, and the strange flow of etchings that were inscribed upon every inch of its curved walls appeared to rest just below the surface of rock.

Apoletta and the others, however, had no time to ponder the strange phenomenon. They pushed ahead of the sphere, hurtling and colliding past one another. A horrible sound, like breaking ice floes, roared at their heels. Apoletta glanced back long enough to see the coral giving chase behind them, with its lances firing out and striking the walls.

She looked ahead, but the walls had seemingly vanished and with them, all rumblings of sound. She'd fallen in the dim-lit dark, diving down toward a great black maw. Apoletta suddenly understood why they called the place the Dead Well.

Faint light emanated from the luminescent inscriptions covering the wall, each letter naught but an ember, but together in strength they tempered the darkness. Were it not for the salt lichen and barnacles covering the walls, their glow would have been greater. Swimming down and down, Apoletta felt as though she were a torch dropped down a well, seeing only a narrow ring of stone as she plummeted.

The script covered all, except where great squid-faces stared back with impassive gazes, and where ledges with columned arcades swept the circumference of the well. On those ledges at spaced intervals were round tunnels.

Though they swam, Apoletta and her companions felt as though they were falling down the great shaft. And yet they swam hard, for the pit did little to slow the coral's continued advance. Behind them it spread across the walls, devouring lichen and barnacles, and casting the way they'd come into darkness. The barbs and lances continued to shoot out, filling the shaft with something like teeth, but none quite reached them.

Only at the last moment did Apoletta spy a large tunnel diverging to the side, its opening scratched by large claws. She yelled, drawing the attention of the others, and dived for the mouth. The others struggled behind. The coral raced for that tunnel as well.

They were too slow. The coral got there moments ahead of them. Apoletta veered away, squealing to warn the others. Coral spears shot out toward them. One impaled a dart-lancer through his fluke. The coral pinned him and raced across his flesh, calcifying and devouring him in moments. The others bolted in all directions, back to the safety of the pit's heart.

Apoletta darted around one spear, then another, in her bid to evade the coral. Something cut into her flipper. A hot flash of pain followed. She looked down in horror; a spear barb had nicked her, and the coral draped Anhalstrax's tunnel with its deadly crust. They swam deeper into the pit. Apoletta struggled to keep up with the others, but her body felt consumed by flames and sharp pain. Her vision grew blurry.

Suddenly, the shaft grew wider, almost doubling in diameter. They had entered a giant chamber. Rows of columns lined the circumference of the walls, resting upon a twenty-foot ledge. Above them the columns were stacked, forming rings upon rings of columns. The vast, dark chamber was lit only by the wan glow of hidden script.

Below, walkways extended from the walls to a dais in the center of the shaft. Three walkways remained intact; the fourth, a long one, was broken. They led to a large, circular platform, which appeared an altar of sorts; the stone was pitted and ancient.

Everyone slowed down and peered around.

The coral had yet to overtake them. Apoletta stared back. The coral had stopped at the mouth of the giant chamber. It remained in place, lances poking at the empty pit, no longer moving but neither withdrawing. It had apparently reached its limits.

Utharne, returning to sea elf form and flushing the water with the warmth of his change, swam up to her. "Apoletta, are you——?"

Apoletta jerked away. She abandoned her porpoise form, immediately doubling over. As had happened with Anhalstrax, the small tendrils of coral inside of her lacerated her flesh and ruptured her blood vessels. Apoletta screamed, feeling as though her mouth were filled with white-hot teeth trying to swallow her. She retched and fell unconscious.

"Apoletta?" a voice whispered.

Apoletta opened her iron-heavy lids to find Utharne watching her. They rested inside a smaller tunnel.

"Do not touch me!" Apoletta said, trying to back up against the curved wall. "I am infected." Her legs wouldn't budge, however. She gazed down; coral covered her legs up to her knees. The nausea returned; her right arm tingled. It lay heavy at her side, covered in a coral crust.

Brysis swam to her side. She laid a gentle hand on Apoletta's cheek and tried soothing her.

"You can't infect others," Utharne said. "We've already moved you."

Apoletta's heart sank. "It's inside me," she said, resigned, too tired to care and humbled by her defeat.

"We know," Brysis said.

"I tried to heal you. Cast protections against curses and poisons. I think—think, mind you—that I slowed its pace."

"But it will overtake me all the same."

Brysis averted her gaze, but Utharne kept his steady. "Maybe. Or maybe it'll stop."

Apoletta doubted that, but she didn't want to surrender hope either. "Perhaps," she said. "Where are we?"

"In smaller tunnels," Brysis said. "Away from the coral. It hasn't moved. The others are keeping an eye on it from a safe distance."

An awkward silence followed. Apoletta caught the glances that Utharne and Brysis exchanged. She hurt badly, and her body swelled with heat. It was difficult to think.

"What?" Apoletta finally managed to gasp. "What have you not said?"

"Tell her," Brysis said.

Utharne spoke reluctantly. "I can't heal away this sickness. But perhaps I could dispel the touch of chaos. In you, I mean. The coral creature is certainly a child of whim."

"What do you mean?" Apoletta asked.

"Perhaps I could reverse the effects of the coral. Reverse your petrifaction. But," Utharne added with a deep sigh, "I've spent my share of miracles. I may have the strength for one more miracle. But I don't have the right spell. I must pray to Abbuku."

"For how long?" Apoletta asked, a catch in her voice.

"I can only pray in two hour's time, when the sun crests the horizon. It's only then that Abbuku's grace will be upon me. It's only then that I may be renewed."

"Do I have that long to live?" Apoletta asked.

"I don't know," Utharne whispered. "Even if we reverse the effect of the coral, I do not know if that will be enough to heal you. And I will be spent. I'm sorry."

"Then we have no choice but to wait and pray," Apoletta

whispered. She set her head back upon the stone wall and immediately lost consciousness.

In her fevered delirium, Apoletta barely heard the voices around her. She could no longer distinguish real voices from those fond memories her mind insisted upon reliving. She was in Istar, young again by decades, with Zebulah, her husband.

"I'm growing old," Zebulah said, sitting on the ledge of the cavern's pool.

"We all grow old," Apoletta replied. She swam past the spiked sea turtle and set her jade trident on the ledge. With little effort, she pulled herself out of the water, trailing her wet silver hair.

"I'm aging faster. I'm catching up to my natural age," Zebulah said.

Apoletta studied him, running her hands through his graying hair. The light streaks seemed to be growing thicker. "What about the magic of the daggers?" she asked.

Zebulah reached to the side and produced two daggers with ivory shell handles. "I have drained them of their magics. I needed them to breathe water and cast spells of divination. They were useful in that respect. They aren't strong enough to prolong my life."

"Magic will return," Apoletta said. "You will see, my love."

"It's been gone for years now. I . . . I could be dead within two years."

"Hush, do not say that," Apoletta whispered. "The fact that magic remains trapped in some items is certainly hopeful. Have not your kind discovered the power to leech—?"

"Whatever trinkets I've robbed of magic, they haven't helped me to survive under water."

"We'll find a way," Apoletta whispered. "Until then, take my trident."

"I can't," Zebulah said.

"You must," Apoletta said. She leaned in and kissed Zebulah, handing him the weapon. "The magic within my trident will nurture you for a while."

Zebulah remained silent; he studied the trident in his hands, ashamed by what he felt he must do. Apoletta held on to him, even after her thoughts filled with water and Zebulah dissolved in her arms. Her feet turned to stone, the green flagstone of turtle shell. It spread through her body, racing for her brain. And it felt hot, the warmth threatening to conquer her.

Voices filtered in.

"It's ready!"

"Hurry! If it reaches her heart—"

"Hush! Let me concentrate."

Apoletta opened her eyes, catching a hazy glimpse of Utharne wreathed in blue fire. Her body felt heavy, as though she were out of water, submerged in stone. She wondered what that would be like, swimming through stone.

Suddenly, the weight dissolved, her body releasing its grip on her lungs, her heart, her soul. The heat vanished, and she shuddered at the sudden chill. Something light and delicate touched her skin. She felt buoyant again. Her body tingled with blood flow, and she welcomed her limbs back.

Apoletta shoved away the deliriums and fell back into her comfortable dreams.

"You did it!" she heard a female voice in the distance.

"Let her sleep," a male voice replied. "Let her sleep."

Apoletta mumbled her gratitude and drifted away.

❖ ❖ ◆ ❖ ❖

Brysis threw her arms around Utharne, catching him off guard. "You did it!" she exclaimed. She glanced at Apoletta, feeling absurdly hopeful.

"We all need rest, I fear."

"You more than others," Brysis replied. "Sleep. I will keep you safe."

Utharne smiled. It did not take much to encourage him . . . nor did it take much to fall asleep.

Wartide swam slowly, well behind the surviving magori, dark sea elves, and motley undead. The mood was somber. Their ranks had been devastated by the fight with the dragon and by their master's appearance. Still, at least among the magori, there was unquestioning support for Blazewight.

Wartide stretched his skin as he moved. One problem with getting healed was that his flesh felt tighter, no longer limber. As he moved, Naranthil swam up and told him that Zebulah was watching him carefully. Studying him, really.

"Zebulah knows I'm planning something," Wartide said. "But he's also preoccupied with that silver-haired Dargonesti . . . Apoletta."

"If I may ask," Naranthil asked cautiously. "You seem to want Apoletta to survive."

"Blazewight is scared," Wartide replied. "He fears Apoletta and her friends."

"What does a dragon have to fear of mortals?"

"History," Wartide said. "Who felled the dragon overlord Beryllinthranox? Mortals. Brynseldimer? Khellendros? Malystryx? Mortals, each time."

"But those were unusual circumstances. Gods acting through their agents."

"Perhaps. But Blazewight fears the same is happening with Apoletta, and he's certainly no overlord. He's a shell of what he once was. He means to grow more powerful but at our expense."

"So you're using Apoletta to distract him?" Naranthil said.

"Not I," Wartide said. "Apoletta and her band are doing the job for me."

"To what end?"

"You shall see," Wartide said. "Meanwhile, Blazewight has been forced to act precipitously, believing his time is short. He's preparing the rituals. Unfortunately for him, the Legion Coral has been stretched to its limits. It blocks their escape but cannot pursue any further."

"Why not?" Naranthil asked.

"Because, there's something inside the deep well that gives pause to even the deadly coral. It's a creature of such horror that even Blazewight dares not antagonize it."

Brysis occasionally pinched herself to stay awake. Ornathius, Apoletta, Arrovawk, and Utharne slept while the baby-faced dart-lancer named Timathian and the Dimernesti soldier, Brightshore, kept watch over the strange coral from their tunnel's mouth. Brine-Whisker also slept with his companion, while Echo Fury kept Brysis company.

Brysis stroked Echo Fury's head and watched his lids grow heavier.

Echo Fury's eyes snapped open in alert.

Brysis rose to stand, which in turn woke up both Ornathius and Arrovawk. Both were well trained, their hands seeking their blades almost instantly.

"What is it?" Ornathius whispered.

Brysis whispered back, "Echo Fury hears something." With that, she melted into the warmth of her porpoise form. With stronger hearing, it took her but a moment to locate the noise, but once she did, she changed back.

"Singing," Brysis hissed.

Arrovawk smirked.

THE ALIEN SEA

"Get Timathian and Brightshore back here," Brysis whispered.

"Why?" Ornathius asked, almost laughing. Only then did they hear a whisper in the darkness: a soft singing, halfway between a melodic hum and lullaby; something altogether beautiful and sad, like soft fingers strumming a long-abandoned spider's web.

"I've heard of only one thing that sings in dark places," Brysis whispered urgently. "Get the others, now!"

"Apoletta, wake up," a voice said.

Apoletta wanted to sleep longer, half remembering her beautiful dream. Her mother held her, cradling Apoletta's head on her chest and singing her a lullaby—a sad, beautiful melody. Apoletta stroked her mother's long, silky green hair. She could have stayed in that happy memory forever.

Apoletta mumbled in response, but something rested gently over her mouth. She awoke with a start, the dream vanishing. Brysis had her hand on Apoletta's lips, keeping her quiet. Apoletta shook her head, trying to awaken, but she still heard her mother's singing.

"What?" Apoletta asked, confused. The singing continued; it echoed in the catacombs around them. The voice wasn't from her dream.

"Shh," Brysis advised. "It's still quite far away. But just in case."

Apoletta sat up, draped by the heavy blanket. She checked her arms and legs; aside from some stiffness and tender flesh, the deadly coral had vanished.

"So Utharne did have one miracle left for me. The spell worked," Apoletta said, gratefully.

Brysis opened a jar carved from hollowed whalebone, scooped out some yellow caviar jelly, and rubbed the salve into Apoletta's skin. The pleasant floral aroma filled the water, and was followed by a flush of warmth in Apoletta's limbs.

"This should help your stiffness," Brysis said, "and improve the flow of blood."

The singing drifted, moving away. Brysis appeared relieved.

"What was that?" Apoletta asked.

Brysis explained. Quayseen had called it a Desolate Maiden, which are rare creatures only ever glimpsed by a handful of people. They were undead of sorts, with songs to hypnotize their victims and a thirst to drain their lives. Quayseen had once told her how a Desolate Maiden had hunted him in the ruins of a Dimernesti city. He had hidden, but she had always found him. He had never seen her, only heard her. He had said that the Desolate Maiden seemed to circle and circle—Brysis made a spiral pattern with her finger—honing in on her victims. "It is circling us now. We'll have to move soon," Brysis concluded. "According to the tales I heard, it's wiped out entire triton colonies."

"And where are the others?" Apoletta asked. "Utharne? Ornathius?"

"Keeping watch at the other passageways. Listening for the Desolate Maiden's approach. Trying to find another outlet. No luck yet, though. These catacombs are a maze. They stretch on for miles."

"Catacombs? For the squid-people?"

Brysis shrugged. "The niches and alcoves are empty. The fish ate them all, it seems. We haven't opened the tombs."

"Better we don't." Apoletta rested her head against the wall and sighed deeply. "Anhalstrax warned us not to leave the path."

"We didn't have much choice," Brysis replied. "And we do need another way out."

The two sat in silence, pondering their predicament. The coral blocked their escape, and the Desolate Maiden hampered their ability to explore the area.

"I have an idea," Apoletta said suddenly. She brought her head up. "Call the others," she said gravely. "I know how we can escape."

THE ALIEN SEA

Brysis moved through the cylindrical tunnels of the catacombs, past dark niches and the vile script of long-dead tongues. She kicked with her fluke, propelling herself through the corridors and threatening to career into walls at the angles and turns.

The melody seemed to surround her with the call of home: her mother's voice, her father's gentle whispers, Quayseen's laughter. The melody carried no words, only the glow of memories. Brysis struggled to ignore their temptation. When she heard her mother's voice, Brysis forced herself to remember waiting at her deathbed. When her father whispered, she thought of the squid that had killed him. Quayseen laughed, and she recalled his shocked face when an underwater avalanche carried him down into the World Gash.

For each promise made by the Desolate Maiden, Brysis reminded herself why the promise would never be honored.

Then Brysis turned a corner and froze at the sight before her.

The Desolate Maiden filled the corridor with her mass. She was a giant jellyfish whose white skin glowed softly. Where her organs once lay, floated the desiccated corpse of a decaying Dimernesti maiden with hollow eyes, wisps of fragile white hair, and a skull's smile. The Desolate Maiden beckoned Brysis with her outstretched hands, her limbs snaking and weaving just as the jellyfish's tentacles wove and snaked toward her.

The song the Desolate Maiden sang from afar did not compare to hearing it from her own lips up close. The song no longer merely promised home and a golden past. The song *was* home, the love of her mother, her father, her mentor—all embodied in that single being. Brysis watched, mesmerized, as the Maiden approached, growing more attractive with each step. Her flesh returned and her hair grew thick and green, revealing a living sea elf maiden of unrivaled beauty. The jellyfish itself dissolved into a soft radiance.

Brysis slipped free of her porpoise form and extended her hand to touch the Maiden. The Maiden, in turn, reached for Brysis with a tendril of soft light. They were inches away from one another when something struck Brysis hard, jarring her from her fantasy. Apoletta had flown out from the corridor and slammed into Brysis, knocking the breath from both of them.

The illusion vanished; the Desolate Maiden was no longer beautiful or alive. She shrieked, her meal interrupted; as the Maiden lurched forward, a voice filled the corridor.

"Heed me, unhallowed! The Fisher King demands you submit or *flee!*"

Utharne floated in a corridor behind the Desolate Maiden. His arms were outstretched, and Brine-Whisker was at his side with a flame lit on his brow.

The Desolate Maiden, appearing unmoved by the spectacle, turned on Utharne. She swam at him and Brine-Whisker, her melody still spilling from her lips. Utharne turned and swam away, his companion by his side. The Desolate Maiden gave chase.

"Are you hurt?" Apoletta asked Brysis, swimming after Utharne and the Desolate Maiden.

"Embarrassed!" Brysis said, following her, "but unhurt. Tell me this is working!"

"It's working!" Apoletta replied.

Brysis's shoulder throbbed from where Apoletta had struck her, but she continued swimming with all her strength. A moment later, as they approached the corner of an intersecting tunnel, Echo Fury appeared. He'd spotted the glow of the Desolate Maiden as it careened off the glassy walls.

"Don't get too close," Brysis cried out in warning.

Ahead of them, however, Utharne could be heard screaming in pain.

Apoletta, Echo Fury, and Brysis burst into a spherical chamber that measured forty feet in diameter, with tunnels radiating out from it in all directions. The trio arrived just in time to see the

Desolate Maiden, having caught Utharne by the ankle with her ghostly tentacle, pulling him toward her. Utharne writhed in pain, his face pinched as he fought strenuously.

Brine-Whisker darted around the Desolate Maiden, trying to strike her while avoiding her flailing limbs. Echo Fury lunged at the foul creature and struck her tentacle with his bladed fin. Apoletta cast her remaining spell, striking the Desolate Maiden with four arcane missiles, while Brysis drew her rapier and slashed at the Maiden's tentacles.

Echo Fury's wound forced the Maiden to release Utharne; the creature seemed easily enraged and easily distracted.

Utharne and Brine-Whisker scrambled to the safety of a tunnel. Their plan relied on quick-strike tactics. None of them could afford to stand their ground and fight.

"The temple!" Apoletta instructed Echo Fury.

Echo Fury darted away, using his voice and skill to navigate the tunnels. He disappeared down one of the corridors; Apoletta and Brysis turned into porpoises and chased after their dolphin compatriot. The Maiden swallowed the bait and raced after them.

The chase taxed them, however. Apoletta ached, her body protesting and her mind numb. It was bad enough that she'd only just recovered from the coral's petrifying effects, but all her spells had been exhausted and, with them, her last reservoir of strength. Still, they had only one opportunity to defeat the Desolate Maiden, and Apoletta dug deep for energy.

Echo Fury swam fast; Apoletta and Brysis were equally nimble. They darted in and out of corridors, barely catching sight of the dolphin's fluke as it vanished down passageways. Apoletta felt hopelessly lost, and she suspected the same of Brysis. Still they raced, the Desolate Maiden moving behind them in frightening spurts. But the Maiden slowed at the turns, and while fast, she also proved clumsy. Each time the Maiden seemed inches from grab-bing their tails, Echo Fury whirled in a fresh direction, and the two porpoises navigated the corners with greater precision.

Apoletta wondered how—and if ever—the drama would end. The corridor opened into the temple chamber. The walls peeled away, the columns flashed by them, and they swam upward, past the platform and its three surviving walkways. Apoletta cried out, warning the others that the Desolate Maiden had doubled back on them.

In the open water, the Maiden made up for lost ground, bearing down on the three swimmers.

"A little more!" Apoletta urged, horrified. More prayerfully, she added, "Please let this work!"

Echo Fury, Brysis, and Apoletta dived straight for the shaft encrusted with coral. The Desolate Maiden closed to within yards . . . then feet. They swam past the coral lances, skirting as close to them as possible.

"Now!" Apoletta chirped.

Feet became inches.

The three dived sharply away from the coral. Several lances shot outward to spear them but missed. The Desolate Maiden abruptly shifted direction, her tentacles grabbing the easier target: the coral. Her song filled the waters, and the coral in her grip disintegrated.

Cautiously, Apoletta, Brysis, and Echo Fury slowed to watch the struggle. The three were trapped between the Desolate Maiden and the next ledge, where needlelike teeth of coral waited in the narrowed gap. It appeared as though their two adversaries had found each other's toxic embrace. As Apoletta suspected, the living coral proved to be an irresistible meal of opportunity for the undead creature.

The coral lanced the Desolate Maiden with its spears, but the Maiden sucked the life from whatever touched her, preventing the coral from petrifying her. Apoletta watched in grim fascination as the Desolate Maiden's touch wiped out huge swaths of the crust along the walls. The coral retreated, retracting on itself while stabbing out futilely with sharp fingers that instantly died but would cut whomever they brushed, nonetheless.

Apoletta hugged the opposite wall and swam in a very wide arc around the Desolate Maiden, bringing her within striking distance of the lances. Fortunately, the coral pulled away, trying to escape, and the Desolate Maiden drank her fill of the coral. Apoletta and her friends were ignored. Arrovawk, Utharne, and the others arrived in time to see the Desolate Maiden chasing after the coral as it retreated. They followed at a distance.

In moments, the crust withdrew from over the corridor's large mouth, revealing the clawed rim; the Desolate Maiden still voraciously pursued the coral. The way stood clear, though for how long, no one could know.

The expedition darted for Anhalstrax's tunnel and swam through its wide passages as hard and as fast as they could.

Neither the Desolate Maiden nor the killing coral followed.

CHAPTER
The World Gash
14

Apoletta and the others thought they would be glad to leave behind the Dead Well. On tasting the sulfur-laden waters, feeling the near-infernal heat, and entering the vicinity of the World Gash, however, they were instilled with terrible doubts.

The crumbling cliff side from which they emerged from the Dead Well revealed a truly alien sea.

The ocean was dying . . . and dying painfully. The World Gash had collapsed the seafloor into a pit several miles deep. Mineral particles choked the turbid water, and while they could breathe, it was only with difficulty. Occasionally, Utharne purified the immediate waters through minor miracles, allowing the expedition to draw clean breaths. The small pockets of cleansed water didn't last for more than a few breaths before their taste again turned strange.

Near the cliff tops where they emerged, Apoletta and her compatriots were close enough to see the stormlike ash clouds. She'd never seen near-perfect clouds under water, could never have imagined particles lying in such a state of absolute balance. Once, Brysis supposed the heat from the volcanic fields below and the water's salinity created those conditions, but Apoletta had little doubt that was false. The Impaling Throne shaped the seafloor and waters of the World Gash, according to the silver seal, and it likely kept the underwater clouds in perfect form and suspension.

After the expedition had spent a moment in stunned awe of their surroundings, they set about swimming down, closer to the seafloor some miles below them. Brysis insisted that the waters tasted less foul deeper down, with the storm clouds above drawing the poisons into them and out of the World Gash. They traveled in silence through the gray waters.

The waters did indeed improve, if only barely. It also grew warmer. Brysis advised them to be careful not to overexert themselves. Water stole heat from the body faster than air. That also meant when the water proved too hot, it trapped warmth inside the body and exhausted the swimmer with heatstroke. The deepwater Dargonesti were in far greater danger of that exertion than the shallow-water Dimernesti.

Because of the turbidity, it grew more difficult for the elves to see. They traveled close together, wary of anything and everything in the thick haze. Finally, Apoletta and the others realized they could see more easily. The waters had grown lighter.

"If Solinari's silver light touches the Yawning Deep," Brysis said, "so, too, does Lunitari's red glow."

The nimbus was indeed crimson, but the others didn't realize Brysis spoke facetiously until they saw the volcanic fields covering the seafloor; they spewed their poisons into the water and heated it to uncomfortable levels. The magma flows, bloody veins on the black and cracked landscape, flickered through the haze of rising steam. Water and fire met, twisting the rivers of magma into tortured glass and obsidian.

The expedition had seen all they cared to see for one day. They settled upon the wide ledge of a great hill that rose three hundred feet above the seafloor. The hill was likely once a section of cliff that crumbled away as the World Gash expanded.

Apoletta took first watch with Utharne. She studied her spells while he read his scriptures. The others slept deeply. Finally, Apoletta put her book down.

"Do you wish to talk?" Apoletta asked Utharne.

"No. Perhaps." He looked up from his reading. "I can't find it," he said.

"What?" Apoletta asked. She moved closer to him.

"This place. I can't find where this place fits. In the scriptures, I mean."

"I still don't understand."

Utharne handed her a thick volume of treated vellum bound in turtle hide. "Where?" Utharne said. "Where is it written that these places exist? That they must exist? That the gods created them to teach us some lesson?" He indicated the World Gash. "They talk of blessed places, beyond this life, but why aren't any of these blessed places here now?"

Apoletta remained quiet, simply listening.

"The World Gash isn't in there," Utharne said, motioning to the book. "It isn't in the scriptures. The places of promise are, but no mention of the places of misery. No mention that this is foretold. And do you know why? Because the gods did not foresee this! It's almost as though the gods have lost control. Over their own creation, I mean. They promise us paradise in an afterworld because they can't make promises for this one."

"You cannot believe that," Apoletta said as gently as she could.

"I don't know what to believe. How can they allow such evil in this world?"

"I do not know. But maybe we are intended to fight evil, as part of our lesson."

"Perhaps," Utharne said, his voice subdued. "But I once measured my faith by this book's weight. I questioned this book. I questioned myself. And in seeking answers, I found myself. Now this place, everything I've seen, throws my questions and answers into turmoil."

Apoletta nodded. "I'm sorry," she said. "I understand."

Utharne stared out across the tortured vista.

Everyone awoke, uncertain if it was morning or evening. The perpetual red-orange dusk persisted, and they'd lost track of day and night. They continued on their way, heading for the heart of the World Gash, with Brysis as their able guide.

They had little food left, and the plentiful game was gone. Utharne took to purifying the corpses of the fish they found, but even his miracles could not shake the taste of death from their flesh. It did not matter. They had lost their appetites. Still, Brysis and Arrovawk caught carrion-eating crabs when they could, to nurture their strength.

Through the first day, until they found a mountainous pile of stones to rest upon, the companions saw sights that would forever haunt them: a slow, persistent rain of dead fish; fields of skeletons and corpses being picked clean by legions of carrion crabs and red-krill clouds; landscapes sculpted of black volcanic glass.

The ghastly panorama worsened on the second day. The seafloor ruptured. Trapped steam and giant gas bubbles drifted up through the cracks. The companions raced to escape the billowing gas that suddenly materialized and rose for hundreds of feet above them. It blocked their way and seemingly extended for miles. The water spiked in temperature. By the time the companions fled the area, their skins were cooked and dry.

More such eruptions hampered their travels, but they were warned in advance by Brine-Whisker and Echo Fury, who were able to sense the unnatural events before they occurred.

The second day became the third, then the fourth. The members of the expedition felt numb with exhaustion; sleep was no respite, for it was as though they traveled through the World Gash in their dreams and awoke to discover they must keep going.

Finally, Brysis and Echo Fury returned from a scouting foray to announce something troubling ahead. They were guided to a trench that was no more than a dozen feet across. They did not know its length, but it seemed like all the other cracks in the glassy seafloor. It could extend over dozens of miles, for all they knew.

Carefully, they leaned over to study the furrow and discovered that black ink filled that particular trench. Unlike squid's ink, which dissolved into a fine cloud, it appeared to be liquid of a different viscosity. It was thicker, and while its surface misted and roiled, it kept its form; it did not spread, dissipate, or diffuse. In fact, it appeared to flow, a dark current that was colder and more shadowy than the surrounding waters.

Apoletta and Utharne exchanged knowing glances. The ink looked similar to that which spilled from Veloxua's eyes and mouth. Brysis nodded, sharing their thoughts and suspicions.

"Best to avoid it," Apoletta said.

"Actually, we finally have a clear direction," Brysis said.

"I understand," Apoletta said. "The darkness flows from somewhere. We must follow it back to its source."

Brysis nodded. "Perhaps we will find what feeds it."

"Will this take us into the heart? Of the World Gash, I mean," Utharne asked.

Brysis traced the path of the trench with her eyes as it vanished into gloom. "I believe so, yes."

"Wonderful," Utharne muttered. "I suggest we bed for the night."

"Is it night?" Arrovawk said, grumbling. "Can't tell a damn thing down here."

"Agreed," Apoletta said. "Let's get away from the trench, though. I do not trust this place."

"Get some rest," Brysis said. "Tomorrow's bound to be difficult."

"Isn't every day?" Arrovawk replied.

THE ALIEN SEA

The next morning—or what passed for morning in the World Gash—the companions rose, ate enough crab meat to silence their hunger, and continued on their way through the broken seascape.

A few hours into their journey, the waters grew increasingly turbid, and it was more difficult to breathe. Their eyes and gills stung. Brysis pointed to the soft-looking gray silt that covered the volcanic glass and obsidian ground.

"Stay clear of the bottom," she instructed. "Don't disturb the ash, or you will suffocate."

A thick layer of volcanic ash covered the seafloor. The waters were increasingly acidic and salty.

For safety's sake, the group rose well above the seafloor to avoid agitating the ashen sediment into an abrasive cloud. The ground vanished into the mists below, though occasionally Brysis dived down to check the path of the trench. One time, she came back and advised them.

"Sink carefully," she instructed. "No kicking. Use the air in your lungs to control your descent."

"What is it?" Apoletta asked.

"I want to show you something," she said before dropping down and vanishing.

The others followed, breathing out enough air to sink slowly to the bottom. Even Echo Fury swam carefully, though Utharne held Brine-Whisker to stop his eager companion from darting away.

Thick layers of ash covered the seafloor, rendering it indistinct.

"What are those mounds?" Utharne asked, pointing to dozens of knolls.

"That's what I wanted you to see," Brysis said. "Don't follow me." Brysis dropped farther, floating above the ash-covered mound and kicking lightly. A small gray cloud blossomed. Brysis waited patiently until the ash settled again, revealing a patch of what lay beneath.

A glassy, white eye surrounded by blue-gray skin stared at them. It didn't blink, nor did it focus on anyone specifically. It merely stared, the life long gone from its gaze.

"It's a whale," Apoletta said. She gazed at the other mounds. "All of them?" she asked in shock.

"I count dozens more," Brysis said. She floated up. "All of this. This entire place is an abattoir. It's not a graveyard; it's more a mass grave." She looked to Arrovawk. "I was never trying to be arrogant—in Dimernost. But how do you explain this? How do you tell others what you've seen when it is so fantastical?"

Arrovawk said nothing. He studied the mounds, his eyes darting from one to another. "You're wrong," he said, finally.

Brysis stared at him, her face robbed of expression.

"I count over a hundred mounds," Arrovawk replied. "It isn't just one pod that died here."

Apoletta looked to Utharne, but his eyes were closed, his mouth moving in prayer. He was offering the pods their last rites, she realized, having seen him do the same in the cave with Maleanki. Regardless of his crisis of faith, Utharne could not help but play the priest. To Apoletta, that showed true faith—the power to believe even when riddled with doubt.

Brysis signaled them to rise up when Echo Fury poked her.

"What—?" Ornathius was about to ask, but Brysis interrupted him with an outstretched finger.

Brysis placed another finger over her lips, tapped her ears, and pointed to Echo Fury. Echo Fury heard something nearby, something close enough that it might be listening to them. Everyone waited.

Brysis's eyes widened. Apoletta heard it next; the mad chitter of the magori. It came from the shadow-filling trench underneath them. Brysis pointed up urgently. Everyone swam furiously in that direction.

Apoletta cast her spell to hear thoughts. Although the trench was well outside her reach, nothing seemed to have followed them.

"The magori are large," the dart-lancer, Timathian, said in a low voice. "How could they fit in that narrow trench?"

"The trench is only narrow at the top," Brysis responded. "Beneath the lip, it widens."

"Right," Arrovawk responded. "That means maybe they ain't chasing us now because—"

"Because they're trying to find a way around," Utharne said.

"We have to assume the worst. We have to continue moving," Apoletta said.

"Away from the trench," Brysis said.

Apoletta nodded. "A wise suggestion. Lead on, Brysis."

With an appreciative nod, Brysis led the companions a mile north before veering west again. Everyone remained quiet, fearful of the magori, afraid of what new horrors they might find.

Two long hours into the journey, the sky above their heads lit with a ghostly flash. Another flash followed. Brysis reappeared frantically through the gloom.

"Dive!" she screamed and promptly vanished below. They followed without hesitation, diving through the murk and coming upon the seafloor within moments.

Twisted ropes of black magma crust scarred the ground, but no ash covered the area . . . at least, not until the first snowflakes of gray appeared. Ash was falling from above in lazy drifts, and more flashes lit the heavens.

Brysis swam around erratically, looking for . . . something.

"What's happening?" Utharne asked.

"Ash fall!" Brysis said. "We need shelter now!"

The companions separated briefly, swimming far enough apart to lose sight of one another. Finally, Brightshore called out.

They found him hovering above a rent in the ground. The fissure measured several yards across before it stopped.

"We'll suffocate in there!" Brysis said. She brushed the growing ash from her shoulders. The ash burned only when it lingered too long on the skin.

"No," Brightshore said. He pointed to the edge of the fissure, which formed a tunnel.

"No more bloody tunnels!" Arrovawk growled, but everyone ignored him. The ash fall grew heavier. It became increasingly difficult to see and even more so to breathe.

"Wait here!" Brysis said. She turned into a porpoise and swam into the fissure. Echo Fury followed.

A moment passed, then another. Utharne cast his miracles, purifying the water around them, but the snow increased in volume, cutting visibility to a few feet. The companions moved constantly, trying to brush the burning ash from their skins. Finally, Brysis returned and chirped.

"Follow her!" Apoletta cried. "Hurry!"

Brysis reentered the crevice, and the others followed on her fluke. They entered the dark tunnel with its broken, jagged walls, away from the ash fall. The fissure was deep and warm, though its walls narrowed thirty feet down. Below that, only a child could slip through. The tunnel itself continued forward, thinning at points, expanding at others.

Brysis returned to her sea elf body. "Where's Echo Fury?" Apoletta asked.

"Further inside. Exploring," Brysis said.

"What's happening outside? With the ash, I mean. And those flashes?" Utharne asked.

"The flashes were lightning. From the ash cloud."

"Underwater lightning?" Timathian asked. "How is that possible?"

"The clouds aren't natural," Brysis said. "Nothing makes sense here. Abbuku's laws are upturned."

Apoletta shot Utharne a glance, but he said nothing.

"Then are we safe here?" Ornathius asked.

"For now," Brysis said. She motioned to the strange lichenlike growths on the wall. "We're in a magma fissure. It's been dormant long enough for life to start growing back. As for the tunnel. . . ." Brysis trailed off.

"What is it?" Apoletta asked.

"Well. We've encountered, what? Five or six trenches thus far?"

"At least," Apoletta replied. "Formed by the collapse of the seafloor."

"I'm not so sure," Brysis replied. "They all seem to point in the same direction. West."

Apoletta thought about that a moment. "So they radiate from a common point?" she asked.

Brysis nodded. "Whatever's happened here," she said, "it's because something happened to the west. At the heart of the Gash."

"So what do we do?" Ornathius asked. "Wait for the ash to stop falling?"

"We don't know how long that'll take," Apoletta replied.

"Let's wait for Echo Fury to return," Brysis said. "Discover what he's learned."

Echo Fury returned after two hours. During that time the ash fell unabated, though little of it reached them. Some of the companions slept where they floated, while others waited patiently. Apoletta focused on her spells. Finally, they heard the war dolphin's bark.

According to Echo Fury, the fissure not only continued, but it widened considerably. They followed Echo Fury deeper into the tunnel, finding that it not only widened, but that it sometimes rose up, exposing itself to the seafloor. In those patches, the ashen snow fell heavily, forcing the companions to dart across the open veins until the fissure submerged once more and they could continue deeper into the darkness.

CHAPTER
City of the Blood Shoal
15

The ash continued falling. The companions swam until exhaustion forced them into a troubled sleep. They awoke with no sense of the time that had passed. Throughout the journey the tunnel remained true and straight, though it did breach the surface repeatedly. At one juncture of exposed tunnel, they discovered the disposed remains of large fish. At another, they hid as a patrol of undead zombies passed overhead.

After another hard day's travel, the companions decided to rest. Unable to sleep, both Brysis and Echo Fury left to scout ahead and to hunt for food. Everyone was tired of crab.

Apoletta had barely fallen asleep when someone gently nudged her. She opened her eyes and found Brysis staring at her.

"Anything?" Apoletta asked, stirring quickly.

"Perhaps everything," Brysis whispered urgently. "I found a city."

Apoletta had never imagined a city like the one before her, a city built in descending depths rather than height. Like the Dead Well, it was a gigantic cylindrical shaft that had been excavated into the ground, with a diameter of more than five hundred feet. Where a coral plug sealed the Dead Well to the outside ocean, the city's roof opened freely to the sea above; more significantly, the sky above the city was clean and free of sediment. In fact, the city's waters seemed rich in fish and wild groves of seaweed.

The gigantic shaft contained rings of ledges, a hundred feet wide, with ancient buildings stacked upon them. They ranged in size and importance, with temples, apartments, recessed amphitheatres, warehouses, palaces, and shops all fighting for space upon the crowded shelves. The builders of the city had carved the palaces and temples flush with the barrel walls; their interiors likely penetrated far into the rock itself. Such important buildings bore pilaster entrances, columned fronts, and pediment roofs.

The minor buildings appeared strange indeed, as though someone had constructed them with melting wax. Walls curved into one another with few sharp edges, and their roofs rose like dollops of cream. Many bore the ravages of time, their walls crumbling and their roofs collapsed upon their interiors. Age had sheared away some ledge segments, burying the shelves below the time-worn ledges under rubble and debris.

In those places where no buildings occupied the walls, dark windows and tunnel mouths suggested a labyrinthine city stretching far into the rock.

Perhaps the most distinct feature of all, however, was the large trench that bisected the shaft. At one time, the shaft must have been pristine and perfectly cylindrical. Something must have happened, however, to shatter the very seafloor. The trench cut across the seafloor and across the shaft, dividing the city in half and sending out a spider's web of smaller fissures and rents. The trench looked like a jagged sword stroke cut down the shaft's length, slicing a deep cavity into the surrounding seafloor.

The companions were in a crevice just outside the shaft. As they stared at the vista and crowded about their tunnel's edge, Brysis nudged Apoletta and pointed down the trench.

Apoletta glanced down and saw a world lost in shadow, lost in ink. Writhing, boiling darkness filled the trench, occasionally lashing out like wild lightning to snap against the cliff wall. Apoletta followed the oily river that flowed in the trench and realized that upon reaching the shaft it appeared to cascade over the edge.

No, she realized with a start, it was the other way around. The darkness flowed upward from the shaft, over the lip and into the trench.

"By the gods," Ornathius whispered. "What is this place?"

"Home," Utharne responded. Everyone turned to look at him, but he pointed out. "To them, I mean."

Everyone followed Utharne's gaze to the specklike forms of the magori and dark sea elves who swarmed around the top of the shaft. They ruled the domain. It was their home.

Everyone elected to remain deep inside the tunnel, well away from the trench leading to the shaft city. At first, they could not sleep; their terrified minds raced as they tried to fathom the World Gash. They had traveled far, endured many horrors, and beheld an entire city of shadows and evil whose existence had been lost to history.

Utharne loathed the place. He railed against its builders, the squid-people, the eaters of thoughts. Everything they built despoiled the seafloor and left behind scars that would never heal. They had violated nature itself. Arrowawk agreed then unwisely mentioned the dwarves as equal culprits, an accusation that drove Utharne into silence.

After that, nobody felt like talking. Everyone lay quietly and let sleep slowly overtake them. Apoletta bade Timathian to keep watch, and Timathian complied.

Apoletta was grateful for Ornathius's support and protection; she felt guilty for the betrayal she had planned. What she had to do, however, she had to do alone. She would not jeopardize anyone else's life in that gambit.

So, quietly, she found the pack Ornathius had carried for her, near where he was sleeping, and shouldered the heavy burden. She silently bade her friends farewell and headed for the tunnel's mouth, where Timathian was stationed. He had yet to notice her, so she blurred her outline, as she'd done as a child, to conceal herself further.

Apoletta removed a small ball of wax from her pouch and whispered, "And Daydra marveled at the jester dolphins as they mimicked her calls." The warmth in her belly pulsed and ebbed, and she felt the required kernel of heat rise into her throat.

With that, Apoletta allowed a small whisper to slip from her lips, one that carried past Timathian on the kernel of magic. He thought he heard movement closer to the tunnel's mouth—a phantom noise that blossomed from the kernel—and moved forward to investigate. Apoletta moved with him until she found a small crevice in the wall. He swam less than a dozen feet ahead of her before pausing. She slipped inside the crevice. Timathian returned, satisfied he had heard nothing important, and swam past her.

Apoletta waited until he was gone; then she approached the tunnel's mouth. With a deep sigh, she stepped out into the trench and swam against the oily flow toward the city.

The Mahkwahb fisherman fished alone. He hunted with a small javelin and a net from his niche in the ruins of the ledge, giving chase to a yellowtail diver that would feed his family for a week. The large fish darted through the gaps of the fallen walls, evading his attempts at spearing it. Finally, he chased it around a corner and nearly ran into someone.

In his surprise he dropped his net and lowered his javelin for a moment—but only a moment. The "someone" was another sea elf—a Dargonesti with pale skin and long silver hair. The Mahkwahb snarled and raised his weapon, but the sea elf proved quicker, her spell at the ready. Light struck him, the kaleidoscope of colors stunning him with their blinding hues. By the time he had recovered, he found a dagger at his throat.

"Annoy me and I'll pry open your throat," she hissed. "If I am found, you will die first."

The Mahkwahb stopped moving.

"Zebulah," she said. "Where is he?"

Someone jostled Utharne. He opened his eyes in time to see Ornathius move past him, pushing everyone awake.

"Apoletta is gone," Ornathius said.

"What?" Brysis cried. "Gone where?"

"Who was on guard?" Utharne asked, jolted into action.

"I was," Timathian said miserably. "But I didn't see her go by me."

"I find it unlikely she'd return back the way we came," Ornathius said. "She must have slipped past you! Were you asleep?"

"No!" Timathian protested. "I was awake, I swear!"

"Did Echo Fury sense anything?" Utharne asked. "Dolphins stay half awake, don't they?"

Brysis shook her head. "Echo Fury sleeps fully. It's his elf nature." She turned to Timathian. "Did you notice anything out of the ordinary last night?" Brysis said. "Anything strange?"

"Anything to make you leave your post?" Utharne asked gently.

"No," Timathian said. "Wait, yes! At one point I heard a faint noise near the mouth of the cave. I went to investigate."

"Show us," Brysis said.

As the companions followed Timathian, Ornathius grabbed Utharne by the arm, pulling him back. "Something is missing,"

Ornathius whispered. "Apoletta entrusted me with a package. It was why she sent Slyphanous to Istar . . . to retrieve this package."

"What's inside it?" Utharne asked.

"I don't know! But she said to guard it with my life. She said it was more important than her own safety, if I were to choose between her and it."

Just then, Brysis called out.

Utharne and Ornathius found everyone hovering around Brysis, who was inspecting a small niche in the tunnel.

"She hid here," Brysis said. "Likely distracted Timathian, hid in here as he swam by."

"Forgive me," Timathian said. "I didn't know."

"Not your fault," Utharne said, laying a hand on the young elf's shoulder.

"But why?" Ornathius said.

"Zebulah," Brysis and Utharne both said without hesitation.

"We must find her," Brysis added.

"And risk all our lives?" Arrovawk said. "No! She made her choice."

"Not a matter for debate," Utharne said, joining Brysis. "Captain Ornathius?"

"I know my duty," he replied. He sounded angry, not that Utharne blamed him. At that moment, they all felt betrayed.

The Mahkwahb fisherman guided Apoletta to a rundown manse. An avalanche had collapsed the ledge on either side and destroyed part of the building. Rubble lay strewn across the floors while erosion had eaten the color and lines of the frescoes.

Apoletta tied and gagged the Mahkwahb before scouting the building's interior. The Mahkwahb had said that Zebulah made his lair there alone; Apoletta believed him; he was obviously afraid for his life.

After a moment of composing herself, Apoletta called out.

"Zebulah!" she said, her voice dominating the vast silence of the reception hall. "Zebulah!"

A moment passed before the red-robed Zebulah emerged from the darkness.

"We need to speak," Apoletta said. "I've come to save you." Though what form that salvation took, Apoletta remained unsure. In one hand she palmed a crystal rod tied with a strip of fur. In her other, outstretched hand was nothing, nothing but the hope of saving Zebulah. As far as she was concerned, Zebulah had but one chance to convince her he wanted to be saved. Otherwise she would kill him for his actions, for what he'd become.

Zebulah studied her, his gaze fixed. "Why?" he asked, his voice shattered and dry.

"Do you doubt my love for you?" Apoletta asked. "Or do you overestimate your master, this dragon of steam?"

Zebulah eyed her carefully, saying nothing.

"Yes, I've seen him," Apoletta said. "What is he? He looks weak."

Zebulah clenched his fist and stepped forward. Suddenly, he grimaced at something, his features softening. His fists unclenched.

Apoletta reached into her pouch with her free hand and produced her favored copper coin. "Perhaps you are not as eloquent as you once were, but I can still listen."

She cast her spell and sifted through the noise to reach Zebulah's thoughts. A disembodied voice filtered through, a woman whose tone seemed infinitely mercurial.

"Don't kill her," the woman said, her voice a remembered echo.

Memories of Zebulah and Apoletta, their bodies knotted together in lovemaking.

"Who's speaking for you?" Apoletta asked.

Images of Apoletta filled Zebulah's thoughts: Apoletta kissing him, him teaching her new magic.

"No, it's not me speaking," Apoletta said. "Who is this female?"

One word floated into prominence: Mistress.

Before Apoletta could react, more images filtered into her mind. There was a red-haired Mahkwahb accompanying Zebulah; she spoke to him in whispers, wearing a conspiratorial smile on her face.

"What does she want?" Apoletta asked. She hoped to draw something out of Zebulah, some voice of reason. His shifting thoughts and memories, however, made him seem deranged.

Zebulah's thoughts suddenly dropped away; the woman's presence intruded forcibly on his memories. A single image manifested itself, and Apoletta saw the contents of her package, the one Slyphanous had retrieved and Ornathius had safeguarded.

Apoletta inhaled sharply and straightened. She hadn't anticipated this. "Yes," Apoletta said, thinking quickly, "I hid it," which was the truth. "Because I wish to bargain."

Zebulah smiled, his lips cracking at the pitiful attempt by Apoletta to save her own—

"No," Apoletta said. "I wish to bargain for your life, not mine. Your freedom . . . your memory."

Zebulah hesitated. He blinked, confused, as though he hadn't heard her demands correctly. Finally, with a startled and broken voice, he said, "Come, and meet someone."

The hours had passed with growing futility. Brysis and the others had entered the shaft city, but they didn't know where to look for Apoletta. There seemed little hope of finding her among the hundreds of buildings. Disheartened, they returned to their hiding hole.

On reaching the tunnel Echo Fury cried a staccato burst and darted away. The others, familiar with the war dolphin's peculiarities and his sharp instincts, tried to disperse. A thick mist poured out of the tunnel's mouth, accompanied by the mad chitter and cackling of the magori. The mist revealed only their dark silhouettes, but there seemed a multitude.

Moving rapidly, the magori fell upon the stunned companions, their blades already drawn and busy. Brysis and the others had no chance but to form a circle and fight.

From out of nowhere, a group of tattooed sharks appeared. They barreled through the magori pack, biting eye stalks, limbs, and heads with their rows of teeth. The companions managed to back away and regroup. The sharks wheeled and attacked again even with acid blood dripping from their mouths and staining the water; some changed into Mahkwahb, and the magori were devastated by their trident thrusts.

The companions warily eyed the Mahkwahb sharks that circled them; one dark sea elf with a tattooed body, white hair, and elongated incisors swam over to them. He wore a green loincloth and bore a blood-coral trident. He stopped several feet from the companions, studying them with an equal measure of distrust and dislike.

"Come with us," he instructed. "Quickly, before another patrol discovers you."

Arrovawk leaned close to Utharne and whispered, "When a shark invites you to dinner, it's because you're the dinner."

"Who are you?" Brysis said.

"You call us Mahkwahb, but we are Blood Shoal," he said, jutting his chest out.

"Why did you help us?" Utharne asked. He did not trust the rogue sea elves, the exiled Dargonesti and Dimernesti. "And where do you want to take us?"

The Mahkwahb sighed with an exasperated air that suggested he was not patient about such matters. "We go to see your friend, Apoletta. And we helped you because I'm told we have a common cause."

From the trench, the Mahkwahb escorted the companions through a series of interconnected buildings. Two sharks swam through the ruins first, scouting ahead and mapping a clear passage. From there, they entered the labyrinth of corridors and tunnels carved within the stone walls of the shaft. Despite the complicated and confusing route, the Mahkwahb knew their home well; they never once encountered magori or any of the undead that resided in the upper warrens of the city.

Neither group spoke to the other; instead, an uncomfortable silence prevailed between them; both sides still harbored an animosity.

From the tunnels, the group entered the dungeon of a castle; its waters were still murky from the age-old filth of misery. The walls were soaked with old blood.

Through the dungeon, the companions entered the main chamber of a hollowed-out temple with a domed ceiling and broken columns. Floating above the dais made from a huge turtle shell waited the red-robed figure of Zebulah and a Mahkwahb with long, clay-red hair, bone-powder tattoos on his blue skin, and coral armor. Apoletta waited with them.

CHAPTER
The Bargain
16

While relieved to see her friends, Apoletta noticed their stern glances.

"Well," Wartide said. "I brought you your friends unharmed. As promised."

"Apoletta," Utharne asked. "What is this? Why did you bring us here? To this unhallowed place?" Utharne cast a look of disgust at the turtle shell.

"Unhallowed?" Wartide said, baring his fangs. "This is the sacred Temple to the Turtle-Goddess Zeboim! You stand in her glorious presence, fish-worshiper!"

Utharne pushed forward, ready to answer the insult against Abbuku, the Fisher King. The other Mahkwahb in the room also appeared ready to attack Utharne and his companions with their tridents and rapiers. Apoletta quickly interceded.

"Stop!" Apoletta shouted, swimming between them. She pointed to Wartide. "I swear on my own blood that if anyone comes to blows, my weapon will be lost to you!"

Wartide held up his hand with a smirk. The other Mahkwahb lowered their weapons slowly.

"What have you done?" Brysis asked. "They murdered Anhalstrax. Whatever bargain you have struck, it dishonors her sacrifice!

I will not participate in such a decision."

"Nor I," Utharne said.

Arrovawk simply crossed his arms defiantly; Ornathius and Timathian looked away, uncomfortable and torn between their own anger and their sense of duty.

"Please," Apoletta said. "Listen to what Wartide has to say, and then hear my words. Then if you still disagree, you may leave safely."

"What!" Wartide said.

Apoletta barely glanced at him. "On your word. You promised."

Wartide smiled a shark's grin, offering a slight bow. "You hold me at a disadvantage," he said. "Very well. They may leave if they wish. No harm will befall them."

Apoletta nodded in satisfaction, waiting for Wartide to begin.

"We serve a dragon named Blazewight," Wartide said simply, though evidently pained by the admission, "but it is not a willing servitude."

"He treats you well for slaves," Brysis said, challenging Wartide with her own fierce gaze.

"We are fodder," Wartide said.

"Why should we care?" Utharne asked.

"Perhaps you shouldn't," Wartide said with a low growl. "But Blazewight controls a powerful artifact . . . a weapon from an age when the world was too young to write its first words."

"So it is true! The Impaling Throne?" Brysis said. "We've heard of it."

"Then have you heard what it is capable of doing?" Wartide asked. He waited with a feral smile before their silence goaded him on. "Like a thorn that pierces the skin, it draws forth blood from the world beneath. And not just any blood," Wartide said. "The venom-blood of Chaos. This Impaling Throne straddles here and where here ought not to be. It is a pinprick of a portal between the two worlds—that of ours and that of Chaos."

Wartide paused melodramatically. "The Winding Thorn, as it's also called, twists the lands here to mirror those over there. The blood of Chaos spills into our domains and tortures these seas to reflect its own realms. And Blazewight has been using the Winding Thorn to rip that hole wider, to spill more venom-blood here."

They were all horrified. The last time Chaos rampaged through their world, less than half a century ago, mountains burned, oceans fell into great rifts, islands vanished, and even the sun halted its journey across the sky. The last time Chaos reigned, the blood of heroes and villains alike washed the lands red, and the world itself almost died. Apoletta herself had nearly abandoned Istar when Chaos's foot soldiers, the magori, tried invading her city. Then, with Chaos's defeat, the gods seemingly vanished from Krynn—though it was really the trickery of the Dark Queen Takhisis—and magic fell silent. The last time Chaos appeared on Krynn augured an unparalleled dark age in history.

"Why does Blazewight do this?" Utharne asked. "Why would he open those doors again?"

Wartide smiled at Utharne's question, arriving at his most savored secret. "Because," Wartide said, studying them all, "Blazewight wants to return home. Or rather, he wants to bring his home here."

The shock electrified the room. The companions stared at one another then at Apoletta.

"Blazewight is a dragon of Chaos?" Utharne finally asked.

"Blazewight was a red dragon," Wartide explained. "He became a fire dragon after entering a pact with Chaos to survive the destruction of the world. The pact turned his scales black, with magma coursing just beneath the skin."

"A fire dragon," Brysis repeated. "Living under water?"

Wartide again proffered his maddening smile. "Smart girl," he said. Wartide explained that after Chaos fell and the dragon overlords emerged, it appeared that Blazewight imagined himself capable of joining their ranks. He killed off lesser dragons to steal their skulls and fashioned a skull totem before running afoul of Malystryx. The great red Malys would not tolerate any rivals. So Malys struck at Blazewight."

"What happened?" Brysis asked.

"Blazewight fell victim to a terrible affliction that almost killed him. His own magma blood soared like a fever. His own flames threatened to consume him from the inside out. Blazewight retreated into the sea, to keep from burning up."

"That is why he's shrouded in steam!" Brysis said.

"Real damage was done," Wartide said. "His body has become charcoal. Were it not for the pressures of the deep, Blazewight would flake and crumble away slowly. He would die a prolonged, horrible death. Were it not for water, he would burn up completely."

"And yet he is powerful enough to enslave you?" Brysis asked with a grin intended to annoy Wartide.

"He is a dragon!" Wartide said. "And weak for a dragon is still stronger than you or I, girl. Besides he is supported by other minions of Chaos, the magori, who have found their way here. They've remained unflinchingly loyal to him. And while he has thinned their numbers, hurling them against various threats, they do not seem to mind."

"Where do we fit in? In this grand scheme, I mean?" Utharne asked.

Wartide looked to Apoletta. Apoletta nodded with a small sigh.

"Blazewight killed Anhalstrax and others," Apoletta said, "because he's ready to widen the rift and did not want to risk further interference. He believes his powers—his prowess—will return to him once the blood of Chaos transforms the region into his domain. He seeks healing in the very darkness that spawned him. He is preparing this ritual as we speak."

"So," Utharne said, looking at Wartide. "You need our help because Blazewight will destroy you? Once the rift opens, that is."

"Yes," Wartide said.

"And how are we supposed to help?" Arrowawk said. "What do we have that will be of any value to you?"

"Ah," Apoletta said. "That is where I come in. I brought a dragon-lance with me."

Again, the entire room lapsed into charged silence. Apoletta watched the reaction of her speechless companions while Wartide stared with bemused indifference. Even Zebulah, off to the side, appeared lost in thought, wrestling with one of his inner demons.

"With the dragonlance," Wartide said, "we will strike at Blazewight when he is at his weakest, when he is focused upon the ritual. If we fail in our mission, Chaos will bleed into this world and poison the oceans. More importantly, my people, the Blood Shoal, will die. Either we will die, or we are fated to be Blazewight's twisted pawns forever. I am pledged to ensure that neither happens."

For a long time nobody said anything. Apoletta's friends appeared stunned by the revelations.

"They need time to think," Apoletta said to Wartide. "I need a moment with them."

"No," Wartide said. "I want their decision now. Blazewight has already begun his preparations. He may cast the ritual within the hour, or the day. I don't have time for indecisiveness."

"No," Apoletta said. "You must give them what time they need. Try my patience further, and you can forsake any hope of using my dragonlance against Blazewight, much less finding where I've hidden it."

Wartide scowled, studying Apoletta closely. Finally, he turned and dismissed them with a flick of his arm. He joined the other Mahkwahb at the edges of the room, far enough away for the companions to speak privately but not so far that they could escape very easily. Only the still-silent Zebulah remained close by, hovering.

Apoletta approached the group, but Brysis and Arrovawk were manifestly angry, and the others refused to meet her gaze.

"You have every right to be mad," Apoletta said.

"It's not my place to question milady's orders," Ornathius mumbled, looking away.

Apoletta sighed. "Would you have allowed me to speak with Zebulah? Any of you?"

"No," Brysis said, glancing at Zebulah, "and even now I question your motives."

"My motives?" Apoletta said. "We had no idea what we faced. We expected nothing like this, and yet our mission was to stop the World Gash. We entered this crisis blindly. I weighed the risk and took a chance that Zebulah might provide some crucial answers."

"Why didn't you mention all this before?" Brysis asked.

"You brought a dragonlance," Utharne said accusingly, his jaws clenched. "You sent Slyphanous to retrieve the weapon, correct?"

"Yes."

"Which means you knew about Blazewight before we witnessed the fight with Anhalstrax. And still, you didn't tell us what you knew . . . or suspected."

"No," Apoletta admitted. "But I was not certain there was a dragon involved. My source"—she glanced at Zebulah—"remained suspect. You all would have said as much. I brought the dragonlance in case."

Utharne started as though jolted. "Wait," he said. "Did you tell Zebulah you were bringing the lance?"

"No," Apoletta said.

Utharne raised his voice, loud enough for Wartide to hear. "Then why does it seem like Wartide has been waiting for the dragon-lance to arrive? Like we were part of his plan all along?"

The question caught Apoletta off guard. Wartide certainly had not acted surprised when Apoletta mentioned the dragonlance. In fact, he seemed ready to bargain with her from the moment Zebulah brought her to him. Apoletta turned to face Wartide.

Wartide came over, a grin splitting his face. "The Goddess Zeboim counsels me. She sees all, knows all," he said.

"Zeboim," Utharne repeated, his voice cold enough to chill the waters.

"She speaks to me and to Zebulah. It is she who brought you here to help my people."

"Then I will not help," Utharne said. "I will not aid Zeboim's machinations."

Wartide barked with cutting laughter. "Like god, like priest. What has Abbuku done to save these waters? It is Zeboim who fights for her people, conspires to resist the menace from another world. It is Zeboim who brought you here to fight the dragon and stop the World Gash from consuming the oceans."

Apoletta groaned, turning to Zebulah. "Zeboim speaks through you?" Apoletta asked ruefully. "She sent you so that I might come to your rescue with the dragonlance?"

Zebulah smiled, though in truth, the smile was ambiguous. It almost seemed like Zebulah hadn't realized this truth before Apoletta uttered it. His smile faltered and vanished; he turned and swam away. Wartide, grinning still, followed after him.

Apoletta turned to her friends. "I am sorry," she whispered. "If you wish to leave, you are free to do so. But I must stay and help." She turned to follow Zebulah.

Brysis stopped her. "How do you know Wartide won't kill you? Kill us all? Once you surrender the dragonlance?" Brysis asked.

Apoletta offered a tired smile. "I still have some tricks left. We hold the advantage. But I will not begrudge you if you leave. I'd like you to trust me one more time, but understand that you feel betrayed."

"You stay, I stay," Ornathius said quickly.

"I follow Captain Ornathius," Timathian said after a moment's hesitation.

"We'll stay," Brysis declared, stroking Echo Fury's head. "We promised to protect you . . . even from yourself, if need be."

Apoletta nodded, offering a troubled smile.

"I follow Utharne," Brightshore stammered.

They all looked at Utharne.

"I . . . don't know," Utharne said. "I need time to think about this decision." He wandered away. Brine-Whisker followed at his side, as did Brysis.

"Hey!" Arrowawk cried, indignant. "In case you're wondering . . . I vote to leave! But I can't leave alone. If Utharne goes, I go. If he stays . . . well, I guess I'll have to stay too."

Apoletta offered a noncommittal nod before swimming after Zebulah.

Utharne stood in the shadows of a twisted column, watching from a second-story balcony as the Mahkwahb below polished the great turtle shell. Brysis could see he was mired in thought; even Brine-Whisker kept his distance.

Brysis edged closer. She cleared her throat; Utharne barely moved.

"So much for the polite approach," she said, standing next him.

"I'd prefer to be alone."

"And I'd prefer to be home." She motioned around her.

Utharne grunted.

"Still feeling sorry for yourself?" she asked. If diplomacy didn't work, perhaps needling him would.

"I'm not . . . I'm not feeling *sorry* for myself."

"Then what?"

"Must we discuss this? Here? Now?"

"Where else?" Brysis asked, swimming around to face him. "If you're looking for the proper place for a quiet, thoughtful conversation, that's at least a week's travel away."

"Fine!" Utharne said. "You want to hear my thoughts? I envy them." He motioned to the Mahkwahb.

"What!" Brysis asked, startled. "Them? Why?"

"Because their god acts in their favor."

"They worship Zeboim! Whatever they receive, it must accrue to her benefit first."

"She's helping them fight a dragon. She speaks to her followers directly, guiding them. No mystery, no signs or portents."

"She rules them like a tyrant and controls their actions," Brysis said.

Utharne threw his hands up. "What am I supposed to think? Abbuku leaves us to flounder about, to seek meaning in the meaningless."

"Abbuku helps us in his own way. Zeboim is blatantly purposeful. She wants the Mahkwahb to fawn over her. Idolize her. Abbuku doesn't need slaves. He doesn't need that kind of devotion."

"Have you ever considered, then, that he doesn't need his worshipers? That he doesn't need us? Perhaps we suffer through our misery because to Abbuku, it doesn't matter. Zeboim? Abbuku? Tyranny or misery. Which can I stomach more? Perhaps I'm better off without either one. Without any of the gods. Do you know what faith is? It's another set of teeth on a shark. Another tentacle on a squid. Another avenue for dying slowly."

Brysis shook her head, appalled. "You dishonor the Dimernesti with those words."

"What do you want me to say? Huh? That I forgive the gods for letting my wife suffer! Do you know what my last kindness for her was? The only kindness I could offer her? I gave her a merciful death! Her last kiss was from me . . . her executioner!"

Brysis said nothing. She looked away, made uncomfortable by his confession.

"And after I stopped her pain," Utharne said. "I went to find what was left of my children."

Brysis nodded in understanding. "I lost Quayseen," she said. "He died saving me because I was foolish."

"Did you love Quayseen so much that without him you were nothing but a ghost to this world? An echo?" Utharne said, his voice rising.

"When Quayseen died, I lost my second father. Losing my father twice is not easy!" Brysis said, shouting back. "I'm sorry your wife died. I'm sorry about your children. But they are no longer suffering. So why are you prolonging your own misery?"

Utharne said nothing. He simply stared at Brysis, his mouth open.

"You claim you cannot forgive the gods," Brysis said. "But I think you are looking for their forgiveness . . . for what you did." With that, she turned and left.

Utharne watched Brysis leave. He wanted to reach out and stop her; to apologize for his harsh words. The past two weeks, he had felt everything slip from his grip. But he felt numb. His old wounds had reopened, cutting him deeper than he ever imagined.

He looked around to find Brine-Whisker, but his companion, his oldest friend, had also left. Utharne closed his eyes and wept.

Apoletta swam through the corridor and spied Zebulah turning another corner. She gave chase, finally catching up to him.

"Leave," Zebulah croaked.

"Haven't you been alone long enough?" Apoletta asked.

Zebulah turned to face her. He pulled back his cowl, his eyes glowing red with arcane fire. "Not your husband," he hissed.

"Mistress loves me."

"She uses you."

Zebulah said nothing, but made no move to leave. The red in his eyes guttered to a candle yellow.

"You never offered her your loyalty, did you?" Apoletta asked. "She took it."

Zebulah was quiet a moment, but finally he looked at her. She could see the curiosity etched across his face, in the way his brow wrinkled.

"The dragonlance," he said. "I wielded that weapon before, didn't I?"

Apoletta winced at the memory. She straightened, defiantly.

"Tell me," he said, his eyes burning brighter.

Apoletta stood her ground. "Very well," she said, her voice grim. "When magic fled the world, you learned to leech magic from magical objects."

Something in Zebulah's eyes flickered in recognition.

"At first, I gave you what I had, my own magical trinkets. It allowed you to survive in the ocean with me. But it wasn't enough. Each year, you aged faster and faster; your life had already been extended beyond normal time, and the magic was fading. Behind my back, you took to leeching magic from the city's twenty-four dragonlances."

Understanding flooded across Zebulah's face. "I remember," he rasped.

Apoletta could see in his face the memories returning: the sea elves holding him down, Zebulah fleeing the city.

"You cast me out! You betrayed me!"

"You left me no choice!" Apoletta said, the humiliation of the moment sparking her temper. "With the dragons murdering each other for their skulls and the overlords carving their domains in our flesh, the dragonlances were our only means of defense! I could not let you condemn all of Istar, no matter how—" Apoletta hesitated.

"No matter how . . . ?" Zebulah asked, his eyes narrowing into slits.

"How much I loved you," Apoletta said.

Zebulah winced, another memory dislodged and returned. He remembered something else and was struck hard. Apoletta immediately understood the nature of that memory; she'd seen that look of utter humiliation and shame on his face once before.

She had not exiled Zebulah; she had protected him from the others. He had fled Istar in shame and self-imposed exile.

Zebulah and Apoletta floated there, neither able to meet the other's gaze, the gap between them widening in the silence.

Utharne hovered inches above the floor, his arms outstretched to his sides, his eyes closed. He focused on everything that once brought him courage and strength; he thought of his wife and family . . . and of Abbuku. But the once roaring hearth of his faith felt cold and dead with a winter's frost upon it, and the temple inside his soul had gone quiet.

Suddenly, something flickered in his mind, and his despairing thoughts were swept away. The image in his mind was huge, and Utharne caught a glimpse of a turtle shell that filled the sky.

His eyelids jumped open, and Utharne breathed heavily. Is this what a god feels like? Utharne wondered.

Carefully, he shut his eyes, feeling a rush and swell. His mind was filled with the huge image. Before him waited a great turtle, its shell spiked with sea mountains, wrinkles like the waves of green seas, and two deep shafts for eyes.

"Priest," a woman said, her voice stolen from the cries of rocks. "You know me."

Utharne averted his gaze; whether or not he waited in the presence of a goddess he did not know. The one in his mind was divine, certainly. "I know you," Utharne whispered.

"Attend to me, priest, and your fortunes will be greater than the stars have numbers. The ocean will be your treasure box, the land your footstool. Am I not generous?"

"Your generosity humbles me," Utharne said, careful in his words. "The legends of your munificence do not do you justice. But I am a mere rector of Abbuku. I have nothing worthy to offer you."

"True. Your loyalty is admirable, though misplaced. When has Abbuku last spoken with you? Last praised you for your allegiance? Last rewarded you for your devotion?"

Utharne started to answer, "Never," but the word died on his lips. He thought of Brine-Whisker, a friend and companion unlike any other.

"Why do you hesitate?"

"Forgive me," Utharne said quickly. "But I must consider this question carefully."

"Consider?" the voice said with a growl. "Am I not beautiful? Powerful? Am I not worthy of your praise? Your devotion?"

"Yes, and more. But I must think on this matter," Utharne said. "I doubt you'd want an impetuous fool for a follower. For a priest, I mean. Are you not worthy of deep contemplation? Should I not reflect on your generous offer? Your blessing is no trifle."

The giant turtle paused, a little pleased. "Very well. Then consider the matter. But do not tarry. My patience is not infinite, but my appetite for misery is."

Utharne opened his eyes. He breathed hard, his heart pounding. After a moment of settling his strung nerves, he thought about Zeboim's words. It was the first time a god had appeared to him, much less spoke to him; the experience thrilled and terrified him equally.

Is that what he wanted? The attention? Did he deserve such attention? Utharne didn't know anything anymore.

CHAPTER
Farewell Friend
17

A blue-haired Mahkwahb raced through the temple, trident at his side, crying out as loud as he could, "It's starting! It's starting!"

Mahkwahb from all corners raced to the windows and doorways, peering over one another to see the commotion.

Apoletta entered the main floor and found her friends and her strange allies clustered together. For a moment, the three branches of sea elves had forgotten they despised each other. They stared out the temple's circular half doors, watching in horror as tendrils of insoluble ink wafted up from somewhere deep inside the shaft. The tentacles of ink twisted and corkscrewed upward; any fish that touched the ink died instantly. A helix of dead fish and feasting magori wound itself around the black ribbons.

Wartide faced Apoletta and her friends and demanded their answers. In turn, each said their decision remained the same . . . until the issue was put to Utharne and Arrovawk. Arrovawk squirmed a moment, looking to Utharne for commitment.

"Staying," Utharne said, his eyes downcast. "I may abandon my principles, but I won't abandon my friends."

Arrovawk sighed and also agreed to stay. Wartide did not appear impressed and instead demanded the weapon right away.

They'd run out of time.

"We'll retrieve it together," Apoletta said.

"Fine," Wartide replied. He pointed to his two lieutenants. "Begin the attacks on the magori. Send out raiding bands. Keep them guessing, and try to scatter them."

"What about the undead?" Apoletta asked. She glanced at Zebulah, despite herself.

"Most will help us. Some won't," Wartide said.

"How'd you arrange that?" Brysis asked.

"Do you forget? We serve Zeboim. When we die, we return as undead in continued service to her glory. Now enough chatter. Take me to the dragonlance!"

Apoletta peered out the door, searching. She pointed to the ledge across and above them.

"Care to be more specific?" Wartide said.

"No," Apoletta said. "Lead on."

Wartide obviously did not enjoy being led around by the nose. He shot Apoletta a venomous look before turning to swim inside the temple.

"This way," he said. "Keep up."

As the companions streamed after Wartide, Apoletta paused long enough to thank Brysis, who simply nodded in response.

She also glanced gratefully at Utharne. "Where is Brine-Whisker?" Apoletta asked.

Utharne shook his head. "I fear I've lost him." With no other explanation, he, too, followed Wartide.

Mahkwahb bands ambushed several magori patrols swimming through the buildings and tunnels to reach the shaft. The fact the magori did not expect their "allies" to betray them enabled the Mahkwahb to draw close and strike ruthlessly. Before the magori could react, the dark sea elves had driven tridents through their backs, trapped them in nets, and crushed them under rocks, or used spellcraft to paralyze them for deadly pummeling. The braver Mahkwahb plunged their daggers into the dying bodies of their enemies and used the magori's corrosive blood to draw scar patterns into their own skin.

The Mahkwahb ambushed one group of magori with the aid of the undead. As the patrol passed through an alley, three hooded and tattered wraiths drifted through the surrounding walls. They swarmed the magori, reaching into their foes with their insubstantial hands and pulling out dark, gauzy tendrils. The magori weakened, once their wills and strengths were torn from them; they dropped their weapons and buckled. The Mahkwahb then wielded their wickedly curved blades and unleashed a barrage of cutting blows. One magori broke free, filling the water with its clouding mists, and escaped into the shaft.

The magori's piercing shriek seemed to fill the waters; the pursuing Mahkwahb hesitated. The wraiths, however, would not let their quarry escape so easily. In the shaft's open waters, the three wraiths overtook the desperately fleeing magori. Swarming over it, they dived their spindlelike arms into its chest and cracked open its carapace.

All the magori shrieked in rage at the violation. A flock descended upon the three feasting wraiths. But the undead turned and charged. Few magori had weapons capable of harming something incorporeal. The wraiths tore through their opponents as magori weapons passed harmlessly through them; the cackling undead drained some opponents and cruelly killed others.

Mahkwahb wizards, priests, and sorcerers, hiding in the buildings, swam near the fray, unleashing their spells. Lightning forked out and struck one group of magori; another bunch vanished in a cloud of steam; water hammer spells rendered others senseless. Dozens of arcane missiles zigzagged through the melee, striking targets. The magori unleashed a volume of obscuring mist, and soon a white fog enveloped the heart of the city's shaft. Mahkwahb spellcasters darted back into the safety of the labyrinth, drawing the enraged magori into additional ambushes.

Somewhere, at the bottom of the shaft, Blazewight was roaring in fury. His voice shook the sediment free of the walls, and it urged the magori on, telling them they did not fight alone. The Mahkwahb had betrayed Blazewight and threatened his plans. Blazewight's roar promised retribution. And his retribution came swiftly.

Up, through the darkness of the trench from which the shadows bled, the Legion Coral rose into the city core. Its lacelike surface appeared more ragged and less pristine than before; its battle with the Desolate Maiden must have cost it dearly, but it still possessed a ferocious appetite, and it still served as the will of Blazewight's reckoning.

The companions, along with Zebulah, Wartide, and several of Wartide's guard, swam frantically through the tunnels. They'd barely reached the ledge where the dragonlance was sequestered when the attacks across the city began. All around them, it seemed, the magori in the shaft danced around curls of rising ink.

The labyrinth truly confused Apoletta, and she lost track of the way they had come. Tunnels curved and drifted into one another, and the buildings looked similar.

Outside the windows they passed, they could see that bedlam had gripped the core. Sea elves were firing spells into a growing cloud of fog. The magori gave chase to the Mahkwahb. A misty pillar rose, black with magori blood and the plumes of ink. All the while, Wartide led them deeper into the knot of tunnels and passageways.

The Legion Coral impaled fish and straggling magori on its lances. It absorbed them into its mass. The magori saw the sphere's approach and tried to flee. A Mahkwahb wizard cast pauper's spells at the creature, striking it with a cold, bluish ray and darts of light.

The coral ignored the wizard, instead striking a nearby building. The crust immediately spread across and infested the building . . . then the one next to it. The wizard tried to flee, but it was too late. Three lances shot forth and impaled him. One moment he was flesh; the next, he was calcified and added to the Legion Coral's mass. The spreading, crusting coral covered a third building in moments . . . then a fourth.

Like wildfire through a haystack, the coral spread, penetrating corridors and tunnels. It devoured those magori foolish enough to remain in its path and flooded into the niches where Mahkwahb lay in wait. And with each death, more victims added to its mass.

"Where?" Wartide shouted, yelling as he spun to face Apoletta.

"I'm lost. We are too far inside. I don't know!"

Wartide turned, presumably to lead them closer to the shaft wall, when three creatures materialized behind them. Although wraithlike, their bodies were composed entirely of undulating indigo fire. Both groups stopped, surprised to encounter one another. The creatures shrieked and lunged forward. Surprisingly, Zebulah darted in front of Apoletta and pushed her behind him. Wartide's guards charged the enemy.

Glancing at him, Apoletta realized Zebulah seemed uncertain as to why he'd just done that. He appeared almost embarrassed.

Utharne joined the charge, but his stance was not very confident as he prepared to try to cast out the undead. He hesitated. Apoletta realized that his faith had weakened without Brine-Whisker.

But the Mahkwahb fiercely engaged the undead creatures, hacking at their flaming bodies and screaming when they suffered their blighted touch. Wartide backed the companions away from the main fight and redirected them through another corridor.

"We must find the weapon!" he said. "Everyone's life is forfeit. Except for yours, naturally," he said to Apoletta with a sharp grin.

Apoletta said nothing. Instead, she looked at Zebulah. "Thank you," she whispered.

They approached another intersection, but even though they were all on alert, they nearly jumped when a black figure darted into their path and barked loudly. Wartide reared back with his trident, but Apoletta grabbed his wrist.

Brine-Whisker unleashed a series of happy barks and struck Utharne hard enough in the chest to send him feet over head. Utharne recovered and hugged his companion.

"I'm sorry," he whispered. "I'm sorry."

"Not as sorry as you're about to be," Wartide said.

Wartide was looking in the direction from which Brine-Whisker had come. Apoletta joined Wartide and gazed at the scene unfolding before her. Down the corridor, through a door that peered outside, they could see a coral mass spreading across the buildings.

"The Legion Coral," Wartide said.

"It's coming here," Apoletta replied. "We must hurry!"

"Outside, then!" Wartide said, charging through the door. To reach the dragonlance, Apoletta knew, they had to expose themselves to danger.

◆◆◆◆◆

The coral crust spread across more buildings. Nobody knew how far it dug inside the tunnels, but the screams of the Mahkwahb and disloyal undead filled the waters.

Abruptly, the coral stopped spreading and wavered, almost as though it'd reached the limits of its strength. Then, slowly at first, but increasing in speed, ripples spread across the coral, growing to waves that bulged the crust before settling down. Then the coral began to slide across the face of the shaft like a millipede. While it no longer grew in mass, it slid across buildings and ledges, scouring everything in its path. Several of the structures that it had coated and consequently abandoned collapsed from the strain.

The companions darted through the alleys of buildings, catching glimpses of the horror.

"The coral!" Apoletta shouted.

"I know," Zebulah said. The coral mass was less than two hundred feet away.

"Where's the weapon?" Wartide said, eyeing the coral through every window, every broken wall, every gaping hole they crossed.

"I don't know!" Apoletta replied. "None of this looks familiar."

Wartide spun around. "This is absurd! Do not test me, Dargonesti!" he yelled. "You will not spoil years of planning!"

Ignoring Wartide, Zebulah swam between them. "Think calmly," he said.

Apoletta thought for a moment and suddenly found peace in the storm of the moment. "Fate," she whispered, the word itself flooding her with serenity.

"What?" Zebulah asked.

"Fate is immutable," Apoletta said with a smile. It was not her time to die. The Speaker had said as much. Then it came to her.

"There." She pointed at a building several dozen yards away.

This building lay broken in several places, its windows hungry mouths. But it was free of the deadly coral covering. Apoletta swiftly swam to it. "I buried it in there."

The others followed. The coral was less than a hundred feet away; it frightened them, cracking and snapping as it moved, constantly breaking and rearranging itself to devour more territory.

"We don't have enough time," Wartide said, watching the coral.

"No, we don't," Utharne agreed. "But we will make the time. I have faith in my friends." With that, Utharne swam straight for the coral. "I will delay it," he shouted. Without hesitation, Brine-Whisker followed.

"No!" Apoletta cried, starting after him, but Zebulah grabbed her, and Ornathius pushed her back as he swam after Utharne.

"I will help him!" Ornathius yelled.

Apoletta stared in shock. She could no longer hear the shouts of Wartide and Arrowawk, or Zebulah's words. Brysis slapped her hard.

Stunned, Apoletta slapped Brysis back. "Good!" Brysis said. "Now get the dragonlance before we all die!"

After a moment Apoletta nodded and, with a heavy heart, cast a last glance at brave Utharne; she swam into the building.

The coral was seventy feet away and approaching rapidly.

Utharne, Brine-Whisker, and Ornathius hovered before the approaching coral, a mere fifty feet away, the snapping and reforming of its mass an unnerving thunder.

"You should have stayed with Apoletta," Utharne told Ornathius.

"She would have wanted me to help you," he said. "And . . . Vanastra tried to save one of my men. I now assume her obligation to protect you."

Forty feet away, the crust seemed to increase its velocity.

Utharne smiled. "Thank you, Captain. It was a pleasure to know you. But you will not die. For me, I mean." With that, Utharne touched Ornathius and muttered a prayer of protection. Ornathius tensed.

Thirty feet away.

With a smile, Utharne then turned to Brine-Whisker. "Beloved friend," he said, the only words that expressed the indescribable love he felt for the seal. "You never deserted me. No matter how often I threatened to leave you. You spoke, and I failed to listen. You gave, and I failed to see. I'm sorry. I can see and hear you clearly now."

The birthmark of the blue flame on Brine-Whisker's brow flared once, then again. He barked, and the mark turned into a bright blue flame that spread over all three of them. Utharne smiled, feeling invigorated for the first time in years. His faith felt renewed; the strength of Abbuku filled him. It welcomed him into its forgiving embrace.

Twenty feet away.

Blue flames danced in Utharne's eyes as he invoked his first miracle.

Ten feet.

Then Utharne spoke another prayer, exactly the same words and intonation as the first. He knew it would work, though part of him was saddened at the thought he might not live to know its effect. But he did not dwell on that. Instead, he focused on his wife, his son, his daughter.

"They wait for me," he said, tears dissolving, then cast his final miracle.

The coral had reached their feet; sharp lances flew out in all directions. To Ornathius's obvious horror, the coral veered clear of him and Brine-Whisker, the lances missing their marks. The crust would not, could not, touch them. Utharne had protected them.

Utharne completed his last miracle just as three lances impaled him—one through his arm, another through his torso, and the third through his thigh. He screamed in excruciating agony; for a white-hot moment he could neither think nor see anything. He felt the coral trying to grow inside him, trying to spread, but it was hampered. His last miracle, the same one he used on Apoletta to save her, worked inside him. The coral could not devour him. He focused past the pain, willing himself to think beyond the moment.

Ornathius hacked at the three lances, cutting each at a stroke. He grabbed Utharne as he collapsed, taking the priest in his arms. He stared out at the coral, which had stopped . . . hesitated. It did not continue its advance. Instead it quivered and shook, cracking along its surface like dried mud.

"What did you do?" Ornathius asked in amazement.

"Fire," Utharne gasped. "Fought fire with, uh, with fire."

The coral at their feet retreated, pulled back by some mysterious tide.

"Sometimes I can, uh, can summon monsters to my . . . aid," Utharne said, groaning. "Coral is a collection of, ah, of life. Perhaps it is a . . . monster of life. So I turned it upon itself. Two spells . . . two patches of rebel coral I created. So it . . . it devours itself."

"You've done it!" Ornathius said, kissing Utharne on both cheeks.

"Not yet," Utharne whispered weakly. "Leave me."

"I will not!" Ornathius said. "Perhaps the dark sea elves have a priest—"

"No," Utharne whispered. "The coral is not, ah, not dead. I must try one last thing. Please. If I . . . uh . . . uh . . . do not . . . then all will be lost."

"I cannot leave you here!" Ornathius protested.

"You must," Utharne said. "Do this for me. Protect Apoletta. That is your duty. Hu . . . hurry." Utharne coughed blood.

Ornathius looked around, uncertain. "Brine-Whisker?" he called.

Utharne smiled, blue flames caressing his ailing body. "Go. I . . . I am no longer alone. I never was."

Ornathius looked at the coral that had retreated inward, still devouring and falling upon itself. He finally settled Utharne on his side, so he didn't rest on his wounds.

Utharne heard Ornathius swim away.

His vision dimmed, the coral retreating. A phoenix of blue flame grew in the darkness, its fingerlike wings stretching around him to cradle him. The world turned to light and azure fires, and beyond that, a hint of endless blue oceans.

"My love," a gentle voice said, calling from the seas. "How I've missed you. See how your children have grown. . . ."

Smiling, Utharne let one last miracle slip past his lips; the phoenix rushed through him, and through him, it touched the world for the better.

"Wonderful," Utharne whispered.

Ornathius spun around at the sudden howl of fire and the eagle's screech that filled the shaft. Utharne was floating up, face to the sky, his back arched. Around him, a tornado of blue flame spun and scoured the coral with its touch.

The inferno grew hotter still, the featherlike tips of flame tinged white.

Ornathius shielded his eyes.

Apoletta scrambled through the building, swimming and pulling on the edges of doorways and pushing through debris to propel herself faster. The others followed on her heels, bumping into one another and snarling in frustration. The sound of rolling thunder increased in pitch; the Legion Coral seemed moments away from spilling over them.

Into the empty basement with its vaulted ceiling, Apoletta raced for a pile of flotsam leaning against the door. She pulled away a slab of rock, revealing an ordinary bag beneath no larger than a saddle bag.

"Here it is!" Apoletta cried triumphantly. The thunder grew louder.

Wartide roared angrily. "That bag's too small! That can't be it!" He pulled the bag from Apoletta's grip. Brysis and Timathian swam forward to attack Wartide, but Apoletta held up her hand.

"The coral!" she yelled.

Wartide pulled at the bag's buckles and opened it. Inside rested the head of a sharp lance. The metal glittered with a strange, almost mirror-silver sheen. Sinister teeth and flat horns pointing in both directions lined its razor edge, while down its center lay floral etchings and decorative carvings with sharp patterns.

"Where's the rest of it?" Wartide screamed in frustration.

"Inside!" Apoletta replied.

Wartide, mystified, peered inside. It was a bag larger inside than out—another arcane trick. The dragonlance would stretch to its full length of eight feet when brought out of the bag. The strange silver of its metal came from fallen stars, while leather bindings and carved patterns decorated its shaft.

Wartide reached inside and grabbed the dragonlance. Abruptly, he cried in pain and pulled back his smoking hand. He dropped the bag and rubbed his wrist.

Apoletta fixed Wartide with a cool gaze. "Only those of virtue may wield the dragonlance. Or did Zeboim not tell you that?"

The coral snapped and rumbled overhead and all around them. "You needed us to bring you the weapon. And you need us to use it," she added.

"Apoletta!" Brysis urged, but Apoletta did not budge.

"On your word, Wartide," Apoletta said. "My friends and I will be allowed to leave here and return home unharmed, unmolested by you and the others. On your word, Zebulah is restored."

Wartide said nothing for long moments. Finally, he grabbed the bag and shoved it back into Apoletta's hands. "On my word," he said. "So says She."

"Now," Apoletta cried. They turned and headed for the nearest egress. A moment later, they were outside and swimming fast above the buildings. Apoletta could not help but wonder why the coral had not overtaken them and why, as she waited, arguing with Wartide, she somehow knew that nothing would happen to her. The others must have wondered as well, for as one all they turned to look behind them.

A tornado of white and blue flames had engulfed a ledge, back where Utharne and Ornathius had made their stand. They could not stare at it directly, so bright were its fires. Instead, they caught glimpses of the tornado disintegrating and devouring the coral.

"Utharne! Ornathius!" Apoletta cried abjectly.

"Not yet," Wartide said, just behind her. "We haven't won yet." With that, he looked down, down into the trench below, where ribbons of ink were roping upward.

CHAPTER
The Battle
18

The battle raged inside the shaft, with many of the undead aiding the dark sea elves. Many undead served Zeboim as matron of their new sanctuary, the oceans, and thus served her desires. It was her desire that the Mahkwahb should win and turn the Blood Shoal city into her vast temple. Those undead born under Chaos's mark, however, fought with equal zeal, determined to turn the World Gash into their throne on Krynn.

Wartide gathered twelve able warriors and several wraiths to assist them and proceeded to take a roundabout course to Blazewight's chambers.

The companions followed, quietly descending through abandoned passages. The rich and wealthy who once dwelled along the ledge rings had likely built their empire on the backs of whatever poor wretches once lived in the deeper tunnels. The passageways grew increasingly tight, the walls rougher and darker with misery's stains. Echo Fury almost filled the tunnels with his size.

Finally, Wartide stopped and faced the companions. "The trench that split the city open also extends beneath here. We are there now, at the trench. We cannot venture deeper; tunnels are collapsed or split open and exposed. We must enter the shaft in order to enter the trench. The magori undoubtedly await us," he added with a grin.

"What will we find?" Brysis asked, pointing down with her chin.

"A large chamber," Wartide said. "It rests beneath the city, below everything else. Blazewight found it and forced us to excavate it. It contains the Impaling Throne."

"You know the magori. What should be our plan?" Apoletta asked.

"Do not bother using your talents to hide," Wartide said. "The magori see everything regardless. My chosen warriors will lead the charge and break open a path for us. As we reach Blazewight, the rest of us will mount the attack. You," he said to Apoletta, "will lie in wait until Blazewight can be taken by surprise. Then strike him with the lance."

"What of the steam?" Brysis asked. "Won't the heat from his steam kill her?"

Wartide shook his head. "The steam lessens while he casts magic near the throne, near Chaos. His curse abates enough to serve us, not him."

With that, the Mahkwahb turned and swam through another tunnel. They approached an open archway and accelerated through it. As each Mahkwahb burst past the opening, they turned into sharks; a couple were sheathed in coral armor, but most were covered in bone-white tattoos. They dived out of sight. Apoletta, her bag strapped on her back, followed after Brysis and Echo Fury, darting through the archway.

Apoletta found herself at the bottom of the cylindrical shaft, its fractured floor twenty feet below her. The ornate carvings of tentacles and eyes peered up at her through gaps in the debris strewn around the lip of the fissure. The trench, wide enough for the dragon to slip through, sliced into the floor and rose up on opposite sides of the shaft's walls. From the trench, guarded by a handful of magori, billowed tendrils of darkness.

THE ALIEN SEA

The sharks and wraiths charged their former allies, flying through or past them. Several sharks trailed away, enemy blood flowing from their mouths, while two fell lifeless. The wraiths had nothing to fear from that lot, however, and within moments Wartide's party had slaughtered the magori. A breath later, wraiths rose from their bodies.

Apoletta suppressed a shudder and followed the sharks and wraiths deeper down, past the edges of the trench. They followed the columns of ink as their guide ropes.

The raiding party plunged past split tunnels and open passages pitting the rock face, the blackened rock speeding by in a blur; the shadow ribbons shifted and snaked across their path. One shark stumbled into an ink stream. He shifted out of shark form, screaming at whatever nightmares invaded his mind and clawing at the air. He veered away, slamming his head against the stones, again and again, trying desperately to dislodge whatever had roosted in his skull. Clouds of blood and black ink spilled from his wounds.

The other sharks did not slow. Neither did Apoletta and her companions, no matter how much his suffering pained them. They finally understood what had happened to Veloxua.

The trench walls curled away to reveal a chamber one hundred feet in height; the companions flew through the roof of its large dome. From the ceiling hung heavy chains with hooks, a twisted mosaic depicting various humanoids suffering hellish tortures in black fire spread across its surface. Smokey obsidian glass comprised the walls; they seemed to hold corpses embedded just beneath the surface.

The Impaling Throne was in full prominence, coming to half the chamber's height. It was a spiraled thorn the color of aged bone, cracked in places. A groove ran along its twisted length. From the thorn's red tip, an ebony fire flickered, a kernel of chaos; the black flame slowly spread down the throne. The floor of the entire chamber reflected the night sky on a still pool of what might have been oil. From the oil curled the inky smoke.

Apoletta gaped at the scene. Blazewight was curled around the thorn, his body nestled inside the winding groove. It was a throne for dragons, she realized.

Blazewight's body still bled steam but in pitiful wisps compared to the clouds that had once surrounded him. She could see the dragon better in that situation: his body was made of charcoal and burning embers, with a dim yellow glow beneath; in places, chunks of burned flesh were missing, showing angular gashes and the hint of gray bone. His wings were like burned masts without their sails. His mouth whispered rapidly as he performed the ritual.

From the shadows of the room and ink-stained floor, more than a dozen magori flooded forth, screeching. They set upon the intruders, and suddenly the magori, sharks, wraiths, war dolphins, and remaining companions were fighting amidst the plumes of ink.

Blazewight focused on the ritual, briefly opening his ember-lit eyes to observe the fight. The ebony flame continued to spread, engulfing five more feet of the throne.

He must be close to completing the ritual, Apoletta realized, if he risks ignoring his attackers.

It was a wild battle. Two magori wrestled one shark into the black ink, followed by another. Both Mahkwahb screamed and twisted, making them easy prey for the spearing.

The Mahkwahb fought ferociously. They darted past magori, biting quickly or brushing against their foes with their coral armor. The sharks maneuvered their enemies around so the wraiths could attack them from behind. Wartide, fighting now as a sea elf, reveled in the combat, spinning among the magori, wielding his trident with impunity.

All too quickly it grew impossible to see through the murk: magori fog mixed with ink; ink mixed with blood; blood mixed with mist. Black flames engulfed half of the spiraled thorn, and sticky strands of oily miasma clung to Blazewight. The flames inside the fell dragon dimmed.

Zebulah, staying close to Apoletta, unleashed two spells to blind his opponents and hurled missiles of light. Otherwise, he held his strongest magics in reserve. Brysis, Brightshore, and Arrowawk kept a distance from Apoletta, spearing and stabbing at any opponent within range. Echo Fury and Timathian darted around the group, ramming magori from behind and upending them long enough for someone else to land a killing blow.

An armored shark, one of Wartide's lieutenants, made a foolish run for Blazewight. The dragon's eyes snapped open, and he opened his mouth to utter a guttural spell. A loud chime followed, like the peal of a crystal bell, and the shark's coral armor shattered, lacerated the elf with deep gashes. Shark's blood filled the water, and it tumbled to the ground.

Blazewight closed his eyes and returned to the ritual; the ebony flames had retreated a foot or two back up the thorn because of the distraction.

The wraiths turned the battle in the companions' favor. The sharks only wounded the magori, but they were weakened enough for the undead to kill them. With each magori slaughtered in that fashion, another wraith appeared to tip the struggle in their favor.

The battle plan appeared to be working . . .

. . . until Blazewight again opened his eyes, his voice incanting loudly in the knotted tongue of some arcane language. The words chilled Apoletta. The flames extended down another dozen feet, almost reaching the oily floor. Tendrils of darkness snapped from floor to thorn, thorn to floor.

"Stop him!" Wartide cried.

"Help them!" Apoletta urged the others. She extended her arms. "Beneath the waves, the thunder traveled for days to seek counsel with Daydra," she exclaimed, casting a water-hammer spell. The warmth in her belly flared, and she drank in a sip of seawater. A large sphere of water near Blazewight's head vanished. The ocean rushed in to fill the void, and the resulting turbulence shook the dragon.

In the same instant, three wraiths and five sharks wheeled on Blazewight. Zebulah, too, spun to face his former master and unleashed a crackling bolt of lightning that echoed thunder off the chamber walls. Blazewight shrieked either from frustration or pain, but the flames on the thorn retreated a couple of feet, revealing the bone beneath.

"No! I'm not done!" Blazewight cried.

Apoletta and Zebulah cast missiles of light and turned magori into temporary allies to hurl at Blazewight. Timathian and Echo Fury swam closer, as did Arrovawk and Brightshore, engaging the remaining enemy. Blazewight stared at the attackers, his ember eyes blazing, the glow illuminating cracks beneath his charcoal skin. The steam around him grew thicker. A wall of flame appeared between him and his attackers, creating a bulwark of fire. It burned several magori and sharks, sending them scrambling away in panic.

"I'm ready for you," Zebulah said. He muttered a spell beneath his breath and opened his hand. The quartz rock in his palm vanished. The water around the fire crystallized and turned to ice with the snap of a glacier. Ice wall and fire wall met, producing a tremendous fog. The ice evaporated completely; the fire survived in patches. The sharks turned into sea elves and dived through the gaps, charging with their tridents. The wraiths fluttered over the dragon, driving their tattered arms up to their shoulders inside him.

And the black flame retreated another two feet.

"Betrayers! Foul maggots!" Blazewight cried. He unwound himself from the Winding Thorn, no longer caring that the flames jumped back up. He landed upon the floor, sending tremors through the walls and crushing a shark under his claw. His neck snaked back, and he issued a deafening roar. In his mouth, the sun seemed to rise. His head snapped forward, and the yolk of the sun burst open. Black fire, red flames, and steam filled the room, immediately burning mist, igniting blood, and boiling the water.

Apoletta, Zebulah, and Brysis escaped the flames, but others did not. The fire instantly cooked the unlucky ones, cracking skin and scouring away their features. It scorched the wraiths into tattered gauze shreds. The gel-like fire stuck to flesh and cloth with the persistence of tree sap. Those that burned continued to burn.

Arrovawk fell away, trying to smother the flame on his arm, but as he did, Brightshore followed, keeping two magori at bay. In a sudden fit of rage, or perhaps lunacy, Arrovawk whirled around, screaming in pain and waving his fiery limb in the faces of the magori. Terrified, they fled. Brightshore then helped Arrovawk snuff the flames.

Timathian and Echo Fury seemed to have disappeared, but too much steam, mist, blood, and ink filled the water to see clearly. Brysis glanced about desperately, meeting Wartide's eyes, just before Wartide turned and gave the nod to Apoletta.

Apoletta shouted to Brysis. "Go, find him!"

"I can't leave you!" Brysis said.

"Find Echo Fury; then help me!" Apoletta said, swimming away. To her relief, Brysis swam away to locate her friend.

Apoletta remained at the periphery of the room, near the ceiling, slowly circling behind Blazewight. Zebulah stayed in the forefront, casting his spells at a distance, but Wartide and the others drew closer. They tried weakening Blazewight with their blows. As fragile as he'd become, however, he remained a dragon—a force of reckoning.

Blazewight spun around and cast more spells as he moved to crush enemies and their spell-allied magori with claws and tail, magic and fire-breath. The dragon unleashed a rolling, steaming ball of fire at a group of Mahkwahb, who promptly burned up.

Apoletta continued to maneuver behind the dragon, though she felt the rising heat from the steam of his body. Then Blazewight reared his head again and spewed another gout of flame. Everyone seemed to vanish at the moment he breathed, Wartide included.

More bodies floated, lifeless, their identities burned away. Apoletta could no longer tell friend from enemy. She saw none of her companions. She muttered a prayer and a curse in the same breath. Only then did she realize she'd been fumbling with her bag buckle for a few moments now. She tore open the flap, staring at Blazewight.

The dragon had moved away from Apoletta, biting into this survivor or that corpse. Apoletta pulled forth the dragonlance. She'd trained with it before, and its weight felt right in her hands. The surge of power thrilled her soul and filled her with strength. Apoletta pushed off from the domed ceiling toward the dragon. He had yet to notice her.

As she approached, Blazewight neared a motionless, armored dolphin. The dragon opened his mouth to bite into Echo Fury.

Apoletta could not help herself. "No!" she screamed.

Craning his neck, the dragon turned to face her, his mouth was still open but frozen. Apoletta was not close enough for him to strike at her. Before either of them could react, a blood-colored bolt of energy struck Blazewight on the side of his head. He spun to face the new attacker, bits of charcoal floating free of the wound.

It was Zebulah, who quickly cast another spell and darted away.

Apoletta had her distraction. By the time a frustrated Blazewight turned to seek her out again, Apoletta was upon him. She drove the dragonlance and her hands through the steam cloud surrounding his back. She screamed triumphantly but also in pain. The lance cracked his brittle charcoal skin and wedged itself deep into his flesh.

Apoletta relinquished the lance; her hands were blistered and burning. She could not uncurl her fingers; they were gnarled in agony. Trying not to faint, trying not to heave, Apoletta swam blindly away, only dimly aware of Blazewight's shrieks and roars, his wild dance of staggered movements. The dragonlance hung from the dragon's flesh, bobbing precariously. Blazewight tried shaking it loose, but he could not reach it. His skin crumbled. His wing bones fell off, the long ulnae disintegrated into ash, and his humeri dwindled to nubs. He snapped off several of his claws in his jerky convulsions.

When at last Blazewight realized he could not shake the thornlance loose, he wheeled to find Apoletta, his jaws and fangs gaping. The sun rose behind his teeth.

"Apoletta!"

Apoletta turned in time to see Zebulah flying at her faster than she'd ever known him to swim. It was a retreat spell, she realized. Drawing on the last of her wits, she cast the spell—the same one that had saved her in the trench during the storm.

Flames curled past Blazewight's lips.

Zebulah almost reached her.

"And though robbed of land, Daydra could run alongside the swiftest dolphins!" Apoletta cried as Zebulah grabbed her and they both kicked away. A column of red and black fire blossomed forth. Apoletta screamed at the searing heat that enveloped her, but Zebulah pushed her out and away from the flames, shielding her with his own body. He, too, shouted in pain.

In a moment, they escaped the explosion of heat. Zebulah let go, his grip suddenly limp. Apoletta spun to catch him, only to discover the horrifying truth: His legs had been burned away. Nothing remained below his knees; above were blackened stumps and bone.

Apoletta caught her husband under his shoulders and tried lifting him. They both sank slowly.

"Leave me," he whispered.

Apoletta shook her head. "N-no," she said with a growl. She looked over Zebulah's shoulder. Blazewight was moving ponderously toward them, his front claws disintegrating with each ghastly footfall. More of his skin had peeled away, revealing a skull's grin.

He loomed over them and stretched his mouth, eager to devour them.

Apoletta caught a movement behind Blazewight. A dolphin . . . Timathian?

"Hold on to me," Apoletta whispered. "Do not let go."

Zebulah nodded weakly.

Blazewight reared his head back.

"Now!" Apoletta said, turning into a porpoise.

Timathian dived straight for the dragon, straight for the dragonlance butt that was sticking out of the steam cloud. With a sickening crunch, Timathian rammed the lance deeper down with his head. The martyred blow also killed Timathian, of that Apoletta had no doubt; he dropped away, his skull cracked open . . . he'd sacrificed himself for them.

Blazewight roared with impossible pain and fury. More of his body fell away.

Apoletta nudged Zebulah. Instinctively, he grabbed her dorsal fin. She pushed through the water, out from under the disintegrating dragon. His death throes shook the walls.

Racing as fast as she could, Apoletta pulled up into the trench. Her wounded flippers ached. Wartide was there already, swimming ahead of them, and she also spotted a hurt Arrovawk and Brightshore. Her own strength felt depleted. Another porpoise pulled alongside Apoletta, nudging Zebulah. Apoletta shapeshifted back to her sea elf form, and both she and Zebulah threw arms around Brysis's dorsal fin.

A squeal tore through the water behind the trio. Apoletta turned in time to see an injured Echo Fury trailing them, and behind the war dolphin, a terrible phoenix of steam and charcoal scales.

The dragon was still lurching and scraping himself over the trench walls and careening off outcroppings, the dragonlance in his back skipping off the rocks. And with each step of his advance, more of him disintegrated; his wings were gone already, his claws stubs, and his ribs exposed across his eaten flanks. When the dragon opened his mouth to roar, Apoletta saw the severed, burned log of his tongue wagging loosely in his mouth.

Brysis cried a warning, and Apoletta dodged as a large boulder fell past them and more rained down. The Mahkwahb were trying to crush Blazewight, bury him with the very stones they'd excavated under his tyranny. More boulders and rocks sailed past the companions.

Apoletta glanced back at Blazewight. A large rock struck him in the shoulder. His arm disintegrated. The fires inside him were dim. But he refused to die. Even with three ragged limbs, he pursued them with unholy rage.

Apoletta, Brysis, Zebulah, and Echo Fury cleared the lip of the trench where the Mahkwahb were rolling stones and boulders over the edge. Apoletta let go of Brysis's dorsal fin and allowed Brysis to bear Zebulah away.

Despite the piercing pain in her hands, Apoletta pulled from her pouch a piece of seal fur tied around a crystal rod—the weapon she'd intended to use against Zebulah earlier.

"And though dim the sky," Apoletta said, "so much the better to witness her fury!"

The last of the warmth faded from Apoletta's belly. Lightning raced along her arms and lanced out from her fingertips, striking the trench wall above Blazewight's head. A section of wall broke free, the trench collapsing. Apoletta watched as a large stone fell upon the dragon's skull. Blazewight's head exploded into charcoal and ashen debris; the stone plummeted through his body, demolishing anything that had ever been alive.

CHAPTER
Zebulah's Memory
19

The rain of debris as well as Apoletta's lightning bolt had collapsed the trench and buried the vile chamber beneath. The Mahkwahb cheered their victory and made sacrifices of their magori prisoners. Still, they eyed the strangers among them with distrust. The Dimernesti and Dargonesti had served their purpose and should be killed; the dark sea elves and undead seemed united on that subject. Since Wartide had yet to speak his mind, however, the Mahkwahb locked the surviving companions in an empty warehouse.

A wounded Ornathius had rejoined his compatriots, most of whom bore some injury. Brysis and Echo Fury suffered from acid burns; fire mauled Arrovawk's arm. Apoletta's hands were burned and twisted, and Ornathius had suffered a cut to his ribs. Only Brightshore seemed relatively unharmed. Ornathius told them all about Utharne's valiant stand, and they told him of Timathian's noble sacrifice.

Of them all, Zebulah suffered the worst.

Zebulah continued to burn slowly, the embers inside and outside his undead body refusing to gutter. He said it was because of his brittle flesh. His body had disintegrated from the waist down, and yet he hung on, cradled in Apoletta's arms.

"Fate," Zebulah said, his voice rough.

Apoletta stared down at Zebulah.

"Before the battle," he continued. "You said 'Fate is immutable.'"

"It means," she whispered, "knowing what I know now, I would not change a single thing. Meeting you, taking you for my husband . . . meeting you again. I love you, Zebulah. No matter what has come to pass, you will always be my husband."

"I stole from you," Zebulah rasped.

Apoletta eyed him. "Do you remember more now?"

"I remember enough," he said, after a moment. "When I fled Istar, I stole a dragonlance, didn't I?"

Apoletta offered him a sad smile. "You took two."

"I'm sorry," he whispered. "I thought I was scared of growing older, growing powerless, but I was scared of losing you . . . leaving you alone. And yet, I managed both."

Trying to speak, Apoletta choked with emotion. Instead she caressed Zebulah's face and kissed his cold forehead. "Are you in terrible pain?" she asked.

Zebulah shook his head, furrowing his brows. "Strangely, I feel . . . nothing. Even now. I look at you and I remember loving you, but they are hazy memories. Uncertain."

"Do you remember what happened to you? After you left Istar?"

"I wandered, I think. The ocean felt empty without you. I—" Zebulah paused, confused. "I gradually exhausted the magic of the dragonlances, looking for more magic to preserve me. When that was done, I . . . I think I died," he said.

Wartide stepped through the doorway with three priests behind him. They wore bloody vestments made from the carapace armor of the recently slaughtered magori.

Wartide quietly regarded them for a moment. "Tend to their wounds," he said.

"Sire?" one of the priests asked, obviously continuing a debate that had begun outside.

"Do not question me!" Wartide snarled. "Heal them enough to send them on their way."

The priests bowed their heads and cast their healing crafts on their unwanted guests. The companions cringed at being touched with Zeboim's holy spells, but in regaining some mobility, some comfort, they grudgingly offered a nod of gratitude.

"You kept your promise to me," Apoletta said to Wartide, flexing her healed fingers. "What about your promise to Zebulah?"

"We plan to keep it," Wartide said. "But 'restore him,' you said?"

"Human, alive with his memories," Apoletta said, glancing at her suffering husband.

Wartide shook his head. "No, no. The memories certainly, but as for the human . . . he died long ago. He drowned trying to rob an underwater tomb, his magic spent. Of course he couldn't move on, like so many others. The gods were gone—the river of souls trapped."

"But the gods returned and reopened the river of souls!" Apoletta argued. "Everyone else was allowed to continue on their journey, so why is he cursed to remain unde—" Apoletta stopped, her eyes widening. "Zeboim. Zeboim turned him into an undead."

Zebulah's eyes opened. "Yes! I remember dying," he whispered. "I drowned."

"Zeboim found him," Wartide said. "She restored his body and returned him from the dead."

Anger coursed through Apoletta; everything fell into place. "She used Zebulah to get to me," Apoletta said. "To get the dragonlances into your hands. She was planning this for years?"

"Would you expect anything less from a goddess?" Wartide asked, surprised. "She turned Zebulah into this *thing*, and I introduced him into Blazewight's service. Once Blazewight began preparations to open the final portals to Chaos, it was time to draw you into the intrigue, counting on your love for your husband. At the mere mention of a dragon, you provided us with the necessary weapon and your own brave help. For that, you and your friends will leave here unmolested. For that, Zebulah continues on his way."

"Wait!" Apoletta said. "He can continue? He won't be tainted by his actions? He will no longer have to be undead? He will not be damned?"

"I suppose. 'Restore him' means whatever it means. It will restore him to the point of death."

Apoletta hesitated. She'd risked so much to save her husband only to lose him anew. She wanted back the life she once shared with him; she wanted back the man she remembered, the man she had loved and would always love.

But wasn't it more important that he find the peace denied him for so long? And hadn't she already had the chance she longed for, to amend the misunderstanding that had caused them both to suffer? Wouldn't they part loving each other?

With a heavy heart, Apoletta nodded. "Give me a moment, then?"

Wartide sighed, giving her a casual flick of the wrist. "The rest of you," he said to the companions, "prepare to depart. Leave these waters and never return. These are Blood Shoal lands now, and neither Dargonesti nor Dimernesti will be tolerated here. We remain under the protection of Zeboim—She who protected us from Blazewight and She who engineered his downfall. You would be wise to remember that."

The companions stared grimly at Wartide. In truth they would be happy to leave that place. Whether or not they would ever return, despite his threats, well, they made no promises.

Apoletta caressed Zebulah's cheek. The ember flames had eaten half his body, but he seemed free of pain. His look of calm detachment, however, had been replaced with concern.

"Where am I?" Zebulah said, his memories slowly returning. And with the wide eyes of memory, the man Apoletta remembered said, "Beloved, I . . . I hurt you."

"Shh, my love," Apoletta said. "Never. You could never hurt me."

"I love you. You know that, don't you? I would never hurt you."

"You haven't, dearest."

"Then why do I remember hurting you?" he said, his voice cracking. She tasted his tears in the water. "I remember it clearly . . . I think, I . . . I. . . ."

"It was only a dream," Apoletta whispered. "And all dreams fade in the morning." She drew closer to his face and let her hair cascade like a silver curtain around his head. Nobody else mattered; only the two of them existed in the world, that moment.

Zebulah blinked. "A dream?" he whispered.

"Only a dream."

"Am I dreaming now?"

Apoletta leaned in and kissed her husband on the lips. She could feel him fading, eroding in her hands, pouring like silt through her fingers.

"I feel so light," he whispered. "So tired."

"You suffered your nightmares for so long," she replied, her heart aching. "You deserve your sleep."

"I don't want to leave you."

"Never," Apoletta said. "Sleep . . . dream of better things. I'll be here when you wake up."

"I will never leave you," Zebulah vowed, his eyes growing heavy. He blinked, the glow in his eyes vanishing. Behind them lay the familiar gentle brown color she always remembered. He smiled. A flicker of blue flame filled his pupils, as though reflected from afar.

"So beautiful," he whispered, his eyes fluttering closed.

Apoletta kissed Zebulah a final time. A sigh escaped his lips and brushed hers. He turned to mist in her embrace.

Behind her veil of silver, Apoletta wept.

No victory celebrations awaited the departing heroes, no grateful, cheering denizens to thank the companions. They left in silence, stared at by the others in silence.

Apoletta carried the earthly remains of Zebulah in a simple jar whose mouth she sealed with wax. For all the pain and hardship of the past week, however, she felt calm. The gods had chosen to return to an unfinished chapter in her life, completing that volume of her existence. What remained was to open a new page and begin writing anew.

Fate or consequence.

Neither . . . either . . . she would handle both with the same determination that bore her through those signal events and the previous night.

Apoletta paused to stare back at the Blood Shoal city. She could barely make out its clean-water dome in the murk of the World Gash. Despite Wartide's bravado and threats, Apoletta knew she would return to Mahkwahb waters, to the Mahkwahb city. His pronouncement of their "exile" amounted to nothing less than a declaration of war.

The next time they met, it would be a fight to the death. Zeboim would never permit the Mahkwahb to remain complacent. She would dispatch them to conquer the neighboring waters in her name. She would invite more undead to befoul the ocean.

Apoletta could not risk leaving a terrible weapon like the Impaling Throne in Wartide's possession. The artifact thorn would survive calamity and avalanche. Apoletta did not doubt that the device continued to function beneath the tons of debris and Blazewight's fall of ash. The dome of clean water surrounding the city remained in place, but for how long?

Apoletta joined the others, knowing she would return, but first they had to find their way out.

"Where to?" she asked Brysis.

Brysis surveyed the waters ahead: the dwindling ink rivers, ash storms, poison clouds, and magma fields. The landscape was bleak, but there was hope.

Apoletta nudged Brysis, pointing to the dark shape darting

through the water. Its black body, smaller than a porpoise, was almost dewdrop in form. While hard to see through the murk, they all recognized the blue candle flame that flickered upon its forehead.

Apoletta smiled. "Follow him," she said. "He'll guide us home."

EPILOGUE

The festivities almost made Apoletta forget her terrible experiences of more than two months previous. Colored bladders and shells decorated the coils of seaweed festooned from the ceiling, while the delegates dressed in their finest liveries and spoke with one another in civil tones. The Dargonesti and Dimernesti had worked alongside one another for the past three weeks to ready the shallow-water keep for the wedding.

However, since returning to Istar, Apoletta had labored to ensure their experiences, their sacrifices, would not be forgotten. Their harrowing struggles had found believers among the Dargonesti and Dimernesti alike, thanks to their respective Speakers.

Of the two sea elf races, the Dimernesti had had a greater stake in the crisis, and their involvement was passionate. Utharne's death resonated with his people, especially when a powerful isolationist like Arrovawk and a certain Dargonesti captain spoke of his courage with equal ardor. The Dimernesti had thrown themselves into the wedding preparations, and while there were still many dissenters among the shoal elves, Arrovawk used his considerable influence to bring those sea elves under his thumb.

In Dimernost, the Temple of the Fisher King saw more worshipers returning to the fold. Priests in their sermons recounted the tales of Brine-Whisker leading the companions from the darkness before vanishing and Utharne's stand against the Legion Coral. Bards told the same tales, with embellishment, in crowded taverns. Certainly, they exaggerated the story of Utharne's bravery—with grand flourishes describing the titanic struggle between Zeboim and Abbuku—but the message was understood.

The gods were still around. They had not abandoned their children.

In comparison, the Dargonesti behaved more cautiously, more somberly. A growing internal strife affected the Dargonesti. Speaker Treyen Silverwake supported the wedding, though Apoletta knew it was because he felt the future of his people was no longer in his hands. The wedding would happen, regardless of Watermere; Istar could not turn its back on the alliance. But power had shifted from Takaluras to Istar.

Apoletta had invited delegates from the cities of Dargonest and Darthalla. Speaker Aquironian sent representatives to the wedding, though matters between the various Dargonesti enclaves remained tense. Apoletta hoped the occasion would force all the sea elf races and factions to set aside their differences and work together. At the very least, the wedding would provide a good start.

Apoletta also invited the other races to attend. While not all of the friendly species credited the companions' accounts of events in the World Gash, most sent delegates to witness the historic proceedings.

Apoletta hovered above the stage and looked out across the sea of faces in the great hall. The roof had long collapsed, but that allowed those of great size to remain outside while still observing the proceedings. The sea giant Boddenson had come with two companions. The three sea giants came well armed and appeared disappointed not to have faced any threats. The ocean strider Ashkoom had returned with two of Shakhall's daughters. Brysis embraced them all when she first saw them, and the two daughters, in turn, embraced her as kin. Brysis told them what the Matriarch had said—how Shakhall hunted in vast oceans as clear as the sky. That brought them some comfort. Brysis, the three ocean striders, and Echo Fury watched together.

Among the throng of Dargonesti, Dimernesti, and water-breathing Qualinesti who crammed into the hall were other races who sat and waited quietly. Merfolk delegates included the volatile Athiana, and the brathnoc delegates of Hygant also sat quietly. The brathnoc had sent diplomats to visit Dimernost and arrange an alliance with the sea elves.

New to the prospective alliance were several triton warriors with their silver-blue scaly legs ending in fins, their silver upper-bodies, and long blue-green hair. Despite their harrowing war with the sahuagin, the triton folk appeared friendly and eager to make allies.

Apoletta raised her arms and called for attention. She motioned down to the two figures standing side by side, both covered in robes, holding each other's hands. Behind the elf male stood Captain Ornathius in his gleaming red crab armor, while behind the female stood Arrowawk, shifting uncomfortably in his heavy robes.

"You are present for an auspicious moment in sea elf history: the joining of the Dargonesti and Dimernesti as one family," she proclaimed, motioning to the male sea elf in black robes and seashell-braided hair of green. "Here waits Berrion Silverwake, youngest son of Speaker of the Moon Treyen Silverwake and grandson of our ancestral champion Nakaro Silverwake." She then indicated the young elf maiden in white robes and with copper bands in her hair. "Here waits Mercy Windspeaker, wise daughter of Ressata Windspeaker and granddaughter to the great Speaker of the Sea Nuqala Windspeaker."

Apoletta smiled at the bride and groom, both of whom blushed with the innocence of youth. "Before I step aside so that our two priests might wed you two together," Apoletta said, "I wish you all the love and happiness that I have known in my life."

She faced the throng. "Behind them stand Captain Ornathius and Arrovawk, heroes of the World Gash," she said. "They represent what has passed and will be remembered—blood spilled and intermingled between our two people, our shared tragedy. Berrion Silverwake and Mercy Windspeaker represent the blood to be shared through the future of their children . . . the blood to come. They are our best hope, the best of Dimernesti and Dargonesti and all the sea elves and esteemed races gathered here—the brathnoc, tritons, ocean striders, merfolk, sea giants, and others of the shallows and the deep. We, all of us, are kith and kin. It is our duty, and in our natures, to help one another."

Apoletta offered a sad smile, for the merging of their two races through the ceremonial marriage also signaled the gathering of two armies. The future offered promise, but it also exacted a price. "Near three months ago, we began this journey to cement our alliance in hopes of peace. But we must be honest with ourselves. It is the prospect of war that brings us closer together. We share our enemies, so why not share our allies and resources? The World Gash still awaits us, and our foes are preparing and gathering their numbers. But I choose to rejoice in our union. And I can think of no better ceremony to symbolize our alliance than with one that is a celebration of love."

Undead and Mahkwahb worked shoulder to shoulder, removing the rubble from the trench. Wartide floated above, watching them toil; he tossed bits of the dead fish in his hands to the thorny turtles swarming around him. He did not mind their snapping bites.

The excavation work taxed his people; the fissure's collapse was far more extensive than before. Still, the city emerged less damaged than expected.

THE ALIEN SEA

Wartide watched as a wraith crawled up through the rocks of the trench. It floated toward him.

"Well?" Wartide asked, enduring the bite of another sea turtle.

"The ink has retreated," the wraith whispered, its voice doubling upon itself. "But the Impaling Throne is undamaged."

Wartide nodded. "Dig faster!" he called before turning his attentions to the strange creature that waited nearby. The reptilian visitor had black and green striations across its scaly skin; fishlike eyes; webbed digits; frills on its arms, legs, and back; and a mouth filled with sharp teeth. Wartide turned into a shark, which allowed him to communicate with the creature, whose species spoke telepathically with sharks. He swam up to it.

Why should we help you? the creature asked, its raspy voice jabbing at his mind. *We can take this city for ourselves if we want to. After all, it's more suited to us.*

I could fill the shaft with fresh water, Wartide responded. *I know your species cannot breathe fresh water well.*

You lie, the creature said. *You have no such power.*

Is it also a lie that the World Gash drives your people away like refugees? Wartide asked. *The volcanic fields, the ash storms . . . all, our doing.*

The creature snarled.

I could change that. Make the World Gash hospitable for your people. Give them better hunting grounds.

The creature paused. *What do you want in exchange?*

An alliance, Wartide said. *The Mahkwahb, the undead . . . and the sahuagin.*

We don't need your alliances.

But you do, a woman's voice said. She filled both their minds. The sahuagin looked around and bared his fangs.

Who speaks?

A very powerful ally, Wartide said.

Your blood enemies, the tritons, are about to gain new allies, the woman said. *The sea elves stand with them. Tell me, are you strong enough to fight Dargonesti, Dimernesti, and triton?*

The sahuagin said nothing.

Speak to your king, ambassador, Wartide said. *Tell him we offer this alliance and a new home for your people. Tell him, together, we can reshape the oceans and destroy both our enemies. He has an ally in the city of Zeboim.*

And what do you get in return?

The woman said nothing, so Wartide spoke. *It has come to our attention that your people have found something in a remote catacomb pit of the squid-people.*

Perhaps, the sahuagin said, his lids narrowing.

Was it a giant twisted thorn? Wartide asked. *Near fifty feet in height? The color of bone and shadow.*

Perhaps, the sahuagin ambassador repeated with a sly smile. *And perhaps we found two such sculptures.*

Two thorns? Wartide asked.

But you ask us to join an alliance against an enemy we do not fear! the sahuagin said incredulously. *The sea elves!* he added, his laughter a hiss.

No, the woman said. *The real enemy is the woman who will lead the sea elves, brathnoc, and tritons against you. Her name is Apoletta, and so long as she lives, you will never rule the seas. Give us the two thorns, and we will help you kill her.*

The ambassador hesitated. *I know something of this Apoletta. And there is something in what you say. I will speak with my king,* he said before swimming away.

Wartide shifted out of his shark's skin and watched the ambassador leave. "What if he doesn't give us the two artifacts?" he whispered.

"It is enough at the moment that we know they exist. Whether the sahuagin join us or not, we will take the other Impaling Thrones for ourselves," the woman said. "And with the three thorns, I will flood the continents and leave naught but a world of ocean."

"Glory be to Zeboim," Wartide whispered.

A NEW TRILOGY FROM MARGARET WEIS & TRACY HICKMAN

THE LOST CHRONICLES
Dragons of the Dwarven Depths
Volume One

Tanis, Tasslehoff, Riverwind, and Raistlin
are trapped as refugees in Thorbardin, as the
draconian army closes in on the dwarven
kingdom. To save his homeland, Flint begins a
search for the Hammer of Kharas.

Available July 2006

For more information visit **www.wizards.com**

FOLLOW MARGARET WEIS FROM THE WAR OF SOULS INTO THE CHAOS OF POST-WAR KRYNN

The War of Souls has come to an end at last. Magic is back, and so are the gods. But the gods are vying for supremacy, and the war has caused widespread misery, uprooting entire nations and changing the balance of power on Ansalon.

AMBER AND ASHES
The Dark Disciple, Volume I
MARGARET WEIS

The mysterious warrior-woman Mina, brooding on her failure and the loss of her goddess, makes a pact with evil in a seductive guise. As a strange vampiric cult spreads throughout the fragile world, unlikely heroes – a wayward monk and a kender who can communicate with the dead – join forces to try to uproot the cause of the growing evil.

AMBER AND IRON
The Dark Disciple, Volume II
MARGARET WEIS

The former monk Rhys, now sworn to the goddess Zeboim, leads a powerful alliance in an attempt to find some way to destroy the Beloved, the fearsome movement of undead caught in the terrifying grip of the Lord of Death. Mina seeks to escape her captivity in the Blood Sea Tower, but can she escape the prison of her dark past?

AMBER AND BLOOD
The Dark Disciple, Volume III
MARGARET WEIS

February 2007

For more information visit **www.wizards.com**

IN THE WAKE OF
THE WAR OF SOULS...

The power of the Dark Knights in northern Ansalon is broken.

The Solamnic order is in disarray.

And in a shrouded mountain valley, an army of evil gathers.

Against them stand a mysterious outlawed warrior, a dwarf,
and a beautiful enchantress. With the aid of two fugitive
gnomes, they will hold the banner of Good against the forces of
darkness. And from the ashes of war, a new Solamnia will rise.

THE RISE OF SOLAMNIA TRILOGY
BY DOUGLAS NILES

Volume I
LORD OF THE ROSE

Volume II
THE CROWN AND THE SWORD
June 2006

Volume III
THE MEASURE AND THE TRUTH
January 2007

For more information visit **www.wizards.com**

ELVEN EXILES TRILOGY
PAUL B. THOMPSON AND TONYA C. COOK

The elven people, driven from their age old enclaves in
the green woods, have crossed the Plains of Dust and harsh
mountains into the distant land of Khur. The elves coexist
uneasily with surrounding tribes under the walls of
Khuri-Khan.

Shadowy forces inside Khur and out plot to destroy the elves.
Some are ancient and familiar, others are new and unknown.

And so the battle lines are drawn, and the great game begins.
Survival or death, glory or oblivion — these are the stakes.
Gilthas and Kerianseray bet all on a forgotten map,
faithful friends, and their unshakable faith on the
greatness of the elven race.

SANCTUARY
Volume One

ALLIANCES
Volume Two
August 2006

Volume Three
June 2007

For more information visit **www.wizards.com**

TALADAS TRILOGY
CHRIS PIERSON

The War of Souls is over. Takhisis is dead. On Ansalon, heroes and gods have banded together to save the world from destruction. A new peace, of sorts, has taken hold.

Half a world away, on the continent of Taladas, the troubles are just beginning. Sorcery, long thought lost, has returned to the world. Disasters wrack the land, nations clash, and dark forces stir in the aftermath of the Godless Night.

An ambitious barbarian unites the tribes, a victorious general returns, and an elven thief tracks a mysterious enemy. One will live, one will die, and one will wish for death. For ancient powers are waking in Taladas.

BLADES OF THE TIGER
Volume One

TRAIL OF THE BLACK WYRM
Volume Two

SHADOW OF THE FLAME
Volume Three
March 2007

For more information visit **www.wizards.com**

DragonLance
THE NEW ADVENTURES

A Practical Guide to Dragons
By Sindri Suncatcher

Sindri Suncatcher—wizard's apprentice—opens up
his personal notebooks to share his knowledge of these
awe-inspiring creatures, from the life cycle of a kind copper
dragon to the best way to counteract a red dragon's fiery
breath. This lavishly illustrated guide showcases the wide
array of fantastic dragons encountered on the world of Krynn.

The perfect companion to the Dragonlance: The New
Adventures series, for both loyal fans and new readers alike.

Sindri Suncatcher is a three-and-a-half foot tall kender,
who enjoys storytelling, collecting magical tokens, and
fighting dragons. He lives in Solamnia and is currently
studying magic under the auspices of the black-robed
wizard Maddoc. You can catch Sindri in the midst of
his latest adventure in *The Wayward Wizard*.

For more information visit www.mirrorstonebooks.com

For ages ten and up.